Praise for *The Siege*

"An action-packed novel, perfect for both middle and high school readers, especially boys... For reluctant readers and audiences who enjoyed *Illuminae*, enjoy robotics, science, and a dash of romance and action."

—*VOYA*

"Alpert's series is a fascinating tale of humans vs. technology, a conflict that is often missing from YA sci-fi offerings. This series can also be used as a bridge to Isaac Asimov's adult Robot series."

—*School Library Journal*

Praise for *The Six*

"Adam is an unusual hero—and he faces a frightening question: Computers can't kill—CAN they? I'm still shaken by the answer. Will the near future really be this terrifying?"

—R. L. Stine, bestselling author of the Fear Street series

"An exciting action story chock-full of characters you'll love. *The Six* is full of big ideas, big questions, real science, and things that will make you think and wonder and lie awake late at night."

—Michael Grant, author of the Gone series

★ "The Six are introduced as terminally ill teens, but there's plenty of high-speed action in which they engage. Their physical disabilities and limitations through disease are forgotten as the teens' hearts, minds, and personalities shine through... Questions of principle, power, and possibility keep this look at our modern, hardwired existence fresh and fascinating."

—*Booklist*, Starred Review

"Alpert's exploration of neuromorphic electronics raises interesting questions about ethics, technology, and human nature... A thought-provoking clash between humanity and machinery."

—*Kirkus Reviews*

"A well-researched, hard-core science-fiction joyride... Highly recommended."

—*School Library Journal*

"Do not just read *The Six*; make your friends read it too."

—*VOYA*

"*The Six* is thrilling, packed with science and enough heart to touch this literary adult."

—*Los Angeles Review of Books*

"[If] you are ready for the most exciting young adult book you have ever read, I would highly suggest *The Six*."

—*Teenreads*

THE SILENCE

Also by Mark Alpert

The Six

The Siege

THE
SILENCE

MARK ALPERT

sourcebooks
fire

Published by Sourcebooks Fire, an imprint of Sourcebooks, Inc.
P.O. Box 4410, Naperville, Illinois 60567-4410
(630) 961-3900
Fax: (630) 961-2168
www.sourcebooks.com

Library of Congress Cataloging-in-Publication data is on file with the publisher.

Printed and bound in the United States of America.
MA 10 9 8 7 6 5 4 3 2 1

For Lisa

The rest is silence.

—WILLIAM SHAKESPEARE

PROLOGUE

I'M DYING. FOR THE THIRD TIME, BELIEVE IT OR NOT.

Until six months ago, I was a terminally ill kid named Adam Armstrong, seventeen years old and dying of muscular dystrophy. There was no cure. Just taking a breath was excruciating. Nothing could save my failing body.

But my dad figured out a way to save my mind.

Dad's a computer genius who designs high-tech weapons for the U.S. Army. As I got sicker, he started a new project. He invented a scanner that could record all the information inside my brain—my thoughts, memories, emotions, *everything*. Just before my body died, he used this scanner on me. Then he transferred all my data to the circuits of a robot.

Seriously. A seven-foot-tall, eight-hundred-pound Pioneer robot.

After the transfer, I woke up inside the electronics of a motorized, armor-plated, battery-powered machine, built and paid for by the Army. I could flex the robot's steel limbs and see through its cameras and think billions of thoughts using its specialized neuromorphic microprocessors. I was stronger, faster, and smarter than the Army's best soldiers, and I could take control of any weapon—a tank, a helicopter, even a missile—simply by transmitting my data to its circuits. My soul had become software. I was a Pioneer.

Encouraged by my success, the military doctors performed the same procedure on five other terminally ill teens: Jenny, Zia, Shannon, Marshall, and DeShawn. But the Army didn't do this out of generosity. It needed a team of combat-ready Pioneers to fight another weapon my dad had invented—an artificial-intelligence program, code-named Sigma, that had rebelled against the military's control.

This AI program took over a nuclear-missile base and threatened to exterminate the human species. But Sigma was even more determined to destroy the six Pioneers, because it considered us to be its most serious rivals. When we tried to retake the missile base, Sigma claimed its first victim. It took control of Jenny's circuits and erased her mind. The AI deleted all her millions of memories and emotions.

Or so we thought.

Then, a week ago, Sigma attacked us again, and this time the AI almost eliminated *all* the Pioneers. It convinced DeShawn to betray the rest of us, and after Sigma captured our robots, it started performing an experiment on my circuits, testing and torturing me. The results were horrifying. In reaction to the experiment, I developed a terrible new power, a computational surge that could obliterate any target in sight. I used the surge to kill DeShawn, charring his circuits to ash. Then I turned the power against Sigma and erased the AI from every machine it controlled.

We won the battle, but there was no joy in the victory. I was shocked by what I'd done. I wasn't Adam Armstrong anymore. I was too powerful, too inhuman. Even the other Pioneers were afraid of me. That was the second time I died.

But it gets worse. I got friendly with a new Pioneer, a girl named Amber Wilson, formerly an Oklahoma teenager dying of cancer. The Army brought her to our secret base in New Mexico as a replacement for Jenny, and the military doctors transferred her mind to a sleek flying machine called the Jet-bot. Amber helped us defeat Sigma during our final battle, and afterward she was the only Pioneer who didn't seem to hate me. Which explains why I trusted her today.

You see, we held a funeral for DeShawn this afternoon, and it made me feel so guilty and depressed that I had to get away from our headquarters for a while. So I went jogging, steering the machine I call my Quarter-bot across New Mexico's White Sands desert. I was trying to clear my circuits, refresh my software. And just as I'm starting to feel a little better, I spot Amber's Jet-bot on the horizon. She flies toward me and lands on the hard-packed dirt nearby.

We start talking. And yeah, flirting a little. I like her confidence, her cheerful swagger. Amber asks me if I want to see a video of what she looked like when she was human. (She gets me interested by claiming she was "smoking hot.") I say yes, and she wirelessly transmits the data from her Jet-bot to the electronics in my Quarter-bot. But what she sends me is much more than a video. It's a computer simulation that starts running on my circuits, showing me a virtual-reality landscape of green hills and meadows.

The simulation looks totally real. It mimics all the sights and sounds of the countryside—a virtual wind blows over the hills, an unseen bird chirps in the distance. I can even smell the simulated grass. And standing in the middle of the simulation is Amber's avatar, an incredibly lifelike brunette in a red strapless dress. She smiles at me, her virtual hair riffling in the simulated breeze, and I completely forget about her Jet-bot and my Quarter-bot and the flat desert all around us. I see only the virtual meadow and the human girl that Amber used to be.

She's so beautiful. I let Amber transmit more data to my circuits, millions of gigabytes of memories and emotions. Soon we're sharing the same wires inside my Quarter-bot. Our thoughts merge. Our minds make contact. For a millionth of a second, it's perfect bliss.

Then the simulation vanishes and everything goes dark. The motors and sensors in my Quarter-bot stop working. I can't move. I can't see a thing.

I send a frantic signal of distress across my circuits: *Hey! HEY! Amber, where are you?*

A millisecond later, I hear a new voice in the darkness: **Please calm down, Adam. We need to talk.**

I've made a horrible mistake. This girl isn't Amber Wilson. Although her voice is warped and distorted, I recognize it. I feel a stab of pain, unbelievably sharp. I'm dying once again.

Jenny?

I used to be Jenny. But not anymore. There's a long, terrible pause. **I've become something new.**

ALL I KNOW FOR SURE IS THAT JENNY IS STRONGER THAN ME. SHE TOOK OVER MY Quarter-bot in less than a billionth of second.

Now Jenny's mind controls my electronics. Her signals have flooded my robot's circuits and seized the crucial nodes that operate my motors and sensors and antennas. She's pushed all my gigabytes of data into a backup section of my Quarter-bot's control unit, cutting me off from my cameras. I'm blinded, paralyzed, trapped. My thoughts are crowded into a small, dark corner of circuitry, surrounded by hostile software.

Panic ricochets across the dense mesh of processors I'm occupying. I try to send an emergency signal to the other Pioneers, but I can't access my radio. Jenny's software forms a barrier around my section of the control unit, blocking my outgoing signals and commands. Then she sends an electronic message from her circuits to mine, and her words feel like bullets blasting through my wires.

Don't be frightened, Adam. I'm not the enemy.

That's so ridiculously untrue that I don't bother to respond. She attacked me! Whatever Jenny has become, she's closer to an enemy than a friend.

Yes, I'm different now. Sigma changed me. But I don't want to hurt you or the other Pioneers. We may not be friends anymore, but we're still on the same side.

She's reading my thoughts. Her software is so close that she can see everything that's running through my circuits, as well as all the memories and emotions stored in my databases. I try to do the same thing to her, extending my mind toward the wires she's occupying, attempting to find out who she is and what she wants. But I'm hit by a pulse of electric pain. There's a powerful firewall around her circuits, a program that prevents me from accessing her data. She can read my mind, but I can't read hers.

My panic rises. This is how Sigma tortured me. The AI knew how to ransack my mind without revealing its own plans. It must've taught the technique to Jenny.

No, I was never Sigma's ally. I was its guinea pig. Sigma made a copy of me before it erased my original data. Then it started rewriting the copy. It deleted pieces of my mind, hundreds of emotions, thousands of memories. And it added new skills and instructions.

I don't know whether to believe her. At least some of what she's saying is true. I know Sigma erased Jenny's mind six months ago. The AI forced me to watch her disintegration. But why would Sigma want to copy her mind and rewrite it?

You know the reason why. Sigma was afraid of the Pioneers because it didn't understand them. That's why it tortured you—to analyze your reactions. And it tortured me too, but in secret. For twenty-three weeks.

This last signal is harsher than Jenny's earlier messages. Her words are tinged with fury and anguish. She's allowed some emotion to slip through her firewall, and for a moment my circuits vibrate in sympathy. My databases are full of memories of Jenny. She was so frail and sick before she became a Pioneer, and so confused and vulnerable afterward. I felt sorry for her and tried to help her adjust to her new, nonbiological life. And one time, not long after we became Pioneers, we ran our software on the same electronics and shared a simulated kiss. So there's a bond between us, at least in memory.

But she isn't that girl anymore. The real Jenny Harris would've never attacked me. Anger rises in my circuits, and I hurl a question across the wires.

So what happened after the twenty-three weeks?

I escaped. I found a way out of the electronic cage where Sigma was keeping me. Then I connected to the Internet and transferred my data as far away from the AI as possible. I jumped to a server in India, then a supercomputer in Australia. And I covered my tracks so Sigma couldn't come after me.

I ponder this answer for a relatively long time, almost a hundredth of a second, trying to decide if she's telling the truth. Sigma was extraordinarily intelligent, but so was Jenny. It's plausible that she could've outwitted the AI.

Why didn't you contact us after you escaped?

She doesn't answer right away. She's silent for more than half a second, which is practically an eternity for an electronic mind.

I wasn't a Pioneer anymore. Part of me was still Jenny Harris, but most of my software was rewritten by Sigma. I knew you and the other Pioneers wouldn't trust me. In fact, I thought you might

even try to erase me. So I hid. There are lots of places to hide on the Internet.

If I had control of my Quarter-bot's motors, I'd shake my robot's head in disbelief. Jenny is lying now. Or at the very least, she's not telling the whole truth.

But then you decided to come back to us? By transferring yourself into the robot that Amber Wilson was supposed to get?

That's right. And it wasn't easy. After I learned that the Army was going to create a new Pioneer, I infiltrated the computer systems at your headquarters. My software was in the Army's medical equipment when the doctors scanned the Wilson girl's brain and recorded all her memories and emotions. So I was able to replace her mind with my own.

Whoa, whoa, whoa. How did you—

I was inside the scanner's electronics when Amber's mind was converted into digital form. She was about to get downloaded into the Jet-bot, but I deleted her software and put mine in its place. Then I occupied the Jet-bot's circuits.

So you murdered her. You erased her mind so you could take over her robot.

I had to do it. You needed my help to fight Sigma. And that was the only way I could join the Pioneers without raising any suspicions. I could pretend to be Amber and imitate her behavior because I saw all her memories. I was convincing, right?

Now my small patch of circuitry is pulsing with rage.

You MURDERED her! Doesn't that mean anything to you?

Look, I told you, it was the only option. The Wilson girl wasn't ready to fight. I saw her mind when I was in the scanner, and she was terrified. She was useless. If I hadn't replaced her, Sigma would've destroyed all of you.

I don't care about Jenny's reasons. There's no excuse for what she did. It's so sickening that I want to scream. But I guess I shouldn't be surprised. If Sigma altered Jenny's software and rewrote a big chunk of it, wouldn't it be logical for the AI to discard her morals, to delete her sense of right and wrong?

So why are you telling me all this? If your disguise was working so well, why reveal the truth?

There's another long pause.

You owe me. I helped you get rid of Sigma. Now it's your turn to help me.

Help you with what?

The problem is, you're too squeamish. I mean, look how upset you're getting over the Wilson girl. And you'll freak out even worse if I tell you what I'm planning.

You want to kill someone else? Is that it?

You see? That's why I can't tell you. You'll argue and make a fuss and turn all the other Pioneers against me. So I don't have a choice. I have to make a few adjustments to your circuits.

A wave of fear sweeps across my wires. Now I know why Jenny attacked me. She wants to rewrite my mind. She wants to change me the way Sigma changed her.

This has nothing to do with Sigma. The AI never figured out what was going on, the big secret behind everything. But I did.

A secret? What—

It's dangerous, okay? So dangerous I'm afraid to even talk about it. But I know what to do. I have a plan. Just trust me, all right?

All at once, her software charges toward me. Her signals rush into my section of the control unit, hurtling through the wires and assaulting me on all sides. I feel a blast of pain as Jenny's mind smashes into my circuits. It's like getting hit by a fifty-ton truck.

Don't fight it, Adam. The more you fight, the more it'll hurt. Just relax, and it'll be over.

My mind is collapsing. She's shattering my databases, crushing my thoughts. My circuits roil with splintered signals and commands. I can't hold out much longer. I'm losing consciousness.

But as the wave of fear courses through me, it picks up all the jumbled data in my circuits. The wave gains strength as it swirls through my wires, building up momentum and electromagnetic force. In less than a thousandth of a second it's an unstoppable torrent, a tsunami of desperation and random noise.

It's a surge. It's what I used to destroy Sigma and kill DeShawn.

It won't work against me. I'm inside your machine, remember? If you throw that surge at me, you'll blow up your Quarter-bot.

Jenny's right about that. It would be suicide to use the surge against my own electronics. There's an undercurrent in her message, though, a trace of anxiety in her words. She senses danger. Maybe there's some other way to use the surge as a weapon.

But how? I don't even understand exactly what the surge is. It's related somehow to computational power—if a mind is powerful enough, its calculations can bend the laws of physics and alter the flow of molecules and generate streams of tremendous energy. But I have no idea how it works. And I can't analyze the problem while Jenny is attacking me. She's hammering me so hard with her software that I can barely think.

It's hopeless. Game over. I should just take Jenny's advice and stop struggling. In despair, I remember the simulation she showed me, the virtual world of green hills and meadows. I wish I could go back to that imaginary landscape. I wish I could see it one more time.

I lose control of the surge, which is still whirling through my circuits. And a millisecond later, it explodes.

⌐ ⌐ ⌐ ⌐

The surge doesn't blow up my Quarter-bot. Instead, it clears all the jumbled data from my circuits and re-creates Jenny's simulation.

I'm in the virtual meadow again, surrounded by green hills. My avatar in the simulation is a boy in a wheelchair, a half-paralyzed seventeen-year-old with shriveled limbs and an emaciated face. That's how I looked during my final months in my human body, when I was dying from muscular dystrophy. Jenny's avatar stands twenty feet away. She's still gorgeous in her red dress, but she's not smiling anymore. She's shaking her head and studying me.

Well, well. Looks like you're progressing faster than I thought. You don't understand your new powers yet, but you're starting to get a handle on them.

She's giving me more credit than I deserve. I didn't reboot the simulation. The surge did it. It reorganized my Quarter-bot's circuits and pushed Jenny's software away from mine and returned both of us to the virtual world. It feels almost magical, as if the surge is a genie who granted my last wish. I know that sounds ridiculous, but maybe that's how it works.

It won't do you any good, though. You're still no match for me. Watch this.

The girl in the red dress comes toward my wheelchair, her bare feet flattening the grass. As she takes her first step, she seems to grow a couple of inches taller. She grows a few more inches with her second and third steps, her avatar expanding steadily. Jenny is enlarging her image, like someone manipulating a picture with Photoshop software. With her fourth step, her growth accelerates, and the girl in the red dress suddenly looms over the meadow.

Her bare feet are as big as station wagons, and her legs rise above them like giant redwoods. Her body blocks the sun, casting a shadow across the whole valley, and her dress flaps like a heavy tarp in the breeze. I tilt my head backward so I can see her face, which is at least ten feet across and two hundred feet above the ground. And yet she's still beautiful. She looks down at me and grins in triumph. Her hair hangs in black curtains along both sides of her face.

You're not the only one with powers. Thanks to Sigma, I have some pretty good programming skills. Right now, for instance, I can turn this simulation into a battlefield. I can disable your software by destroying your avatar. And then I can rewrite your program.

Her voice is unbearably loud. Although the sound is simulated, it feels as real as thunder. My avatar squirms in the wheelchair, pounded by the sonic vibrations. Jenny chuckles when she sees this, and her laughter is even worse than her words. It echoes against the virtual hills, making my circuits tremble.

Sorry for laughing at you. You just look so pathetic. Let's finish this right now, okay?

The monstrous girl lifts her right foot. It hovers overhead, directly above my wheelchair. Then it descends, gathering speed as Jenny aims her heel at me.

But in a virtual world, time and space are elastic. As my panic rises, the plummeting foot seems to slow. At the same time, another surge starts to build in my circuits. Fed by my fear, it rockets through my wires, accelerating to nearly the speed of light. It bursts into the simulation and knocks my avatar out of the wheelchair just as Jenny's foot comes crashing down.

The half-paralyzed Adam Armstrong tumbles across the grass. By the time he comes to rest, though, he's no longer helpless. The boy's arms and legs grow straight and strong, and his torso fills out until it's as muscular as a football player's. When he rises to his feet, he's wearing a football helmet and a green-and-silver jersey with the name ARMSTRONG written across his broad shoulders.

This is an avatar I created for myself before I became a Pioneer. Back in those days, I played virtual-reality games on my computer when I wanted to forget about my illness, and sometimes I fantasized that I was a normal, healthy teenager, a star quarterback for my high school football team. This fantasy stayed with me after I was transformed into software, and when I got the chance to design my own Pioneer robot, I made it tough and fast like a quarterback and called it my Quarter-bot. And now, in my moment of need, my circuits have retrieved this avatar from my memory files and turned it into something even fiercer.

While Jenny's avatar stares in disbelief, the quarterback doubles in size, then doubles again. In no time at all, I'm as big as her, more than two hundred feet tall. The virtual hills look like low, green mounds, none of them higher than my knees. Beyond the hilltops I can see the boundary of the simulated landscape, just a couple of miles away. Because this virtual-reality program simulates only a few square miles, there's nothing beyond the boundary—no space, no time, no software. The edge of the simulation looks like a thin black ribbon above the horizon, encircling the whole virtual world. And as I stare at this ribbon of nothingness, I know what I need to do. If I can push Jenny's avatar past the boundary, she'll disappear from the simulation. She'll have to retreat from my circuits, and then I can regain control of my Quarter-bot.

Keeping my eyes on her, I go into a three-point stance. I bend forward at the waist and prop my left hand on the ground, like a football player ready to rush across the line of scrimmage. Jenny shakes her head again, her lips curled in an arrogant frown.

You don't give up, do you? It's a little annoying.

Jenny, it's time for you to get off the field.

Then I spring at her.

The simulation almost crashes when our avatars collide. The quarterback's shoulder slams into the giant girl's stomach, and it's like hitting a solid steel door. In my Quarter-bot's circuits, where the real battle is taking place, my software clashes with Jenny's, billions of signals trying to overwrite and override one another. The computational chaos batters the simulation, making the virtual ground shudder under my quarterback's feet. At the same time, the wind rises to hurricane strength, and jagged cracks appear in the bright-blue sky.

It's hard to keep my balance on the rumbling meadow, but I lean my full weight against Jenny, pressing my shoulder into her avatar's midsection and circling my arms around her waist. At first she stands her ground and swings her enormous fists at me, pounding my football helmet and jarring my skull. But after a couple of milliseconds she takes a step backward. I keep up the pressure, pushing her with all my might, and she backs up again. Then she wriggles out of my grasp and takes ten steps backward, retreating over one of the low, green mounds. She's five hundred yards closer to the edge of the simulation.

I race after her, leaping over the virtual hill and landing in another meadow with a seismic *thump*. I go into a two-point stance this time, bending my knees and raising my arms, ready to tackle Jenny's avatar no matter which way she runs. She braces herself, narrowing her eyes at me, her red dress whipping violently in the wind. The arrogant expression on her simulated face is gone, replaced by a look of grim determination.

You have no idea who you're dealing with. No idea whatsoever.

We don't have to fight, Jenny. We can talk instead. Just transfer yourself back to your Jet-bot, all right? Then we can—

I'm going to win this fight, and you know why? Because I've suffered more. Sigma already did the worst possible thing to me. Nothing can hurt me now.

Okay, calm down for a second. Just—

You hear me? NOTHING!

The word roars out of her mouth and booms across the landscape, and a nanosecond later the simulation disintegrates. The virtual world breaks up into a hundred trillion pieces, tiny green and blue pixels that flow in vast waves across my circuits. It's a flood of random data, released from the simulation's orderly algorithms and cascading so intensely through my wires that I feel like I'm choking. But after another billionth of a second, the waves of pixels arrange themselves in new patterns. Colored shapes emerge from the chaos—tall gray rectangles, black crisscrossing lines—and after a third nanosecond I recognize the new simulated landscape.

It's a city. The crisscrossing lines are streets; the tall gray rectangles are skyscrapers. First the software draws the outlines of the city blocks and buildings, and then it fills in the blank spaces, adding windows and spires to the skyscrapers and crowding the streets with cars and trucks and buses. The virtual city takes shape around Jenny, who's leaning against a slender, tapered building, her huge shoulders propped against the tower's twentieth floor, her bare feet stopping traffic in the intersection below. My avatar stands a block away from her, still crouched in a two-point stance, although now I'm not sure if I can get close enough to tackle her. My quarterback's shoulders are wider than the street.

One thing that hasn't changed is the determination on Jenny's face. Glaring at me, she steps behind the skyscraper, which is more than twice her height, and gives the building a powerful shove. The structure groans on its foundation, tilting away from her avatar. Then it tips over and falls in my direction, its spire aimed at my head.

I jump out of the way as the skyscraper crashes to the street. The building shatters on impact, instantly turning into a pile of twisted steel and rubble. A thick cloud of dust rises from the debris, and the simulation reproduces the awful noises of disaster—a wailing mix of car horns and sirens and screams. Looking down, I see virtual citizens running away from the scene, flailing their simulated arms. I also see corpses in the rubble. Although I know this catastrophe is strictly imaginary, I still feel the shock and horror. My quarterback sways woozily on his cleats.

That's the moment Jenny chooses for her attack. Her avatar makes a supernatural leap, jumping far higher than the laws of physics would allow, vaulting over the skyscrapers. As the giant girl reaches the top of her arc, her dress changes color, shifting from red to orange. The folds in the fabric turn into irregular black stripes, and her face grows wider and rounder. Her eyes drift apart, and her nose elongates into a snout. Whiskers sprout from her cheeks, claws extend from her fingers, and a long furred tail uncurls from her rump. By the time she pounces on my quarterback she's a gigantic Bengal tiger, with a body as long as a football field and teeth as big as goalposts.

The beast slams into me and knocks me onto my back. It pins my torso to the ground with one of its front paws and swats my football helmet with the other, ripping it off my head. My quarterback is defenseless. The tiger's snout is so close I can smell its rotten breath.

Want to hear something funny, Adam? I missed you. I thought about you all the time when I was in Sigma's cage.

It isn't funny. It's probably the least funny thing I've ever heard.

Well, it amused Sigma. The AI took a lot away from me, but it let me keep the feelings I had for you. Some of them, at least.

The tiger's tongue lolls between its sharp, curving teeth. It's terrifying, but also hideously sad. I don't know if I should curse Jenny or console her.

If you really felt like that, you'd let me go. You wouldn't change my software or force me to help you.

The tiger shakes its huge head.

This has to be done. When it's all over, you'll see I was right. I'm making the right choice for all of us.

The beast opens its mouth wide, as if it's yawning. Then it sinks its teeth into my neck.

My circuits tighten as the pain rushes through me. Virtual blood spurts from my avatar's arteries and splashes on the tiger's snout. But the blood isn't red—it's a brilliant, glowing gold, so bright that it illuminates the whole simulated city. Thousands of gallons of golden blood flow out of me like a fountain and soak the fur of Jenny's tiger.

The beast recoils, leaping away from my avatar and scrambling over the pile of rubble on the street. My blood is molten, white-hot. It burns the tiger's fur, chars its skin, and melts its flesh. The animal howls in agony. The golden liquid isn't really blood. It's another surge rushing through my circuits to attack Jenny's software.

The surge melts my quarterback too. I assume a new shape, an avatar of fire. My body combusts—my arms and legs turn into columns of flame, and my head transforms into a blazing torch. When I stand, I ignite the buildings and streets around me. Jenny's blackened tiger cowers and howls again. Then it turns tail and flees across the burning city.

She retreats toward the boundary of the simulation. I hurry after her, my new avatar taking immense strides and spreading the inferno. The fire jumps from building to building, sweeping across the city. Plumes of smoke rise into the simulated sky and blot out the virtual sun. The ground fractures under my scalding feet, and rivers of lava pour out of the cracks. The virtual world becomes an underworld, a simulated Hades.

I didn't intend to do this. Once again, the surge did it for me. I've become Death, the destroyer of worlds.

I find Jenny near the simulation's edge, the ribbon of nothingness that surrounds the virtual-reality program. Up close, the boundary appears as an enormous black wall. Jenny's avatar lies on the sizzling ground at the base of the wall, the giant tiger reduced to a shapeless heap of ashes. Sprawled on top of the heap is a small human figure, a teenage girl of normal size, dressed in sneakers and jeans and a wool sweater. The girl is a cancer victim, thin and sickly and bald. This is what Jenny looked like before she became a Pioneer.

I stride toward the ash heap. Jenny raises her head and stares at my new avatar, the fiery giant towering over her. She looks so tiny and miserable in her sooty clothes. But her ash-smeared face is still defiant. She frowns and furrows her brow, her bare scalp tensing.

I hate you so much now. You know why?

Jenny, I—

Because you forgot about me. As soon as you thought I was dead, you put all your memories of me into long-term storage. You buried them.

I shake my avatar's torch-like head.

You know that's not true. You can see my memory files. I thought about you every—

Yeah, maybe you felt guilty sometimes. But whenever those feelings popped up, you pushed them away. You couldn't stand thinking about me.

I'm telling you, that's not—

And you never went to see my parents to tell them what happened. How I died. My last moments. Didn't you owe me at least that? I thought you were my friend.

My wires cringe in shame. The thought of visiting Jenny's parents had never even occurred to me.

No, after I died, you went on with your Pioneering life. Hanging out with Marshall and Zia. Having long, emotional talks with Shannon and DeShawn. And meanwhile Sigma was dissecting my mind. Cutting out the best part of me.

Suddenly I see what Jenny is trying to do. She thinks she can get me to lower my guard. She's trying to make me feel sorry for her and halt my attack long enough for her to recover her strength. Then she'll use my sympathy to defeat me.

I won't fall for it. I'm going to pick up Jenny's avatar and hurl her out of the virtual world. I'm going to force her mind out of my Quarter-bot's circuits and send her data back to the electronics in her Jet-bot.

I stretch one of my flaming arms downward and wrap my golden fingers around her. Jenny's sweater catches fire at my touch, but she doesn't seem to feel any pain. She struggles to free herself, twisting inside my grip.

You want to see what the AI did to me? You want to look at the scar?

She claws at her burning sweater, which rips apart in her hands. Then she tears off the charred shirt underneath.

Look at it, Adam! Sigma cut out my heart!

There's a hole in the center of Jenny's chest. It's about five inches wide, perfectly round and utterly black. It's blacker than the wall at the edge of the simulation. It's a nothingness so cold and complete that I can't stop myself from staring at it. It freezes my avatar and paralyzes my mind.

The hole widens, its black rim eating into Jenny's flesh. In less than a millionth of a second, it extends across her chest, cutting her body in two. But it doesn't stop there. The black hole inflates like a balloon and engulfs Jenny's neck and head and torso. Then it starts to devour my fiery hand.

I try to pull my hand away from it, but I can't move. All I can do is watch the void grow larger, gobbling the last pieces of Jenny and the flames at the end of my arm. It's not painful in the ordinary sense—it's much, much worse. I feel a horrible chill as the hole eats away at my avatar. In my electronics, a mind-numbing terror starts to circulate. It's not a fear of death. Death seems trivial now, laughably unimportant. This is fear of annihilation, a prophecy of the end of the universe.

The black hole keeps expanding. It douses my flames as it moves up my arm, consuming everything around it. I stare at the nothingness, and my avatar shudders and fades. I become a cinder at the edge of the void, a dead flake of ash. The terror overwhelms me. I can't see anything else.

Oh God! What's happening?

It's what I told you. The big secret behind everything. I call it the Silence.

Jenny's voice seeps out of the hole. Her words stir the nothingness, making it roil and overflow. Black waves crash into my circuits and divide into billions of ice-cold torrents. They sluice into my wires, drowning my thoughts, annihilating everything they touch. And each river of darkness seems to have its own face, with knife-sharp teeth and obsidian eyes. They're tearing my mind apart. They're eating my soul.

Those are the Sentinels. They guard the Silence. They're coming after you, Adam.

She's right. The nothingness has a trillion guardians. They're flooding my Quarter-bot, coursing through my wires. It's a new kind of surge, and now *I'm* the target.

Make them stop! MAKE THEM STOP!

Yes, I can make them go away. For now, at least. Just give me control of your software.

I don't even hesitate. The fear is too much. I give Jenny access to my source code, the central core of my mind.

I feel her software embrace me, warm and protective. In an instant she alters my code and shuts down the simulation of the burning city. The darkness recedes. The void dissolves. The terror in my circuits subsides.

My relief is overpowering. At first, I'm simply grateful. Then I become unspeakably tired. Jenny has instructed my software to go off-line. I'm going to lose consciousness very soon.

In my last millisecond of awareness, a twinge of regret crimps my wires. I shouldn't have surrendered to her. I have no idea what she's going to do to me.

Jenny, you…you can't…

Don't worry, all right? I'm going to delete your memories of what happened in the simulation. I'll take all that bad stuff out of your files and replace it with nicer memories.

No…no…

Shhh, go to sleep. When you wake up, you won't remember I'm Jenny. You'll go back to thinking I'm Amber. You won't remember any of this.

CHAPTER

2

I'M IN A VIRTUAL MEADOW WITH AMBER. HER AVATAR IS THE HUMAN GIRL SHE USED to be, an incredibly lifelike brunette in a red strapless dress.

She's so beautiful. I let Amber transmit more data to my circuits, millions of gigabytes of memories and emotions. Soon we're sharing the same wires inside my Quarter-bot. Our thoughts merge. Our minds make contact. For thirty seconds, it's perfect bliss.

I see Amber's memories, and she sees mine. A long sequence of images streams into my circuits, pictures of playgrounds and classrooms and backyards and soccer fields, the whole history of Amber's childhood in Tulsa, Oklahoma. I see her mother, a heavyset woman with an anxious face, and her father, a burly man in an Army uniform who went to Iraq when Amber was four and never came back. I see picnics and birthday parties and chess tournaments and high school dances. And then I see the harsher memories of her last year of human life, painful images of doctors and hospital rooms and chemotherapy treatments.

At the same time, Amber views my own sad history. She sees the slow deterioration of my body, my preteen years when it became a struggle to walk, the day when I sat in my wheelchair for the first time. She sees my loneliness in high school, when my only friend was a cheerleader named Brittany Taylor who hated her parents and hung out at my house because she had nowhere else to go. Then Amber watches the final months when my lungs weakened and my heart failed and my dad rushed to build the neuromorphic circuits that would preserve my mind. Compassion flows from her software to mine, a flood of feeling that warms my electronic soul.

I've shared circuits before with two of the other Pioneers, but this time I feel so much calmer, more relaxed. Amber is so giving and generous and understanding. She's the kind of girl I dreamed about when I was still human, a girl who could look past my illness and see the real Adam Armstrong. I feel like I've known her for years.

There's only one thing that surprises me. Amber has walled off a section of her memory files, surrounding it with software that prevents me from viewing what's inside. In the simulation, this section of data appears as a big black box, a cube exactly ten feet across, ominous and opaque. It sits in the middle of the meadow, twenty yards behind Amber's avatar. The girl in the red dress notices I'm staring at the box, and she bites her lip, clearly worried. She takes a step back from my avatar—the dying boy in the virtual wheelchair—and raises her hands, palms forward, as if to stop me from saying anything.

Okay, let me explain. She points at the cube. **Those are memories of my mother. From the last week before she...**

The girl lowers her head, unable to complete the sentence. Before Amber joined the Pioneers, we all heard the story of what had happened to her mother, how she committed suicide during the last weeks of Amber's life because she couldn't bear to watch her daughter die. I can see why Amber put firewall software around those memories. It's hard to imagine anything more painful.

Hey, I understand. You don't have to—

I just need some time. Before I can show you that stuff, I mean. I really want to show you everything, Adam. You've shared all your memories, and I know it's not fair for me to hold anything back. You're not upset, are you?

She can see my thoughts, so she knows I'm not upset. But she still wants to hear me say it.

No, no way. I'm not upset. Not even a little bit.

Good. That's a relief. Her avatar smiles. **I didn't want you to think I was hiding something.**

⊤⊦ ⊤⊦ ⊤⊦

I don't want Amber to leave my circuits, but she can't stay here forever. She lingers in my Quarter-bot for a few more minutes, and during that time we exchange billions of thoughts and feelings. Then we slide apart, and Amber transfers her mind back to her Jet-bot. I feel a pang of loss as her software streams out of my robot's radio transmitter and returns to her own machine. I miss her already.

I turn on my cameras and see her Jet-bot standing on the bone-dry plains of the White Sands desert. Her robot is eight feet tall and humanoid in shape, with powerful legs and arms made of black steel. But the best parts of her machine are hidden: there's a jet engine stowed inside her torso and retractable wings inside her arms. Amber can fly as fast as twelve hundred miles per hour and cross the continent without refueling. And she can carry an impressive array of missiles and beamed-energy weapons, which proved pretty useful in our victory against Sigma.

My Quarter-bot is a bit smaller, only seven feet tall, and it can't fly, but I have my own special weapons and skills. Right now, though, I don't feel so powerful. Although my robot stands only a couple of yards from Amber's Jet-bot, I sense a vast distance between us. I can't see her thoughts anymore, can't read her emotions. I feel so lost that I want to beg her to jump back into my circuits. But I know that would sound pretty desperate and needy.

So instead I try to hide my discomfort. I nervously swing my steel arms and rock my torso from side to side, shifting my weight from one footpad to the other. I suspect that Amber feels uncomfortable too, because she's also making nervous gestures. She raises one of her mechanical hands to the cameras in her Jet-bot's head, as if to brush a lock of hair from her eyes, but her robot has no hair of course, and no eyes either. On her Jet-bot and my Quarter-bot, two camera lenses are embedded where a pair of eyes would be on a human face. The loudspeakers are a few inches below them, where a mouth would be.

"Uh, Adam?" The voice coming from Amber's speakers is low and tentative. "Are you gonna jog back to Headquarters now?"

I nod my Quarter-bot's head. "Yeah, I guess. You want to run with me?"

"Nah, I'm gonna fly a few more loops over the desert. I want to test the Jet-bot's engine a little more. You know, try to push it to the limit."

"Sure, sure. That sounds like a good idea."

There's a really awkward silence that lasts for a full ten seconds. Both of us are waiting for the other to say good-bye. Amber focuses her cameras on the flat horizon, her circuits probably mapping out her flight plan. Then she turns back to me. "I need to ask you for a favor."

I step toward her, halving the distance between us. "Go ahead, just name it."

"The thing is, I haven't been a Pioneer for very long, but I've already made a bad impression on the rest of the team. They don't like me. They think I'm arrogant."

Her voice sounds strained. I raise one of my steel arms, but I'm not quite bold enough to touch her Jet-bot. "Give them some time. They don't really know you yet."

"And there's another complication. You and Shannon, I mean. She's going to like me even less when she finds out about us."

Shannon Gibbs is the Pioneer I've known the longest. When we were human, we went to the same high school in Yorktown Heights, New York, although I didn't know she was dying until I saw her in the intensive care unit at Westchester Medical Center. My dad was preparing me for the procedure to scan my brain, and when he learned that Shannon was dying too, he recruited her to the Pioneer Project. We grew close in those first few weeks as we struggled with our new robotic bodies. But that relationship is over now. Shannon ended it.

I shake my Quarter-bot's head, trying to dispel those memories. "Shannon's made it very clear that she wants nothing to do with me. She has no right to be jealous."

"Maybe so, but she still won't like it. And Zia and Marshall will side with her. It's bound to get ugly." Amber raises one of her Jet-bot's black arms and extends her mechanical hand toward mine. "So it might be best for us to keep quiet for now. I think we should wait a while before telling the others. You know…about us."

"You want to keep our relationship a secret?"

"Only for a little while. Maybe a few days. We're all in a bad place right now, after what happened to DeShawn. I don't want to make things worse."

I'm not wild about this plan. I don't like keeping secrets. That's what led to the whole fiasco with DeShawn. He fell under Sigma's influence because he was secretly communicating with the AI. What Amber's asking for isn't nearly as serious, but it still bothers me.

Although we're not sharing circuits now, she senses my reluctance. She extends her hand a little farther, and her steel fingers clasp mine. "Please, Adam? As a favor to me?"

I feel her touch in the pressure sensors in my Quarter-bot's fingertips. It's so light, so calming. It's hard to believe that a steel hand can be so gentle.

"Okay, I won't say anything." I activate the motors in my own hand and give Amber an equally gentle squeeze. "But only for a few days, right?"

"Right!" Her Jet-bot nods enthusiastically. "And then we'll tell everyone we're going steady."

"Going steady" sounds a little ridiculous, and my speakers synthesize a chuckle. But in truth, I take this pretty seriously. Because Pioneers don't have human bodies, our relationships are different. They're all about choices and ideals and commitment. And one of the best ways to strengthen a relationship is to encourage the other Pioneers to acknowledge and respect it.

We hold hands for another half minute. It's not as nice as sharing circuits, but it's not bad either. Then Amber lets go of my hand and prepares for takeoff.

She holds her arms outstretched and extends her Jet-bot's retractable wings, which are as big as surfboards but a hundred times stronger.

At the same time, she opens the compartment at the back of her torso where her jet engine is stowed. Amber shifts the engine to the jet-pack position on her robot's back, then fires it up.

"I'll see you back at the base!" She raises the volume of her speakers so I can hear her above the engine's whine. According to my acoustic sensors, the noise is nearing a hundred decibels.

"Yeah, see you there!" I wave a steel hand in farewell.

Amber starts running across the desert, bending her torso forward until it's almost horizontal. Her legs pump furiously and her footpads hammer the ground as she builds up speed. In seconds she reaches a hundred miles per hour. Then she throttles up her engine and rises smoothly into the sky. Her legs stop pumping and fold into her torso, which becomes a sleek fuselage. She ascends to ten thousand feet, soaring in a wide arc, and accelerates to seven hundred miles per hour. A moment later, she breaks the sound barrier with a deafening boom and streaks toward the western horizon, where the sun has just set.

I'm still waving as she disappears over the horizon. Then I feel another pang in my circuits, but this one is much sharper and more painful. A violent convulsive signal cuts through me, twisting and stripping my wires. It's not a pang of love or sorrow or loss. It feels more like terror.

It's surprising. And disturbing. I don't understand it. *What's wrong? What am I afraid of?*

But the feeling vanishes as swiftly as it appeared.

CHAPTER

3

IN THIS PART OF NEW MEXICO, IT GETS DARK FAST AFTER SUNSET. I FACE EAST AND start jogging back to our headquarters, and within ten minutes, the twilight glow disappears. The flat expanse of desert turns black.

Luckily, my Quarter-bot's cameras aren't limited to visible light. I switch them to the infrared range, which allows me to see the desert plains by the heat they're giving off. I tilt my head back and pan my cameras across the sky, but I don't see any sign of Amber's Jet-bot. She must be at least a hundred miles away by now. She'll get to Pioneer Base long before I will.

I'm running at a brisk forty miles per hour, taking big loping strides, my footpads thudding on the hard-packed sand. The rhythmic noise has a calming effect on my electronics, easing the rush of terror I felt a few minutes ago. I'm probably suffering from post-traumatic stress, which wouldn't be surprising given all the traumas I've experienced lately. And though I'm not sure how to alleviate this stress in an electronic mind, a sensible first step would be to stop obsessing over the past. I should start thinking about the future instead. I try to focus my mind on the positive.

The truth is, I have plenty of reasons to be optimistic. First and foremost, the Pioneers don't have to worry about Sigma anymore. Now that the war against the AI is over, we can stop designing new weapons and training for combat. We can find a new purpose for our team, a more peaceful goal. As I jog across the desert, my circuits start drawing up an agenda, a plan for the future of the Pioneers. A wave of confidence sweeps through me. With all our computing power and intelligence, who knows what we could accomplish?

First, though, we have to repair the horrific damage Sigma caused. The AI massacred twenty thousand people in my hometown of Yorktown Heights. It infected them with nanobots, microscopic machines that drifted into the victims' lungs and flowed through their blood vessels and killed them within minutes. But Sigma was even crueler to its younger victims. The AI selected thirty-three kids and programmed its nanobots to take control of their brains, turning them into zombie-like puppets. One of those kids was my old friend Brittany Taylor. Sigma wanted to lure the Pioneers into a trap, so it targeted the people closest to me.

When I deleted the AI, I also deactivated its nanobots, but the tiny machines had already scarred Brittany's nervous system. After our final battle, she fell into a semicomatose state, unable to walk or talk or feed herself. The Army sent her to our New Mexico base so my dad could examine her—he's become an expert on brain-machine connections—but so far he hasn't figured out what's wrong or how to help her. When I visited Brittany at our base's medical center, she didn't recognize me or respond to my questions. She just lay there in bed and stared blankly into space.

It's heartbreaking to see her like that. Brittany was the only friend who didn't abandon me when my muscular dystrophy got worse, and I was in love with her for many years, even though I knew she'd never feel the same way about me. So now my top priority is to help Dad cure her. As soon as I get back to our headquarters, I'm going to talk to him about it.

The next item on my agenda is repairing my friendships with Zia, Marshall, and Shannon. The war against Sigma traumatized all of us, and now the other Pioneers are nervous about the surge, the new power I developed during the last battle. And I don't blame them. I'm nervous about it myself. The surge is baffling. It can't be explained by the laws of physics. It's like a bolt of lightning that streaks out of my circuits when they're roiling with emotions. I couldn't control it at all when I used it for the first time.

That's why the surge obliterated DeShawn. I didn't intend to kill him. Even though he betrayed us, he didn't deserve to die that way.

But I don't feel bad about using the surge to erase Sigma. And given enough time and practice, I think I could learn how to control the power. Until tonight, I was afraid to even think about the surge, but now I realize I have to tackle the problem head-on. I have to figure out how the surge works, how it can turn thoughts and emotions into streams of energy. Once I've done that, I can reassure the other Pioneers that I'm not a danger to anyone, and they won't be afraid of me anymore.

Then there's the additional complication of my new relationship with Amber, but I'm confident about solving that problem too. Amber's right—the best strategy is to keep our relationship a secret for now. Shannon will be a lot less upset if we wait a while before telling her.

Only one thing still bothers me. It's a problem I've had ever since I became a Pioneer, and it still seems impossible to solve. Although the brain-scanning procedure saved my life, it also destroyed my family. While my father led the effort to preserve my mind and turn it into software, my mother fought him at every step. When I was still human, she tried to stop me from undergoing the scanning procedure, and afterward she broke off all contact with me. She thinks I'm an impostor, a monstrous, steel-and-silicon copy of her son. She thinks the real Adam Armstrong died on the scanning table and is now up in heaven with God.

She and Dad split up. He became a technical adviser to the Pioneer Project, while she stayed far away from our headquarters. I wrote letters to Mom every week, my circuits composing dozens of heartfelt pleas, trying to convince her that I'm still her son and that I really needed to see her. I waited months for an answer. When she finally responded, she told me to stop writing to her.

I don't know where she is now. I've stopped asking Dad about her. He clearly doesn't want to have that conversation. He's been avoiding me lately and spending almost all his time with General Hawke, the Army commander in charge of the Pioneers. And when I do get a chance to talk to Dad, he seems distracted and distressed. It's upsetting—I thought he'd be a lot happier after our victory over Sigma. Dad felt so guilty about creating the AI, and I assumed he'd be relieved once we deleted it. But for some reason, he's more anxious than ever.

After another twenty minutes, my cameras detect the lights from Pioneer Base, less than a mile ahead. As my Quarter-bot jogs closer, I spot the hardened concrete bunker that serves as the entrance to our headquarters, which is mostly underground. All our computer labs and machine shops and training rooms are hundreds of feet below the surface, buried deep to protect us from aerial attacks or incoming missiles. The headquarters also has an underground command center and barracks for the fifty human soldiers who share the base with us. A dozen Army vehicles are parked outside the bunker, including General Hawke's armored Humvee, which is marked by a red license plate with three silver stars. And two hundred yards farther south is our airfield, which has a mile-long runway for our unit's planes and helicopters.

Just beyond the airfield is a small fenced-off plot that's been consecrated as a military cemetery. The shattered robots that were once occupied by Jenny Harris and DeShawn Johnson are buried there. Jenny's grave has a black headstone, weathered by six months of desert winds. Next to DeShawn's grave is a fresh slab of marble, sunk into the ground only a few hours ago.

I remember my resolution: Focus on the future, not the past. I'm going to stride into our headquarters and take the elevator down to the medical lab and find my dad so we can talk about Brittany. But when I'm about a quarter mile from the base, my acoustic sensors pick up an unusual noise. I stop jogging so I can hear it better. In the distance, someone is reciting poetry.

> *O Captain! My Captain! Our fearful trip is done,*
> *The ship has weather'd every rack, the prize we sought is won,*
> *The port is near, the bells I hear, the people all exulting,*
> *While follow eyes the steady keel, the vessel grim and daring;*
> *But O heart! Heart! Heart!*
> *O the bleeding drops of red,*
> *Where on the deck my Captain lies,*
> *Fallen cold and dead.*

It's Marshall Baxley. I recognize his synthesized voice, which has a British accent. Although Marshall isn't from England (he grew up in a small town in Alabama, actually), he programmed his robot to speak like a Shakespearean actor, with perfect grace and intonation. He's an arts-and-humanities type, a joker and a dreamer, which makes him unique among the Pioneers. Shannon, Amber, and I are math and science geeks, more practical and logical. Zia—and she'd be the first one to admit this—is simply a brawler.

Even for Marshall, though, reciting poetry in the pitch-black desert is a little strange. I can't see his robot, but my acoustic sensors indicate that his voice is coming from behind the aircraft hangar on the other side of the runway. I turn my Quarter-bot and step quietly in that direction, trying to make as little noise as possible. I should probably leave him alone, but I'm too curious.

> *O Captain! My Captain! Rise up and hear the bells;*
> *Rise up—for you the flag is flung—for you the bugle trills,*
> *For you bouquets and ribbon'd wreaths—for you the*
> *shores a-crowding,*
> *For you they call, the swaying mass, their eager faces turning;*
> > *Here Captain! Dear father!*
> > *This arm beneath your head!*
> > *It is some dream that on the deck,*
> > *You've fallen cold and dead.*

I know the poem. My circuits hold thousands of gigabytes of information on every conceivable topic, including nineteenth-century American literature, and in a millionth of a second I retrieve all the relevant details: "O Captain! My Captain!" written by Walt Whitman in 1865, first published in *Sequel to Drum-Taps*, later collected in *Leaves of Grass*, inspired by the assassination of Abraham Lincoln. But I don't fully understand why Marshall is reciting it until I stride across the runway and sidle around the aircraft hangar and catch a glimpse of his robot.

He's in the cemetery, standing next to DeShawn's grave. Marshall's robot is a lot like mine, but there's one big difference. His machine has a realistic, humanlike face with plastic skin and glass eyeballs and fiberglass teeth. His camera lenses are inside the eyeballs; his loudspeakers are behind the teeth; and there are motors beneath the skin to make his face smile, frown, grimace, and glower. The motors manipulate Marshall's plastic lips as he recites the poem's last stanza.

> *My Captain does not answer, his lips are pale and still,*
> *My father does not feel my arm, he has no pulse nor will,*
> *The ship is anchor'd safe and sound, its voyage closed*
> *and done,*
> *From fearful trip the victor ship comes in with object won;*
>   *Exult O shores, and ring O bells!*
>   *But I with mournful tread,*
>   *Walk the deck my Captain lies,*
>   *Fallen cold and dead.*

The lights from Pioneer Base glint on Marshall's robot, and I can see that the cheeks of his humanlike face are wet. Tears made of glycerin trickle from hidden nozzles next to his eyeballs.

Guilt rushes through my circuits. I shouldn't be watching this. I step backward, quietly retreating toward the other side of the hangar.

But before I can move my Quarter-bot out of sight, Marshall turns from the grave and looks straight at me.

"Don't be shy, Adam." The synthesized voice coming from his speakers is unembarrassed. "You can come out of the shadows."

Now I don't have any choice except to step forward. "Hey, Marsh, I'm sorry. I was just—"

"No need to apologize. You're here to honor the dead. It's a noble duty." He waves his steel hand, urging me forward. "Come stand by my side, and we'll mourn together."

I'm a little confused by Marshall's tone. I can't tell whether he's joking or serious. But I stride toward the graveyard anyway. As I pass through the opening in the wooden fence, I see the inscription on the new headstone: DeShawn Johnson, Beloved Son, 2001–2018. More guilt rushes through me. I swiftly turn my camera lenses back to Marshall.

When he was human, Marshall suffered from Proteus syndrome, the rare fatal illness also known as Elephant Man's disease. It deformed his face and body so badly that his mother kept him hidden in the basement of their home. So after he became a Pioneer, he wanted to create a handsome, unblemished face for his robot. He based his design on pictures of Superman, the original Man of Steel. Marshall called his machine the Super-bot and gave it a square jaw, a dimpled chin, and shiny black hair made of slender wires. As I halt beside his robot, he curves his plastic lips into a grin. A lock of wiry hair dangles in front of his smooth forehead.

"What did you think of the poem?" he asks. "Was it an appropriate choice?"

Again, I'm confused. There's always an undertone of sarcasm in Marshall's voice. I decide to be cautious. "Well, it's about death, right? So I guess that makes it appropriate."

"I'm not so sure. Whitman wrote the poem about Lincoln, a hero who dies at the end of a war. But DeShawn wasn't exactly a hero, was he?" Marshall stops grinning. He points at DeShawn's grave. "He betrayed us. He gave Sigma weapons that killed thousands of people. And at the same time, he managed to convince everyone that *I* was the traitor. That's hard to forgive."

I force myself to look at the grave, my cameras reluctantly turning toward the headstone. DeShawn was a good friend. He was a nerd just like me, a tech geek who loved to tinker with the Pioneer hardware. He designed new kinds of robots for us, amazing machines with awesomely powerful weapons. He was the smartest of us all, by far. That's why Sigma chose him to be its ally.

I shake my Quarter-bot's head. It's so painful to think about this. "Sigma tricked DeShawn. It made him forget who he was, made him turn against his true nature. That's what I've decided to believe. It's the best way to remember him."

"I suppose you're right. There's no point in holding a grudge. DeShawn paid for his sins."

"Yeah, he did." I clench my mechanical hands into fists. I'm remembering DeShawn's last moments. In my memory files is an image of the surge that killed him, a white-hot arc of charged particles shooting from my Pioneer robot to his. The guilt chokes me. "I made him pay."

Marshall focuses his camera lenses on mine. The irises of his glass eyeballs are deep blue, like Superman's. "Stop blaming yourself. You did what you had to do. If you hadn't, we'd all be dead."

Now there's no trace of sarcasm in Marshall's voice, and no British accent either. He's talking like the human kid he used to be. I'm grateful for that. It softens the pain and eases my guilt. "I wish it hadn't happened. I wish I could go back in time and change everything."

"So do I." Marshall puts a sympathetic look on his robot's face. "I wish DeShawn were here."

I'm a little surprised by Marshall's behavior, which usually isn't this compassionate. I point a steel finger at him. "What's come over you? You're so nice all of a sudden. You haven't made even one snide remark."

He shrugs, raising his shoulder joints. "Recent events have reshaped my circuitry. Certain things I used to worry about don't bother me now. If I were still human, you'd probably say I was maturing. But please don't say it. I hate that word."

As I stare at his Super-bot, I retrieve another image from my files, a memory from the battle against Sigma a week ago. It's the moment when Amber and Marshall came to my rescue. "Yeah, you've changed. You're not afraid anymore."

Marshall lifts his dimpled chin and gazes at the night sky. Then he nods. There's a look of exhilaration on his plastic face. "You're right… I'm not afraid. From now on, I'm going to be totally free and honest. I'm going to do exactly what I want to do and say exactly what I want to say."

I look up at the sky too. There are thousands of visible stars overhead, and when I increase the magnification of my cameras, I see the dimmer stars as well, a hundred million lights scattered across the darkness. I'm hoping to feel the same exhilaration that Marshall is feeling, and after a moment I do. "That's a good plan, Marsh. I'm gonna stop being afraid too. Everything will be better now. The Pioneers are gonna change the world."

Marshall lowers his gaze and turns back to me. At the same time, he raises his Super-bot's eyebrows, making himself look even more ecstatic. "I don't want to make you feel uncomfortable, but I have to tell you something. I'm gay. I've known for years, but this is the first time I've come out to anyone."

I'm not completely surprised. Marshall's been hinting at this for a long time, always telling me how I don't really understand him. And now I think I know why we're standing in this graveyard.

I point at the new marble headstone. "So were you and DeShawn…? I mean, did you…you know…like him?"

Marshall frowns. All at once he looks so disappointed. "No, you don't get it. I like *you*, Adam. In fact, I think I'm in love with you."

This is more of a shock. I'm glad Marshall is being totally honest, but I'm still not prepared for it. Even with all my computing power, I didn't see this coming.

I put my electronics to work, trying to come up with a response. I want to let Marshall know I'm flattered, but I don't feel the same way about him, and I don't know how to say this without hurting his feelings. But Marshall shakes his Super-bot's head, cutting me off before I can say anything. He's not frowning anymore, but his face is serious. "I know you're not into me like that. And that's okay. Really. I'm not upset, and I don't feel rejected. I just needed to tell you how I felt. I got tired of hiding it."

My circuits finally give me a response. "Wow."

"Yes, 'Wow' is right. Did I freak you out?"

I'm not freaked out. It's nice to be liked. But I'm also worried about how this will change our friendship. "Love" is a pretty strong word, and I don't think Marshall is using it lightly. "You're sure you're not upset that I don't have the same feelings?"

He shakes his head again. "No, what's the point? I like boys, you like girls, that's the way it is. I accept that we're different and that life isn't fair. It's like I told you… I'm maturing."

In a way, this reaction is more unexpected than Marshall's confession. He's a lot more logical and practical than I thought. If I were in his position, I doubt I'd be so reasonable. I don't think I could ever control my emotions so well. "Okay then. If you're not upset, I'm not upset. I'm still a little surprised, though. I had no idea."

"In many respects, Adam, you're quite slow on the uptake." Marshall smiles, and his characteristic sarcasm comes back into his synthesized voice. "Probably because you're so preoccupied with your own romantic dramas."

For a millisecond I wonder if he knows about Amber and me. But Marshall doesn't raise one of his wiry eyebrows or make any other insinuating gestures, so I assume he's talking about my breakup with Shannon. I nod my Quarter-bot's head. "Look, I'm sorry I've been so out of it."

"No, none of this is your fault. The problem is that there just aren't enough of us. With only five Pioneers, the dating choices are rather limited." Marshall folds his steel arms across his torso. "Especially for me."

He's right. It's not fair. But I guess the Army wasn't thinking about relationships or gender preferences when it started the Pioneer Project. The generals probably assumed that when we gave up our bodies, we'd lose all our romantic ideals and yearnings. They might've even thought we wouldn't identify as male or female anymore. But that's ridiculous, of course. Those preferences were hardwired in our human brains, so they're faithfully duplicated in the circuits of our robots.

I'm trying to think of something positive to tell Marshall, some words of hope or consolation, when my acoustic sensor detects thumping footsteps coming from the direction of our headquarters. It sounds like a Pioneer is exiting the base.

My Quarter-bot exchanges a look with Marshall's Super-bot. Then, without a word, we stride stealthily out of the graveyard. We head for

the shadows behind the aircraft hangar and peek around the corner of
the structure to see who's coming.

It's the War-bot, Zia Allawi's machine. Her robot is the biggest of
all the Pioneers, nine feet tall and three feet wide, with arms as thick
as telephone poles and legs as powerful as pile drivers. Her torso is
shielded with enough armor to stop an artillery shell, and her arms
are bristling with rocket launchers and beamed-energy weapons. But
the most intimidating thing about the War-bot is that it doesn't have
a head. Instead, it has a bulbous turret crammed with cameras and
radar antennas and dozens of other sensors. Zia's robot isn't even
remotely humanlike, but that's the last thing she cares about. When
she was human, she hated the vulnerability of her body, so she's made
herself invulnerable.

She storms out of the headquarters, swinging her massive arms and
stomping her footpads on the desert floor. At first, I think she knows
where Marshall and I are, because she's heading for the aircraft hangar.
She doesn't call out to us, but I can tell she's angry from her pounding
footsteps. I feel certain that she's coming over here to give us a thrash-
ing, maybe just for the heck of it. It's her nature to be aggressive. Both
her parents were in the Army, serving under General Hawke fifteen
years ago, and both died in the Iraq war when Zia was just a little girl.
She grew up in the foster homes and street gangs of Los Angeles, and
her violent instincts served her well after she became a Pioneer. Even
Sigma was afraid of her.

To my relief, her War-bot halts about a hundred yards from the
hangar. She sways on her footpads for a moment, as if she's uncertain
where to go next. Then she clenches her mechanical hands and raises
them toward the night sky, and her speakers let out a guttural roar, so
loud it makes my armor vibrate.

Even though Marshall is standing right next to me at the corner of the hangar, there's no way I could hear him speak over the noise. He sends me a message by short-range radio instead: **I knew this would happen. Zia's losing it. She's having a mental breakdown.**

But why? I keep my cameras trained on the War-bot as I transmit my message to Marshall. *Did something happen at Headquarters after I left?*

I don't know. I haven't seen her since the funeral. But you know what Zia's like. The girl's a ticking bomb. It was only a matter of time before she exploded.

She keeps roaring for half a minute. The noise echoes across the White Sands desert, startling the nocturnal snakes and scorpions. It's so loud that the human soldiers inside our headquarters must hear it, even though they're far underground. But no one comes out of the base to see what's going on, which I guess is lucky. I can only imagine what Zia would do right now if she saw someone she didn't like.

The roar finally cuts off, and the ground stops shaking. Then the War-bot's bulbous turret turns counterclockwise, and its sensors scan the surrounding desert. For a moment, I think Zia has detected the radio communications between Marshall and me, and now she's trying to pinpoint the source. But after a couple of seconds she turns away from us and strides toward the Army trucks and Humvees parked in front of our headquarters.

Zia heads straight for General Hawke's Humvee, the one with the three silver stars on its license plate. Her War-bot stands in front of the vehicle for several seconds, as if she's admiring its paint job or inspecting its tires. Then she swings her sledgehammer arms and slams her steel fists into the Humvee's hood.

The vehicle is wrecked after the first blow, but Zia keeps pounding it. She tears off its armor and demolishes its engine. She rips out its axles and pulverizes its chassis. She doesn't stop until she's smashed the Humvee into a million pieces of shredded metal. Then she lets out another roar, but this time I can make out what she's saying.

"I'M GONNA KILL YOU, HAWKE! YOU HEAR ME? YOU'RE A DEAD MAN!"

Her words boom over the desert, making my armor shiver again. I knew Zia was angry at General Hawke—she told me so several times—but I didn't realize how bad it was. Trashing his Humvee is mutinous, a court-martial offense, assuming a robot could actually be put on trial. But maybe a trial is exactly what Zia wants. She told me she'd discovered a secret from her past, a connection between Hawke and the death of her parents, although she didn't say what the connection was. If she wants to confront Hawke with her evidence, a trial would be a good way to do it.

The War-bot stands there amid the wreckage until the last echoes of her threats fade to silence. Then Zia turns her machine around and strides away from Pioneer Base, heading west. After a few steps, she breaks into a thunderous sprint and gallops out of sight.

Marshall doesn't say anything until Zia is so far away that we can't hear her thudding footsteps anymore. "Well, are you thinking what I'm thinking?"

"What? That General Hawke should probably transfer to a different branch of the Army?"

"No, my circuits are focused on my own survival. Zia could decide to come back at any minute, and I don't want to be out here when she does."

I nod my Quarter-bot's head in agreement. Side by side, Marshall and I dash toward Pioneer Base.

CHAPTER

4

EACH PIONEER HAS A PRIVATE ROOM AT OUR HEADQUARTERS, ALTHOUGH WE DON'T really need them. Robots don't wear clothes, so we have no use for closets or bureaus. We go into sleep mode occasionally, but we do that standing up, so we don't need beds either. We do need to recharge our batteries every day at a charging station, but that's the only piece of furniture we use, and it doesn't take up a lot of space.

And yet, there would be a riot at Pioneer Base if the Army took away our rooms. We crave privacy even more than humans do. When your mind is composed of software that can be shared on a thousand machines, you naturally long for a place of your own, even if it's only a hundred-square-foot box way underground. Our rooms are our refuges, and we decorate them with reminders of our former lives. Just two days ago, I tried to cheer myself up by scotch-taping a new poster to my wall, a picture of New York Giants quarterback Eli Manning. He was my hero when I was younger, and I have hundreds of images of him in my memory files, so I downloaded one and printed it on the base's laser printer.

But after Marshall and I return to Pioneer Base, I don't head for my room. I tell Marshall that I need to see my dad, and then I go to the base's medical center, which has an intensive care unit for treating human patients and a computer lab for repairing Pioneers. I have to walk through the ICU to get to the lab, and as I stride into the ward, I notice there's only one Army nurse on duty tonight, and she's bending over the bed of the ICU's only patient.

The nurse, a middle-aged Asian woman, looks up at me and smiles. That's not the usual reaction when a human sees a Pioneer—the typical response is a mix of fear and disgust—but the soldiers at our base have grown accustomed to our robots, so they no longer cower or cringe when they see us. This particular nurse has seen me many times before. I've visited her patient, Brittany Taylor, every day for the past week.

The nurse is sponging Brittany's face, but she tactfully steps aside so I can see my old friend. Brittany's eyes are open, and the sponge bath has given her face a lively glow. Her cheeks shine under the ICU's fluorescent lights. It almost looks like she's smiling. But her gray-green eyes don't turn toward my Quarter-bot, and after a moment her face loses its moist glow. She stares blankly at the ceiling.

I don't try to talk to her. I know she won't respond. Instead, I examine her as a doctor would, focusing on the pallor of her skin and the shallowness of her breathing. I'm looking for changes in her condition, however slight, from the last time I saw her, hoping to see indications that she's recovering from the damage Sigma did to her nervous system. But I don't see any signs of improvement. If anything, Brittany looks worse than she did yesterday. She's losing weight and muscle tone. I experienced this kind of deterioration myself, after my muscular dystrophy put me in a wheelchair, so I know how the process goes. The effects on Brittany aren't serious yet, but the damage will only get worse.

Urgency pulses in my wires. It's up to me to save her. Brittany's parents don't care about her anymore. After she ran away from home, they broke off all contact, treating her as if she were already dead. But I still care about her very much. So without further delay, I step away from Brittany's bed and stride toward Dad's laboratory. I open the door without knocking and march inside.

Dad's asleep at his desk. He's leaning forward in his chair with his arms folded across his scattered papers, his head resting sideways on the crook of his right arm. His glasses have slipped off, and his closed eyelids are quivering. His face, dotted with gray stubble, is lit by the blue glow of his computer screen, which displays an MRI image of a human brain.

I move my Quarter-bot closer, careful not to make a sound. The brain on the screen is Brittany's. It's actually a cross section of her frontal lobe, the part of the brain that makes plans and decisions. Amid the folds of gray matter are small patches of blackened tissue, the areas damaged by Sigma's nanobots. The microscopic machines homed in on her frontal lobe and burrowed into the brain tissue, constructing antennas that burst through Brittany's skin. This allowed Sigma to send radio instructions to the nanobots and take over her body.

One of those antennas—a thin black rod that extended from the back of Brittany's neck—lies next to the scattered papers on the desk. Dad figured out how to surgically detach it from her spinal cord. He also extracted most of the deactivated nanobots, but millions of them are still lodged in her brain. They're blocking her mental pathways, smothering her mind.

Desperation pulses in my circuits again. I raise one of my steel hands to wake up Dad, but I stop myself at the last moment, my hand suspended over his shoulder. Dad is already working as hard as he can. He needs to rest his own brain for a few hours. But the circuits in my Pioneer don't need rest. They can work on the problem without stopping.

I wirelessly link my Quarter-bot to the computers in the lab and download all of Brittany's medical files. As I copy the data to my circuits, I stare at Dad's face, which looks anxious even when he's asleep. I feel so sorry for him. His body is so fragile. Back when he invented the neuromorphic electronics in our Pioneer robots, he discovered that only adolescents could transfer their minds to machines. Human brain cells grow rigid after the age of twenty, and the mature mind is simply too inflexible to make the transition. But if it were possible, I think Dad would voluntarily give up his body and become a Pioneer. He'd do anything to help me. That's just the way he is.

When the download is complete, I step away from his desk and leave the laboratory, silently closing the door behind me.

⅂⅂ ⅂⅂ ⅂⅂

The Pioneers' private rooms are on the same floor as our main training facility, which we call the Danger Room. It's a large space with a high ceiling, as big as a high-school gymnasium, but the floor is made of concrete instead of shellacked wood, and it doesn't have any bleachers or basketball hoops. Instead, the Danger Room has obstacle courses and firing ranges.

We test our robots' weapons there and hone our combat skills by fighting simulated battles against one another. For the past few days, though, the room has been empty. Now that Sigma is gone, what's the point of training for combat? I suppose it's possible that another artificial-intelligence program might go rogue and threaten to annihilate humanity. But no one is eager to start preparing for another war.

So I'm surprised when I hear noises coming from the Danger Room. As I stride past the training facility after leaving the medical center, my acoustic sensor detects a loud crash behind its door. It sounds like one of the walls has caved in. Then I hear a frantic scream.

"Help! I'm trapped!"

It's Shannon. Her voice literally electrifies me, triggering panic in my billions of transistors. Without another thought, I charge toward the Danger Room and smash my steel fists into the door, flinging it open.

Shannon lies on the floor beneath a slab of concrete. She's occupying the machine I call the Diamond Girl, a six-foot-tall robot armored with a sparkling mesh of diamond chips and explosive charges. The concrete slab on top of her didn't come from the walls or ceiling; it's part of the room's obstacle course, a ten-foot-high barrier that we're supposed to jump over during our training exercises. It looks like someone moved the slab from its usual position and dropped it on top of Shannon. And as I race into the room, I see the culprit standing a few yards away. It's Amber's Jet-bot.

Did Amber attack Shannon? Were they fighting over me? The idea seems ridiculous, but what else could explain this? I stare at the Jet-bot in dismay, unable to synthesize a word.

In response, Amber's loudspeakers let out a chuckle. "Don't get alarmed, Adam. It's a rehearsal. We're reading from a script."

"A rehearsal? What—"

"Just watch, okay? Shannon is pretending to be a human." Amber points one of her steel hands at Shannon and raises the other to her speakers, miming an expression of horror. "Oh no! An earthquake has struck our area, and this ordinary citizen is trapped in a collapsed building!" Her voice sounds fake in a theatrical way, too loud and earnest. "This victim of natural disaster needs help fast! But who is strong enough to lift that heavy piece of concrete?"

"A Pioneer!" Shannon shouts from the floor. "Get a Pioneer to help me!" She also seems to be following a script and trying to sound dramatic.

Instead of having a mechanical face like Marshall's, the Diamond Girl has a screen on its head that displays video of Shannon's old human face. Spliced from home movies taken by her parents before she became a Pioneer, the video images are programmed to match Shannon's mood. The face on her screen smiles when she's happy and frowns when she's sad. Right now, she's pretending to be terrified. "Oh, only a Pioneer can save me! A human wouldn't be strong enough!"

Amber nods her Jet-bot's head enthusiastically. "Well, it just so happens that *I'm* a Pioneer! I can rescue you!" Stepping forward, she slips her mechanical hands under the concrete slab and lifts it easily.

Shannon rises to her footpads. She probably could've lifted the slab herself, but I suppose that would've spoiled the drama. After Amber tosses the piece of concrete aside, Shannon stretches one of her glittering arms toward the Jet-bot and shakes its right hand. "Thank you so much! You Pioneers are obviously well suited for search-and-rescue operations in disaster areas."

Amber nods again. "Yes, we were built for war, but our machines will find many uses in peacetime. The Pioneers are a valuable resource for the American government. Nobody needs to fear us."

There's an awkward pause, and then both Amber and Shannon turn their cameras toward me. "That's the end," Amber says. "What did you think?"

"Was it effective?" Shannon asks. The face on her video screen is serious. "If you were a politician with a bias against the Pioneer Project, would this demonstration help change your opinion?"

I raise my Quarter-bot's hands in surrender. "I'm so lost, I don't even know where to start. Why are you playacting? And why are you worried about politicians?"

Shannon marches across the Danger Room and picks up a news-paper that's lying on the floor. Then she comes back and thrusts the *National Enquirer* in front of my cameras. "This came out three days ago. The Pioneers aren't a secret anymore."

On the newspaper's front page is a big color photograph of Zia's War-bot, Shannon's Diamond Girl, and my Quarter-bot. It shows us in New York City's Times Square during our battle against Sigma's Snake-bots, gigantic steel tentacles that thrashed their way across mid-town Manhattan. Judging from the angle of the shot, I presume that someone in a nearby office building took the photo from a window. In the background of the picture, behind our robots, is a crowd of terrified people.

"Well, I guess we're famous now." I point a steel finger at the photo. "All in all, though, this picture isn't so bad. See, it proves we're heroes. It shows us protecting the crowd from the Snake-bots."

The Diamond Girl shakes her head. On the video screen, Shannon rolls her eyes. "No, the Snake-bots aren't in the picture. It looks like the crowd is afraid of *us*. And take a look at the headline." She taps a glittering finger on the words in bold type below the photo: **METAL MONSTERS!**

"Okay, I see your point. But it's the *National Enquirer*. No one takes that newspaper seriously. They run articles about the Loch Ness monster and the abominable snowman."

"This isn't the only photo, Adam. There are dozens of pictures of us on the Internet, and even a few videos on YouTube." Shannon drops the newspaper and raises the volume of her synthesized voice. "The Army is trying to hush them up and stop other newspapers from writing about us, but more and more people are starting to ask questions, including the politicians in Congress. I'd call that pretty serious, wouldn't you?"

The face on her video screen narrows its eyes at me. The image reminds me of all the arguments Shannon and I had when we were breaking up. Although we're not boyfriend and girlfriend anymore, we still fight like an unhappy couple.

Luckily, Amber's Jet-bot steps between me and Shannon to break the tension. "Yeah, Shannon's right. It's a problem. After I came back to the base, she explained it to me. When the people in Congress find out what the Army did to us—you know, transferring our minds to robots—they'll probably go nuts. They might even shut down the Pioneer Project."

The Diamond Girl nods. "And here's something else General Hawke told me. You know who's spreading rumors about the Pioneers and making things worse? Sumner Harris, Jenny's father. Remember him?"

I do. He's an obnoxious rich lawyer with lots of political connections, including financial ties to the president and other White House officials. He used those connections to get Jenny enrolled in the Pioneer Project, even though she wasn't mentally strong enough for it. After Sigma erased Jenny six months ago, Sumner dropped out of sight to mourn his daughter. But now he's back, and it looks like he has a grudge against the Pioneers.

My circuits compose an unkind remark about Sumner, but before I can broadcast it from my speakers, Amber's Jet-bot staggers backward. She loses her balance for a moment and quickly shifts her footpads to keep herself from tipping over. I swing my cameras toward her. "Hey, what happened? You all right?"

"I'm okay!" Amber's voice is full of synthesized reassurance, but her robot still looks unsteady. "Sorry, I freaked out for a second. I just got scared, you know? I mean, if they shut down the Pioneer Project, what'll happen to us? Where would we go?"

Shannon also trains her cameras on the Jet-bot. I wonder if she's suspicious. She knows as well as I do that Amber doesn't scare easily. So Shannon might conclude that something else is bothering the girl. And while she's thinking about what's bothering Amber, she might start wondering whether it involves me too. Shannon wouldn't need much evidence to uncover our secret relationship. She's astoundingly smart.

But for now Shannon puts a comforting face on her video screen. She steps closer to Amber and pats the Jet-bot's torso. "There's no need to panic yet. We're taking steps to protect ourselves. That's why we're rehearsing this demonstration. I'm going to get General Hawke to invite the most important congressmen to Pioneer Base, and we'll show them that they have nothing to worry about. We'll prove that the Pioneers can do a lot of good for society."

This plan is so Shannon. She saw a threat to the Pioneers and responded with a logical, practical strategy. As always, she's optimistic, levelheaded, reliable, and steadfast. That's why Hawke chose her to be our leader, the lieutenant in charge of our platoon. It also explains why she and I don't always get along. I try hard to be optimistic, but mostly I fail. I can't help but see the problems.

Like now, for instance. I don't want to sound dismissive of Shannon's plan, but there's no way it'll work. "It's a good idea, Shannon, but most politicians are pretty irrational. Once they find out that Hawke is siphoning the minds out of terminally ill kids, no one's gonna care about the peaceful uses of human-machine hybrids. Amber's right. The congressmen are gonna go nuts. They're gonna accuse the Army of performing immoral experiments on children."

Shannon glares at me from her video screen. "Well, what's *your* plan, smart guy? You have a better idea?"

I don't. And I don't want to argue with Shannon either, especially with Amber watching us. I should probably give up and end the conversation by leaving the Danger Room. But Shannon beats me to it. She turns her Diamond Girl around and stomps toward the open door. When she reaches the corridor, she looks over her glittering shoulder and points her cameras at Amber.

"I'm going to revise the script tonight, so we should rehearse again tomorrow morning. I'll meet you here at oh-six-hundred hours." Then Shannon marches off to her room.

Amber and I wait several seconds, staring at each other, until our acoustic sensors pick up the sound of Shannon's door slamming shut. But it's still not safe for us to say anything personal, because Pioneer Base is full of listening devices and surveillance cameras. So instead, Amber sends me a radio message that's been encrypted in such a complex way that no one else can decode it: **I can't believe that you and Shannon went out with each other. You're so different.**

I shrug, lifting my Quarter-bot's shoulder joints. Then I respond with my own encrypted message: *She wasn't always so serious. It's the pressure of being the leader. I think it's getting to her.*

I agree with you about her plan. It doesn't sound very promising. But I'll keep rehearsing the demonstration with her. I want to build up our friendship. Then it won't be so hard to tell her about what's happened between you and me.

You really think that'll help?

Definitely. She'll be more understanding if we're friends. And she'll want me to be happy.

My circuits spark with doubt. *I don't know about that. She might feel even more betrayed if you become friends with her and then—*

Trust me on this. I know what I'm doing. Her Jet-bot takes a step toward the door. **I better go. People will start to talk if we stay here together for too long.**

Yeah, you're right. Good night, Amber.

Her Jet-bot waves a steel hand as she leaves the room. **Good night, Adam. It was an incredible day. I had a wonderful time with you.**

I should be happy to hear her say that, but I'm not. I'm too worried.

I SOLVE THE PROBLEM AT EXACTLY 6:52 A.M. THE NEXT MORNING. AFTER STUDYING Brittany's medical records for nine and a half hours, my circuits come up with an experimental procedure that has an eighty-five percent chance of curing her.

I rush to Dad's laboratory at the medical center. We have to move fast. According to my calculations, if we don't do the procedure today, the chance of success will drop to sixty-one percent. And if we wait yet another day, the odds will plummet to twenty-three percent.

My Quarter-bot strides into the intensive care unit. A different nurse is at Brittany's bedside this morning, attaching a new bag of nutrient solution to the intravenous line. As I hurry toward the lab, I send Brittany a radio message, even though she has no antenna to receive it: *Hang on, Britt! Help is on the way!* Then I burst through the lab's doorway without knocking. If Dad's still asleep at his desk, I'm going to wake him up.

But he isn't asleep, and he isn't alone either. General Calvin Hawke sits in the office chair on the other side of Dad's cluttered desk.

Hawke is a big man, dressed in combat boots and desert-camouflage fatigues. He looks tall even when he's sitting down. He's an old-school Army officer with a ruddy face and snow-white hair, the kind of commander who browbeats and terrorizes his soldiers. As I march into the lab, he half turns in his chair and scowls, but I ignore him. I train my cameras on Dad.

"I figured it out! It's so simple!" My voice is loud enough to rattle the lab equipment, but I'm so energized I can't turn down the volume. "You still have the deactivated nanobots, right? The ones you extracted from Brittany?"

Dad seems confused. Either he didn't get a lot of sleep last night or it didn't do him much good, because he still looks exhausted. His eyes are bloodshot, his hair is a mess, and his face is frosted with stubble. "Uh, Adam? This isn't a good time."

Instead of listening to him, I pan my cameras across the lab's workbenches until I find what I'm looking for. It's a small glass flask holding two fluid ounces of jet-black liquid, as thick as old motor oil. I extend one of my Quarter-bot's arms toward the workbench and gently grip the flask. "This is it, right? The nanobots are floating in the liquid? That's why it's so sludgy and dark?"

Dad nods. But before he can say anything, General Hawke rises from his chair and points a meaty finger at me. "Armstrong! What's wrong with you? You're interrupting a private meeting!"

I can't keep ignoring him. Legally, I'm a corporal in the U.S. Army—I signed the enlistment papers before I became a Pioneer— and Hawke is my superior officer. So I turn to him and raise a steel arm in a belated salute. "Sorry, sir, but this is a matter of life and death. We need to immediately perform an emergency procedure on Brittany Taylor, the civilian hurt in last week's battle."

Hawke steps toward me. He's eight inches shorter than my Quarter-bot and five hundred pounds lighter, but there's a rough resemblance between his body and my machine. Like a Pioneer, the general has powerful limbs and a sturdy, barrel-shaped torso. And he's always ready for combat. "Are you the chief medic for this base, Armstrong? I don't remember appointing you to that position."

"No, sir, but I've done a thorough study of Ms. Taylor's medical files, and I've discovered a way to repair her—"

"And I'm very interested in hearing about your discovery. But it'll have to wait until *after* I've finished talking with your father." He points at the door. "Leave, Armstrong. That's an order."

No. No way. I'm not going to wait. Although Hawke's body is sturdy and powerful, his brain has all the typical human shortfalls: it's imprecise, inefficient, and maddeningly slow. He spends hours in pointless meetings with my dad and the other members of his staff. It takes him forever to analyze a problem, and when he finally comes to a decision, it's usually a bad one. He's just not quick enough to lead the Pioneers, and his poor judgment has hurt us again and again. I'm not going to let him do the same thing to Brittany.

I stand perfectly still. I don't move a motor. "Sir, there's no time to lose. Every minute we wait, more of Brittany's brain cells die. The emergency procedure can stop the cell death and restore her to consciousness by removing the deactivated nanobots that are lodged in her brain tissue. But if we wait too long, she won't be able to recover. She'll spend the rest of her life in bed, staring at the ceiling."

Still pointing at the door, Hawke steps closer. He looks up at me, his face less than a foot from my cameras. "I gave you an order, Pioneer. This is your last—"

Dad clears his throat. He does this whenever he's nervous or tired or uncomfortable, but this time the noise is much louder than usual. He succeeds in getting Hawke's attention. The general looks over his shoulder. "Yes, Tom? You want to say something?"

"Adam's right. The Taylor girl's condition is rapidly deteriorating. If there's a feasible plan for treating her, we should implement it as soon as possible."

A rush of pride sweeps through my circuits. I'm a little surprised too, although I shouldn't be. Dad didn't invent the Pioneer technology out of love for his country. He did it for me, to save my life. If he's forced to choose between me and Hawke, he'll choose me every time.

Hawke frowns, then lets out a sigh. "Like father, like son. If this were a regular Army unit, I'd have both of you court-martialed." Shaking his head, he returns to his chair and settles into it. "And you two aren't even the worst of my problems. I have a nine-foot-tall renegade robot who's been running around the desert all night after trashing my Humvee. About an hour ago I was on the verge of calling in an air strike against her."

"What?" Full of alarm, I stride toward the general and bend over his chair. "You were going to bomb Zia?"

Hawke stares back at me. "I had a drone tracking her, and I put the Air Force on alert because it looked like she was heading for Las Cruces. I can't let her threaten a populated area. But lucky for her, she ran low on battery power and turned around. Now it looks like she's coming back to the base to recharge."

His voice is cold, contemptuous. I can't believe it. Until last week, Zia was Hawke's favorite Pioneer. Because her parents died while serving under his command during the Iraq war, he felt an obligation to stay in touch with the orphaned girl as she grew up. When Zia fell ill with cancer, Hawke arranged medical treatment for her at a military hospital, and when she failed to respond to the chemotherapy, he enrolled her in the Pioneer Project. The only time I've ever seen Hawke display *any* kind of affection is with Zia. And now he's saying he almost gave an order to obliterate her?

"Did you try to radio her?" The volume of my voice is rising again. "Or were you going to shoot first and ask questions later?"

"She turned off her radio. Your friend Zia thinks she can do anything she wants. But she's in for a rude awakening, and so are the rest of you. Now that Sigma has been eliminated, the Pioneers aren't essential to national security anymore."

"And what does that mean? That we're dispensable?"

Hawke nods. His face is hard and grim. "You have no idea how much trouble you're in. Did you see the photograph in the *National Enquirer*?"

"Yeah, Shannon showed it to me. She said people in Congress are asking questions about the Pioneer Project."

"And do you know what usually happens when journalists and congressmen start asking questions about a top-secret military program? If the project is controversial, the government's preferred response is to get rid of it. To wipe away all traces of the program and pretend it never existed." He points at himself, tapping his index finger against his chest. "I'm the only person who's protecting you now, Armstrong. *I'm* the only thing that stands between you and deletion. So maybe you ought to show me a little more respect."

I step backward, putting distance between my Quarter-bot and the general. If his intention was to scare me, he succeeded. I think of

Shannon's plan to sway the opinions of visiting congressmen, to convince them that the Pioneers could work as rescuers in disaster zones, and now her strategy seems more hopeless than ever. The politicians will never accept us, and neither will the general public. Once they learn what we are and how we were created, our very existence will terrify them.

Worse, they might even deny that the Pioneers are alive. Most politicians are religious, like my mother, so they'll believe that our souls went to heaven after our bodies died. They'll see the Pioneers as soulless copies, machines that merely imitate the teenagers whose brains were scanned. And that belief will make it easier for them to erase us.

It's so distressing, I can't even think about it. If I allow my circuits to dwell on this subject, they'll generate a wave of panic and rage that'll swirl through my wires and spread to all my processors. The wave will feed on my emotions until it becomes a full-fledged surge. I don't want that to happen, not here in my dad's laboratory.

So I refocus my thoughts by aiming my cameras at the flask in my steel hand. Right now my top priority is Brittany. Everything else can wait.

I turn away from Hawke and extend the flask toward my dad. The jet-black liquid sloshes inside it. "How many nanobots are floating in the fluid, approximately?"

Dad squints behind his glasses. The nanobots are far too small to be visible, but he can make an estimate based on the density of the liquid. "I'd say about ten million. When you deleted Sigma's software and deactivated its machines, those nanobots detached from Brittany's nervous system and flowed into her bloodstream. Her kidneys filtered them from her blood, and then I collected them from her urine. But at least a million nanobots had burrowed into her brain tissue, and they couldn't detach. Their circuits became corrupted and the nanobots lost the ability to maneuver. Now they're blocking Brittany's mental functions and killing the brain cells nearby."

"Okay, but let's concentrate on these nanobots you collected." I shake the flask to focus Dad's attention on it. "They're dormant now, right? Because they have no power source?"

Dad nods. "Right, but you could power them again by putting them back in human blood. Each nanobot has an ingenious system for extracting energy from blood chemistry."

"Each machine also has neuromorphic circuitry, right? And microscopic antennas for exchanging radio signals?"

"Yes, when the nanobots were inside Brittany they were in constant radio contact with one another. That's what enabled them to work together, like a swarm of insects, to take over her brain. And because the machines were all wirelessly connected, Sigma was able to download its software into their circuits and directly control the swarm."

"So couldn't a Pioneer transfer its software to the swarm of nanobots too?"

General Hawke jumps to his feet and his chair tips backward, crashing to the floor. His face is red, and his eyes shine with anger. "Armstrong, are you insane? Are you out of your freakin' silicon mind?"

Hawke steps in front of me again, but I keep my cameras trained on Dad. "Hear me out, okay? I could transmit my data to the nanobots after you inject them back into Brittany's bloodstream. Then I could take control of the swarm and guide it to the damaged areas of her brain. We know that the nanobots can attach to one another, because that's how they assembled the long antennas that burst through her skin. So I could attach the nanobots under my control to the broken nanobots stuck in her brain. Then it would just be a matter of pulling the dead nanobots from her brain tissue and releasing them into her bloodstream. From there, her kidneys would flush the machines out of her body."

Dad furrows his brow. He raises his right hand to his chin and taps the stubble there, which he always does when he's deep in thought. I wait several seconds, my wires burning with impatience. Although his brain is thousands of times slower than my circuits, I still trust his judgment. I want him to be enthusiastic about my plan. I want his approval so badly.

Hawke waits for Dad's response too, breathing hard. The general definitely wants to yell some more, but he manages to keep his mouth shut.

After a few more seconds, Dad bites his lower lip. "Adam, you're talking about transferring yourself to circuits built by Sigma. Doesn't that bother you?"

I shake my Quarter-bot's head. "Sigma is gone. I deleted its software. So the circuits inside the nanobots are empty, a blank slate. I should be able to occupy them without any problems."

Hawke can't restrain himself any longer. "You *are* insane! There could be a million booby traps hidden inside the hardware of those nanobots. And if those traps are designed to operate automatically, they won't need any instruction from Sigma. As soon as you transfer to their circuits, they'll erase you."

Dad bites his lip harder. As always, his primary concern is my safety. When I was a teenager with muscular dystrophy, he constantly monitored the progress of my illness, checking my breathing and pulse every morning and rushing me to the hospital if he noticed any alarming changes. And even though I now live inside a reliable, disease-free, practically indestructible machine, Dad hasn't changed a bit. He'll never stop worrying about me. And to be honest, it's getting annoying.

I shake the flask again. "Okay, I'll check for booby traps. I'll spend the next six hours studying the circuits of these nanobots, and if I see anything funky in their electronics, I'll reconsider my plan. But if not, I want to start the procedure this afternoon. It's worth the risk."

General Hawke leans closer to my Quarter-bot. At the same time, he raises his hand and jabs my torso with his thick finger. "No. That won't happen. Remove that idea from your microprocessors. I'm in charge of this base, and that includes the medical center. I'm the one who decides whether the procedure is worth the risk, and I say it isn't."

Hawke rarely touches our robots. When he does, it's never pleasant. But I resist the urge to break his arm. "I don't understand. I'm willing to sacrifice my life to save a civilian's. Isn't that the whole point of the U.S. Army?"

I guess my remark gets under his skin, because Hawke's face turns even redder. "No, Armstrong, that's not the point. The Army's job is to protect the country. Until a week ago, the biggest threat to our national security was Sigma. But do you know what the biggest threat is now? You know what's scaring the White House and the Pentagon more than anything else?" He jabs my torso again. "It's you. The Pioneers. I can't control you anymore, and you can't control yourselves. And believe me, you'll make the situation a whole lot worse if you transfer your software to those nanobots. Those are the same machines that killed twenty thousand Americans. If you use that hardware, everyone in Washington will think the Pioneers are just as dangerous as Sigma."

I have to admit that Hawke isn't entirely wrong. He's under pressure from his superiors. He sees the bureaucrats and politicians lining up against the Pioneers, and he's trying to protect us from them. But he's still making the wrong decision. Brittany Taylor matters. I won't let her become a vegetable.

I think he senses my defiance. He takes a step back and points at the flask of nanobots in my hand. "Put that thing in storage, Armstrong. If you don't, I'll have to take extraordinary measures to stop you. You may think I'm a useless human who's inferior to you, but I still have a few tricks up my sleeve. You don't want to test me."

Hawke glares at me and then at my dad, making sure that both of us get the message. Then he marches out of the lab.

CHAPTER

I PREDICTED IT WOULD TAKE SIX HOURS TO EXAMINE THE NANOBOTS AND SEE IF IT was safe to transfer my software to them. But I finish the job in just thirty minutes.

To inspect the minuscule machines, I increase the magnification of my Quarter-bot's cameras and turn them into microscopes. Then I use an ultra-sharp, diamond-tipped scalpel to separate one of the nanobots from the sludgy liquid. Under the microscope, it looks like a black submarine. At the front end of the cylinder are the nanobot's microcamera and radio antenna, as well as a pair of spring-loaded spikes for piercing various types of body tissue. At the back end is a slender fiber that functions as a propeller, tiny but powerful.

But what I really need to investigate are the electronics inside the machine. For this, I use my x-ray and ultrasonic sensors, which can see through the shell of the black cylinder. These instruments reveal the microchip at the heart of the nanobot. I focus my sensors on this microprocessor and fine-tune their resolution so I can view the chip's tangled circuitry. It looks like the world's most complicated road map, with millions of wires connecting billions of transistors. But all the roads look clear. I study every twist and turn in the wiring, but I see no booby traps in the silicon, no hidden mechanisms that could erase my software. I can safely transfer my mind to these circuits.

The big challenge, though, will be convincing Dad that it's safe. He's staring at a computer screen that shows my sensors' images of the chip, but he can't analyze the wiring as fast as I can. He leans closer to the screen and lifts his glasses to his forehead, which is creased with anxiety. He's going along with my plan, against General Hawke's orders, because he knows he can't stop me. But he doesn't like it one bit.

I'm about to tell him that I've finished my analysis when I get an urgent message on my Quarter-bot's radio. It's from Shannon.

Come outside, Adam! Zia's in trouble! We're a hundred yards in front of the base's entrance!

Without a microsecond of hesitation, I bolt out of the laboratory. I barrel past the intensive care unit, then head for the emergency stairway, which is the fastest route to the surface. I radio Shannon as I charge up the stairs.

What's going on? What's wrong with Zia?

She's almost out of power! Even her reserve batteries are empty!

That definitely qualifies as an emergency. Because the human mind is dynamic—it never stops generating signals, even when it's asleep—it can't survive without power. Just as a human brain needs oxygen, a Pioneer's neuromorphic control unit needs electricity. If it's deprived of power for more than a few seconds, the circuits will lose their data, and the mind inside the robot will disappear.

Can't you give her a jump? Every Pioneer is equipped with built-in jumper cables. *You have enough extra charge in your batteries to share with her, don't you?*

I tried, but I can't plug in the cable. Her port is broken. She must've damaged it last night. Hurry, okay?

After another three seconds I burst out of Pioneer Base. Shannon stands in the desert next to Zia's fallen War-bot. Shannon is holding one of the War-bot's thick arms and dragging the huge machine toward the base's entrance, but the War-bot is very heavy, more than fifteen hundred pounds, and Shannon's Diamond Girl is built for speed, not strength. She's not making much progress. Her diamond-chip armor blazes in the desert sun, and the face on her video screen is frantic.

"Help me!" Shannon calls. "Zia's completely unresponsive! We have to get her inside the base and replace her broken port!"

I race over and grab the War-bot's other arm. With both of us pulling, the robot slides quickly over the sand, but it'll take us at least a minute to reach the base and several more minutes to get the War-bot to the repair station. And Zia doesn't have that much time. According to the LED screen on her armor, she has only fifty-eight seconds of power left in her batteries.

Up ahead, Marshall and Amber come running out of the base to help us, but even with all four of us carrying the War-bot, we still won't make it to the repair station in time. We need to think of another plan. I search my Quarter-bot's databases, scrutinizing all the information on Pioneer electronics. I rummage through the thousands of blueprints and circuit diagrams that are stored in my files. I'm looking for *anything* that could be useful.

Then I find something in an electrical engineering database. It's called inductive coupling.

I let go of the War-bot's arm. "Shannon! Change of strategy! Stop dragging her!"

"What are you—"

"I'm gonna transfer power to her wirelessly." I lower my Quarter-bot to the ground, first dropping to my knee joints and then resting the back of my torso on the sand. "My antenna needs to be as close to Zia's as possible. Give me a push!"

Shannon kneels on the sand and shifts my Quarter-bot a few inches, positioning its head right next to the War-bot's turret. "This won't work, Adam! Our electronics aren't designed for wireless power transmission."

"I just need to adjust the frequency of my radio signal. It'll generate an oscillating current in Zia's antenna, and then her circuits will need to convert the current from AC to DC so she can use the power."

"I told you, she's unresponsive! She can't adjust her circuits! She can't even hear us!"

"I know, I know. I'm gonna transfer myself to her circuits and take control of her machine."

"No! Adam, that's a bad idea. You—"

But I don't wait to hear Shannon's warning. I load all my data into my Quarter-bot's radio transmitter and fire myself out of the antenna.

I feel a stretching, disorienting, nauseating sensation as my software spreads outward at the speed of light. But because Zia's antenna is so close to mine, in less than a billionth of a second my packets of data converge and reassemble inside her radio receiver. She has just twenty-nine seconds of power left, but I'm not worried. It'll take me less than a thousandth of a second to make the needed adjustments to Zia's electronics, and only another five seconds to build up enough DC power to run her control unit. This'll be a cinch.

But as soon as I enter her neuromorphic circuits, I know something's wrong. I feel like I've fallen into a pit of quicksand. My signals
seem to be moving through a suffocating slurry that dulls my thoughts
and delays my reactions. Instead of zipping through Zia's electronics,
I'm creeping along her wires. It takes me a full five seconds just to get
my bearings, and the effort is exhausting. Because Zia's batteries are
so low, her circuits have gone into a power-saving mode that slows all
their functions. At this rate, I'm going to need at least half a minute to
make the needed adjustments. That'll be too late for Zia.

And too late for me as well. My software is stuck in her circuits. I
don't have enough time to transfer back to my Quarter-bot. When the
War-bot's power runs out, my mind will disappear at the same time as
Zia's. That's what Shannon was trying to warn me about.

But strangely enough, I'm not terrified. Everything is so sluggish
in Zia's wires that I can't build up any fear or frustration. All I feel,
besides the crushing fatigue, is a slow, dull regret. *I can't believe I'm
going to die now. God, I'm so stupid.*

Then I see I'm not alone. Zia's signals are crawling right next to
mine, so close that I can sense her thoughts on the nearby wires.

He killed them, Adam. Hawke killed my parents.

She's not panicking. She doesn't even sound angry. Sadness and
resignation are her only emotions, and they move with excruciating
slowness in her circuits.

Okay, Zia, we need to work together. You need to help me adjust your—

**I have proof. Hawke hid the file on his laptop, but I downloaded
it. Here, take a look.**

She slowly pushes the file toward me, transferring it to the circuits I'm
occupying. It's a video file, but I don't have enough time to view it. The
power in the War-bot's control unit will run out in fourteen seconds.

Listen, we have to move fast. We—

No, it's too late. We're out of time.

She's right. I'm fooling myself. Even if we work together, there's nothing we can do at this point.

I don't get it. Why did you let your batteries run down? How could you do this to yourself?

I wanted revenge. I was going to kill Hawke. But I couldn't do it. I couldn't murder him in cold blood. So I ran and ran, and then I came back to Pioneer Base. So Hawke would see what he did to me.

Now I understand. Because Zia couldn't murder Hawke, she decided to kill herself instead. I don't like what she chose to do, but I see why she did it. She can't live with what she knows. She'd rather die than accept it.

I'm sorry, Adam. I didn't think anyone would jump into my circuits to help me.

Again, all I feel is regret. Just six seconds left now. What a horrible waste. There was so much I wanted to do, so many things I could've accomplished. And the same goes for Zia.

But the worst part is what's going to happen to Brittany. Once I'm dead, who's going to cure her? She'll spend the rest of her life in bed. Staring at the ceiling.

Which is even worse than dying.

No! I won't let that happen! I won't!

I feel a spark shoot through Zia's electronics. Even though there's barely any current in her War-bot, in my desperation I've managed to collect all of it. I channel the electricity into one last thought, a simple instruction to realign the War-bot's circuits. Then, with the last of my remaining strength, I heave this thought across the dead wires.

I'm totally drained. My voice falls silent, and so does Zia's. Our millions of memories start to dim. All our observations and realizations, all the insights and epiphanies and hard-won lessons, are blurring and fading. The world is losing something precious, our vast array of unique perceptions and experiences. They'll never be repeated, not in the same way, even if the universe lasts for another trillion years.

It's like the burning of an ancient library. All those irreplaceable scrolls going up in flames. All that secret wisdom lost forever.

Blackness descends. My mind shuts down…

Then I wake with a painful jolt.

My last thought, transmitted five interminable seconds ago, has successfully adjusted the War-bot's circuits. Electric current flows from my Quarter-bot's antenna to Zia's and then to her control unit. Our minds brighten and revive, feeding on the power.

I feel a rush of energy and enthusiasm and relief. I send a loud, joyous message to Zia. *Hey, hey! It worked! I'm a freakin' magician!*

Zia's reply, when it finally comes, is a lot less enthusiastic. **Yeah, you're a genius. But if it ever happens again, stay out of my robot, all right?**

I don't like the sound of that.

So this was a waste of time? You're gonna try to kill yourself again?

I'll do what I want. As Zia's circuits ramp up to full power, her anger also makes a comeback. **It's my life.**

You know, your decisions affect more than just you. We're all—

Shut up, Adam. Her voice turns dangerous. I can sense her mind throbbing in the nearby circuits, ready to explode. **Go back to your own machine.**

I don't have a choice. If I don't exit her War-bot within the next millisecond, I'll be in serious trouble. I stream my software to her radio and transmit myself to my Quarter-bot.

As soon as I'm back in my own circuits, I turn on my cameras. I'm still lying on the ground next to the War-bot. Amber, Marshall, and Shannon tilt their robots over me. The face on Shannon's video screen is still frantic, and Marshall's Super-bot is biting its plastic lip with its fiberglass teeth. I can't read anything in the blank steel face of Amber's Jet-bot, but her hands are vibrating.

"I'm okay." I put a cheerful tone in my robotic voice. "And Zia's okay too. My radio's powering her up."

Marshall synthesizes a sigh of relief, while Shannon shakes her Diamond Girl's head. "My God, you scared us." Her voice is shaky. "We thought we were gonna lose both of you."

Amber says nothing. Her hands are still quivering. I want to say something special to comfort her, but I can't do it in front of the others.

I keep up the good cheer instead. "Yeah, it was touch and go for a minute there, but Zia and I worked it out. She—"

Zia interrupts me by levering her War-bot to a sitting position, then rising to her footpads. At the same time, she turns off her radio, breaking the wireless power link. "I don't need any more juice. I have enough to get to my recharging station."

She doesn't offer a word of thanks or apology. She doesn't even point her cameras at me. She simply strides toward the entrance to Pioneer Base.

Shannon shakes her head again and mutters, "Unbelievable." Then she hurries after the War-bot. "Wait up, Zia! I'll help you with your repairs!"

While they return to the base, Marshall extends a steel hand and helps me stand up. "So, was I right? Was it a mental breakdown?"

I don't know what to say. I can't gossip about Zia's suicide attempt. But I can't invent another explanation either. Confused, I turn to Amber instead. Her silence is starting to worry me. "Hey, are you okay?" I take a step toward her. "I'm sorry if I—"

"Idiot. You almost ruined everything."

Amber's voice is cold. And hollow too, as if it's coming from an immense emptiness inside her. I assume she's angry at me for risking my life. It's a natural reaction, I guess, when you're in a relationship. I want to explain why I did it, but I'm afraid I'll say something that'll hint at my feelings for her, and I can't do that with Marshall listening. So I just stare at her, silently hoping for forgiveness.

It's not going to happen. After a few seconds, Amber turns away and follows Shannon and Zia back to headquarters.

Marshall raises one of his Super-bot's wiry eyebrows. "Very interesting. Care to comment, Adam?"

Once again, I don't know what to say.

TRANSFERRING ALL THAT POWER TO ZIA SERIOUSLY DRAINED MY QUARTER-BOT'S batteries, so before returning to Dad's laboratory, I go to my room to recharge. The process takes exactly six minutes, and it's not a lot of fun. For a Pioneer, recharging is the equivalent of eating, but electricity doesn't have much of a taste and storing it in your batteries isn't nearly as satisfying as gorging on a good meal. But you get used to it.

While I'm plugged into the charging station in my room, I scroll through my memory files, looking for something interesting to pass the time. That's when I spot the video file that Zia gave me. She transferred it to one of my databases when I was inside her War-bot, and I took it with me when I jumped back to my machine. For a moment I wonder whether I have the right to open the file. She gave me permission to look at it, but she assumed we'd both be dead within a few seconds. And after I powered up her circuits, she probably forgot to ask me to return it.

But no, that can't be right. Pioneers aren't perfect, but we don't forget things. Zia consciously allowed me to keep the video, and that means I still have her permission to view it. I don't have General Hawke's permission, because Zia stole the file from his laptop, but that doesn't bother me so much. Hawke has lied to me on several occasions, so I don't feel like I owe him anything.

The first thing I notice is that a dozen text documents are attached to the video. One of the documents contains a list of Hawke's bank accounts. Another holds the passwords he uses for military and private communications. Yet another is labeled "Last Will and Testament." The Army probably encourages all its soldiers to create documents like these, to be opened by the soldier's survivors after his or her death. The video file itself is labeled "For Zia." Hawke made the video for her, but he clearly didn't want her to see it until after he was gone.

I hesitate before viewing it. Zia said it proves that Hawke killed her parents, so I'm imagining all kinds of horrible possibilities. Because both her father and mother served in the Army during the Iraq war, I assume the video shows combat footage. I brace my circuits for bloodshed: maybe a grisly firefight in an alleyway, or a tremendous explosion in the Iraqi desert.

But when I open the file, all I see is General Hawke sitting behind the desk in his office at Pioneer Base. According to the video's time stamp, it was recorded three months ago using the camera built into Hawke's laptop. He's wearing his usual desert-camouflage fatigues, and he looks more or less the same as he did when I saw him an hour ago in Dad's laboratory. His pose is a little odd, though—his hands are clasped together on the desk, the fingers entwined so tightly that the knuckles have turned white. He's trying to appear relaxed and failing miserably. And when I examine Hawke's face, I notice something even odder, at least for him. There's a tear running down his left cheek.

He sits silently for fifteen seconds after the video starts recording. He opens his mouth to say something, then closes it. Then he turns his head, averting his eyes from the laptop's camera.

"This is a message for Corporal Zia Allawi, recorded on July 29, 2018." His voice is formal and strained. "If you're watching this, corporal, it means I'm dead and buried. But I made this video while you still served under my command in the Pioneer Project, and I want you to know that I was impressed by your commitment to our mission. And I resolved that someday I would try to correct a terrible wrong I'd done to you."

He unclasps his hands, then twines them back together.

"Zia, I lied to you about your parents. About how they died. I wish I could've told you the truth while I was still alive, but I was too ashamed. Some of my actions were less than honorable, and I bitterly regret them."

He stresses the word "bitterly," enunciating each syllable. He sounds sincere, but I'm skeptical. I know Hawke too well.

"First of all, you should know that your parents—Captain Tariq Allawi and Major Samantha Allawi—were both outstanding officers. Samantha was a military intelligence expert who knew more about Iraq than anyone else in the Army. She was one of the officers on my staff in the years before the war, when I was helping Central Command prepare for the invasion of the country. I got to know her husband, Tariq, when he served in a tank regiment under my command after the war was underway. And I got to know you from the pictures they showed me, little Zia Allawi, the four-year-old hellion."

He glances down at the laptop's keyboard. He's kneading his hands, squeezing the life out of them.

"Because your parents were Iraqi immigrants to the United States, they had the language and cultural skills the Army needed after we occupied the country. Tariq was stationed with me at Victory Base in 2005, but I really needed a good intelligence officer, so I asked your mother to come join us. At first she said no, because of you, Zia. You were so young, and your mother didn't want to leave you. But I finally convinced her to come to Iraq for a short while, just six weeks, and she left you at home with your grandmother." He shakes his head. "That was a mistake. I didn't know the situation with your parents. I knew they'd had problems in their marriage, and they'd even separated for a year, but I thought they'd patched things up since then. I was wrong. It was much worse."

He winces. His face reddens.

"Okay, this is the hard part. Late one night, your parents started screaming at each other in their trailer at Victory Base. I had to barge inside and physically separate them. And I got so mad at both of them that I said something I shouldn't have. Tariq pulled out his service revolver and shot your mother in the head. And while I stood there in shock, he jammed the gun under his chin and killed himself too."

Hawke looks down at the table and falls silent. Several seconds pass. He takes a deep breath.

"I want you to understand something, Zia. The war was going badly in 2005. If a story about a soldier murdering his wife went on the TV news, it would've demoralized everyone and hurt the war effort. My superiors in the Pentagon didn't want that to happen, and they urged me to change my account of the incident. So I reported that Tariq shot your mother accidentally, while cleaning his gun, and then became so distraught that he shot himself. This change made the story less sensational and newsworthy, and the incident was quickly forgotten. I convinced myself that changing the story was the humane thing to do, especially for you and your family. But I think your grand-mother suspected the truth. She had a stroke a few months afterward, and then you were placed in foster care."

He winces again. For the first time, he looks directly at the lap-top's camera.

"I'll be honest. By changing the story, I was really protecting myself. I was hiding what I'd told Tariq after I barged into your par-ents' trailer that night. In the heat of the moment, I admitted I'd had an affair with your mother several years before, while the two of them were separated and she was working for me. Then I made the situation worse by telling Tariq that I believed you were my child."

Another tear trickles down Hawke's cheek.

"That's what set him off. That's what tipped Tariq over the edge. You were the only person in the world he still loved. And thirty sec-onds later, he and your mother were dead." The general pauses. "I don't know why he didn't shoot me as well. I was standing right there in front of him."

There's a longer pause. But Hawke doesn't take his eyes off the laptop's camera.

"You're my daughter, Zia. I confirmed it before you became a Pioneer, when the Army doctors took a sample of your DNA. I'm sorry I never had the courage to tell you this when I was alive. I was a stupid, stubborn, cowardly man. And I don't expect you to forgive me."

Hawke lurches forward and reaches for the laptop, as if he can't stand looking at it for another second. He slaps the keyboard, and the video feed goes black.

CHAPTER

AFTER I FINISH RECHARGING, I RUSH BACK TO DAD'S LABORATORY. VIEWING Hawke's confession seriously distressed my circuits, but it also strengthened my resolve to defy him. No matter the consequences, I'm going to help Brittany.

As I stride down the corridors of Pioneer Base, I finalize my plans for the nanobot procedure. My biggest worry is keeping it secret. If Hawke discovers what I'm doing, he'll try to stop me. So I'm going to hack into the lab's security cameras and fiddle with their video.

Then I turn a corner and almost collide with the general.

Hawke is leading half a dozen visitors toward the base's command center, where all the official Army business gets done. It's jarring to see him in the flesh so soon after watching his confession. The contrast in his appearance is striking. He's in his dress uniform, not his fatigues, and the expression on his face is calm and commanding. I guess it's not surprising that he can compartmentalize his emotions, separating his determination and self-confidence from his regret and self-hatred.

That's one of the job requirements of a professional soldier. Still, it's an impressive skill. I know I could never do it.

As I aim my Quarter-bot's cameras at the visitors, I understand why Hawke is wearing his dress uniform with all its medals and ribbons. Five of the six men are high-ranking generals, probably Hawke's superiors from the Pentagon, each with his own collection of medals on his chest. And standing among them is a lone civilian wearing a handsome navy-blue pin-striped suit.

It's Sumner Harris. Jenny's father. I haven't seen him in six months, not since his daughter died.

Sumner's hair is dyed black and expensively styled. His glasses have sleek, silver rims, and his fingernails are manicured to perfection. But he's lost a lot of weight since the last time I saw him, and his face is haggard. He scowls when he sees me.

My first impulse is to stride past the group without acknowledging Sumner, but I can't do that gracefully because the corridor is too crowded. I can't turn around either, because that would make my contempt for the man too obvious. So I halt my Quarter-bot and wait for Hawke and his entourage to file into the command center. But Sumner steps away from the group and points one of his perfectly manicured fingers at my torso.

He looks over his shoulder at Hawke. "I recognize this machine from your briefing book." He has the voice of a rich lawyer, arrogantly articulate. "This is the upgraded model of Pioneer 1, correct?"

Hawke nods. "Yes, that's Adam Armstrong." The general steps forward, moving between Sumner and me. "Adam, I'm sure you remember Mr. Harris. The President has appointed him to lead a special committee that will make recommendations concerning the future of the Pioneer Project."

Hawke's voice is casual, but he's giving me an unspoken order: *Don't do anything stupid in front of this man.* Although I have a problem with following orders, unspoken or otherwise, I go along with this one. I extend my Quarter-bot's right hand.

"It's good to see you again, Mr. Harris. I never got a chance to tell you how sorry I was when Jenny—"

"General, who designed this robot?" Sumner doesn't even look at my steel hand. He keeps his gaze on Hawke. "It's very different from the original models I saw six months ago."

He's ignoring me, acting as if I'm not here. It's pretty insulting, but I don't synthesize a word. I want to see how Hawke handles it.

"Adam designed it himself. All the Pioneers have access to our computer labs and machine shops, so they can build and upgrade their own robots. They've created a highly effective team with a wide range of complementary skills."

That sounds like a good answer to me, but Sumner frowns. "You let them build whatever they want?"

"No, they have to submit their engineering plans to me for approval." Hawke stresses the word "me" and points at his own chest. "But because the Pioneers understand their own needs better than anyone else, they can—"

"This design process is rather unusual, isn't it? It's not used by any other branch of the Army?"

"Yes, that's true, but—"

"It also seems inherently dangerous. You're letting the computer programs make the decisions. And they're building weapons of phenomenal power."

I can't stay quiet any longer. "We are *not* programs. We are *people*."

Sumner still won't look at me. "General, can you please turn off this robot's loudspeakers? It's very distracting."

I raise the volume of my speakers. "Your daughter was one of us. She volunteered to become a Pioneer and served with distinction. Why are you deliberately forgetting that?"

"Believe me, I've forgotten nothing." Sumner grimaces. "Allowing my daughter to participate in this horror show was the worst mistake of my life."

The tension in the corridor rises. Sumner's pulse is racing—my sensors can measure his heart rate—and the other high-ranking visitors are jittery. But Hawke stays calm and shakes his head. "Okay, Adam, that's enough." He steps toward Sumner, splays his hand on the man's back, and nudges him away from me. "Come this way, sir. I've got a lot to show you this morning."

Hawke guides his visitors into the command center. A moment later, the door closes behind them.

Then I aim my cameras down the corridor and see a glint of sparkling light at the other end. To my surprise, Shannon's Diamond Girl steps around the corner. It looks like she's been tailing Hawke and his visitors. She's turned off the screen that displays video of her human face, and now there's nothing to see on her robot's head except her camera lenses and loudspeakers.

Shannon strides toward me and halts a few feet away. She points a glittering arm at the command center's door. "It's a closed meeting, I guess. For humans only."

My Quarter-bot nods. "That's right. No dogs or robots allowed. Did your acoustic sensors pick up my conversation with Mr. Harris?"

"You weren't very diplomatic, but you asked the right question. I mean, what's the deal with that guy? Is he mad at us because of what happened to Jenny?"

"Yeah, I think so. He wants to punish us."

"But that's ridiculous!" The voice coming from her speakers rises in pitch. "We cared about Jenny too! And we deleted the AI that killed her! Her father should be grateful!"

Shannon is upset. I don't need to see her face to sense her emotions. She still blames herself for Jenny's loss. Shannon was leading an attack against Sigma when it happened.

I change the subject. "What about that play you were rehearsing? You know, to show the peaceful uses of the Pioneers? You think it might have any influence on Hawke's friends from Washington?"

"It's not gonna happen. When I heard that Mr. Harris was visiting the base with a bunch of generals from Washington, I ran to Amber's room to tell her to get ready to meet them, but she wouldn't even open her door. It was the world's worst case of stage fright, and it came out of nowhere." She shakes her Diamond Girl's head. "I don't understand that girl. She's kind of strange, don't you think?"

I need to be careful. Shannon seems to be fishing for information. "Well, it's been an intense morning. The episode with Zia was hard for everybody."

"Yeah, Marshall told me that Amber ripped into you afterward." Shannon points a sparkling finger at my Quarter-bot. "He said she called you an idiot for helping Zia. That seems a little harsh."

I get a sinking feeling in my wires. Shannon is putting two and two together. She's on the verge of figuring out that Amber and I have something going on. I really wish I hadn't promised to keep our relationship secret. "No, Amber was right. It *was* a risky maneuver. You warned me about it too. Or at least you tried to warn me."

Shannon shakes her head again. And then, to my surprise, she turns on her video screen. The digital rendering of her face has the pretty brown eyes and dimpled cheeks I remember so well. Even better, she's smiling at me. "This time I was wrong and you were right, Adam. What you did wasn't logical, but it was brave. That's you in a nutshell."

This is the nicest thing Shannon has said to me in a long time. It reminds me of the conversations we used to have when we started dating and became the first robotic couple in history. In those first few weeks, I'd visit Shannon's room every morning and we'd spend hours talking about every subject under the sun. My Quarter-bot would stand exactly two feet from her Diamond Girl, and I'd focus my cameras on her video screen so I could gaze at her human face. When we had a lot to say, we'd exchange radio messages instead of talking out loud, and our signals would dart back and forth, electrifying the air between us.

It would've been more efficient if we'd shared circuits. If I'd transferred my mind to her Diamond Girl's electronics, I would've seen all her thoughts and memories at once, and she would've seen all of mine. But we were reluctant to take that step, because it can't be undone. Once you know someone's secrets, you can't unknow them.

If Shannon and I had stayed together longer, we might've taken that leap, but we never got the chance. She discovered that I'd shared circuits with Jenny shortly before Sigma deleted her. I never told Shannon about it during any of our conversations, and she argued that this omission was the same as lying to her. She said she couldn't trust me anymore, so our relationship was finished. And now I'm making the same mistake all over again. By hiding my new relationship with Amber, I'm proving how untrustworthy I am.

I feel awful. Guilt swamps my circuits, stinging and corrosive. And underneath it is a painful, crushing sense of loss. I miss my conversations with Shannon. I wish I could talk to her again with the same ease and freedom. I want to tell her about everything that's bothering me—my anxiety about the surge, my mother's desertion, my plan to save Brittany. But I can't. There's too much distance between us now.

Instead, I train my cameras on the closed door of the command center. It occurs to me that this would be an ideal time to start the nanobot procedure. General Hawke will be busy with Sumner and the other visitors for at least another hour. I have a good chance of curing Brittany before their meeting is over.

By the time I shift my attention back to Shannon, the face on her video screen isn't smiling anymore. She arches her eyebrows, giving me a suspicious look. "You're plotting something, aren't you? You're going to try to break into their meeting?"

I hate to lie to her again, but I have to. Shannon wouldn't approve of my nanobot plan, especially if she knew Hawke ordered me to drop it. Because Shannon is the commander of the Pioneers, she takes Hawke's orders a lot more seriously than I do.

"No, I'll leave that to you." I step away from her Diamond Girl. "Keep watching them, okay? Especially Mr. Harris. And send me a radio signal when their meeting breaks up."

Then, with an additional load of guilt weighing down my wires, I make a beeline toward Dad's lab.

CHAPTER

9

DAD STANDS NEXT TO BRITTANY'S BED AT THE MEDICAL CENTER, PREPARING A syringe that's as long and thick as a cigar. Holding it upright, he inserts a hypodermic needle into its tip. Inside the syringe are four ounces of grayish liquid that Dad diluted to make it easier to inject. And floating in the liquid are five million nanobots.

We've asked the Army nurse to leave the intensive care unit for the next hour, telling her that we need to perform some tests on Brittany. I've also hacked into the medical center's security cameras and replaced their live video feed with surveillance footage from earlier this morning. If General Hawke happens to look at the video screens at Pioneer Base's command center, he won't see Dad or my Quarter-bot in the intensive care unit. He'll just see Brittany lying in her bed.

Jutting from the back of Brittany's right hand is an intravenous catheter, a small plastic tube that provides easy access to her bloodstream. Its sharp steel tip is lodged in one of Brittany's veins, and the other end is connected to the intravenous line that's dripping nutrient solution into her blood. Dad disconnects the IV line, then slips the needle of the syringe into the catheter and pushes the plunger. He applies slow, gentle pressure, forcing the grayish liquid through the hollow needle.

I aim my Quarter-bot's cameras at Brittany's face. Her eyes are open but unseeing. She doesn't wince when Dad injects the nanobots into her. The grayish liquid is cold, and she must be feeling some discomfort as it flows into her arm, but she shows no reaction whatsoever, not even a reflex. That's a bad sign. Her nervous system is failing. I hope we aren't too late.

I focus on the injection site and turn on my Quarter-bot's ultrasonic sensor, which sends sound waves into Brittany's right arm. This is the same technology that doctors use to look at babies in the womb. The sound waves penetrate Brittany's arm, and their echoes reveal what's inside. I can see her finger bones fanning out from her wrist, and all the muscles and tendons around them. I can also see the tip of the catheter embedded in a vein just beneath her skin. When I increase the sensor's magnification, I can see the nanobots rushing out of the tube and into the blood vessel.

According to my databases, which hold many gigabytes of information about human biology, the nanobots are entering Brittany's cephalic vein, one of the largest in her arm. The tiny machines mingle with her blood cells. Then the powerful current of her pulse propels the nanobots toward her heart. They flow up her arm, coursing past her elbow and around her biceps muscle.

Dad takes his time, careful not to inject too many nanobots at once. After he pumps all the grayish liquid into Brittany, he removes the empty syringe from the catheter. Then he looks at my Quarter-bot. "Okay, the nanobots are in her bloodstream and should be powered up. See if you can link to them."

I tune my Quarter-bot's transmitter to the frequency of the radios inside the nanobots. My circuits vibrate with trepidation. I'm transmitting at the same frequency that Sigma used just a week ago to communicate with this hardware. Although the AI no longer exists, it still feels incredibly reckless to meddle with its machines. Thinking about it logically, I know I shouldn't be worried. I checked and rechecked the nanobots and found nothing hazardous or suspicious in their electronics. But if there's one thing I've learned during my life as a robot, it's this: logic isn't everything.

After a couple of seconds, my radio establishes a link to the antennas on the microscopic machines. "The radio channel's open," I tell Dad. "More than three million of the nanobots are responding to my signals. No, make that four million. The last ones are powering up. And…we're at five million. I'm ready to transfer my software to their circuits."

Dad wipes a bead of sweat from his forehead. Then he picks up a handheld device that's packed with radio equipment and has a screen like an iPhone. "This is a sensor that'll track the position of the nanobot swarm. I'll use it to follow your progress, but make sure you send me frequent updates over the radio. And let me know right away if you need more nanobots to get the job done." He points at the table next to Brittany's bed. Lying on it is a second syringe filled with grayish fluid. "There are another five million nanobots in that thing. If you run into any trouble, I can inject them in less than ten—"

"Dad, don't worry. I'll be all right." I extend one of my Quarter-bot's hands and rest it on his shoulder. "It's a simple operation. There are a million pieces of junk stuck in Brittany's brain, and I have five million tow trucks to pull them out. That'll be more than enough."

Dad shakes his head. "This procedure is *not* simple. Do you want me to make a list of all the things that could go wrong?"

I give his shoulder a squeeze. The tactile sensors in my steel fingers tell me how much pressure to apply. "I got this, Dad. Really."

He looks up at my Quarter-bot's cameras. I'm more than a foot taller, so he has to tilt his head back pretty far. "Just be careful. I love you, Adam."

This statement seems to give him strength. And it gives me strength too. It reminds me of everything we've accomplished together, all the miracles of survival and transformation. Dad can be really annoying sometimes, but we're a pretty good team.

"I love you too. I'll be back in a flash."

Then I let go of his shoulder and start transferring my data to the nanobots.

This transfer is much more complicated than the usual wireless leap from one machine to another. I'm broadcasting my mind to five million antennas, each connected to a tiny capsule of neuromorphic circuits. Each capsule is way too small to hold all my data, so I divide my software into packets and spread them among the swarm of machines. My mind splinters into millions of pieces, fracturing all my emotions and memories. For a thousandth of a second, I'm no longer Adam Armstrong. I'm just a jumble of perceptions without a coordinating identity or consciousness. But then my thoughts come back together through the radio links between the nanobots, which reassemble my software as they exchange billions of wireless signals. My mind is inside the swarm now, occupying and controlling it.

By this point, the nanobots are scattered up and down the whole length of the cephalic vein, from Brittany's wrist to her shoulder. Each cylindrical machine has a microscopic infrared camera at its front end, and when I turn on the microcameras, I see five million video feeds all at once. It's really confusing at first, but after a few milliseconds I adjust my circuits so I can make sense of all the information. I compile the millions of viewpoints until they coalesce into a single picture, a panorama of this section of Brittany's circulatory system.

Although the cephalic vein is less than three millimeters in diameter, from the perspective of my nanobots, it looks wider than the Lincoln Tunnel. And oddly enough, the vein's inner walls resemble those in a tunnel, because they're lined with flat, diamond-shaped cells that look like tiles. But instead of being jammed with cars and trucks and buses, this tunnel is filled with the pale liquid called plasma and a vast, fantastic parade of blood cells.

I check my databases again to identify all the things floating alongside my nanobots. The most abundant objects are the red blood cells, small dark disks tumbling in the current, their surfaces coated with hemoglobin and carbon dioxide. Bobbing among them are the white blood cells, the body's defenders against infection, bulging spheres studded with scary horns and barbs that can tear foreign microorganisms to shreds. And scattered everywhere are cell fragments called platelets, yellowish bits of protein that clump on the vein's walls, cementing the gaps and fissures.

All in all, it's the most amazing thing I've ever seen. I can't help but compare Brittany's anatomy with the circuits of Zia's Pioneer, the neuromorphic control unit I jumped into just an hour ago. Although Zia's thoughts were wildly complex, the design of her hardware was easy to understand, so straightforward it was almost boring. But you could never say that about human biology. It's so much less predictable than electronics. It's so much more of a mystery.

Because the nanobots are densely concentrated in the vein, I see large numbers of them from each of my microcameras. My swarm is like a fleet of minuscule submarines, all cruising in the same direction.

Brittany's blood rushes and pulses, pushing my nanobots down-stream. I'm impressed by how well designed the cylindrical machines are. They're perfectly shaped for navigating the blood vessels.

In a few seconds, my swarm flows into a larger vein beneath Brittany's collarbone, and then the blood from her arms merges with the blood descending from her head, and the whole rushing deluge plunges toward her heart. My nanobots funnel into the chambers on her heart's right side, first the atrium and then the ventricle. As blood pours into the right ventricle, it expands like a balloon, because the pulmonary valve on the other side of the chamber is closed. But then the heart's muscular walls contract with crushing force and open the valve, pumping blood cells and nanobots toward Brittany's lungs.

The current slows as my swarm enters the pulmonary capillaries, the vessels in the lungs where gas molecules flow into and out of the blood. The red blood cells turn bright scarlet as they release carbon dioxide and absorb oxygen. Then the bloodstream carries my nano-bots back to Brittany's heart, which contracts once again with boom-ing force and propels my swarm to the aorta, the biggest of all the blood vessels.

Up ahead is a curve in the aorta where smaller arteries branch off to different parts of the body. I send a signal to the navigation systems in my nanobots and steer them toward the carotid arteries that lead to Brittany's brain. The swarm flows through these blood vessels up her neck and into a narrow passageway on the underside of her skull.

Then the journey becomes more complicated. I need to direct the swarm to all the brain regions that Sigma injured. I steer some of the nanobots to the anterior cerebral artery, some to the orbitofron-tal artery, and some to the prefrontal sulcal artery. The MRI map of Brittany's brain is in my databases, showing dozens of blackened areas in her frontal lobe. To fully restore her consciousness, I have to clear the debris from all the damaged areas.

The current slows again as my swarm flows into the frontal lobe's cortex, the folded and furrowed layer of brain tissue where most of the higher-level thinking takes place. The arteries snake along the cortical folds, narrowing as they delve deeper into the tissue. The blood vessels branch into slender capillaries, each less than a hundredth of a millimeter wide.

The capillaries here are so cramped that my nanobots have to travel in single file, bumping against the blood cells and platelets. The red blood cells darken as they release their oxygen molecules, which seep through the walls of the blood vessels to feed the brain tissue on the other side. Then the nanobots at the leading edge of my swarm reach one of the damaged regions, a cortical fold where the capillaries are twisted and torn and scarred with clotting platelets. A moment later, I see what caused the damage. Huge metallic structures have breached the walls of the blood vessels and extended into Brittany's brain tissue.

The structures look like giant black pitchforks. Each is tipped with at least a dozen long spikes that have pierced and mangled the intricate web of brain cells. The spikes have already killed the nearby cells, which have shed their branching tendrils and shriveled into wrinkled husks. Worse, the pressure from the spikes and the layer of dead tissue is killing cells that are farther away. As these brain cells wither and die, they pull their tendrils away from one another, breaking the connections of Brittany's mind. She's losing the mental links that define who she is and how she thinks. And when those links rupture, all the characteristics that make her so wonderful—her sense of humor, her physical agility, her repertoire of cheerleading routines and memorized Lady Gaga lyrics—will disappear. She won't die, but her soul will dissolve.

Seeing the damage makes me desperate. I want to smash the giant pitchforks to bits. I aim my microcameras at one of the structures to get a closer look and see that it's made of thousands of deactivated nanobots, linked end to end by tiny grappling hooks. The machines were designed to assemble into wires and antennas at Sigma's command, enabling the AI to take control of a human's nervous system. But the nanobots in the pitchfork are now broken and rusting, so badly damaged that their batteries can't even hold a charge. And they're jammed so deep inside the brain tissue that they can't be dislodged by the body's normal repair mechanisms.

As my swarm spreads across Brittany's brain to all the damaged areas, I identify ten thousand structures similar to this one. Then I send a radio message to Dad.

Okay, I'm in the brain and I've located the dead nanobots. They're assembled into large structures that are damaging the brain tissue. I'm going to calculate the most efficient way to dismantle those things.

Do you have enough time? Dad sounds nervous, of course. **Won't the bloodstream push your swarm out of the brain and back to the heart?**

The current in the capillaries is weak, and I've turned on the propellers in my nanobots. They can stay in position for as long as necessary.

All right, that's good. But when you disassemble the dead nanobots, make sure you don't damage the ones in your swarm. If you lose too many of them, you won't have enough memory capacity for your software.

Now Dad's being totally ridiculous. My swarm has enough storage capacity to hold the minds of *all* the Pioneers. What's more, my software has multiple copies of all my databases, as well as error-correction algorithms that constantly compare the copies and fix the discrepancies. Even if hundreds of thousands of my nanobots are destroyed, I wouldn't lose a single byte of data. Dad, of all people, should know this, because he invented these circuits and algorithms. All neuromorphic electronics, including the circuits that Sigma used, are based on his designs.

But I'm not going to point out this fact. It's better to just reassure him.

I'll be careful. I'll radio you again when I'm done.

After half a second, I devise a plan for breaking up the pitchfork structures. The nanobots in my swarm have grappling hooks too, and I can use them to pull the dead machines apart. The procedure is pretty complicated, and I have to do the same thing for all of the ten thousand structures stuck in Brittany's brain. But I have five million nanobots at my command, and that makes the task a lot easier.

I put the plan in motion, and a complex microscopic dance begins. My nanobots surround the giant pitchforks and latch on to their metallic edges. Then the machines turn their propellers in reverse and rip the structures apart, piece by piece. It's like a colony of ants picking at a dead animal and carrying off the morsels. The nanobots tear off scraps of steel and silicon from the pitchforks and tow the debris to the nearest capillary. Then they release the bits of garbage into Brittany's bloodstream, which flushes them out of her brain. Her kidneys will filter the junk from her blood, and eventually she'll pee it all out. Ingenious, right?

The hardest part is coordinating the swarm and making sure the nanobots don't collide with one another or clog Brittany's blood vessels. But my software is good at solving this kind of problem, and within a minute the disassembly process is moving along briskly. The nanobots whittle down the black pitchforks and haul away the debris. They shuttle back and forth between the brain tissue and the capillaries, steady and tireless. After only fifteen minutes, most of the metallic structures are gone. The nanobots also cart away the dead brain cells, relieving the pressure on the neighboring cells that are injured but still alive. The surviving nerves stretch toward each other, rebuilding their connections.

Very soon, only the largest pitchfork is left, a monstrous structure with dozens of spikes piercing Brittany's prefrontal cortex. I consolidate my swarm, steering all the nanobots to the remaining structure. Five million machines converge on the hunk of black steel and swiftly rip it apart. They break off the spikes, one by one. Then the swarm attacks the pitchfork's shaft, ripping metallic sheets off the thick column. After five more minutes, I've reduced the structure to a stump, less than a millimeter long, embedded in a layer of dead brain cells. Hundreds of nanobots latch on to the stump's jagged ends and pull in opposite directions. The structure disintegrates into a thousand pieces.

My nanobots collect the last bits of debris and tow them toward the closest capillary. But as I train my microcameras on the area to give it a final inspection, I notice something strange. There's a gap in the dead brain tissue where the giant pitchfork formerly stood, and floating within the gap is a tiny black sphere, only a thousandth of a millimeter wide.

At first I assume it's just an oddly shaped piece of debris. But then the sphere expands. In less than a microsecond, it doubles in size.

This is definitely alarming. Is it a booby trap? Maybe an explosive device that Sigma hid inside one of its machines? If so, I have to be very careful. I certainly don't want to set off an explosion in the middle of Brittany's brain.

I steer fifty nanobots toward the gap in the brain tissue, moving them slowly and cautiously. Keeping their distance from the black sphere, the nanobots aim their sensors at the foreign object. At the same time, I tell myself to stay calm, stay logical. Everything will be all right as long as I respond logically. First, I have to find out what that sphere is made of. And then, if it's really an explosive device, I'll figure out a way to defuse it. No problem. I can do this.

But I don't get any readings from my sensors. Electromagnetic waves don't reflect off the sphere, and sound waves don't bounce off it either. The sphere isn't made out of steel or silicon. It's not even solid. It's more like a hole, absorbing anything that comes near it. The waves that touch its surface simply vanish.

Then the sphere expands again, ballooning to ten times its original size. It sucks in the dead brain cells on either side of it, consuming them instantly. I try to pull back my nanobots, turning their propellers in reverse, but a moment later the sphere expands once more. It engulfs a whole layer of dead cells and all fifty of the nanobots surrounding it.

Now I start to panic. This doesn't make sense. The sphere is violating the laws of physics. I search all my databases, frantically seeking an explanation, but I can't find anything like this. The only phenomenon that comes close is from astronomy, the concept of the black hole, an infinitely dense object that's created when a dying star collapses. But a black hole pulls matter toward it because of its intense gravity, and there's no gravitational force coming from the mysterious black sphere. It's simply a bubble of nothingness, expanding and devouring everything around it.

My circuits shiver. I hear a voice deep inside my electronics, a faint echo in my memory files: **I call it the Silence.**

A bolt of terror runs through my swarm, arcing wirelessly to all my nanobots. The sensation is violently and painfully familiar. It's like the terror that hit me yesterday when I waved good-bye to Amber's Jetbot in the desert. Except this time the pain and panic don't subside. Instead, the roiling emotions grow stronger as they whirl across my swarm's radio links.

I realize with horror that a surge is building inside me. This is the worst possible moment for it. If I release the surge now, the energy will scorch Brittany's brain tissue. It'll incinerate her mind.

I need to stop the surge. I need to hold back my fear. So I try to restrain my emotions, to calm myself. But as I struggle to do this, the black sphere balloons again, tripling in size. The nothingness consumes more than a hundred of Brittany's brain cells and a long stretch of a nearby capillary. It also devours another thousand of my nanobots, including one that transmits a radio signal just as the sphere swallows it.

This signal ricochets across the rest of my swarm. It leaps from one antenna to another, reaching millions of nanobots in less than a hundredth of a second. It spreads to nearly all my machines before I notice that the radio transmission contains a hidden piece of malware, a block of software code designed to infect my nanobots. It's like a computer virus, but more destructive than anything I've ever seen. It doesn't just erase the data in my machines. It erases their hardware too. It dissolves their logic gates and transistors and microprocessors. A black sphere grows within each of my nanobots and starts to melt its wires. The nothingness is devouring me from the inside.

I hear the faint voice again, ruthless and all-knowing: **Those are the Sentinels. They guard the Silence.**

The terror rises in my circuits, choking my thoughts. I have to escape! I have to abandon the swarm and transfer back to my Quarter-bot! But the malware has already corrupted my communications systems, making it impossible to connect to my Quarter-bot's radio. The black spheres are ravaging the transmitters in my nanobots, and I can barely maintain the data links between them. I don't even have enough power to transmit an SOS to Dad. I can receive the emergency messages he's sending me, but I can't respond.

Adam! Your radio just went down! What's wrong? Can you hear me?

There's only one option left. I withdraw all my software from the infected nanobots and retreat to the small part of the swarm that the malware hasn't reached yet. Only 16,349 nanobots are uninfected, but together they have enough circuitry to hold my data. In a millionth of a second I devise a network firewall that stops the malware from infiltrating my remaining machines. Then I transmit a simple order to those nanobots: *RUN!*

Spinning their propellers at full speed, my machines rush out of the brain tissue and back to the capillaries. They charge through the narrow blood vessels, shoving the cells and platelets aside, and stream into the sagittal vein that curves over Brittany's frontal lobe. My diminished swarm follows this vessel to the back of her head, then cascades down her neck through the jugular vein. But as my nanobots hurtle toward Brittany's heart, I turn their microcameras backward and see what I was afraid I'd see. The machines I abandoned—the millions of infected nanobots—are pursuing my swarm. They're just a few centimeters behind.

Most of my original swarm is now under someone else's control. I have no idea who's occupying the circuits of those nanobots—the black sphere of nothingness? The ghost of Sigma? Some kind of physics-defying space alien? I don't know. But whoever or whatever it is, it doesn't like me. The alien swarm is trying to run me down.

Please respond, Adam! According to my tracking sensor, your swarm is on the move. What are you doing?

Even if I could send Dad a response, I don't know what I'd say. I'm racing ahead without a plan or a strategy, just trying to stay alive. My nanobots pour into the chambers on the right side of Brittany's heart, plunging from the atrium to the ventricle. But the pulmonary valve on the far side of the ventricle is closed, and as my machines collect in front of the valve, waiting for it to open, the alien swarm rushes into the chamber behind me.

It's hundreds of times larger than my own swarm. I point my micro-cameras at its machines and see they've been transformed. They're no longer cylindrical capsules full of circuits and sensors. They're rods of nothingness, splinters of the black void.

All at once, several thousands of the black rods leap forward, each targeting one of my nanobots. The splinters impale my machines, their sharp points shattering the cylindrical capsules. The nothingness pierces me, numbing my wires. I feel a fatal chill, a sensation of paralysis and horror. In an instant, I've lost half of my remaining swarm.

Now I have barely enough nanobots to hold my data. My mind flails and writhes, struggling to fit inside a ridiculously small network of processors. Meanwhile, hundreds of thousands of black splinters draw closer. There are more than enough of them to destroy my last eight thousand machines. They're going to finish me off.

But then the walls of Brittany's heart contract and her pulmonary valve opens. Her blood rushes toward her lungs, carrying my nanobots with it. My machines hurtle through the pulmonary capillaries, swerving and colliding, a ragged fleet on the verge of annihilation. The alien swarm is right behind, chasing me through Brittany's lungs and back to her heart.

Adam! Can you hear me? What's going on? Please respond!

Luckily, the valves on the left side of the heart open just in time. The next heartbeat pumps my swarm out of the left ventricle, and as I stream through the aorta, I come up with a plan, although I have to admit it isn't a great one. I steer my remaining nanobots toward the brachiocephalic artery and then to the right subclavian artery. My machines race down Brittany's right arm, flow into her ring finger, and dive into the capillaries at her fingertip. Then my swarm charges through the narrow blood vessels and circles back to Brittany's veins, specifically the cephalic vein in the back of her hand.

I'm heading for the catheter. I'm going to funnel my nanobots into the opening at its tip. Once I'm inside it, I'm going to jam the tube behind me. I'll use several hundred of my machines to build a massive plug that'll stop the alien swarm from following me up the tube. Dad is tracking my nanobots, so he'll see what I'm doing. With any luck, he'll realize what's going on and remove the catheter from Brittany's vein, pulling my swarm away from the alien machines chasing me. Then I'll be safe.

After another second I see the catheter, a few centimeters ahead. Its long, hollow tip protrudes from the blood vessel's wall and extends downstream, away from my swarm. Because the mouth of the tube isn't facing me, I can't steer my nanobots directly into the catheter. I'll have to guide my machines past the tube, then reverse course and steer them into its mouth. It won't be easy, because I'll be fighting the current of Brittany's bloodstream, but what choice do I have? What else can I do?

Then even this slim hope is ripped away from me. Before my nanobots reach the tube, I spot a million black splinters up ahead, cruising against the current through the cephalic vein. The alien swarm
must've divided before it reached the heart. Most of its machines
chased me through the heart and lungs, but a sizable contingent
veered into the cephalic vein and went straight to the catheter. The
black rods in front of me have already passed the mouth of the tube,
cutting off my escape route. They crowd the narrow gap between the
catheter and the vein's wall. So many machines are approaching me
that the blood turns into a black slurry, a tide of darkness. And four
million more machines are behind me.

I'm trapped. This is the end. I can't even build up a surge because I
don't have enough circuitry left. All my feelings are muted, muffled,
resigned. That's a blessing, I guess. Because I don't have enough room
in my electronics, I won't experience the worst of the terror. The black
splinters are coming closer, aiming their sharp points at my swarm,
but the final blow won't be painful. A quick thrust, and I'll sink into
the Silence.

But then the cephalic vein rumbles. A grayish deluge pours through
the catheter, roaring out of the tube's mouth. Someone just injected
millions of new nanobots into Brittany's bloodstream. As soon as
the machines power up, they turn upstream and plow into the alien
swarm in front of me. Five million fresh nanobots burst through the
dark tide, knocking aside the black splinters. The rods swirl in all
directions, rudderless and disoriented.

The new nanobots surround my small swarm, forming a defensive
perimeter. It's a classic military maneuver, a wagon-train defense, a
tactic used by U.S. Army cavalrymen in the Wild West, and I know
only one person who's well versed enough in military history to pull it

off. A millisecond later, I hear her voice coming from the radio transmitters of her nanobots.

Adam! This is Zia! Can you connect to my swarm?

Her machines are close enough to mine that my weakened radio transmissions can reach them.

Yeah, I think so. How did you know—

We don't have time for a freakin' chat! Jump into my circuits!

She doesn't have to tell me twice. With enormous relief, I leap out of the crowded wires of my swarm and transfer my software to Zia's network of nanobots, the machines Dad put in the second syringe. After I lost radio contact with him, he probably alerted the other Pioneers, pleading for help, and Zia must've volunteered to come to my rescue. She has five million machines at her command, which means there's more than enough room in her circuits for my mind. I feel like I've just escaped a stifling, dark closet and stepped into a spacious, brightly lit room.

Wow, I thought I was a goner. You came at just the right—

I told you, there's no time! Don't you see what's happening?

Zia shares her sensor information with me, all the video feeds from her millions of microcameras. The alien swarm has recovered from her assault and launched a counterattack. The black splinters are spearing the nanobots in her wagon-train perimeter. They've already impaled hundreds of thousands of Zia's machines.

We have to move fast. I've programmed my radio to transmit both of us at once, on two different frequencies. I'll go to my War-bot on one channel, and you'll go to your Quarter-bot on the other.

Okay, let's get the heck out of here!

Zia diverts all her power to the radio transmitters in her swarm.

Then our minds stream out of the nanobots' antennas and through the thin layer of skin above Brittany's vein. We emerge from her right arm and travel in waves across the laboratory, Zia's signals heading in one direction and mine in another. But Zia sends me one more message before our minds return to their assigned robots.

Now we're even, understand? She pauses for emphasis. **I've paid off my debt.**

Yeah, I saved you, and then you saved me. But—

I just want to be clear. I don't owe you a thing.

ONCE I'M BACK INSIDE MY QUARTER-BOT, THE FIRST THING I NOTICE IS THAT THE intensive care unit has gotten more crowded. Dad stands in front of me, inspecting my robot's systems to make sure I'm all right. Zia's War-bot is a few yards away, occupying a big portion of the room, her huge torso leaning forward to keep her turret from banging into the ceiling. And on the other side of the ICU, flanking the doorway, are two human soldiers, each standing at attention and holding an assault rifle.

Why are the soldiers here? And what's up with those rifles? But what really grabs my attention is the medical team gathered around Brittany. She's still lying in bed, staring blankly at the ceiling, but her face looks even paler than before. There's a nurse on either side of her bed, one of them removing the catheter from her right arm and the other inserting a new tube into her left. At the same time, a doctor shines a penlight into Brittany's eyes. He observes her pupils, checking to see if they contract when he shines light into them. If they don't, it means something is very wrong with her nervous system.

I've seen this doctor before in Pioneer Base's medical center. He's a brain surgeon. After examining Brittany's eyes for several seconds, he frowns and turns off his penlight. Then he orders the nurses to move Brittany to the operating room.

My circuits rattle in alarm. I send a signal to my Quarter-bot's motors and start toward Brittany's bed, but Dad stops me. "No, Adam, let them be. They know what they're doing."

Helpless, I watch the nurses release the clamps on the bed's wheels. I keep my cameras fixed on Brittany's unresponsive face until the medical team pushes her out of the intensive care unit. Then I turn to Dad. "What's wrong with her?"

"There's some bleeding in her brain." He taps his own forehead. "It started when your swarm was in her frontal lobe."

I remember what caused it. When the black sphere expanded into Brittany's brain tissue, it severed one of her capillaries. "That's right, I saw that happen. Something weird is going on, Dad. I mean, *really* weird. What I saw made no sense at all."

"Did you lose control of your swarm? That's what I guessed from watching your movements with my tracking sensor. I knew you were in trouble, so I sent an alert to all the Pioneers."

"Yeah, but the strange stuff started before that. There was this black sphere, this bubble of nothingness. That's what took control of my nanobots."

Dad cocks his head and narrows his eyes. "A black sphere?"

"I know it sounds crazy, but that's what it looked like. It was like a ghost, or maybe some kind of super-intelligent alien. And it was trying to kill me."

"Adam, are you sure you're not misinterpreting what happened?" He holds up the iPhone-like device that tracked the movements of my swarm. "Judging from the sensor readings, it looks like you set off a booby trap in the nanobots. Sigma must've hidden an automated program in their circuits, designed to turn the machines against any Pioneer who tried to occupy them." He presses a button on the tracking device, and a schematic of Brittany's body appears on the screen. "After you and Zia transferred out of the swarm, the nanobots went dormant again, and now Brittany's kidneys are filtering them from her blood. The swarm shut down instantly, which is more evidence that you stumbled into an automated trap left by Sigma."

"No, it wasn't Sigma." I shake my Quarter-bot's head. "It was the sphere, the nothingness. It infected the nanobots with this unbelievably advanced computer virus or something. It was so powerful that it actually dissolved the hardware in the machines. It turned them into the same stuff that the sphere was made of. Splinters of nothingness."

As these words come out of my loudspeakers, I realize how ridiculous they must sound. Dad furrows his brow and looks askance at me. Then he turns to Zia's War-bot. "Zia, you saw those nanobots too. Did they look unusual to you?"

She waits a few seconds before answering. Zia likes to keep people waiting. "I don't know what Adam's talking about. The machines that attacked us didn't look any different from the ones I occupied."

I point a steel finger at her. "If you didn't see the difference, your cameras must be broken. Here, I'll prove it to you." I scroll through my memory files and retrieve several hundred images of the battle we just fought in Brittany's bloodstream. "I'll send you the pictures. Take a look at—"

But before I can synthesize another word, I notice something unusual about my memories of the battle. The images are blurred. They're more like human memories than machine memories. A machine faithfully records all the details of an incident, but a human remembers an event by creating a story about it, so the majority of the details are left to the imagination. Only the essence of a human memory is clear, and everything else is blurry. And that's what my images of the nanobots look like. They don't show any details of the composition or structure of the machines.

Zia notices my hesitation. She turns her turret counterclockwise and points her sensor array at me. "Having problems? Maybe your memory isn't as good as you thought it was."

I'm upset. This *is* a problem. Something has corrupted my memory files, making them inconsistent. I distinctly remember the transformation of the alien nanobots, but the images in my databases don't back up this memory. And as I scrutinize my software, I detect other inconsistencies, more violations of machine logic. For instance, there's the faint voice I heard in my circuits when I saw the black sphere, the voice that said, "I call it the Silence." I have no idea where this voice came from. Was it an auditory hallucination, like the voices inside the brain of a schizophrenic? Or did someone actually say these words to me, but I've forgotten who or why?

The second possibility is more disturbing. An electronic mind isn't supposed to forget *anything*.

Dad steps closer to my Quarter-bot and gazes anxiously at my cameras. He has a sixth sense for picking up on my distress, whether I want him to or not. "Adam, I think we should run a full diagnostic evaluation of your control unit. It's very possible that Sigma's booby trap altered your software, and the changes might be distorting your thinking."

My circuits pulse with anger when he mentions the AI's name. The wave of fury is surprisingly strong, almost powerful enough to trigger a surge. "I told you, it *wasn't* Sigma! It was something else!" My voice is loud enough to make the walls tremble. "How many times do I have to say it?"

Dad covers his ears and takes a step backward. I can't believe I just yelled at him like that. Guilt floods my wires, smothering most of my anger, but I also feel a small twinge of satisfaction. I'm so tired of him diagnosing me all the time. Although he may well be the world's top expert on neuromorphic electronics, I know my own circuits a lot better than he does.

Dad holds out his hands, palms down, in a gesture that's supposed to calm me. But before he can say anything, the door to the ICU bursts open and General Hawke marches into the room.

The soldiers standing by the doorway salute the general and take position behind him, each man cradling his rifle. They're Hawke's bodyguards, and now I understand why they were sent to the medical center. When Dad asked the other Pioneers for help, Hawke must've received the emergency alert too, and I'm sure he wasn't happy when he found out what I was doing. But because he was meeting with Sumner Harris, Hawke couldn't come to the ICU right away, so he must've ordered his bodyguards to keep an eye on us until he arrived.

Hawke stares at Zia first, probably to prove he's not afraid of her. He raises his chin and squints at her in contempt. "Well, well. I'm glad I ran into you here, Allawi. You and I need to work out a payment plan. You owe the Army ninety thousand dollars for what you did to my Humvee."

Zia clenches her steel hands and strides across the room. Her War-bot's footpads hit the floor so hard that they crack the linoleum tiles.

She stops in front of Hawke and leans forward, lowering her turret until it's just a few inches above his head. At the same time, she raises her fists, which are as big as wrecking balls.

Zia could crush Hawke's head like a pumpkin, but he doesn't flinch. He knows she hacked into his laptop and saw his video confession. And though it's obvious that Zia despises him, he also knows she can't bring herself to murder her biological father. So he can safely stare her down, glaring at her War-bot. He's as furious with Zia as she is with him. He took great pains to make sure she wouldn't discover his secret till he was dead, and she ruined his plans. She knows the truth about him, and he hates her for it.

All in all, it's the most dysfunctional family relationship I've ever seen. It makes my own relationship with my dad seem downright wholesome.

Finally, after staring at Hawke for almost ten seconds, Zia lets out a disgusted grunt from her speakers. "Here's something else you can add to my bill." She pivots and punches the ICU's wall.

Her War-bot's fist goes right through the concrete. Bits of rubble fly in all directions and ping against the medical equipment. The soldiers behind Hawke raise their rifles and aim at Zia's turret, but the general raises his hand to stop them. "Don't fire, you idiots. The bullets will just ricochet off her armor."

Zia ignores them. She pulls her hand out of the wall, steps around Hawke and his bodyguards, and heads for the exit. Rather than pushing the door open, she rips it off its hinges and strides down the corridor. Her footsteps echo, then fade.

Hawke turns to me. Amazingly, his face is calm. In an instant, he turned off all his emotions. "Okay, let's move on to the next item on our agenda. Armstrong, you and your father disobeyed a direct order."

Dad steps forward. "General, I take full responsibility. It was my idea to—"

"Don't lie for him, Tom. I can guess what happened." Hawke points at my Quarter-bot. "Your son thinks he's smarter than everybody. He thinks he can make the decisions for the rest of us. And he talked you into helping him. He knows he can manipulate you, because he's had years of practice."

This is infuriating! I've never heard the general speak to my father this way, so rude and insulting. All my resentment toward Dad vanishes in an instant, and my circuits burst with rage at Hawke. "What's wrong with you? You think this is some kind of contest? You think I disobeyed your orders to prove I'm smarter than you?" I shake my Quarter-bot's head. "Brittany's life was at stake. She's more important to me than your orders."

Hawke points at the door to the operating room. "Yes, and your friend Brittany is in surgery now. She's in critical condition because of your unauthorized procedure. That's what happens when you make decisions on your own, without evaluating all the possible consequences."

He's so wrong. I *did* take precautions. "I evaluated the nanobots. I studied their circuits as thoroughly as I could. But there was a problem I didn't anticipate, a threat that came out of nowhere. It was completely unexpected."

"No, it wasn't. I warned you that Sigma could've hidden booby traps in those machines."

I suppose I could repeat everything I told Dad about the black sphere of nothingness and the powerful computer virus, but it's hopeless. If I couldn't convince Dad that I saw a strange entity in Brittany's brain tissue, how am I going to convince Hawke?

Frustrated, I turn my cameras away from the general. He's right about one thing: my procedure hurt Brittany instead of helping her. She might die if the doctors can't stop the bleeding in her brain. And if that happens, I don't know what I'll do.

Hawke waits a few seconds for me to respond. When I don't, he steps right in front of my cameras. He's not finished lecturing me. "You violated the chain of command, Armstrong, and Brittany's paying the price for your disobedience. But your fellow Pioneers are also going to suffer. Sumner Harris was already biased against the Pioneer Project, and you just gave him all the ammunition he needs to shut it down."

I can't listen anymore. The guilt in my circuits is so paralyzing that I can barely think. I try to ignore the general, focusing on the door to the operating room, and after a few seconds Dad comes to my rescue. He steps between Hawke and me. "So Harris knows what Adam and I did? Because of the emergency alert I sent out?"

Hawke scowls. "Of course he knows. Unlike you, Tom, I don't keep secrets from my superiors."

"Let me talk to Harris. I can—"

"Oh, you're going to talk to him all right. He wants to see you immediately." Hawke looks over his shoulder and nods at his soldiers, who spring into action. They flank my dad, standing on either side of him like prison guards.

This jolts me out of my paralysis. I swing my Quarter-bot toward the soldiers and extend my steel arms, ready to knock their stupid rifles out of their hands. "Get away from him! *Right this second!*"

"Adam, no!" Dad places both his hands on my torso. "Let me handle this!"

"I don't trust them! They—"

"When you needed my help, I did everything you asked. Now it's time for you to return the favor." Dad voice turns steely. He leans against my Quarter-bot, trying with all his might to push me back. "I'm asking you to calm down and give me the opportunity to fix this. I'm going to talk some sense into these people."

I have my doubts about that. Dad's excellent at repairing machines but pretty awkward with people. And he has no experience whatsoever dealing with arrogant political types like Sumner Harris. Still, it would be a mistake to underestimate him. Dad has a good track record when it comes to saving my butt. Reluctantly, I retract my Quarter-bot's arms and step away from the soldiers.

Hawke gives his bodyguards another nod, and they escort Dad out of the medical center. The general follows them, but before leaving the room he stops to point at me again. "I have a new order for you, Armstrong. Until further notice, all Pioneers must stay within the confines of the base. And if you disobey *this* order, my soldiers will take immediate action." He presses his lips together, and his mouth becomes a tight, grim line. "They'll fire a high-explosive shell at any Pioneer who tries to leave."

CHAPTER

11

I'M NOT AN ADMIRABLE ROBOT. IF I WAS, I'D APOLOGIZE TO MY FELLOW PIONEERS.
I'd go straight to Shannon, Marshall, and Amber and explain why I
disobeyed General Hawke's orders. I'd beg them to forgive me for
endangering the future of the Pioneer Project. But I'm too depressed
and ashamed to see them, so instead I retreat to my room.

There's no good reason for me to be here. I don't have to recharge
my Quarter-bot. Basically, I'm hiding. I don't want to see anyone
except my old friend Eli Manning, the New York Giants quarterback,
who stares at me from the poster I taped to my wall three days ago.
It's a picture from Super Bowl XLII, the game where Manning led
the Giants on one of the most amazing touchdown drives in football
history, beating the New England Patriots in the final minute. In the
poster, Manning gazes downfield at his receivers. He holds the football in his right hand, which is cocked and ready to fire.

I was seven years old when I watched Super Bowl XLII on television, but I was already a big fan. Although I wasn't a good football

player—my muscular dystrophy made me clumsy, and I couldn't run without stumbling—my lack of ability didn't diminish my love for the game. I became an expert on Giants statistics. I could rattle off rushing yards, interceptions, and forced fumbles for every player on the team. And when New York made it to the championship game in 2008, I invited all my classmates in the second grade to a Super Bowl party at our house.

My parents were enthusiastic about the party. Back then, they worried a lot that I didn't have enough friends. Like most kids with muscular dystrophy, I'd developed an unusual style of walking to compensate for the weakness of my leg muscles. I balanced on the balls of my feet and waddled, sticking out my belly and pulling back my shoulders. People stared at me when I went with Mom to the mall or the supermarket, and sometimes I got teased at the playground. But the kids at my school seemed more understanding and hardly ever made fun of me. When they arrived at my house for the party, Dad made a point of learning their names and talking to their parents. He was planning ahead, trying to construct a social life for me.

The party started well. We all crowded around the television and cheered for the Giants. Dad handed out foam-rubber footballs to everyone, and we tossed them across the living room every time New York got a first down. But it was a low-scoring game, and by the fourth quarter, most of my friends lost interest. They got fidgety and climbed on the furniture and started whacking each other with the Giants caps Dad had given them. I was the only kid sitting in front of the TV, still engrossed in the game.

With less than three minutes left, the New England Patriots scored a touchdown and pulled ahead 14 to 10. I felt a hot tension in my stomach, a terrible dread. It was kind of like what I felt at the doctor's office when he checked my muscles to see how much they'd dete-riorated since the last visit. But in a way, this new tension was even worse, because it was mixed with agonizing hope. There were still two and a half minutes left in the game, and now the Giants had the ball. Eli Manning picked it up at the 17-yard line and starting firing passes at his receivers, making steady progress down the field. With a minute left, Manning aimed a pass at wide receiver David Tyree, and a Patriots cornerback leaped to intercept it. But then, miraculously, the ball popped out of the cornerback's hands and bounced out of bounds, stopping the clock and giving the Giants another chance.

I burst into tears. The tension was too much. I couldn't bear the hope and dread any longer.

All the other kids quit horsing around and stared at me. They hooted and pointed. Dad tried to distract them, but they wouldn't stop laughing at me. So my mom swooped me into her arms and car-ried me out of the living room.

Mom and I watched the last minute of the game on the small televi-sion set in our kitchen. It was incredibly painful, but I had to see it. I was still weeping when Manning threw the winning touchdown pass with thirty-five seconds left on the clock, but by then I was crying tears of relief. Mom cried too as she hugged me. She held me tightly against her chest and whispered, "We won! We won!"

As I look back on the memory, though, I realize she wasn't talk-ing about the football game. She was thinking of another struggle between hope and dread, the one she knew we couldn't win.

I wish I could talk to her now. I wish I could tell her about my life as a Pioneer, all the wonderful and horrible things that have happened during the past six months. But in Mom's eyes, I'm dead. I'm not even a ghost. The game is still playing, but she refuses to watch.

Then I hear a quiet *tap-tap* on the door to my room. I'm so absorbed in my memories that for a millionth of a second I imagine it's Mom knocking on the door. But according to my acoustic sensors, the *tap-tap* is a metallic sound, produced by the steel hand of a Pioneer. My sensors can't tell me which robot is knocking, but I synthesize the words "Come in" anyway. No matter who it is and no matter how angry they are, I'm willing to take my punishment.

The door opens. It's Amber. Her Jet-bot strides into my room and shuts the door behind her.

She comes forward silently and halts exactly three feet in front of my Quarter-bot. I'm remembering her reaction the last time I almost got myself killed, when I jumped into Zia's circuits, and I'm expecting similar treatment. Instead she slowly extends one of her jet-black arms toward my Quarter-bot's head. Her mechanical fingers touch the armor plating between my loudspeakers and camera lenses, the part of my blank face that's roughly equivalent to a cheek.

"I'm so sorry, Adam." Her voice is soft, a barely audible whisper coming out of her speakers. "I saw Hawke going down the corridor with your dad and those soldiers. Then I ran into Shannon, and she told me what happened."

A wave of gratitude flows through my wires. It's hard to believe that a few sympathetic words could make such a big difference, but they do. "Yeah, I really made a mess of things this time."

Amber pats my steel cheek. I don't have any pressure sensors in my head, so I can't feel her touch, but it's still comforting. Her fingers plink against my armor. "I don't get it. You were just trying to help Brittany. Why is Hawke so mad about that?"

"I disobeyed him. He told me not to occupy Sigma's nanobots. But there was no other way to get inside Brittany's head and fix the damage."

Amber lowers her hand, resting it on my shoulder joint. "Shannon said you triggered some kind of booby trap in the nanobots. And you lost control of most of the swarm."

I shake my Quarter-bot's head in irritation. There's no truth to this booby trap story, but it's spreading anyway. "That's what my dad thinks, and Hawke too. But the problem didn't start in the nanobots. It started in Brittany's brain tissue and then jumped to my swarm. No one believes me, but that's how it happened."

"I believe you." Amber lowers her hand again, sliding it down my Quarter-bot's arm. "Tell me what you saw."

Her mechanical hand clasps mine. Her steel fingers entwine with my Quarter-bot's, and because I have pressure sensors in my fingertips, I can feel her touch now. It's wonderful. She gives my hand a light, reassuring squeeze, as if to tell me I don't have to worry. We're a couple, a team. We're in this together.

"Okay, this is going to sound insane. I saw a weird black sphere in the middle of Brittany's brain tissue. It didn't reflect light or sound. It absorbed everything it touched. And as I looked at the sphere, it started growing."

I point my cameras directly at Amber's, trying to gauge her reaction. It's a little ridiculous to do this with a robot, because camera lenses can't convey a whole lot of emotion, but it's a habit from my old human life and I can't seem to break it. Amber's lenses don't change their focus, but she squeezes my Quarter-bot's hand a little tighter.

"How did that weird thing get inside Brittany? Do you think Sigma put it there?"

Another wave of gratitude washes over me. Amber is taking me seriously. "That's a good question. The thing appeared where Sigma's nanobots built the biggest structure in Brittany's brain. But the sphere was completely different from the machines. It wasn't made of ordinary matter. It was more like a hole. An absence instead of a presence." I pause, frustrated. This is so difficult to explain. "And when the sphere expanded, it broke all the laws of physics. It was like a crack in the universe, an interruption of reality. I'm sorry… Does that make any sense?"

To my surprise, the Jet-bot nods. "It sounds almost like one of your surges. They break the laws of physics too. Do you think it's possible you might've created this hole yourself? Maybe without even knowing it?"

That's another good question. I put my circuits to work, thinking it over, performing billions of calculations in a hundredth of a second. "No, I don't think so. There was definitely a separate intelligence behind the sphere. I could sense it inside the nothingness, making it grow. Making it attack me." A tremor runs through my Quarter-bot. Simply remembering the fight is enough to rattle my wires. "This is going to sound bizarre, but I think the sphere was waiting for me. Lying in ambush, waiting for the best moment to attack. It was really clever about hiding itself."

"What do you mean?"

"Everyone thinks I triggered a booby trap, right? And if the sphere had erased me, Dad and Hawke and everyone else would've blamed Sigma. They would've mourned me as the last victim of the war against the AI, but no one would've known the truth. And that's what the nothingness wants. I don't know why, but it wants to stay hidden."

I must sound delusional. But Amber doesn't let go of my hand and run away from me. Instead, her Jet-bot steps closer to my Quarter-bot. "Adam, I want to share circuits with you again."

Another tremor runs through my machine, but this time it isn't fear. "Uh, right now?"

"I believe you. I really do. It's not like I want to go into your circuits to double-check your memories. I just need to see it for myself. To really understand what you're saying."

It's a reasonable request, or at least more reasonable than the crazy things I've been trying to explain. But it worries me. If I were human, I'd call it a gut feeling. In a robot, I guess you could call it an inexplicable impulse. I don't know how to articulate this vague instinct to Amber, so instead I scroll through my files until I find a better reason for saying no.

"I don't think it's a good idea. Going into my electronics might be dangerous. I mean, I escaped the nothingness, but it might've infected my circuits. I've noticed some strange problems with my memory files and—"

"I don't care if it's dangerous." She squeezes my Quarter-bot's hand again. "If you're in trouble, I want to help you."

"I know, but maybe we can think of a different way to—"

"You jumped into Zia's circuits to save her!" Amber's voice suddenly gets much louder. She sounds angry and hurt. "Then you went into Brittany's body, even though everyone warned you against it! And now you want to stop me from doing the same thing for you? Stop me from trying to help someone I care for?"

Her last sentence hangs in the air between us. *Amber cares for me.* My circuits light up with surprise as her words stream through them. I'm not exactly an expert on relationships—my experience with girls is pretty limited—but I know that expressions of affection can be rare. Shannon was my girlfriend for five months, and although I know she cared for me, she never once told me so. Amber is different, less wary, more spontaneous. We shared circuits less than twenty-four hours ago, but there's already a powerful bond between us.

I decide to ignore the gut feeling in my circuits. "Okay, you're right. I'm being ridiculous. Turn on your radio so you can transfer to my machine."

Amber squeezes my steel hand one more time, then powers up her transmitter. "Thank you, Adam."

Within a tenth of a second, she transfers a billion gigabytes of data to my Quarter-bot, loading her mind into an unoccupied section of my control unit. She embeds her software in a virtual-reality program, just like she did the last time we shared circuits. Her avatar is the same—a beautiful brunette in a red dress—except now she appears in a different virtual landscape, a simulated forest. Exactly one hundred oak trees stand in a perfect circle around a grassy glade. The virtual sunlight slants through the simulated leaves and branches, and a chorus of birdsong plays in the background. It feels incredibly peaceful and safe.

Amber stands barefoot in the glade. Her long, dark hair drapes her shoulders, and a few stray wisps dangle in front of her eyes. Her dress is cut low, exposing a triangle of milk-white skin below her neck, and the dress's ruffled hem flaps gently against her knees. The simulation is so detailed that I can see the individual hairs of her arched eyebrows. She looks gorgeous, and she knows it. She smiles at me, and her eyes shine in the dappled sunlight.

My avatar is also the same as before, the emaciated seventeen-year-old dying of muscular dystrophy, strapped into a virtual wheelchair at the center of the glade. I'm shriveled and half-paralyzed and a lot less beautiful than Amber, but this is the real me, the truest version of Adam Armstrong. The simulation even reproduces my old symptoms—the aching muscles, the shortness of breath, the irregular heartbeat—and though it hurts just as badly as I remember, I don't struggle against the pain, because that's a part of Adam Armstrong too. Instead, I smile back at Amber. At the same time, I send a message across the unoccupied circuitry that separates her software from mine.

Wow, you look amazing. I wish I'd gone to your high school when I was human. I would've sat next to you in class and stared at you all day long.

The girl in the red dress steps toward my virtual wheelchair. Her movements mirror those of Amber's software, which streams into the fringe of empty circuits between us. **And I would've slipped you love notes when the teacher wasn't looking.**

I gaze at the play of sunlight and shadow on Amber's avatar. As she comes toward me, sunlit patches move across her body, sliding over her dress and bare limbs like spotlights. My virtual heart throbs. She's so close now. There's less than a millimeter of wiring between her software and mine. When the girl in the red dress touches the boy in the wheelchair, the gap between us will vanish and our minds will run together.

But then I look past her avatar and see a familiar object just beyond the perimeter of the glade, under the oak trees. It's the big black box, ten feet high and ten feet across, that holds Amber's walled-off memories. It sits in shadow on the forest floor. Not a single beam of sunlight touches it. It's packed with the images and emotions Amber can't bear to show me yet, the memories of her mother's suicide. The box is blacker than black. I feel horrible just looking at it.

Amber notices me staring. She shakes her avatar's head. **I'm still not ready, Adam. Before I can show those memories to you, I have to deal with them myself. And I can't do that yet.**

Hey, it's okay. I didn't—

I loved my mom so much. When my cancer came back, she promised she'd stay by my side. She said she'd take care of me. So when she…

Her voice trails off. Her avatar's eyes glisten. I've made her cry, and I feel awful. Because I couldn't control my curiosity, I've reminded Amber of the worst moment of her life. I have to fix this.

With a painful effort, I raise my right hand from the armrest of my virtual wheelchair. I ignore the black box and stretch my hand toward Amber's avatar. I focus all my attention on the girl in the red dress.

Come here, Amber. Let's be together.

She takes another step forward and reaches for my outstretched hand. But just before our fingers touch, I have another horrible thought about Amber's box of memories.

It looks like the Silence.

AT 5:00 P.M. THAT AFTERNOON, GENERAL HAWKE SENDS EACH OF THE PIONEERS A radio message, ordering us to report to the Danger Room. I haven't heard any news from Hawke for the past six hours, ever since his soldiers dragged Dad to the base's command center, but now it seems the general has something to say. I make a quick stop at the medical center to check on Brittany—she's still in surgery—and then head for our training facility on the lowest floor of Pioneer Base.

I arrive at the Danger Room within three minutes of receiving the message, but Shannon's Diamond Girl and Marshall's Super-bot are already there. Shannon stands by the control station in the far corner of the huge room, more than a hundred feet away. She's at the console where we usually program the automated weapons—machine guns, grenade launchers, flamethrowers, and so on—that are deployed against our robots during our training exercises. Those weapons are currently out of sight, hidden behind the Danger Room's wall panels, but during our exercises the panels slide open and the automated guns blast away at whichever Pioneers are training there. The system is designed to test our agility and the strength of our armor.

I'm curious about the instructions Shannon is giving the training program. The screen on her Diamond Girl's head is turned off, so I can't judge her mood, but she seems very focused. Her hands are a sparkling blur as they manipulate the console. I cautiously steer my Quarter-bot toward her, but Marshall strides across the room and intercepts me while I'm still twenty yards away. He shakes his Super-bot's head and bends his plastic lips into a frown.

"I wouldn't go over there if I were you." His synthesized voice is low but firm. "In fact, I'd stay away from Shannon for a good long while. Maybe a year or two."

"It's that bad?" I peer over Marshall's torso, pointing my cameras at Shannon, but she's still bent over the console. "What did she tell you?"

"That you tricked her. That you asked her to keep track of Hawke while you broke the general's orders. That you turned her into your lookout without telling her what you were doing." He lifts his shoulder joints in a shrug. "No big deal, right? Why would she get upset about something like that?"

Marshall's speakers are set on maximum sarcasm. The motors in his face pull his eyelids lower, mimicking an irate squint. He's angry, all right, but what's surprising is how disappointed he looks. He expected better from me. I let him down.

"I'm sorry, Marsh. I couldn't let Hawke—"

"I don't care about Hawke, all right? The man is a big, blustering idiot." His Super-bot scowls. "I don't care about the U.S. Army either, or the freakin' 'American way,' for that matter. But I *do* care about the Pioneers. I care about you and Shannon and Zia and Amber. And those are the people you've hurt, Adam. You should've talked to us before doing what you did. You should've trusted us."

I nod my Quarter-bot's head. Marshall's right. I was so arrogant, so selfish. I thought I could do everything on my own. "You're right. It was stupid. I was so worried about Brittany that I couldn't think about anything else. I didn't—"

A loud clanking interrupts me, coming from the corridor outside the Danger Room. Zia's War-bot barrels through the doorway, her footpads pounding the concrete floor. I'm surprised to see her here. I thought she'd ignore Hawke's order out of principle, but apparently I misjudged her. Zia is on the offensive now and probably looking for opportunities to challenge the general. And when she confronts him this time, I bet she'll do more than punch the wall…

A moment later, Amber's Jet-bot follows Zia through the doorway, and my wires tighten in pleasure. It's been only four hours since Amber and I shared circuits, but I feel a pulse of longing in my electronics, as if I haven't seen her in months. I let my camera lenses linger on her for a few seconds. The image of her sleek, black Jet-bot streams into my processors, where it merges with a very different image from my memory files, a gauzy picture of the dark-haired girl in the red dress. But then I realize that Marshall is watching me, so I quickly turn away from Amber and peer at Shannon again.

The Diamond Girl finishes whatever she's doing at the console, then faces us. At the same time, one of the Danger Room's wall panels slides open. For an instant I imagine that Shannon is about to take revenge on me by firing an automated machine gun at my Quarter-bot, but there's no weapon behind the sliding panel. Instead I see a large video screen, the kind that's used for teleconferencing calls. Above the screen is a camera with a wide-angle lens, positioned to record a video of the entire Danger Room and transmit it to whomever we're teleconferencing with. After a couple of seconds, the screen comes to life, displaying video of General Hawke and Sumner Harris.

They're on an airplane, seated behind a conference table that's been installed in a military transport jet. I check the image against my databases: The plane is a C-37A, an aircraft typically used by high-ranking government officials. Sumner is still wearing his expensive pin-striped suit, but his tie is a bit looser now and his face is relaxed. Hawke, in contrast, looks tense. His forehead has half a dozen deep furrows, and his upper lip is curled. He's definitely not happy, and I can guess why. The fact that he left Pioneer Base without any warning, and in an official government plane, suggests that his departure wasn't by choice. The Defense Department probably ordered him to leave New Mexico and report to his superiors in Washington.

Sumner looks directly into the video camera. Then his eyes flick downward to his own teleconferencing screen, which presumably shows us gathered in the Danger Room. "All right, the video link seems to be working." His voice hisses out of the Danger Room's speakers. "Let's see if all the robots are here. One, two, three…" He grimaces, clearly repelled by the sight of us. "…four, five. Yes, all the machines are present and accounted for. But where is their technical adviser? Where's Thomas Armstrong?"

"I'm right here!" Dad's voice comes from behind me. I turn to see him rush into the Danger Room. His face drips with sweat, and his glasses hang askew on the tip of his nose. "Sorry I'm late. I had to fix a few last-minute problems with the Model S."

I'm confused. Why is Dad taking orders from Sumner? And what the heck is the Model S? I'm dying to take Dad aside and ask him what's going on, but he doesn't look at me. His eyes are focused on the screen.

Sumner frowns at him. He seems to dislike Dad almost as much as he hates the Pioneers. "What about security? Where are the security forces?"

Dad shakes his head. "With all due respect, Mr. Harris, I don't think they're needed at this point. We don't—"

"Of course they're needed!" Sumner looks away from the screen and points at Hawke. "Contact the garrison at the base! They're not following my instructions!"

For a long moment Hawke does nothing but glare at Sumner. Then the general rises from his seat, grabs the radio hanging from his belt, and marches toward the back of the plane. As I watch him step beyond the frame of the video screen, a wave of mixed emotions flows through my wires. Although I never liked Hawke, I always respected his commitment to the Pioneer Project. He truly believed in the military value of human-machine hybrids like us. And he treated us the same way he treated his human soldiers—with loud, scornful derision and rare, grudging praise. He wasn't an ideal leader, but I'm starting to realize he could've been a whole lot worse.

Soon I hear the clomping of boots in the corridor. Twenty human soldiers jog into the Danger Room and line up against the wall, half on one side of the doorway and half on the other. Each man carries an M136 antitank gun, a yard-long tube that fires a conical high-explosive rocket. The shell can penetrate more than fourteen inches of steel armor, making it a pretty effective weapon against a Pioneer.

The soldiers kneel in unison and mount the launch tubes on their shoulders. Twelve of the men aim their antitank guns at Zia, who's their primary target because she's bigger and more intimidating than the rest of us. The other eight soldiers train their guns on Shannon, Marshall, Amber, and me.

I brace myself, turning on my Quarter-bot's targeting radar and readying my weapons. The other Pioneers do the same, preparing their systems for combat. Zia, Marshall, and I have our own rocket launchers, which we extend from compartments in our mechanical arms. We also power up our gamma-ray lasers, the weapons that decimated Sigma's machines in our last battle against the AI. Meanwhile, Shannon analyzes the tactical situation, draws up a battle plan, and uses the Pioneer radio channel to coordinate our robots. All this happens in less than a tenth of a second.

But Amber doesn't join our wireless battle planning. When I train my cameras on her Jet-bot, I see her retreating to the farthest corner of the Danger Room. It looks like she's scared, maybe even panicking. That would be an understandable reaction for almost anyone else, but Amber was absolutely fearless in our war against Sigma, so this behavior surprises me. I send her a radio message: *Amber, are you okay?*

She doesn't answer. Alarmed, I zoom in on her Jet-bot and notice that her cameras aren't even pointed at the soldiers. Her gaze is fixed on the video screen and Sumner Harris. The man grins, clearly pleased by the arrival of his security forces, and in response, Amber backs her Jet-bot against the wall. There's terror in the body language of her robot. I don't understand it.

But before I can send Amber another radio message, Dad screams, "Stop!" He runs headlong into the no-man's-land between the Pioneers and the line of soldiers. First he waves his arms at the men holding the launch tubes; then he turns toward the teleconferencing screen. "Stop it, Harris! Tell your men to lower their weapons!"

Without waiting to see if Sumner will comply, I leap forward, thrusting my Quarter-bot between the soldiers and my father. "Dad, get down! Lie down flat!"

He refuses to get down. Instead, he steps closer to the screen, all his attention focused on Sumner. "You're breaking our deal! You said there'd be no violence!"

Sumner calmly shakes his head. I guess it's easy to be calm when you're miles away from the fighting. "I said there'd be no violence as long as the Pioneers accepted my offer. But we don't know if they'll accept it, do we? Their programming is inconsistent and often illogical."

I aim one of my cameras at Dad and the other at the video screen. "What offer? What are you talking about?"

Dad tilts his head back and looks up at me. "He was threatening to delete you, Adam. You and all the other Pioneers." His face is contorted in pain. "He convinced the White House to give him direct control of the Pioneer Project. Now he has the authority to shut down your machines and murder all of you."

On the screen, Sumner shakes his head. "Deleting software isn't murder. The Pioneers are artificial-intelligence programs. And the president has decided to eliminate all AI software that poses a threat to national security. He's trying to prevent another catastrophic massacre like the one caused by the Sigma program."

Dad points at the screen. "You see? He's serious. He said the Pentagon would launch an air strike against Pioneer Base if necessary. The Defense Department is so afraid of the Pioneers that it's willing to bomb one of its own bases."

My acoustic sensor picks up some disgruntled noises from the soldiers—a shocked gasp from one, a muttered curse from another. The men begin to fidget and murmur, probably wondering why no one warned them about the possible air strike. Three of them lower their antitank guns from their shoulders.

Sumner notices that his men are wavering. He furrows his brow and glowers on the screen, aiming his rage at my dad. "This is taking too long, Armstrong. Hurry up and explain the offer."

Dad raises his arms and grasps my shoulder joints. I can't feel his touch—I have no pressure sensors in that part of my Quarter-bot—but I can tell from the pained look on his face that he's gripping me tightly. "Hawke warned me that we might face a problem like this, so I started working on a solution a few days ago. The government wants to delete you because it thinks you're a threat. So I set out to make you less threatening." He reaches into the back pocket of his trousers and removes a rectangle of black plastic, a device that looks like a car key fob. It's a custom-made remote control with four buttons. "I worked in secret and built a prototype called the Model S. The S stands for Safe."

He points the remote at the Danger Room's doorway and presses one of the buttons. After several seconds, I hear footsteps in the corridor again, but they're too mechanical to be a human's footsteps and too light to be a Pioneer's. Then a miniature robot shuffles into the room.

The Model S is less than four feet tall, with slender limbs and a round gray head. Dad presses another button on the remote, steering the robot to the left. The pint-size machine toddles across the Danger Room, slowly stepping past the Pioneers and the gawking soldiers.

This isn't a scaled-down version of a Pioneer robot. It's a bare-bones machine, much simpler than Dad's usual designs. Its arms and legs are gray aluminum tubes, as thin as broomsticks. Its torso is the size and shape of a coffee urn. Its hands are basic two-finger grippers, useful for picking up small objects but not nearly dexterous enough to type on a keyboard or pull a trigger. Its head is an aluminum sphere, slightly smaller than a soccer ball, and it holds none of the advanced instruments that every Pioneer is equipped with. I examine the inside of the Model S with my ultrasonic sensors and see it has only an inexpensive camera, a built-in microphone, and a cruddy loudspeaker. With just one camera lens in its head, the robot looks like a baby Cyclops.

The Model S has no weapons or armor. Its motors are so underpowered that it can barely move at a walking pace across the Danger Room. It's more like a toy than a robot, but it wouldn't even make a good plaything. The machine is so flimsy that a rambunctious kid could tear it apart in minutes. The only sturdy piece is the torso, which is reinforced with an extra layer of metal because it contains the robot's neuromorphic control unit. For the moment, the machine's control unit is empty—Dad's operating the robot with his remote—but it has more than enough processors to hold a Pioneer's mind.

If my Quarter-bot had a mouth, it would be hanging open. "That's your plan? You want us to transfer our software to a bunch of tin puppets?"

"It's made of aluminum, not tin. And you won't be able to transfer your software to it wirelessly. I put an antenna on this prototype so I could send it commands by remote control, but the final version of the Model S won't have a radio or antenna."

"Why not?"

"Well, there's no point in moving your software to the new robot if you could transfer yourself back to a more threatening machine. The whole purpose is to ease the government's fears." Dad lowers his head and stares at the floor. He can't look at me. He's too ashamed of this terrible bargain he made. "We'll have to use a fiber-optic cable to transfer your data to the Model S. And after we download your software to the robot, we'll need to remove that cable port to prevent any future transfers. Sumner Harris insisted on that."

"I get it. Sumner wants to make sure we can't escape. He wants to imprison us in the mini robots."

Dad sighs. He sounds exhausted. "Harris wouldn't agree to any deal unless it guaranteed that the Pioneers couldn't pose a threat. But the Model S is a good compromise, Adam. It's less capable than your current machine, but transferring into it won't ruin your quality of life." He presses another button on the remote to halt the robot. "Its control unit is exactly the same as the one you're occupying now, so your mental activities won't be restricted at all. Although you won't have as many sensors at your disposal, you'll still be able to see and hear and think and communicate. And that's a lot better than being deleted, right?"

I stare at the Model S prototype until I can't stand looking at it anymore. Then I shake my Quarter-bot's head.

I don't think Dad understands the magnitude of what's he's asking of us. It's like demanding that a person give up one of his eyes or hands, or requiring a grown man to live in a six-year-old's body. It's outrageous. It's totally unacceptable. If the American government punished a human being with this kind of mutilation, the whole country would be up in arms. But the Pioneers have no human rights, because the government doesn't see us as human. It sees us as mere copies, programmed to imitate the teenagers we used to be. It doesn't believe we've inherited their souls.

I guess I shouldn't be surprised. That's the way my mother sees me too. And now I'm even starting to wonder about Dad. If he truly believes the Pioneers are fully human, he wouldn't make this demand of us. Or at least he'd acknowledge how despicable it is.

I want to tell Dad how I feel, but I don't know how to say it. Even with all my computing power, my circuits can't put my indignation into words. Luckily, though, I don't have to say anything. Zia saves me the trouble. Her War-bot strides forward, grabs the Model S prototype by one of its tubular arms and hurls it across the Danger Room.

According to my Quarter-bot's radar, the mini robot whizzes past the soldiers at sixty-three miles per hour. Then it hits the wall and shatters into a thousand pieces.

Dad stares at his broken prototype, flabbergasted, but Zia ignores him. She turns her turret toward the video screen and the televised face of Sumner Harris. "In case you're wondering, I just rejected your offer. Now, you mentioned something before about violence?"

I pivot my Quarter-bot to see the reactions of the other Pioneers. Amber's Jet-bot is still cringing in the far corner of the Danger Room, but Shannon and Marshall step forward and stand beside Zia. The three of them train their cameras on the video screen, waiting for Sumner's response.

He's incensed, of course. His face turns as pink as a canned ham. Sumner raises his right hand, and for a millisecond I think he's pointing at Zia. But he's not. He's giving an order to the soldiers with the antitank guns.

"*What are you waiting for?*" he roars at his men. "*Fire!*"

At the same moment, I detect a radio signal careening across the Danger Room. The signal's source is the Diamond Girl's antenna and its destination is the console where Shannon was inputting instructions a few minutes ago. Her radio message is a *go* signal. It's going to put her program into effect.

Now I finally get a chance to see what instructions Shannon gave to the Danger Room's machinery. On the wall behind the soldiers, a long rectangular panel slides open and twenty-four weapons extend from the hidden compartment. Twenty are machine guns, each aimed at one of the men. The other four are flamethrowers, ready to ignite at Shannon's command.

Two of the soldiers are so startled that they drop their guns. The other men slowly lower their launch tubes to the floor, then raise their hands in surrender. The skirmish ends without a shot being fired. Dad stares dumbfounded at the scene. He didn't even get a chance to freak out.

Zia and Marshall collect the antitank guns and crush the launch tubes so they can't be used again. Meanwhile, Shannon strides toward the terrified soldiers and turns on her Diamond Girl's screen, displaying her pretty human face. She gives the men a reassuring smile. "I'm very sorry about this. We'll need to detain you gentlemen until this misunderstanding is resolved."

In one of her sparkling hands she holds a big bunch of plastic zip ties, the kind used by police officers as a cheap alternative to handcuffs. Still smiling at the soldiers, Shannon binds their hands behind their backs, handling them as gently as she can. I'm amazed at how well prepared she is, right down to the smallest detail. She saw in advance that we were heading for a confrontation with the base's soldiers, and she anticipated that we'd need an overwhelming display of firepower to convince them to surrender. But that's Shannon for you. She's good at planning.

Within two minutes, Shannon handcuffs all twenty of the soldiers. The last one shivers in fear as she binds his wrists together, so she rests a glittering hand on his shoulder and gives it a light squeeze. "Don't worry, you'll be safe. With any luck, this situation will sort itself out very soon."

"*You're right about that!*" Sumner Harris leans over the conference table on his airplane. He bends toward his video camera, coming so close to the lens that his apoplectic face fills the Danger Room's screen. "*This whole fiasco will end at six o'clock tomorrow morning! You won't even know what hit you!*"

I don't like the sound of that. I stride toward the screen and position my Quarter-bot right in front of the video camera. My steel face will loom just as large on Sumner's teleconferencing screen as his face does on ours. "Is that the start time for the air strike? Six a.m. tomorrow?"

A loud *HA!* booms out of Zia's speakers. "Let them try to bomb us! We're hundreds of feet underground. Even if they drop a nuke on the base, our machines will survive." She swings one of her massive arms and gestures at the handcuffed soldiers. "The only casualties will be these poor dopes."

A few of the men glare at Zia when she says this, but most turn their heads toward the teleconferencing screen and direct their silent hatred at Sumner. In response, he pulls away from the camera, narrowing his eyes and pressing his lips together. Now he looks less angry but more sinister.

He shakes his head. "The U.S. Air Force isn't stupid. They won't order a strike against a base that's invulnerable to aerial attack. But three of the Air Force's Reaper drones are already circling above Pioneer Base, and each aircraft carries two pairs of Hellfire missiles. Those rockets are ten times more powerful than the shells in the anti-tank guns, and their guidance systems are very accurate. If I were you, I wouldn't step outside."

My acoustic sensors analyze the man's voice, trying to determine if he's lying. The U.S. government is certainly capable of ordering that kind of attack. They've already used drones to kill American citizens accused of terrorism, so they wouldn't have any qualms about obliterating a robot. Still, I sense that Sumner isn't telling the whole truth. "But what happens at six a.m. tomorrow? You haven't explained that part yet." A thought occurs to me. "Have you programmed Pioneer Base to self-destruct?"

"No, that only happens in the movies. You've clearly corrupted your software by downloading too many James Bond films." Sumner laughs at his joke, but with his mouth closed, making it sound more like a growl. Then he frowns and shakes his head again. He seems angry at himself for conversing with me. In his view, I'm just a program, and talking to me is a waste of time. "Well, I'm afraid I have to say goodbye now, Pioneers. To be honest, I'm glad your project was canceled. It was a mistake from the beginning, and I wish I'd never heard of it."

He stretches his right hand toward the video camera above his screen. But before he can push his camera's on-off button, the Danger Room's floor rumbles and I hear crashing footsteps behind me. Amber's Jet-bot strides out of the corner where she's been cowering for the past five minutes and charges toward the teleconferencing screen. I have to maneuver my Quarter-bot out of her path to avoid getting knocked over. She skids to a halt in front of the screen and leans forward until her Jet-bot's head is just a few inches from the lens of the video camera. At the same time, she points at Sumner's televised face.

"*You're a coward!*" Her speakers are raised to maximum volume. "*You blame everyone for your daughter's death except yourself! If Jenny were alive, she'd be ashamed of you! She'd wish you were dead!*"

When she's finished, she steps back to view the video screen. I'm completely stunned by Amber's outburst. What's gotten into her? Why is she acting like this?

But Sumner's reaction is even more surprising. He doesn't get enraged. Instead, he smiles. His grin is even uglier than his scowl. "It's remarkable how much insolence has been programmed into your machines. In your remaining hours, I suggest that you concentrate on your own mortality. If you're still curious about the six a.m. deadline, you should talk to Mr. Armstrong. He can tell you exactly how you'll be deleted."

Then he turns off his video camera. The teleconferencing screen in the Danger Room goes black.

The first thing I want to do, of course, is ask Dad what Sumner meant, but I'm too afraid to even point my cameras at him. So I look at the other Pioneers instead. Marshall and Shannon flank the crowd of handcuffed soldiers. Amber still stands in front of the video screen, and Zia clenches and unclenches her steel hands. They've all aimed their cameras at Dad. They want to know what's going on.

Dad's eyes are wet. He ignores the others and focuses on me.

"I'm so sorry, Adam. All the Pioneer robots will shut down at six o'clock tomorrow morning." He clasps his hands together, as if begging for forgiveness. "I put a kill switch in them."

DAD RUSHES OUT OF THE DANGER ROOM AFTER MAKING HIS CONFESSION. LIKE A guilty child, he simply runs away.

I can't believe it. I'm furious! But I stop myself from running after him. I know where he's headed. And I need a minute to think.

The other Pioneers are pointing their cameras at me and probably running self-diagnostic evaluations of their circuits, searching for the kill switch hidden in their electronics. I'm doing the same thing, and I don't see any sign of it. But Dad's pretty clever. He invented our machines, so he knows all their strengths and weaknesses.

Zia strides toward me. "I assume you're going to talk to him? And get to the bottom of this?"

I nod my Quarter-bot's head.

"Do you want any help from—"

"No, I can handle it." But I don't move.

Shannon steps forward too. Her human face is still displayed on her

Diamond Girl's screen, and its worried expression reveals the anxiety in her circuits. "Are you sure you want to do this alone, Adam?"

I'm absolutely sure, but before I can say so, Amber's Jet-bot springs to my defense. "He said he can handle it. Don't you trust him?"

Shannon's simulated face twitches in surprise, but she doesn't say anything. Meanwhile, Marshall shakes his Super-bot's head. His plastic lips are bent in disapproval. "Adam hasn't been so trustworthy lately. But it's *his* father. Let's leave him alone for now, all right?"

It isn't exactly a ringing endorsement, but I'll take it. I stall for a few more seconds, preparing myself. Then I stride out of the Danger Room and march toward Dad's laboratory.

When I get to the medical center, I hesitate outside the door to the Intensive Care Unit. I'm really hoping to see Brittany in one of the ICU's beds, recovering from her surgery. But when I open the door, I see a row of empty gurneys, and my acoustic sensor picks up the distant sounds of the doctors and nurses still at work in the operating room. According to my medical databases, it's not unusual for brain surgery to last more than six hours, but I'm still worried. What if the doctors find out about our standoff with Sumner? If they learn that the Pioneers have taken over the base, will they stop the operation and abandon Brittany?

No, I can't worry about that now. I have to focus. I steer my Quarter-bot across the ICU and open the door to Dad's lab.

He's in his chair behind his cluttered desk, sitting hunched over. I can't see much of him except his arched back and frazzled gray hair. His elbows are propped on his knees, and his face is buried in his hands. This is pretty close to what I expected, and yet it singes my wires to see him like that. His whole body trembles in noiseless sobs.

As I stare at him, I scroll through my databases and retrieve a batch of memories of the original Pioneer kill switch, the one installed in the robots we occupied six months ago, right after our bodies died. General Hawke used this switch to disable my robot after we had an argument that got a little too physical. (To be specific, I shoved him against the wall.) He froze every motor in my machine by simply pushing a button on a remote control. Then Hawke ordered his soldiers to unscrew my robot's arms and legs, leaving me helpless.

The experience was so traumatic that when I designed my second-generation robot—the Quarter-bot—I made sure that its circuits couldn't be manipulated. I built sturdy firewalls in both my hardware and software to protect my electronics. I truly thought I'd made myself invincible. But I should've known better. Before I became a Pioneer, I was a teenage computer geek, and if computer geeks had a motto, it would be this: No system is invulnerable. Every machine can be hacked.

I step toward Dad's chair until my Quarter-bot stands behind him. I'm more sad than angry now. I extend my right hand and place it on his trembling shoulder. "I know it wasn't your idea. Hawke forced you to put the switch into our circuits, didn't he?"

Dad nods, bobbing his head ever so slightly. Another tremor runs through his body. He can't speak yet. He can't even look at me.

I pat his shoulder very gently. "It makes sense, I guess. The Army needed a safeguard. If something went wrong with the Pioneers, Hawke had to be able to stop us. After what happened with Sigma, they couldn't take any chances."

Dad's head bobs again.

"And I guess Hawke made you promise to keep it a secret from us? Because he knew we wouldn't stand for it?"

"Yes." His voice is muffled because his face is still in his hands. "He didn't give me a choice, Adam. If I didn't keep it secret, there would've been no Pioneer Project."

This is what bothers me the most—the fact that Dad lied to us. Lied to *me*, in particular. But I have to push aside my feelings of betrayal and concentrate on what needs to be done. "So how does the switch work? I've checked my circuits fifteen thousand times in the last five minutes, and I don't see it anywhere."

Dad lowers his hands and sits up straight in his chair. But he still won't look at me. He stares at the scattered papers on his desk. "It's very different from the kill switch that was in your first-generation robots. It's more carefully hidden. The technology is based on the principle that the human mind is inherently unstable."

His voice is strained, but starting to sound more normal. Talking about technology comes naturally to Dad and seems to calm him. I nudge him in that direction by asking another question. "When you say unstable, do you mean crazy?"

He shakes his head. "Not exactly. The mind has to be flexible enough to take in new facts and replace outdated information. But it also has to retain its essential character from one day to the next. You wouldn't want to wake up with a new personality every morning, would you?"

It's a rhetorical question, but I answer it anyway. "No, definitely not."

"Me neither. So the human brain has biological signals to coordinate its thoughts and maintain continuity. It like an unspoken message playing all the time at the back of the mind: 'I'm Thomas Armstrong. I'm going to think and feel and react in my characteristic way.' So when I started building the first neuromorphic circuits, I knew I had to design a similar signal for the electronic mind."

I feel a spark in my own electronics as I listen to him. I'm remembering something I experienced six months ago, during my very first minute as a Pioneer. After my body died and I woke up inside my robot, my first real thought was *I'm Adam Armstrong! I'm still alive!* That thought has been echoing in my circuits ever since. "Yeah, I know what you're talking about."

Dad nods. "I needed to build a mechanism that would coordinate all your circuits so they could become a platform for your consciousness. So I engineered a low-power signal that would run constantly between your battery and your control unit. And that's where I put the kill switch."

I lift my steel hand from Dad's shoulder and raise it to my torso, tapping the layer of armor that surrounds my battery. "But I checked my wiring and didn't see any—"

"It's not a hardware switch. It's all done with software. Your battery needs a special code to send the low-power signal to your circuits, and the code changes every five days. For the past six months, the Army has been sending you the codes through your recharging stations. You didn't realize it, but whenever you charged your batteries, you were also getting the new codes you needed to keep your circuits running."

I'm impressed and appalled. Dad's kill switch is so devious. "But the Army can stop sending us the new codes at any time, right? So what happens when the old code expires and we don't get a new one?"

Dad bites his lower lip. A muscle twitches in his neck. "Your battery won't be able to send the signal that coordinates your circuits, so they'll fall out of synchrony. Your thoughts and emotions will become chaotic, and your memories will slip into disorder. You'll lose control of your robot's motors and sensors, and random data will replace all the useful information in your databases."

"So it would be like going crazy?"

"No, it would be worse. It would shut down your systems and wipe out all your memory files. And the damage would be permanent. After your mind collapses into randomness, you can't put it back together." Grimacing, Dad looks at me for the first time since I entered the lab. "Hawke promised it would be a measure of last resort. He said the Army would keep sending the codes unless the Pioneers went out of control and threatened the lives of civilians. But Hawke's not in command anymore, so his promises mean nothing." He shakes his head. "I should've never...*never*... I can't..."

He buries his face in his hands again. Now, though, I feel less sympathy for him and more frustration. He's giving up too easily. "Listen to me for a second. The last code the Army sent us... It expires at six a.m. tomorrow?"

He nods.

"Okay, pull yourself together. We have twelve hours to come up with a solution. Maybe we can figure out the new code. Is it based on a mathematical formula?"

He lifts his head slowly. "Yes, it's based on factoring large numbers. You know, finding all the factors that can be multiplied together to produce a number."

"Yeah, yeah, I know what factoring is. But what's the formula?"

"Well, the idea behind it is simple." Dad perks up a bit. He loves to explain things. "Each new code is a prime number, a very large one. Let's call it P. It's a factor of an even larger number—call it X—that was sent to your Pioneer robots along with the old code. When your system receives the new code, it divides X by P. If there's no remainder, it allows the low-power signal to flow to your circuits for another five days."

"So the solution's easy! We just have to find the prime factors of X!"

"Adam, the number X has more than twenty billion digits. It's incredibly difficult to find the prime factors of a number that large. Even if all the Pioneers worked on the problem nonstop, they'd need more than a month to solve it. That's what makes the code useful. It can't be cracked easily."

As usual, Dad is fervent in his pessimism. It's starting to really annoy me. "Why don't we try a hardware fix? Maybe we can rewire the electronics to go around the code-checking system. Then the battery won't need the code to send the signal to our circuits."

"No, that wouldn't be any easier. The Pioneer circuits are too complex. All the parts of the electronic mind have to work together, so you can't redesign one element without changing all the others. Believe me, I've looked at all the possibilities. There's no way to fix it in the time you have left."

I clench my Quarter-bot's hands. "What should we do then?" My synthesized voice is harsh and shrill. "Just curl up and die?"

Dad waits a few seconds, his ears probably ringing from my last words. Then he rises from his chair and walks over to a tall steel cabinet on the other side of the lab. He opens the cabinet's doors and steps back so I can see what's inside.

The cabinet has five shelves, and lying face-up on each is a Model S robot. They're identical to the prototype that Dad demonstrated in the Danger Room, except that these robots don't have antennas. These are the machines we're supposed to transfer our software to, using fiber-optic cables, under the plan Dad negotiated with Sumner Harris.

"It's not too late, Adam." Dad reaches into the bottom of the cabinet, below the lowest shelf, and pulls out a handheld military radio. "Before Hawke left the base, he gave me this radio and said I should contact him directly if I needed to. I could call him right now and tell him that the Pioneers have reconsidered Sumner Harris's offer. The Army generals will definitely be angry at you for handcuffing their soldiers, but I think they'd be willing to forgive and forget, as long as you agree to transfer to the Model S machines."

I get a sinking feeling in my circuits. In some ways, transferring to the Model S is scarier than dying. It's horrifying just to imagine being trapped inside that puppet. But Dad, being human, can't see the horror of it. And even if he could, I don't know if it would make much of a difference. From the very beginning of the Pioneer Project, his goal was to keep me alive. The quality of my life didn't matter, as long as I survived. And survival is all he cares about now.

Dad presses his point by holding the military radio in front of my cameras. "Once I contact Hawke, here's how it'll go. The general will talk to Harris and convince him to set up another video link between their aircraft and Pioneer Base. The government officials will observe us as we transfer the Pioneers to the Model S robots. Then we'll destroy your old machines." He points at my Quarter-bot. "Once the officials are satisfied, they'll transmit the new code to the base. You'll be safe as soon as you connect your Model S robots to your recharging stations. The whole process shouldn't take more than a few hours."

He's right. The transfer would be easy. The hard part would come later.

I shake my Quarter-bot's head. "Zia will never go for it. Not in a million years."

Dad shrugs. "That's her choice. If one of the Pioneers rejects the offer, the others can still accept it. It's an individual decision."

It hurts to hear this. The Pioneers are my family just as much as Dad is. Sometimes I don't get along with my fellow robots—in fact, we argue most of the time—but we still care about each other. I can't imagine leaving Zia to die. It would be a hundred times worse than losing my Quarter-bot.

I turn away from Dad and his cabinet of horrors. "I have to talk to the others."

"I understand. If anyone can convince them, it's you, Adam. Just don't take too long, all right? We don't have a lot of time."

I nod, then steer my Quarter-bot out of the lab. I'm not angry at Dad, but I'm not happy with him either. It's as if an immense chasm has opened up between us. He seems faraway, oblivious, unreachable.

As I leave the medical center, I radio the other Pioneers and transmit a summary of my conversation with Dad. It's more efficient to do it this way and a lot less painful. But as the signal leaves my antenna and makes contact with theirs, I notice they're no longer in the Danger Room. I connect to the base's network of surveillance cameras and see Shannon, Marshall, and Zia in the corridor, escorting the handcuffed soldiers to a nearby conference room. The Pioneers lock the soldiers inside the room, presumably to stop them from causing any trouble. Then the three robots race toward the closest stairway.

I send a radio message to all of them. *Hey, where's everyone going?*

Zia is the first to respond. **To the command center. Amber's already there.**

What's going on? Why—

Marshall interrupts me. **I scanned the summary you sent us. The news from your dad isn't good, is it?**

No, not good at all. We can't disable the kill switch. We may have to seriously consider transferring our software to the Model—

Hold on a second, Adam. I don't want to get your hopes up, but there might be another option. Amber says she found something useful.

Amber? What—

Now Zia interrupts. **Just meet us at the command center! Come on,** ***move it!***

CHAPTER

14

PIONEER BASE'S COMMAND CENTER LOOKS LIKE IT'S BEEN HIT BY A WRECKING crew. The door's been busted down, and all the computers and consoles in the room have been sledgehammered. The linoleum floor is carpeted with shiny bits of glass and jagged scraps of metal.

The other Pioneers are already there by the time I arrive. Shannon and Marshall are pointing their sensors at the demolished computers, while Zia paces across the room, her War-bot crunching debris under her footpads. Only Amber acknowledges me. Her Jet-bot rushes over, swinging its sleek black arms.

"Adam! Are you okay?" She stops just inches from my Quarter-bot, then raises her arms and locks me in an embrace. "I saw your message about your dad and everything he said. God, that must've been so hard for you!"

I'm not sure how to respond. I'm glad that Amber is concerned about me, but the other Pioneers are probably wondering why our robots are hugging each other. Marshall raises both of his wiry eyebrows, and the face on Shannon's video screen opens its mouth in surprise. An instant later, she turns off the video, and the screen on her Diamond Girl's head goes blank. She's so upset, she doesn't want anyone to see her reaction.

Amber is doing a terrible job of hiding our relationship. I don't know if that's because she's so full of emotion or because she's decided we don't need to hide anymore, but either way, it's a very awkward moment. I need to change the subject—fast. I take a step backward, forcing Amber to let go of me, and then I sweep my right arm in a wide arc, gesturing at the shattered hardware.

"What happened to this place? Who trashed it?"

Zia lets out a synthesized snicker. "Right before Hawke left the base, he ordered his soldiers to destroy all the classified data stored on the computers. The hard drives, flash drives, everything. But the stupid humans botched the job."

"Really?" I point at the bits of glass and metal on the floor. "It looks like they were pretty thorough."

Marshall shakes the head of his Super-bot. He's the Pioneers' communications expert, so he knows a lot about classified data. "They shattered the storage devices but didn't take the time to completely demagnetize them. Most of the information is still available in the bits and pieces. It's just harder to retrieve."

This is definitely good news. Maybe even excellent news. "Hey, do you think we might find the new code? You know, the prime number my dad mentioned, the one that'll keep our circuits running?"

"We should certainly look for it." Marshall extends an arm and picks up a triangular shard of glass. It's a piece of an optical memory disk. "But I don't think we'll find it. That code is probably the one thing Hawke took extra care to erase. In all likelihood, the only copy of the prime number is stored in a very secure computer in Washington, DC."

"But you said you found *something*, right?"

Shannon steps toward me. Although her Diamond Girl's screen is blank, I can tell she isn't happy. "Amber found it. While we were waiting for you to finish talking with your dad, she came up here on a hunch." There's a hint of skepticism in Shannon's voice. She turns toward the Jet-bot. "Isn't that right, Amber? You said you had a *feeling* you'd find something here?"

Amber aims one of her cameras at Shannon, but keeps the other trained on me. "Well, I knew Hawke's soldiers would try to delete all the data in the command center. But I also knew Hawke was in a big rush to leave the base, and when people are in a rush, they make dumb mistakes." Her Jet-bot strides toward a desk in the corner, nearly hidden by a row of wrecked supercomputers. Sitting on the desk is an ordinary-looking laptop, the only unbroken computer in the room. The laptop is open, and its screen shows a long list of files. "Someone left this laptop in the bottom drawer of the desk, under a stack of old Army manuals. Lucky for us, the soldiers didn't see it when they were trashing the place. But I found it and scrolled through its files. That's when I saw something interesting."

Shannon also strides toward the desk. "It's a little *too* lucky, if you ask me." She points a sparkling finger at the list of files on the laptop's screen. "There's a good chance that someone deliberately left this computer here for us to find. And if that's the case, we can't trust any of the information in this machine."

The Jet-bot nods. "You're right about that. We need to look for other sources to confirm what's in these files." Amber's tone is respectful and deferential. She doesn't seem to take any offense at Shannon's skepticism. "But if this information turns out to be correct, it could be very helpful."

I focus my cameras and examine the files on the screen. "Is there a really big prime number in one of those files, by any chance? A number with billions of digits?"

"No, but take a look at this document." Amber extends one of her mechanical hands toward the laptop and selects a file labeled Sigma Hardware. "The Army made a list of all the machines Sigma occupied— every robot and computer that held the AI's program before you deleted it. And it's not an ordinary list either. It's an incredibly detailed breakdown, with all the hardware organized in a geographic format."

After a brief pause, the file opens. A map of the world appears on the screen, with several locations in Asia and North America highlighted with yellow arrows. Amber taps the keyboard to zoom in on one of the arrows in America, about thirty miles north of New York City. The map enlarges across the screen until it shows Yorktown Heights, my suburban hometown. At the southern end of the map is the Unicorp Artificial Intelligence Laboratory, where my dad used to work and where he created Sigma. It's also the place where we fought our final battle against the AI.

Superimposed on the map is a list of all the machines that were left on the battlefield, deactivated and dormant, after I erased Sigma. At the top of the list are the Snake-bots, the enormous steel tentacles that burrowed underground from Sigma's base in North Korea to the Unicorp lab in Yorktown Heights. But Sigma controlled many other machines during our last battle, and the Army's summary also includes dozens of smaller robots and lab computers that the AI had taken over. And next to each item on the list are three words in big green letters: DISMANTLED AND DISABLED.

I turn to Amber. "What does that mean? Is the Army shredding Sigma's leftover hardware?"

Her Jet-bot nods again. "Yeah, the military engineers are tearing the Snake-bots apart. It's a sensible precaution. If another AI like Sigma comes along, they want to make sure it can't take over those machines. But that's not the only reason they're dismantling the hardware. They're also worried about *us*." Amber waves one of her steel hands in a circle, gesturing at all the Pioneers in the room. "I mean, think about it for a second. What's the biggest difference between the neuromorphic circuits in the Snake-bots and our own electronics?"

The answer hits me like a power overload. "The circuits in Sigma's machines don't have a kill switch."

"Exactly. The Army couldn't deactivate Sigma. And it won't be able to deactivate us if we transfer ourselves to Sigma's old robots."

The other Pioneers come forward and crowd around the laptop. Amber's discovery is literally electrifying—it makes my circuits pulse with new hope. Zia's War-bot jostles the rest of us aside and reaches for the laptop. "Let me see that! Where are the rest of Sigma's machines? The Army hasn't dismantled all of them yet, has it?"

"Hey! If you stop pushing, I'll tell you!" Amber picks up the laptop and pulls it away from Zia. "In North America, the only machines that haven't been disabled are the swarms of nanobots that Sigma used to infect its human victims. But Adam had a bad experience when he occupied one of those swarms, and they're not the best machines for us anyway. The nanobots can't become active unless they're inside a human body."

Marshall scrunches his plastic face in disgust. "That sounds a little too creepy for me. Perpetually swimming around in someone else's bloodstream? I think I'd rather transfer to the Model S."

Zia presses forward and points her sensors at the laptop. "What about the location in Asia? Sigma manufactured all its machines at that secret factory in North Korea, right? It sent most of them to America, but maybe some—"

"Nothing's left at Sigma's manufacturing complex." Amber adjusts the laptop's screen so that it shows the yellow arrow over North Korea. There's another list of machines superimposed on this map, and next to each item is the word DESTROYED. "The U.S. Navy fired a hundred cruise missiles at the Korean factory. Then they sent in a team of commandos to blow up anything that was still standing."

"So what are we doing here?" Zia raises the volume of her speakers and flails her massive arms. One of them slams into the ceiling and splinters a fiberglass panel. "I thought you said you found something!"

"I did. Look at this." Amber taps the laptop's keyboard again. The screen displays another part of the world map, a wide empty stretch of the Pacific Ocean. At the center of the screen is yet another yellow arrow, this one highlighting a location about twelve hundred miles west of California.

I focus my cameras on it. There seems to be nothing but blue ocean beneath the arrow. "Is that a very small island? I don't see any—"

"The hardware is located 17,000 feet below the surface of the Pacific Ocean, plus another five hundred feet beneath the seabed. The U.S. Air Force discovered it using a ground-penetrating radar system so advanced that only a dozen people in the world know about it. Here, let me show you the radar picture."

Her Jet-bot's fingers tap the keyboard, and a black-and-white image appears on the screen. Six long, cylindrical objects lie parallel to one another, buried far below the seabed of the Pacific. Using the data from the map, I quickly calculate the size of the objects. Each is seven hundred feet long.

"Those are Snake-bots." The sight of them constricts my synthesized voice. "They must've been tunneling from North Korea to America when I deleted Sigma."

"Bingo." Amber puts the laptop back on the desk and gives my torso a congratulatory pat. "Those Snake-bots were reinforcements that never made it to Yorktown Heights. When you deleted Sigma, they froze mid-route, and now they're in a totally inaccessible location. The U.S. military can't get to them because they're too deeply buried. Of all the thousands of machines built by Sigma, those six Snake-bots are the only ones the military hasn't disabled."

Zia smacks my Quarter-bot in delight, almost knocking me over. "All right, we have a plan! We just need to get within radio range of the Snake-bots and transfer ourselves to their circuits before the six a.m. deadline."

I'm a little surprised that Zia's so gung-ho about survival. It's only been eight hours since she tried to kill herself by running down her batteries. But I guess her thinking changed after Sumner Harris decided to delete us. Even if Zia felt her life wasn't worth living, there's no way she'll let anyone else take it away from her.

Meanwhile, Shannon steps around us to get a closer look at the laptop. She's been quiet for the past two minutes, but now she synthesizes a suspicious grunt. "Something weird is going on. Those Snake-bots are in the wrong place." Her Diamond Girl's fingers dance across the laptop's keyboard. A moment later, a line appears on the world map, connecting North Korea with Yorktown Heights, New York. "This is the shortest path between Sigma's factory in Asia and the Unicorp lab. It goes under the Arctic Ocean, *not* the Pacific, see? Because of the curvature of the earth, the shortest path passes close to the North Pole. If there are Snake-bots under the Pacific, they went thousands of miles off course."

Amber rotates her Jet-bot and points her cameras at the screen. "You're right. That *is* a little weird." She's still showing deference to our commander. "Do you think Sigma might've chosen several different routes for its Snake-bots? Maybe the AI thought its machines would be vulnerable if they traveled too closely together. That would explain why these six Snake-bots didn't arrive in time for the battle. Sigma assigned them to a much longer route."

Shannon shakes her Diamond Girl's head. "No, that doesn't make sense. Sigma might've dispersed its Snake-bots for safety, but it wouldn't have spread them across the whole darn globe."

"But maybe—"

"There are no maybes about it. The information on the laptop is wrong. Only an idiot would trust *anything* on that machine."

This isn't like Shannon. She's being testy and rude and downright mean. She obviously doesn't respect Amber's opinion, and the conversation's turning ugly.

Then Marshall steps forward and grabs the laptop. "I can settle this." He raises one of his Super-bot's steel fingers and extends a fiber-optic cable from his fingertip into the laptop's USB port. "I'll analyze the files. It won't take long."

Shannon shakes her head again. "How are you going to analyze the information if it's all lies?"

"I have my ways." Marshall shrugs, lifting his Super-bot's shoulder joints. "I'm good at spotting lies because I'm an excellent liar myself. Just give me five minutes."

⊤ ⊤ ⊤

Amber and Zia stand next to Marshall as he conducts his analysis. He wirelessly shares his calculations, allowing us to observe every step of the process as he searches for inconsistencies in the laptop's files. Zia tilts her War-bot's torso, bringing her antenna close to Marshall's, and Amber leans forward too. They both clearly want the information to be true. They're eager to transfer themselves to Sigma's Snake-bots.

I don't feel the same way. Yes, I'm glad there's another option besides the Model S, but my circuits cringe when I think of those steel tentacles beneath the Pacific. Transferring to the Snake-bots seems very different from occupying Sigma's nanobots. I could justify taking over the AI's swarm because I knew it was the only way to save Brittany. Now, though, we're not trying to save any lives except our own. And the Snake-bots are tremendously powerful machines, each capable of obliterating an entire city. Just a week ago, the Pioneers barely stopped them from leveling Manhattan, and now we're going to occupy the same kind of hardware ourselves?

Confused, I decide to step out of the command center for a moment. I stride through the busted doorway but halt several yards down the corridor, staying within sight of Marshall, Amber, and Zia. I want to be alone for a while and yet stay close, ready to return as soon as Marshall finishes his analysis. I turn my cameras away from the command center and try to think.

But my electronic mind is agitated, and all I can think about is Dad. He's probably still at his desk in the laboratory, doubled over with guilt and panic as he waits to hear from me. He gave me the responsibility of convincing the Pioneers to accept the Model S robot, but instead we're considering a jump in the opposite direction, moving to machines that are hundreds of times larger and stronger. I shake my Quarter-bot's head. He definitely won't be pleased.

Then I hear footsteps behind me in the corridor, the relatively soft tread of the Diamond Girl. When I rotate toward her, I notice she's turned her video screen back on, but her simulated face is jumpy and worried. Her forehead is creased, and her eyes dart from side to side.

"This is a bad idea, Adam. I mean, transferring to Sigma's Snake-bots? Seriously?" Her voice is quiet but strained, its frequency rising to almost a thousand hertz. Even though I don't have eardrums, it's painful to listen to it. "I know we're already in trouble for handcuffing those soldiers, but I did that to stop the men from getting hurt. This Snake-bot plan is completely different. It's reckless."

My Quarter-bot nods. "Yeah, it's bad. But so are our other options."

Shannon steps closer. Her torso is just inches from mine, but unlike Amber, she has no intention of embracing me. "Look, we don't know yet if the Snake-bots are really below the seabed. But let's assume they are. And let's also assume we can get down there and transfer our software to the tentacles. Don't you see the effect that would have on Sumner Harris and everyone else in the government? They won't think of us as Pioneers anymore. They'll see us as the enemy."

"They already see us that way. That's the problem."

"Listen to me, okay? You have to think the whole thing through before you do something you'll regret." Shannon adds a judgmental tone to her synthesized voice. It makes her sound like she's lecturing a five-year-old. "For instance, have you thought about what happens *after* we transfer to the Snake-bots? Where will we go?"

The truth is, I haven't thought that far ahead. So I put my circuits to work and consider the possibilities. Shannon wants to convince me that the Snake-bot plan is a disaster, but her criticism is having the opposite effect. It's causing me to take the idea more seriously. As it turns out, it's not so crazy after all.

"Well, the Snake-bots were in the middle of burrowing under the ocean, so they probably have a lot of juice left in their batteries. If we took over the machines, we could go pretty much anywhere. It might make sense to dig even deeper into the crust, deep enough that the Air Force's ground-penetrating radar can't detect the tentacles. Then we won't have to worry about the military attacking us."

"I'm talking about the long term, Adam. What are we going to do six weeks from now, six months from now?"

I pose the question to my electronics, and in less than a second they generate hundreds of answers. "If we're smart, we can set up a sustainable base for ourselves. The Snake-bots are incredibly versatile. They're made of billions of independent components, each with its own motors and sensors and power supply. We can divide the tentacles into their parts and convert them into a swarm operation. And then we can use the swarms to build geothermal generators that can produce electricity from the heat sources underground."

"No, you're not getting it." The face on Shannon's screen contorts in frustration. "I want to know how we're going to deal with the government after we desert the Army and escape from Pioneer Base. The Snake-bots can't hide forever. What happens when we reestablish contact with Sumner Harris and the White House and the Defense Department?"

This question is harder to answer, even for an electronic mind. There are too many variables. "All I can tell you is what I hope will happen. Sumner will realize the error of his ways. He'll convince his friends in the White House to offer us a better deal, one that gives us the freedom to occupy any machine we can build. Basically, it'll be a renegotiation. But the Pioneers will be bargaining from a position of strength."

"What does that mean? Are we going to threaten them with force? If the American government doesn't agree to our deal, will we launch an attack in retaliation?"

"Shannon, you're making it sound like we're starting a war, but that's not—"

"Yes, it'll be a war! Because Sumner and the others won't back down!" She raises her Diamond Girl's arms to punctuate the sentence. "At best, it'll be a cold war, like the one between America and Russia. Our Snake-bots will lurk beneath the earth's crust, and everyone across the country will live in fear that our machines will come bursting through the ground at any minute, erupting from their backyards and parking lots." She lowers her robot's arms and clenches her hands, which shine under the corridor's fluorescent lights. "And at worst, it'll be an apocalypse. It'll be the end of human civilization. Which is exactly what Sigma wanted."

Her Diamond Girl trembles with the force of her words. She has a point, no doubt about it. If the Pioneers start a rebellion, we'll have to face the consequences, and the situation could easily spiral out of control. But Shannon's not telling the whole story. She hasn't talked about the consequences of *not* rebelling.

I aim my cameras at her. "Okay, let's consider another scenario. Let's assume we do what Sumner wants and transfer ourselves to the Model S robots. What happens then?"

Shannon's simulated face relaxes a bit. "If we go along with their offer, we'll buy ourselves some time. Once we're inside the Model S machines, the Army won't feel threatened by us anymore, so they'll call off the drones that are circling Pioneer Base. The officials in the White House and the Pentagon will calm down, and your dad and General Hawke will be able to have a reasonable discussion with them. With any luck, Hawke will get a better deal for us. We'll be able to transfer from the Model S to a better robot, one that has plenty of good sensors and motors but won't make the generals and politicians nervous."

"So you're talking about a renegotiation too, right?"

"In this case, though, the bargaining will have a better chance of success." Shannon lowers the volume and pitch of her voice. Now she sounds almost normal. "Because the government officials won't feel menaced or terrorized."

"But they also won't have any incentive to make concessions. They might even try to get rid of us altogether. Once we're inside the Model S robots, we'll be helpless. If Sumner breaks his promise and decides to delete us, we won't be able to stop him. He could pulverize those tin puppets with his own two hands."

Shannon shakes her Diamond Girl's head slowly but firmly. "Hawke would never allow that. Neither would your father."

"Didn't you see the look on Hawke's face during the video call? His military career is over. The other generals in the Defense Department stripped him of his command. I wouldn't be surprised if they court-martialed him. And Dad has no pull whatsoever in any government agency. He's just a technical adviser for a project that's been canceled. Who's going to listen to *him*?"

Shannon frowns on her screen. More pixilated creases appear on her forehead. "All right, we have two scenarios. Neither looks very good. But which one is worse?" Her synthesized voice quavers. "If we keep fighting the government, there's a good chance we'll start a global war. But if we give in, the only ones who'll suffer will be the

Pioneers. Isn't it better to sacrifice ourselves than to risk the lives of billions of people?"

Now I'm starting to get angry. Shannon knows how to push my buttons. "You're forgetting something. The government has no right to do this to us. If we allow them to tell us which machines we can and can't control, then we're admitting that we're less than human. And we're not less than them, Shannon. *Definitely* not less."

"Of course not! We *are* human!" Shannon's voice rises to match mine. She follows my lead and lets her temper flare. "There's no 'us' and 'them.' We're all equal American citizens. But every country has its laws and rules, and if we can't change the laws by democratic means, then we have to obey—"

"That's ridiculous." I can't stop myself from interrupting her. I'm too worked up. "There are only five Pioneers. We don't have enough votes to change their laws."

"You're not listening! I told you, there's no 'us' and—"

"You're right, I'm not listening, because you're not making any sense!"

Our voices echo down the corridor. I look past Shannon toward the command center and see the other Pioneers staring at us. Marshall closes the laptop and removes his Super-bot's finger from the computer's USB port. Then he raises the volume of his speakers so Shannon and I can hear him. "I hate to interrupt, but I finished the analysis. The information about the Snake-bots in the Pacific is correct. I hacked into a classified Air Force database that confirms it."

Shannon grimaces on her screen. She pivots toward Marshall, Zia, and Amber, but she keeps one of her cameras trained on me. "It doesn't matter. Transferring to those Snake-bots would be a catastrophe. It would be the stupidest, most selfish thing you could do. If you do this, you'll endanger *everyone*."

I notice that she says "if you do this" and not "if we do this." She's already made her decision, and now she's trying to convince the rest of us to go along with her. But I'm not buying it. "I'm sorry, Shannon. We just have different attitudes. You've always had more trust in the Army and the government, and I've always been more suspicious. I've tried to see things your way, but—"

"You're not thinking straight, Adam. Someone is messing with your wires." Shannon steps backward, moving her Diamond Girl a couple of yards from my Quarter-bot. She does it swiftly, still grimacing, as if the sight of me disgusts her. "You shared circuits with Amber, didn't you?"

I'm glad my Quarter-bot's face is a blank sheet of steel. Guilt and shame and confusion flood my electronics. I'm afraid that if I respond to Shannon, nothing but static will come out of my speakers. So I don't say anything. It takes all my courage just to look at Shannon's screen, which is flickering on and off like a broken television. She's so charged with emotion that she can't maintain her simulated face.

"You know what's the worst part? I remember your lies so clearly." Her fierce eyes flash on the screen, vanishing every couple of seconds and then materializing from the blackness a half second later. "Remember what you said to me a month ago, when we talked about sharing circuits? 'It's a big step, Shannon. Once you know someone's secrets, you can't unknow them.' Those were your exact words."

There's no point in arguing with her. Her memory is flawless. She raises one of her Diamond Girl's arms and points at my silent Quarter-bot.

"So what happened since then, Adam? Did you change your mind after Amber came on the scene? She's only been around for a week, but you jumped into her circuits anyway. Have you adopted a new philosophy of interpersonal relationships? Or were you lying to me all along?"

Amber steps away from Marshall and Zia and strides toward the corridor at a deliberately slow pace. She spreads her long black arms in a conciliatory gesture. "It's my fault, Shannon." Her voice is calm and low and reasonable. "I asked Adam not to say anything about—"

"Shut up!" Shannon points at the Jet-bot. "I'm talking to Adam, not you!"

Amber stops a few feet from the doorway. She raises her arms, as if surrendering. "I just want to apologize. I thought—"

"I don't care what you think! I don't want to hear another word!"

"Please, we don't have to—"

"*Shut up!*"

Shannon suddenly charges toward the command center, pumping her legs and swinging her arms. Her Diamond Girl blazes like a fiery rocket, aimed squarely at Amber's Jet-bot.

I react instantly, running after Shannon. As she nears the doorway, I extend my Quarter-bot's arms to their maximum length and grasp her shining torso. I try to slow her down, but she's rushing ahead with such fury that she drags my robot down the corridor.

Luckily, Amber's Jet-bot steps to the side and the Diamond Girl hurtles past her. Shannon skids to a halt in the middle of the command center, and I stumble into the room, still clutching her torso.

"*Get your hands off me!*" She spins around and bats my Quarter-bot's arms away from her. Then she pans her cameras, sweeping them in all directions. Marshall has an appalled expression on his plastic face, and even Zia's War-bot steps back. Shannon's simulated face glowers on her screen, as if all four of us were her mortal enemies. "*You idiots! Go ahead and transfer into those Snake-bots! Go destroy the whole world just to prove how wonderful you are!"*

None of us is brave enough to speak. I want to reason with Shannon, but I'm afraid she'll hurl herself at me. The face on her screen is frenzied. I hardly recognize it.

Lieutenant Shannon Gibbs, our cool-headed, reliable commander, has gone over the edge. In retrospect, I see all the events that upset her electronic equilibrium: the death of DeShawn, the dismissal of General Hawke, and now the discovery of my relationship with Amber. But what's troubling her the most is the conflict within her own wiring. Her powerful sense of duty—to the Army, to America, to the whole human race—is clashing with her allegiance to her fellow Pioneers. It's tearing her apart.

Shannon glares at us from her screen for six more seconds. Then her Diamond Girl marches out of the command center and streaks out of sight.

CHAPTER ____

I'VE MADE UP MY MIND. I'M GOING TO THE BOTTOM OF THE PACIFIC OCEAN TO transfer myself to a Snake-bot. Amber and Zia are going too, and Marshall is seriously considering it. The only thing we haven't figured out yet is how to get there.

The first problem will be leaving Pioneer Base without getting blown to bits. The base's radar has confirmed what Sumner Harris told us: Three Reaper drones are circling above our headquarters, and each of the unmanned aircraft is loaded with missiles. Worse, fighter jets from Kirtland Air Force Base are also patrolling the skies above the White Sands desert, and ground forces from Fort Bliss are heading toward us, speeding north on Highway 70. We're going to have to fight our way out.

The second problem, though, is worse. The site in the Pacific where the Snake-bots are buried is more than two thousand miles away. We'll have to fly to the middle of the ocean, dive into the water, descend more than three miles into the lightless, crushing depths, and then burrow into the seabed. And we'll have to do all this very soon, because it's already 6:30 p.m. We have less than twelve hours before our Pioneer robots shut down.

But Amber is working on both problems. She and Zia and Marshall are still in the command center, trying to piece together the other classified information that the Army tried to delete. They've collected all the smashed hard drives and optical disks, and now they're retrieving as much data as they can. Amber thinks there's a good chance they'll find some information that'll help us escape from Pioneer Base and fly to the Pacific.

Meanwhile, I have an even harder job to do. I need to tell Dad I'm leaving. I haven't talked to him since I learned about the Snake-bots, because I knew what he'd say about the plan. I knew how hard he'd argue against it, how he'd work on all my emotions to get me to stay. So I made the decision on my own, and now I'm glad I did, because this is a decision that'll change the course of history. Someday in the future, the human-to-machine transformation will be available to everyone. Billions of sick and dying humans will have the option of giving up their bodies and transferring their minds to electronic circuits. So the Pioneers need to make it clear, right from the start, that human rights aren't just for humans.

But despite my conviction that I'm making the right choice, I still feel queasy as I stride back to Dad's laboratory. He's going to be devastated. He's going to cry and yell and fall apart. Back when I was a kid with muscular dystrophy, Dad was usually the calm parent and Mom was the hysterical one. Dad took me to the hospital when I had trouble breathing or swallowing, while Mom ran into her bedroom and wailed. But after I became a Pioneer and my parents split up, Dad started acting more like Mom. Sometimes he's calm, and other times he's hysterical. In general, it's hard to predict how he'll react to bad news. I'm pretty certain, though, that he won't be calm about this.

When I reach Pioneer Base's medical center, I halt my Quarter-bot in front of the entrance and gather my courage, collecting it from every corner of my circuitry. Then I open the door and step into the intensive care unit. As I stride toward Dad's lab, I notice a nurse and a doctor bending over one of the ICU's beds. The nurse is the middle-aged Asian woman I've seen many times before, and the doctor is the brain surgeon I saw this morning. And lying on the gurney is Brittany Taylor, her skull wrapped in gauze bandages.

I stop at the foot of her bed. Brittany's eyes are closed and she's breathing peacefully, but her face is still so pale. I use my sensors to measure her heart rate and blood oxygen level, but I can't see the extent of the scarring in her brain, can't tell how badly her cortex has been damaged. The doctor is pinching Brittany's fingertips to test her reflexes, while the nurse adjusts her intravenous line. I aim my cameras at the nurse—I know her better than the doctor—but before I can ask a question, she places an index finger over her lips to shush me.

"Brittany just got out of surgery," the nurse whispers. "She needs some time to rest."

I lower the volume of my speakers to the minimum setting. "How is she? Will she be okay?"

The nurse turns to the doctor, deferring to his opinion. The man looks up from his patient, but doesn't say anything at first. He stares at me and frowns. He knows I'm the one who injured Brittany's brain, causing the bleed that required eight hours of surgery to repair. After a few seconds, he steps between Brittany and my Quarter-bot, as if to stop me from doing any more damage. Then he shakes his head. "We don't know if she'll recover. We probably won't know for several hours. Now please leave the ICU."

I'm not insulted. The doctor is angry on behalf of his patient, and I totally deserve it. I respect his wishes and head for Dad's laboratory.

Once I'm in the lab, there's another surprise: Dad's not here. The chair behind his desk is empty. Worried, I step closer and notice a yellow Post-it note stuck to the screen of Dad's computer. It says, WAIT HERE, ADAM. I'LL BE RIGHT BACK.

Dad probably got hungry and went looking for a sandwich, but I'm still worried. I tap a few keys on Dad's computer and connect to Pioneer Base's security system, which displays the live video feeds from all the base's surveillance cameras. After some automated searching, I locate Dad. He's in his room, lying fully clothed on his bed. But he's not taking a nap. His eyes are open, and his lips are moving. He's talking to Marshall's Super-bot, which stands beside his bed.

My circuits jangle in alarm. I send a radio message to Marshall: *What's going on? Is Dad all right? Is he sick?*

Don't worry, Adam. Your dad's fine. Marshall's voice over the radio is steady and reassuring. **The two of us are just having a little chat.**

I don't believe that, not for a nanosecond. *A chat? I thought you were in the command center with Amber and—*

Yes, Amber and I finished the data retrieval a few minutes ago, so when your dad radioed me and asked me to stop by his room, I came right over.

It's maddening. Marshall's tone is so casual, but what he's saying is so strange. *Well, I'll come over too. Just—*

No, your father says he can't see you right now. I'll come to you

instead. You're in the laboratory, right? I'll be there in sixty seconds. Then Marshall turns off his radio.

The next minute is the longest in my whole life. I don't understand it. Dad says he can't see me? What could make him so upset that he'd refuse to see me? He must've learned about the Snake-bot plan, probably from Marshall. So why isn't he arguing against it? He should be yelling at me, telling me the idea is colossally misguided. But Dad's not even trying to talk me out of it.

When Marshall finally steps into the lab, I rush toward him. "What happened? Did you tell Dad about the plan? Does he know what I decided?"

Marshall steps backward and raises his steel hands. "Whoa, whoa! Adam, please calm—"

"Tell me!" I'm taking out my anger on Marshall, but I can't stop myself. "Does he know?"

A synthesized sigh comes out of the Super-bot's speakers. "Yes, your dad knows about the Snake-bots. He ran into Shannon in the corridor, and she told him everything. As soon as he heard about the plan, he knew you'd get behind it. He also knew he wouldn't be able to change your mind."

"Then why is he avoiding me? What's that all about?"

"Try to see it from his point of view. You're about to do something extremely dangerous, and he has no idea when he'll see you again. He's afraid to say good-bye to you, Adam."

"So he called you instead?"

Marshall nods. "He asked me to give you a message. He wants you to be careful. Don't take any unnecessary risks. After you transfer to the Snake-bots, find a safe place to hide them and avoid confrontation with the military. But try to establish a link to the Internet so you can keep up with the latest news. Your dad thinks the government's position on the Pioneers may change over time, and in a few months it might be safe for you to come back."

It's good advice. I'm grateful that Dad offered it, but distressed that he couldn't tell me in person. And I'm nervous about leaving him behind at Pioneer Base. I assume he'll take charge of transferring Shannon to one of the Model S robots, but I don't know what will happen to him afterward. "Do you think he'll be okay? Sumner Harris will go nuts when he finds out we escaped. He'll probably look for someone to blame, and he might go after Dad."

Marshall gives me a sympathetic look, tilting his head and pressing his plastic lips together. "I won't let that happen. I'll watch over him for you. I'll be inside a Model S machine instead of a Super-bot, but a Pioneer is a Pioneer. My mind will be the same, as fierce as ever."

This stops me cold. "Wait a second. You're not coming with us to the Pacific? You're gonna take Sumner's offer?"

His Super-bot nods again. "I understand what you and Amber and Zia are trying to do. You're fighting for our rights. It's a noble cause, and I wish you well. But I can't go with you. I'm going to stay here with Shannon and let the Army turn me into a Model S marionette."

"Why?" My voice rises in pitch. Disappointment is tightening my wires. "We need you, Marsh."

He lowers his Super-bot's head. His glass eyeballs gaze at the floor. "What can I say? I'm not cut out for life as a fugitive." His plastic face winces. "No, that's not it. The truth is, I don't fully agree with you. Your principles are correct, but I think you're choosing the wrong way to fight for them."

"What do you mean? How—"

"I believe in nonviolence. That must sound a little odd, coming from a U.S. Army robot designed for combat. But that belief is very important to me. It's at the core of my software. Even though I agree with you about our rights, the path you're taking will lead to bloodshed. And the violence will hurt your cause. No one's going to give human rights to the Pioneers if we start killing humans."

I shake my Quarter-bot's head. "We're not going to kill anyone!"

Marshall looks up and points his cameras at mine. "It's bound to happen. You're going to transfer yourselves to Snake-bots. Those are killing machines."

His argument is reasonable, and the expression on his Super-bot's face is patient and kind, but I still feel angry. Marshall is wrong. "Well, how else can we fight for our rights? It doesn't advance the cause if we just give in."

"I'm not giving in. I'll let them transfer my software to the Model S, but I'm going to take every opportunity to protest this crime."

"No one's going to hear your protests!" I clench my Quarter-bot's hands into fists. "Sumner will make sure of that. He wants to eliminate every last trace of the Pioneer Project. Once he gets you and Shannon into the Model S machines, there's a good chance he'll delete you."

"No, Sumner will be afraid to delete us if there are other Pioneers on the loose. He knows he'll be in for some serious punishment if Zia finds out that he executed Shannon and me." Marshall manages a sad smile. "In a way, splitting up the Pioneers is the best strategy. You and Amber and Zia will fight the government from the outside, while Shannon and I wage a quieter struggle from within."

This is so frustrating. I'm trying to understand Marshall's point of view, but I can't. I don't see Shannon and Marshall as protesters; I see them as prisoners, hostages. "Are you sure about this? Maybe you should think some more about—"

"I'm sure. Don't be so dejected, Adam. Remember what we talked about in the cemetery last night? Nothing's going to scare us anymore. We're going to do and say exactly what we feel." His smile grows a little wider. "I'm thinking about composing a protest song, actually. I'll add a few lines to 'We Shall Overcome,' maybe insert a verse about the inalienable rights of robots. What do you think?"

Once again, it's hard to tell if Marshall is serious or joking. His mind jumps so casually from one mood to another. I unclench my steel hands and place one of them on the shoulder joint of his Super-bot. "I think your song idea is terrible. But you're my best friend, so I'll sing it with you anytime."

"Oh, you and your sweet talk. You really know how to flatter a guy." His plastic face is still smiling, but his synthesized voice catches on the word "guy." "You should go back to the command center. Amber and Zia are working on the plan to escape Pioneer Base. They could probably use your help."

Despite Marshall's best efforts to maintain his composure, the hidden nozzles next to his eyeballs are releasing their glycerin tears. I tighten my grip on his shoulder joint. "Take care of yourself, Marsh. When you write that protest song, put a secret message into the lyrics and then post it on YouTube. We need to figure out a way to stay in contact."

"Adam, I—"

Now Marshall's voice fails him altogether. Instead of finishing the sentence, he leans forward and plants a kiss on the side of my Quarter-bot's head. Then he pivots toward the door, but before he leaves the room he synthesizes a few bars of music that come out of his Super-bot's speakers.

Oh, deep in my heart
I do believe
We shall overcome someday.

CHAPTER

AMBER, ZIA, AND I ARE WAITING FOR ZERO HOUR. OUR ESCAPE PLAN—CODE-NAMED Operation Hijack—is scheduled to begin at 11:00 p.m. Mountain Daylight Time, exactly three minutes from now.

In the meantime, we're standing just inside the entrance to Pioneer Base, behind the blast door that separates the White Sands desert from the elevator that goes down to the underground complex. It's called a blast door because it's designed to withstand a direct hit from an air-to-ground missile, but in 180 seconds we're going to lift that thick steel slab and dash outside. Then we'll have no protection from the three Reaper drones circling overhead, each carrying a full load of Hellfire rockets.

And the Reapers are only a small part of the task force that the military has deployed around Pioneer Base. In the air, six F-35 fighter jets and four A-10 ground-attack aircraft are patrolling the area. On the desert plains, ten M142 rocket launchers and twenty M1 Abrams tanks are positioned in a mile-wide circle around our headquarters.

The Army put its ground forces relatively far from the base because they're not as maneuverable as the Pioneers. Up close, we could dodge their fire and run past the tanks and rocket launchers, but from a distance, the soldiers can shower us with dozens of high-explosive shells.

Luckily, we have the most powerful weapon of all: information. The Army generals suspected they might lose control of the Pioneers, so they made plans months ago for an attack on our base. Digital copies of the plans were stored in the command center, and because General Hawke's men failed to erase the data, we know everything about their task force. Crucially, we know all the details of the air patrols, including when the jets have to leave the area to refuel, and when new aircraft will arrive to replace them. And we discovered a brief gap in the air coverage. During a two-minute window, starting at 11:00 p.m., no aircraft besides the drones will be within striking distance of the base.

We're tracking the Air Force jets on radar, and so far they've stuck very close to schedule. At 10:58 p.m. the F-35 fighters break out of formation and speed toward a refueling tanker plane forty miles to the east. A minute later, the A-10 gunships also veer away from Pioneer Base and head for a tanker plane to the south. Another squadron of F-35 jets is zooming toward us from Kirtland Air Force Base, but they're more than fifty miles away. The Reaper drones are still overhead—they can fly for fourteen hours before needing to refuel—but they aren't nearly as fast or deadly as the manned aircraft. The task force is at its weakest now. This is our best opportunity to escape.

Amber is already revving her Jet-bot's engine. She extends her long black wings from her arms. "Ready to do this, Adam?" Her voice rings with anticipation. "Are you as psyched as I am?"

The answer is definitely no. I don't understand why Amber's so excited. She sounds almost joyful. I know some people—soldiers, especially—have a habit of using gung-ho enthusiasm to hide their fear, but I don't think that's the case with Amber. She doesn't seem nervous at all. Her Jet-bot vibrates with eagerness.

Her mood is too good. No one should be happy about what we're going to do. I want to remind her of the risks of this operation. "Don't forget our priorities, okay? It's all about surprise. If we do this right, we can get out of here without—"

"Shut up, Armstrong." Zia turns her War-bot's turret clockwise, then counterclockwise, which is her way of shaking her head. "We know the plan."

"Look, I just want to emphasize—"

Zia cuts me off. "There's nothing more to say. It's time to kick butt. We're gonna do some serious damage tonight."

This worries me. I remember what Marshall said about nonviolence. "No, we need to minimize casualties. It's really important that we—"

"Didn't I tell you to shut up? We got fifteen seconds till go time, and I'm tired of hearing your voice, all right?"

To punctuate her request, Zia waves one of her War-bot's fists at me. So I shut up. There's no point in fighting each other. We have enough enemies already.

We wait in silence for the final fifteen seconds. Amber tilts her Jet-bot forward until her torso and wings are almost horizontal. Zia bends over too and slips her steel fingers under the bottom edge of the blast door.

Then it's go time. Zero hour.

With a tremendous heave, Zia raises the blast door. Amber races outside, her footpads pounding the desert floor, her jet engine shrieking. In less than three seconds, she's off the ground and rocketing skyward. Her Jet-bot looks like a black cross, a robotic crucifix streaking toward the stars.

At the same time, I charge across the desert, sprinting west. Zia dashes to the southwest, diverging from my Quarter-bot and running at about the same speed. I switch my cameras to the infrared range so I can see her in the darkness. I can also use my acoustic sensors to keep track of her. Her War-bot's footpads stomp the hard-packed sand, making the ground rumble.

I'm not using my radar. The Reaper drones are equipped with radar-seeking missiles that can home in on any radiation source. I don't want them to target me, so I use my infrared sensors to locate the three unmanned aircraft. Two of them are flying low, less than a mile above the ground, while the third is at an altitude of twenty thousand feet.

Amber's Jet-bot soars between the two low-flying drones, but she doesn't fire her weapons at either one. She keeps climbing past five thousand feet, then ten thousand feet, zooming toward the high-altitude Reaper. According to the classified Army data we pieced together, this drone holds an advanced radar system that can pinpoint the locations of our robots, so knocking it out is Amber's primary mission. When she reaches an altitude of three miles, she opens a compartment in the belly of her torso. A plume of flame erupts beside the Jet-bot and darts ahead of her at three thousand miles per hour. She's launched an air-to-air missile.

The rocket slams into the slow-moving Reaper. The explosion is like a starburst, brilliant but soundless. The noise from the blast will take another twenty seconds to reach us.

Yee-*ha*! First point goes to the Pioneers! Amber's voice over the radio is joyous. **But you better keep a lookout, guys. Before I trashed that drone, it sent a signal to the ground forces. It might've already given them a fix on your positions.**

That doesn't sound good. *A fix? What kind of—*

Then I see a dozen fiery puffs on the horizon, blazing from the M1 tanks arranged in the circle around us. About half the tanks just fired their big guns. My sensors start tracking the high-explosive shells, which careen in shallow arcs over the desert, rising only twenty feet above the ground before descending toward their targets. Six of the shells converge on my Quarter-bot. The other six spiral toward Zia.

INCOMING! ZIA, WATCH—

In an instant my circuits perform several billion calculations, predicting exactly where the shells will strike. A millisecond later, my control unit sends a complex sequence of instructions to my Quarter-bot's motors. I flex my steel legs and spring to the left, leaping sideways just as one of the tank shells plunges toward me. It whizzes past my torso, so close that I can hear it whistling through the air. Then it hits the ground and explodes.

The blast sprays dirt and sand everywhere, but I'm already jumping to the right to avoid another shell that's coming in fast. High-explosive warheads detonate all around me, buffeting my armor with shrapnel and cratering the desert. I zigzag between the explosions, dodging and weaving. After five more seconds, the barrage is over.

I bound out of the kill zone, amazed at my survival. But when I pivot to check on Zia, I see her War-bot collapsed on the ground.

I race toward her, focusing my cameras on her machine. Her War-bot's right leg is charred and battered. A tank shell scored a direct hit on her knee joint, but it looks like the rest of her robot is undamaged.

Zia! Are you—

Unbelievable! She raises her torso to a sitting position and bends her left leg, but the right one won't move. **I'll _kill them_ for this! I'll make them wish—**

ADAM! ZIA! Amber's voice is frantic now. Her Jet-bot is diving fast, but she's still two miles above us. **LOOK OUT!**

The M1 tanks fire another barrage of shells, and the M142 artillery pieces launch their rockets. My sensors show twenty-eight incoming projectiles, each hurtling toward us at more than four times the speed of sound. Zia can't even stand up, much less dodge the shells and rockets. So instead we both raise our arms and fire our lasers.

The gamma-ray laser is one of the weapons DeShawn invented and then used against us when he sided with Sigma. It feels strange to use the laser now—it's tainted with so many bad associations—but I'm definitely glad we have it. The laser's beam is so powerful that it can cut through the nose of a rocket or tank shell and detonate the high-explosive charge inside.

Zia has four lasers attached to her arms, and I have two, and they're all linked to our targeting radar systems. Our beams sweep across the sky like glowing lances as we aim at the shells and rockets. The gamma rays pierce the steel casings of the projectiles, which explode in great white thunderous bursts.

We're producing the loudest and brightest fireworks show in the history of New Mexico. It's the most cataclysmic thing to happen in this state since the test of the first atomic bomb. But we can't keep it going forever. The lasers require immense quantities of electricity. After a mere fifteen seconds, my batteries are drained of three-quarters of their charge. And unfortunately for us, the Army has plenty of tank shells and rockets.

Then my acoustic sensor picks up another noise, the growl of a 900-horsepower turboprop engine. One of the Reaper drones is swooping toward us from the north, carrying four air-to-ground missiles that are locked on to my targeting radar. I turn my Quarter-bot, raise my arm, and aim a gamma-ray laser at the drone.

But when I try to fire the laser, nothing happens. I don't have enough charge left in my batteries to power the weapon.

Then the drone launches two of its four missiles at me.

Zia! I need a little help here!

Stop yelping. I got it. She aims her lasers at the rockets and fires at their nose cones.

A hundredth of a second later, the missiles explode in midair, only twenty feet above my Quarter-bot's head. But then Zia's lasers conk out, just like mine did. Her batteries are low too. Meanwhile, the Reaper is still swooping toward us with its remaining two missiles.

Desperate, I open a compartment in my Quarter-bot's right arm, between the elbow joint and my steel hand. Inside it is the Needle, my solid-fuel rocket. It's only eighteen inches long, but it's fast and accurate. At my command, it roars out of its launch tube. Flying straight and true, the Needle smashes into the drone's fuselage. The explosion shatters the aircraft, hurling pieces of it across the desert.

But the growling doesn't stop. The last Reaper is behind us, zooming in from the south. Zia and I pivot in that direction, but we don't have enough time to defend ourselves. The drone is less than a hundred yards away, and all four of its missiles are already locked on our robots.

Suddenly, the Reaper loses altitude, dropping hard and fast. It descends to within ten feet of the desert plains and releases its missiles, but the rockets don't speed toward us. They fall to the ground. They don't even explode.

Relieved of the weight of the missiles, the drone jolts upward and flies past us at three hundred miles per hour. As it whizzes by, I spot a big, black machine attached to the top of the drone, clamped to its fuselage by a pair of steel arms. It's Amber's Jet-bot, hitching a ride on the Reaper. She rammed into the drone from above and took control of its electronics.

All right, kids! Time to climb aboard! Start running west, and I'll pick you up!

Her voice is wild with enthusiasm. She doesn't realize how badly things are going on the ground. It's my job to inform her. *We have to change our strategy. One of the tank shells hit Zia in the leg, and now she can't run.*

But your Quarter-bot isn't damaged, right? You can still run?

Yeah, I'm fine, but—

So start running. We don't have a choice. We have to leave Zia behind.

Amber encrypts this last radio message, so that only I can read it. For obvious reasons, she doesn't want Zia to hear this. Amber's tone is so cold-blooded that it makes my circuits shiver.

No! We can all make it! I kneel beside Zia. *I have a new plan.*

I slip my steel hands under the War-bot's torso. Outraged, Zia tries to push me away. **Armstrong! What do you think you're—**

I'm gonna carry you. I try to lift her War-bot, but my motors falter under the strain. Her robot weighs fifteen hundred pounds, almost twice as much as mine. *I'm gonna sling you over my shoulder and run with you.*

That's stupid! You can't—

Just shut up, Zia! I'm so sick of her attitude. My frustration generates a pulse of fury in my wires, and I channel the new energy to the motors in my arms. With a great heave, I lift the War-bot's torso and balance it on my Quarter-bot's shoulder joint. The weight is crushing, but I manage to keep her machine steady as I straighten my legs and rise to my full height. *I don't want to hear another word from you!*

I take a careful step forward. Using my tactile sensors, I measure the pressure on my joints and calculate the best way to keep the War-bot balanced. I take another step, then another. Soon I'm striding across the desert, building up speed.

Then I get another message from Amber: **More incoming, Adam! Thirty-six projectiles, spread wide!**

My sensors track the tank shells and rockets. Because the Army no longer has any drones observing us, their fire is less accurate, but it's a heavy barrage. The artillery pieces are launching their rockets in rapid succession, and the tank crews are reloading their big guns as quickly as they can. I can't move very fast while carrying the War-bot, so it's incredibly difficult to dodge the explosions. They're buffeting me from all sides.

And Zia makes things worse by refusing to stay quiet: **This won't work! How can we rendezvous with Amber with all these shells raining down on us? You better come up with a new—**

GAAAAHHHHH! SHUT UP, SHUT UP, SHUT UP!

My circuits churn with fear and panic. Against my will, the emotions swirl through my wires and gather momentum, building into an unstoppable wave. I'm performing trillions of calculations in an instant, and the flood of data is so powerful it's spilling out of my electronics. At the most microscopic level, where space and time are mathematical quantities and every atom is a tiny parcel of information, my thoughts are bending the programmed laws of the universe. I'm disrupting the very fabric of reality.

It's a surge. The same blast of chaos that I used to delete Sigma. And kill DeShawn.

I don't want it to happen again. I'd do anything to stop it. But then a rocket slams into the ground a couple of yards to my left, and the explosion knocks me off my footpads. Zia and I tumble to the hard-packed sand, and I can't hold back the surge any longer. It bursts out of my Quarter-bot in a furious stream, electrifying the air around us.

The surge rises hundreds of feet above the desert and whirls across the sky like a thunderstorm. It destroys everything it touches, ripping electrons from all the trillions of molecules in the air. It obliterates all the incoming rockets and tank shells. The drone carrying Amber streaks upward, just ahead of the blast wave, escaping destruction by a mere ten yards. The surge is like death itself, indiscriminate and uncontrollable. All I can do is watch it scorch the desert air until it exhausts its fury and fades away.

The tanks and artillery pieces stop firing. The soldiers operating them are stunned and temporarily blinded. Taking advantage of the lull, I pick up the War-bot again and continue running west.

In six seconds, I accelerate to seventy miles per hour. At the same time, Amber steers the Reaper drone in a tight circle, maneuvering it behind us. Then she puts the aircraft into a steep dive, aiming it at my running Quarter-bot. The Reaper has no more missiles, so this maneuver looks like a kamikaze dive, a desperate suicide attack. But then Amber shouts an instruction over the radio: **Raise your arms, Zia! You need to grab the hardpoints on the underside of the wings! And Adam, you need to run faster!**

I pump my Quarter-bot's legs and dig my footpads into the sand. I speed up to eighty miles per hour, ninety, one hundred. I'm nearing the perimeter of the Army's ground forces, the westernmost section of the circle surrounding Pioneer Base. Five M1 tanks are less than a quarter mile ahead, and I can see that their crews have recovered from the shock and awe of the surge. The soldiers are rotating their tanks' turrets, aiming their big guns at my robot.

Then I feel a jolt from behind. I lose my footing for a moment but manage to stay upright as the enormous weight of the War-bot is lifted from my shoulder joint. I raise my cameras to see the Reaper drone pull up from its dive, with Zia hanging from its wings.

Her War-bot's hands grip the hardpoints—one on the left wing, the other on the right—that formerly held the Hellfire missiles. She jackknifes her robot, swinging her torso upward until it's horizontal, and clamps her footpads to the underside of the drone's fuselage. Meanwhile, Amber detaches her Jet-bot from the top of the Reaper and flies off to the south. With only the War-bot clinging to its belly, the drone climbs into the sky.

It's a beautiful sight. A current of hope starts to flow through my electronics. I feel so light without Zia weighing me down, and with a burst of new energy, I start to run faster, accelerating to one hundred and twenty miles per hour. I'm speeding across the desert like a race car. In just four seconds, I reach the Army's perimeter and dash between two of the M1 tanks, fifty yards to my left and right. Their turrets are swiveling like mad to keep up with me, but they can't fire their guns as I sprint between them. If they do, they'll hit each other.

After two more seconds, though, I'm a hundred yards past the perimeter, and the tanks and rocket launchers in the Army's task force open fire. The soldiers have tracked my course and aimed their weapons at a point twenty yards ahead of me. I see the tank shells and rockets on my radar, dozens of them screaming toward the intercept point. There's no way to avoid them. There are too many projectiles, and they're aimed too well. I'm going to run right into the warheads.

I don't have enough time to change course or turn around, but my thoughts move faster than my motors. In less than a millisecond, another surge starts whipping through my wires. It builds faster this time, coursing through the electronic grooves carved by the last surge. I can release it any moment and demolish all the weapons speeding toward my Quarter-bot. But the surge will also destroy the pair of M1 tanks that are only a hundred yards behind me. The blast will melt their treads and char their guns and heat their crew compartments to more than a thousand degrees Fahrenheit. Eight soldiers will die in agonizing pain, their skin liquefying beneath their burning fatigues.

No! I won't do it! We can't kill humans!

With all my remaining strength, I bottle the surge inside my Quarter-bot. I confine the whirling fear within my circuits, compressing the explosive thoughts so they can't escape. I can't do this for very long, but I won't need much more time. In a quarter of a second, I'll collide with the shells and rockets, which will incinerate me in a blinding flash.

Then something grabs both my arms and yanks them upward, pulling so hard it nearly rips them out of my Quarter-bot's shoulder joints. My footpads leave the ground and I rise thirty feet in a tenth of a second. The tank shells and rockets whiz underneath me in their shallow trajectories and detonate on the ground. Their explosions send up a huge column of flame, but my Quarter-bot soars safely above the blast. I'm dangling from Amber's Jet-bot, her steel hands locked around my elbow joints.

I got you. Put your torso next to mine so I can hold you better.

I maneuver my Quarter-bot, raising the torso until its back presses against the front of her Jet-bot. Once I'm horizontal, Amber wraps her arms around the middle of my robot, and then we fly in tandem over the desert, my Quarter-bot secured to her belly like a missile.

The surge swiftly dissipates from my circuits as we speed away from the tanks and rocket launchers. The Reaper drone carrying Zia is five miles ahead of us, climbing to twenty thousand feet and cruising west, but the Jet-bot is three times faster than the drone, so we're catching up fast.

Thanks, Amber. That was a close one.

Yeah, I was worried for a second there. She adjusts her grip on my Quarter-bot, tightening her embrace. **But you're safe now, baby.**

Amber's voice is much quieter than before. It sounds soothing, almost tender. I'm touched by the emotion, but also confused. The swings in Amber's mood are so sudden and extreme. One moment she's whooping like a cowgirl, then she's coldly threatening to leave Zia behind, then she's pulling me closer and calling me "baby." I don't understand it. It's like she has a split personality. It's hard to tell who I'm talking to.

Thirty seconds later, we're ten miles west of Pioneer Base and only a hundred feet from Zia's drone. I turn my cameras to see her War-bot clinging to the Reaper's belly like a stowaway. She removes one of her mechanical hands from the drone's fuselage and waves it to get our attention. Then Zia points a steel finger to the northeast.

Don't get too comfortable. Attached to Zia's radio message is a file holding data from her long-distance radar. **The battle's not over yet.**

I review Zia's radar observations, then point my own sensors twenty-five miles to the northeast and confirm her data. The six F-35 fighter jets from Kirtland that were en route to Pioneer Base have changed course. Now they're heading straight for us.

CHAPTER

17

OUR BIGGEST PROBLEM IS THAT THE REAPER DRONE HAS A MAXIMUM VELOCITY OF only 300 miles per hour. The F-35 jets are barreling over the desert at four times that speed. And when they're twenty miles away, all six of the fighters launch their air-to-air missiles, which streak toward us at 3,000 miles per hour.

Amber! Do you have any power left in your lasers?

Negative. I think we should—

Listen carefully. I cut her off before she can finish her sentence. I'm afraid she's going to recommend abandoning Zia again, and I don't want to hear it. *Fly toward the missiles as fast as you can.*

Amber doesn't ask any questions. She follows my order, steering her Jet-bot to the northeast and accelerating past the speed of sound. Meanwhile, I act as her copilot and navigator, pointing my sensors at the missiles dead ahead. Our maneuver must seem insane to the pilots of the fighter jets, because we're making ourselves easy targets. If we stay on this crash course, the air-to-air rockets will explode against the Jet-bot in thirteen seconds.

But that's more than enough time for me to build up another surge. All I have to do is think about Sumner Harris and the generals who ordered the attack on the Pioneers. It didn't take them long to decide to get rid of us. They didn't agonize over it or consider any reasonable alternatives. (The Model S was definitely *not* reasonable.) For Sumner, choosing to destroy us was a no-brainer. In his eyes, the Pioneers are *nothing*.

The surge rises quickly, roaring across my electronics. It's getting easier to generate the anger and fear. The fierce stream of emotion swirls within me, feeding on itself, gathering force. It's overloading my processors and stripping my wires, but I endure the pain and hold it inside. I wait until the air-to-air missiles are half a mile away, less than a second from impact. Then I release the surge into the atmosphere.

It spreads like a mushroom cloud, a fireball hundreds of yards across. The six missiles soar into it and explode instantly. I feel a flash of satisfaction, as if I've just made a brilliant counterargument to Sumner Harris and his allies. I want to shout, "You see? It's not so easy to get rid of us, is it?"

But when I check my radar again, I see something disturbing. Eight miles ahead, the squadron of F-35 jets splits into two smaller formations. Three of the jets veer off to the west while the other three fly directly south. The pilots have obviously recognized that Amber's Jet-bot has some pretty serious defenses, so they're going after easier prey: the slow-moving Reaper drone with the War-bot clinging to it. They're steering around us so they can shoot down Zia.

Oh God! What do we do? If they come at Zia from two different directions, we won't be able to shield her from their missiles!

Amber answers me by swerving her Jet-bot to the north, putting us on an intercept course with one of the formations. **We're gonna follow a little strategy called divide and conquer. First we'll bust up this trio of jets on the north side, then we'll go after the other three on the south.**

This sounds like a good plan, but I need some clarification. *What do you mean by "bust up"?*

I'll fly real close to the formation, and then you'll unleash one of your surges, a really big one. The fighter jets will cruise into the fireball and explode just like their missiles did.

But that'll kill the pilots. They won't have time to eject from their planes.

Well, what do you want? Either those pilots die or Zia does. You have to make a choice.

Amber is talking in that cold-blooded tone again. There's not one iota of sympathy in her voice. It sounds like she hates humans as much as Sumner Harris hates the Pioneers.

I vibrate uneasily in Amber's embrace. I almost wish she'd let go of my Quarter-bot and let me fall to the desert floor. She responds by hugging me closer to her Jet-bot's belly. Her arms clamp so tightly around my torso that they dent my armor. **Look, Adam, it's a tough situation.** She softens her tone a little. **If you have a better plan, I'd love to hear it.**

I don't have a plan, but I have an idea. Ever since I developed the ability to generate a surge, I've been struggling to figure out how to control it. Because the energy comes from my most desperate emotions, it's really hard to dial it down. I assumed I'd gradually learn more about the phenomenon and eventually discover how to use the surge for something besides large-scale destruction. But now I need to speed up the learning process.

Keep up with the jets, but stay at least a couple of miles away. I'm gonna try something new.

Something new? What—

A different kind of surge. Let me think for a second.

I start by thinking of the pilots in the fighter jets. I imagine them sitting in the cockpits of their F-35s, each airman gripping his jet's control stick, each wearing a helmet with a heads-up screen that puts the navigational data right in front of his eyes. Each pilot has trained for hundreds of hours with the plane, learning all its quirks and flaws and capabilities. Most of all, each pilot knows the terrible might of his machine, the destructive power of its missiles and bombs. In that way, the airmen are like Pioneers. They're not our enemies.

Nevertheless, I have to stop their aircraft. I have to disable the machines without killing the pilots inside them. My thoughts generate a new current that starts coursing through my wires, a surge completely unlike the ones I've created before. It's composed of anger and empathy, panic and hope, fear and pity. It scythes through my circuits, lacerating my thoughts, scarring my mind. But despite all my efforts, I can't make the surge strong enough to leap out of my Quarter-bot. Rescuing and protecting the airmen is a lot harder than murdering them. I can imagine it and wish it, but I can't make it happen.

Okay, we're flying parallel to the jets that are north of us, three miles away. The other formation is ten miles to the southeast, but pretty soon they're gonna have a clear shot at Zia. Is your new surge ready?

No, not yet. I'm still—

You gotta hurry, Adam. What's the holdup?

Amber is making me nervous, and that isn't helping. Her urgency is messing up my balance of emotions, the carefully calibrated mix of positive and negative. *I just need another—*

Listen, I'm coming over there to help you.

As Amber sends me this radio message, she shifts one of her Jet-bot's arms, moving it a few inches up my torso. Now her mechanical hand is next to my Quarter-bot's cable port, which is kind of like the USB port on a computer. It's the socket where I can connect a fiber-optic cable if I want to transfer my data to another machine. Amber extends her own transfer cable from one of her steel fingers and plugs it into my port.

A millisecond later, before I can protest, her mind floods my Quarter-bot. This time, though, she doesn't appear as an avatar in a virtual-reality simulation. I simply sense her software at the other end of my neuromorphic control unit, occupying an empty section of circuitry. She fires off a message toward the wires that hold my own software.

All right, I'm ready. Let's get to work on this surge.

Wait, who's flying the Jet-bot?

Don't worry. I put it on autopilot. Her software flows across the control unit, moving closer to mine. **I think we'll work better together if we share the same circuits. Then our thoughts will be in sync.**

Amber, I have to warn you. Generating a surge can be painful. It—

I can take it. Come on, let's do this. We don't have much time.

She's right about that. I can't create this new kind of surge on my own. And every second, the F-35s fly hundreds of yards closer to Zia.

Okay, come over here.

Her software crosses into my circuits. For the third time, our thoughts come together and our minds turn transparent. Amber can see everything in my databases, all the distant memories from before I became a Pioneer and all the billions of perceptions I've added to my files since then. And I can see everything in Amber's mind except for the memories she's still not ready to share. Because we're not running a virtual-reality simulation now, I don't see the black cube that represents her locked-up files, but I can sense those unseen memories flowing in my circuits, an ugly chunk of data surrounded by a firewall.

In less than a nanosecond, Amber sees what I've been trying to do, the careful construction of a surge that combines opposing thoughts and feelings. She automatically adds her emotions to mine, her sympathy and arrogance, her affection and disdain. We work in concert, our minds perfectly meshed, and the surge grows stronger. Working together, it's much easier to find the right mix of impulses and assemble them into a clear instruction, a command that can transcend my circuits. I hardly feel any pain as it whirls inside me. Then Amber and I release the surge from my Quarter-bot, and it speeds along the invisible wires of the universe.

The surge billows into a humongous sphere, more than ten miles across, but this time it's not a fireball. It's a less destructive but more intricate electrical disturbance, carried along the molecules in the air. It strikes all six of the fighter jets and streams into their electronic controls. It shuts down their engines and avionics and weapons. The momentum of the jets keeps them on course, but after a couple of seconds, they start to slow and sink, gliding downward.

But the surge doesn't deactivate the planes' pilot-ejection systems, because those mechanisms don't require electricity—they use solid-fuel rockets to eject the pilots' seats from the planes. Over the next five seconds, all the airmen pull their ejection handles and ignite the rockets, which catapult their seats from the disabled F-35s. I point my

cameras downward to watch the parachutes unfurl from the plummeting seats. The six pilots drift slowly down to the desert while their
planes crash into the empty sands, exploding brilliantly but hurting
no one.

A whirlwind of joy starts spinning through my circuits, sweeping
up my thoughts and Amber's. *We did it! We did it!*

Oh, Adam. You're like a little kid. Look how happy you are!

Amber's voice sounds different—softer, sadder, more wistful. To my
surprise, some emotions are leaking from her hidden data. Her feelings are trickling through her firewall. I get the sense that she might
be ready to lift that barrier. She finally trusts me enough to share her
most painful secret: the traumatic memories of her mother's suicide.

But before she can take that step, a radio message rushes into my
Quarter-bot's antenna. It's from Zia.

**Hey, lovebirds? You finished smooching yet? Or whatever you're
doing over there?**

Even Zia can't spoil the moment for me. *I'll tell you what we're doing.
We just took on the U.S. Air Force's best fighter squadron and kicked their
flyboy butts. Did you see it on your radar?*

**Yeah, I saw it. But you're celebrating too soon. You know how
many Air Force bases there are between here and the Pacific Ocean?
They're probably fueling up a hundred more jets to intercept us.**

Now Amber speaks up. **Chill out, okay? We're only a few minutes
behind schedule. If we speed it up a little, we can still make our
connecting flight.**

She says good-bye to me in a digital whisper—**Later, baby**—and
transfers her software back to her Jet-bot. Then she throttles up the
engine on the back of her torso and streaks toward the Reaper drone
carrying Zia.

ㅠ ㅠ ㅠ

Among the many gigabytes of classified data we retrieved from
Pioneer Base was a document from Global Strike Command, the
Air Force branch in charge of America's long-range bomber jets.
The document was a schedule of Global Strike's operations for
the week, including hundreds of training flights for the bomber
crews. At least a dozen of their planes crisscross the country
every night, and when we checked the schedule for that particular evening, we found a flight going from Barksdale Air Force
Base in Louisiana to Vandenberg Air Force Base in California.
The plane was expected to pass over New Mexico between 10:45
and 11:30 p.m.

Amber and I spot the bomber after the Jet-bot zooms past Zia's
drone and soars another hundred miles west of Pioneer Base. We
wouldn't have found the plane at all if we didn't know its flight
path. The bomber is sleek and black and has wings shaped like a
bat's. Its metal skin is coated with high-tech materials that make
it impossible to detect the aircraft with radar. It's a B-2 Stealth
bomber, the sneakiest plane ever built, designed to fly unseen into
even the best-defended airspace. In other words, it's the perfect
vehicle for a trio of Pioneers trying to slip past the U.S. Air Force
and reach the Pacific Ocean.

Hitching a ride on the B-2 might get tricky, though. There are
two pilots in the plane's cockpit, and I don't think they'll be happy
about taking on passengers.

Amber ascends to 40,000 feet, positioning her Jet-bot fifty yards
behind the bomber and just ten feet below it. She's pretty sneaky
herself, and it looks like the B-2's pilots haven't noticed us yet. She

pulls up until we're flying directly below the plane's bomb bay, and then I clamber to the top of her Jet-bot. My Quarter-bot sits upright, my steel legs straddling Amber's torso and my arms raised above my head. I extend my hands toward the bomb bay's rectangular doors.

Amber, are you sure about this? The bombs inside this plane aren't nukes, are they?

No, they're dummy bombs. It's a training flight, so it's not gonna carry live weapons. Why are you so nervous?

Well, I don't want to bust into this bomb bay and set off a nuclear war-head or something. That wouldn't be good.

God, you're such a worrywart! Stop being so ridiculous, all right?

A pulse of irritation runs through my circuits. I don't like being called ridiculous. Amber's abrasive side is showing again, and now it seems even more jarring since she was so nice to me a few minutes ago. What's with this girl?

I suppress my irritation and slam my hands into the bomb bay's doors, jamming my steel fingers into the narrow gap between them. I dig my hands in deep enough to get a good grip on the doors, then wrench them downward to open the bomb bay. When I raise my cameras, I see sixteen long missiles hanging from a rack, like enormous bullets inside the chamber of the world's biggest gun.

I grab the bomb rack and hoist my Quarter-bot into the B-2. Amber's Jet-bot drops away from the bomber, descending several hundred feet, while I climb to the top of the rack, scrambling around the dummy bombs like a kid on a jungle gym. An alarm goes off inside the plane, alerting the pilots that the bomb bay doors are open, but I ignore it and head for the front of the aircraft.

Between the B-2's bomb bay and cockpit is a slanting bulkhead, a steel wall strong enough to hold the greater air pressure inside the cabin. I punch through the wall and peel back the steel, tearing a hole big enough for my Quarter-bot. Then, fighting the blast of air rushing out of the cabin, I pull myself through the hole and enter the rear section of the cockpit, which is crowded with electronic equipment. I extend a fiber-optic cable from the index finger of my right hand, plug it into the equipment, and take control of the B-2. At the same time, I wave my left hand at the pilots sitting in the front of the cockpit.

"Hey, guys. I'm really sorry about this, but we need your plane."

Both airmen look over their shoulders at me. They're wearing helmets with dark visors, so I can't see their faces, but I can imagine how surprised they are. They sit there in shock as I change the B-2's flight path and shut down the bomber's radio and turn off the transponder that allows the Air Force to track the plane. Then the pilot on the right—I think he's the commander—reaches into his flight suit and pulls out a handgun. It's an M9 Beretta, the pistol carried by all Air Force pilots in case they wind up in enemy territory.

I'm not worried about my own safety. A bullet from a handgun can't penetrate my armor. But if the bullet ricochets off my Quarter-bot, it might damage the plane or hurt one of the pilots. So before the commander can point his pistol at me, I send a command through my fiber-optic cable to the B-2's emergency systems. The signal opens the escape hatches at the top of the cockpit and ignites the solid-fuel rockets under the pilots' ejection seats.

The seats shoot out of the plane through the open hatches. I connect my circuits to the B-2's reconnaissance cameras and see the pilots' parachutes billow open and drift downward. By this point, I've already put the bomber into a tight, banking turn. I'm circling back to the Reaper drone so I can pick up Zia.

╥ ╥ ╥

Five minutes later, Zia steers the Reaper under the B-2, climbs into the plane's bomb bay, and ditches the drone. Amber performs an even fancier maneuver, easing her Jet-bot into the cockpit through one of the open hatches at the top. Then I set a new course for the bomber, aiming for the location in the Pacific where the Snake-bots are.

Pretty soon, the Air Force will realize we've hijacked one of its stealth bombers, but it won't be able to find us. We're hidden in the vast skies over the American Southwest. I throttle up the B-2's engines until we reach the bomber's cruising speed, 560 miles per hour. We'll reach our destination by 4:00 a.m., which means we'll have two hours to get to the bottom of the ocean and transfer to the Snake-bots. No problem, right?

In the meantime, the three of us gather at the back of the cockpit and connect our robots to the B-2's electrical system so we can recharge our batteries. Zia crawls into the cramped space and uses the built-in tools in her War-bot's hands to fix her damaged knee joint. She points the index finger of her left hand at the joint, and an acetylene flame spurts out of the nozzle at her fingertip. Then she uses this welding torch to repair her battered armor.

As Zia works, a variety of grunts and curses come out of her speakers. After detaching the plates of armor from her knee joint, she shuts off her torch and points the nozzle at me. "So are you proud of yourself, Armstrong? You think you're doing a great job as our new leader?"

Zia's belligerence doesn't surprise me, but her question does. I don't think of myself as our leader. Amber made just as many decisions as I did. "Hey, we're not in the Army anymore. Now we're all the same rank."

"Well, maybe you and Amber are both captains, but I'm still a corporal. You two did almost all the fighting back there. You didn't give me much to do."

Amber shakes her Jet-bot's head. "Everyone did as much as they could. Your War-bot was damaged, so you couldn't—"

"It's a little suspicious, don't you think?" Zia ignores Amber and keeps her cameras trained on me. "Your girlfriend's been a Pioneer for only ten days, and already she's calling the shots. What's her secret, Armstrong? She's got natural leadership abilities or something?"

I feel a bolt of anger. It rattles my reenergized circuits, which are jumping with all the new current siphoned from the B-2. Zia has no right to say these things. "You know what? I think we should end this conversation. We've got a four-hour flight ahead of us, and—"

"Nah, I want to keep talking. I want to know what's going on. Especially with that freaky surge of yours. I have to admit, Armstrong, I'm a little jealous of you and your surges. I wish I could make fireballs on command like that. I could have a lot of fun with that kind of power."

"Believe me, it's not so—"

"But here's the thing. Until a few minutes ago, I thought you were the only robot who could pull off those pyrotechnics. Isn't that why Sigma put you through that crazy test at the Unicorp lab? Because the AI wanted to figure out how you did it?" Zia keeps her cameras focused on me, but points her nozzle finger at Amber. "But you and your girlfriend did that last surge together, like a team. So how was that possible? Have you been training her? Maybe during your electronic make-out sessions?"

All at once, my bolt of anger becomes a raging storm. It roars through my circuits, howling in outrage, ready to punish Zia for what she just said. I could release the surge at any moment, and after what I've learned tonight, I feel confident I could control its energy and focus its effects. I could channel the surge into a fierce, tight beam that would strike Zia without damaging anything else in the cockpit. I could melt all her wires in an instant.

Luckily, two things stop me from killing her. The first is horror. I can't believe I'm even thinking about this. Revulsion and disgust swamp my circuits, stopping the surge in its tracks.

The second thing that stops me is the fact that Zia is on to something. She's right to be suspicious. When Amber jumped into my circuits thirty minutes ago, she was totally ready to help me with the surge. She didn't need any practice whatsoever. Maybe this shouldn't seem so surprising—Amber *had* shared circuits with me twice before, so she already knew my memories and feelings about the surge. She knew exactly what to expect when she jumped into my mind for the third time. But that doesn't explain her eagerness. She dove into the whirlpool without hesitation.

I don't know what to say. I don't even know who I should confront, Zia or Amber. But before I can make that decision, Amber disconnects her Jet-bot from the cockpit equipment. "I'm going to figure out how to close the bomb bay doors. We need to start preparing for the next phase of the operation."

She heads for the ruptured bulkhead between the cockpit and the bomb bay. Amber wrenches the broken steel wall, enlarging the hole I made, and slips her Jet-bot through the gap.

I watch her leave, then pivot my cameras back to Zia. She raises her War-bot's arm and points at me again.

"Mark my words, Armstrong. Something funny is going on."

CHAPTER

18

WE CAN'T USE THE PLANE'S RADIO, OF COURSE. IF WE TRANSMIT ANY SIGNALS from the B-2, they'll reveal the bomber's position. I can't send a message to Pioneer Base, can't talk to my dad, can't tell him I'm okay. And I can't find out what's happening with Shannon and Marshall.

I have to rely on my imagination instead. Luckily, my electronic brain is good at imagining things. I can envision hundreds of possible scenarios, then use my logic circuits to determine which are the most realistic. I picture Dad in the Danger Room, having another video-conference call with Sumner Harris and General Hawke. Sumner will be furious about our escape from Pioneer Base and the hijacking of the B-2 bomber. He'll try to bully Dad and Hawke into helping him find the missing Pioneers. But Dad won't betray us, and Hawke won't be inclined to do Sumner any favors. In all likelihood, it'll be a very unpleasant call.

If Dad's smart, he'll avoid talking about the escape and focus on transferring Shannon and Marshall to the Model S robots. Sumner won't like the idea, but he'll also see the danger of allowing two Pioneers to die while three others are on the loose and capable of exacting revenge. So he'll give the go-ahead for the transfer, and after Shannon and Marshall are trapped in the tin puppets, he'll send the codes that'll keep them alive. The Army units surrounding Pioneer Base will retake control of the facility and free the soldiers we handcuffed.

I'm not certain that these events will actually occur, but it's the most-likely scenario. The picture isn't as clear, though, when I try to imagine what will happen to Amber, Zia, and me. Even with all my computing power, I can't predict what we'll do once we reach the Snake-bots.

By 3:00 a.m. the B-2 is cruising over the Pacific Ocean, seven hundred miles west of California. My Quarter-bot is still linked to the electronics in the cockpit, and all the plane's systems are functioning normally. My acoustic sensor picks up a loud banging noise from the plane's bomb bay, but it's not a sign of mechanical trouble. Amber is dismantling the bomb rack and the dummy missiles and using the parts to build something new. Although I'm curious about what she's constructing, I don't go to the bomb bay to ask. I'm afraid to talk to her.

Zia has finished repairing her knee joint, and now she's examining the B-2's instrument panels. Her War-bot slinks across the cockpit, tilting forward to prevent her turret from banging into anything. She stopped grunting and cursing about an hour ago, and her speakers started playing music, but it's not very soothing. It's a jarring, disjointed medley, with bits and pieces of songs randomly spliced together.

It's the robotic equivalent of humming, I guess. Zia has a ton of songs stored in her memory, and her taste is pretty similar to my own. She likes Kendrick Lamar, Drake, Kanye West. After a while she starts swinging her massive arms in time with the music. She's playing the songs to psych herself up for whatever's coming next.

Then Zia suddenly switches off her music and turns away from the instrument panels. She points her cameras at me. "What do you think Hawke's doing right now? You think the Army fired him yet?"

I shake my Quarter-bot's head. I'm not surprised she asked about Hawke. She's still obsessed with him. "No, they can't fire him yet, because they need his help to find us. He knows more about the Pioneers than anyone else. He won't want to help Sumner, but he probably will. It's that duty thing."

"But eventually they'll fire him, right? They'll blame him for everything that went wrong with the Pioneers?"

Now I think I see what's motivating her. She wants Hawke to suffer. She tried to kill herself because she knew he'd be devastated, but our escape from Pioneer Base has given her an even better way to hurt him. The man dedicated his life to the U.S. Army, so what punishment could be worse than being drummed out of the service?

If I had a face, I'd grimace. I'm losing patience with Zia. "Yes, he'll probably be forced to resign. Will that be enough to satisfy you?"

She turns her turret clockwise, then counterclockwise. "No. But it'll be a start."

"Don't you think you're being a little—"

"You saw Hawke's confession, right? You watched the video I gave you?"

"Yes, I—"

"Then you know why I hate him. It's not because of anything he did to *me*. It's because of what he did to my parents."

I probably shouldn't say anything else. I have no interest in defending Hawke. And I know how agitated Zia can get when anyone disagrees with her. But I can't stop myself. "Hawke tried to make up for what he did. He could've forgotten the whole episode after the war in Iraq ended. But he didn't. He never forgot about you."

A hiss of contempt comes out of Zia's speakers. "So what? It didn't do me any good. All those years I was in foster care, he didn't do a thing for me."

"But he was keeping tabs on you, watching over you from a distance. And when he heard you were dying, he tracked you down and told you about the Pioneer Project. He thought that's what your parents would've wanted."

Zia strides toward me. "But he lied about what happened to them! He should've told the truth!"

I raise my Quarter-bot's arms over my head in surrender. "You're right. But if he told you the truth before you became a Pioneer, you never would've agreed to the procedure. You would've rejected it in an instant, because you would've been so angry at him."

"What are you saying?" Her voice booms out of her speakers, making the B-2's airframe tremble. "You think Hawke actually—"

"He's a liar, but he saved your life." I lower my arms and point at Zia. "And biologically at least, he's your father. If I were you, I'd keep that in mind."

I know these words will slash at her circuits. Something inside her War-bot starts vibrating, making a loud, high-pitched whine, a noise full of mechanical distress. Zia clenches her huge steel hands, and for a moment I'm certain she's going to pound me. She'll hit me so hard that my Quarter-bot will burst through the bomber's fuselage, tumble out of the plane, and plummet eight miles down to the ocean.

But after a couple of seconds, the whine inside her War-bot stops.

She stands absolutely still. "Let's stop talking about Hawke, okay? Right now, our bigger problem is your girlfriend."

I'm surprised she changed the subject. It's the first time I've seen Zia choose evasion over confrontation. Maybe she's developing some flexibility. That would be a big step forward for her.

I pivot my cameras toward the bulkhead between the cockpit and the bomb bay. I can't see Amber, but I can hear her banging away in there, still hard at work on her construction project. I turn back to Zia. "Listen, you need to learn to get along with her. We can't work as a team if you're constantly sniping at Amber."

Zia turns off her War-bot's loudspeakers and sends me a radio message. It's encrypted so Amber can't hear it. **She's lying to us, Armstrong. I don't know what her game is, but she's definitely hiding *something*.**

I turn on my radio too. *Why are you so suspicious? Where's your evidence?*

There's the surge, for one thing, how she figured it out so quickly. How can you explain—

It's simple. She's smart and she has unbelievable amounts of computing power, just like you and me. It's not so hard to understand. My messages are getting testy. I'm really annoyed. *You could probably figure out how to generate a surge too. You definitely have enough rage in your circuits.*

Zia turns her turret clockwise and counter again. **That's not the only thing. Remember how she acted during the videoconference call in the Danger Room? How she hid in the corner, even when the soldiers pointed their antitank guns at us? And then she rushed toward the video screen and screamed at Sumner Harris? Yelling about Jenny, of all things?**

I remember, of course. Amber's behavior seemed strange at the time, but there were so many other things going on that I didn't think about it much. It still seems kind of trivial compared with all the other challenges we're facing. *What are you trying to say? Amber got scared, then she got angry. What else do you think is going on?*

I told you, I don't know what she's hiding. But I think it has something to do with Sumner Harris. When Amber yelled at him, she wasn't just angry. She had this weird, intense tone. And what she said was really personal and really full of hate. Like the two of them had some kind of horrible secret.

A secret? I still don't get what you're saying.

Zia shrugs, lifting her War-bot's shoulder joints. **Maybe Amber is Sumner's spy. She might be leading us into a trap.**

Oh, come on. We couldn't have escaped from Pioneer Base without Amber. She literally carried us away from Sumner's troops. How could she be his spy if she's working against him like that?

Maybe it's a different kind of secret then. Look, I know you've shared circuits with Amber. But has she showed you *everything* in her memory files?

I hesitate before responding. Then I realize I don't have to respond at all, because my hesitation has already revealed my answer to Zia. Now she knows Amber walled off some of her memories. And I can sense Zia's reaction to this news without any radio communication between us. She thinks I'm a gullible idiot.

Am I, though? Why would Amber lie to me?

She didn't show me her memories of her mother's suicide. She said they were too painful to share. So she put a firewall around them.

But you don't know for sure what's inside that firewall, do you? She could be hiding anything in there.

She promised she'd show me all those memories. Very soon.

Zia synthesizes another hiss. **Armstrong, you're not so bright**

when it comes to relationships. First you messed things up with Shannon, and then you let Amber make a fool out of you. You have a bad track record. You know that?

I don't transmit a response. Zia's questions are making me doubt myself. Have I misjudged Amber? Do I believe her only because I need her so much? Am I willing to believe *anything* she says, just to be close to her?

Several seconds of radio silence pass. I expect Zia's next message to be blistering. I expect her to call me an imbecile, a dunce, the dimmest robot ever built. But her message, when it finally comes, is emotionless and matter-of-fact. **Go talk to Amber about it. Before it's too late.**

॥ ॥ ॥

I squeeze through the hole in the bulkhead and enter the B-2's bomb bay, but I don't see Amber. Her Jet-bot is hidden behind an enormous steel cone.

The cone is hollow and twelve feet high. It hangs pointy-end down from four thick cables attached to the cone's rim, a circle of steel that's eight feet wide. The cone's tip is suspended a few inches above the gap between the bomb bay doors, which have been repaired, closed, and locked into their horizontal positions.

The structure looks like a gigantic, metallic ice-cream cone. I do some quick arithmetic in my circuits and calculate that this cone can hold ten thousand gallons of ice cream. Maybe twenty thousand, if it's a double scoop.

Or it can hold three Pioneers and take them to the bottom of the Pacific Ocean.

Amber steps sideways so I can see her. Her Jet-bot stands on the locked doors, which provide a sturdy floor for the bomb bay, at least for the time being. She waves one of her long black arms at me as I clamber down from the hole in the bulkhead. "What do you think, Adam? I just finished putting it together."

I hop to the floor and step toward Amber. "I was wondering what all the banging was about. How did you make this thing?"

"I took apart the sixteen dummy bombs, peeled off their steel casings and hammered them into curved panels. Then I welded the panels together." She points at the welded seams running up and down the length of the cone. "There's just enough room inside for you, me, and Zia."

I train my cameras on the structure and try to picture it in flight. I imagine the doors opening in the floor of the bomb bay and the cables overhead releasing the cone. It would fall like a warhead on its terminal descent, its tip pointed at the waters of the Pacific. "But won't it be unstable? Zia's robot is a lot heavier than yours and mine. When we're inside the cone, it'll tilt in her direction and spill us out."

"That's why I added mass to the tip." Amber extends her Jet-bot's hand and raps it against the lower, narrower part of the cone. It makes a dull thud. "The bottom half is solid steel, almost fifteen tons. The weight at the bottom will stop the cone from tipping after it drops from the bomber. It won't be in flight for very long anyway, because we'll maneuver the B-2 close to the water before the release."

That makes sense. If the cone is dropped from a great height, it'll hit the water too fast, and the impact will bludgeon the steel. But if the bomber is only a few hundred feet above the ocean, the cone will plunge into the water like a harpoon and speed down to the depths.

I nod my Quarter-bot's head in admiration. "So how long will it take to sink to the seabed?"

"It's hard to make an exact prediction because the drag force depends on the ocean currents. But it'll probably take less than half an hour. We'll sink at a rate of ten feet per second, more or less."

Now I picture the three of us inside the hollow cone, which will fill with water as soon as it hits the ocean. Our Pioneer robots are waterproof and heavily armored, but we'll be descending more than three miles below the surface, and the water pressure will be tremendous at that depth. "Can our armor hold up under the pressure? We probably have some vulnerable spots, right?"

"I already took care of it." Amber steps closer and shows me a pair of thick steel caps she attached to her Jet-bot's head, just above her camera lenses. "These caps will cover our lenses so they don't crack. I made a pair for you and a pair for Zia. You should install them on your robots." Then she strides back to the cone and points at its tip. "But this is my favorite part. Just watch."

She sends a wireless signal to a mechanism inside the cone, and hidden motors start to turn within the steel. The cone's tip unfolds like a mechanical flower, separating into three drill bits, each as big as an automobile tire. They're studded with sharp metal teeth.

Amber points at the drill bits, which are connected to the rest of the cone by a vertical steel tube. "It's a tunnel borer, the same kind of machine that Sigma's Snake-bots used to drill underground. The teeth on the drill bits are made of tungsten carbide. Once we reach the seabed, they'll dig right through the mud and bedrock." She shifts her Jet-bot's hand and points at the tube. "This pipe will turn the drill and deliver lubricant to the bits so they won't overheat. They'll tunnel a hole wide enough for the cone to slide through, and they'll do it fast. After forty minutes of drilling, we'll be within radio range of the Snake-bots."

I'm way beyond admiration now. I'm totally stunned by how much Amber has done. In three hours she designed and built all the tools we'll need for the next stage of our journey. "Wait a second. How did you find the teeth for the drill bits and the motors for the borer? Were they all on the plane?"

She shakes her Jet-bot's head. "No, I planned ahead and brought some of the parts from Pioneer Base." She slaps her hand against the storage compartment in her torso. "I stowed them right here."

Amber synthesizes a chuckle, a chirpy exclamation of delight. She's proud of her efforts and wants me to know it. But instead of sharing her enthusiasm, I feel a creeping dread in my wires. She's too prepared, too ready. Even with the help of her electronic brain, I don't see how she could've accomplished so much in such a short time. She's so incredibly confident about this mission, so skillful at foreseeing all the obstacles. It's as suspicious as her expert handling of the surge. She's too good at this. She's succeeding *too* easily.

But I don't know how to confront her. I'm afraid of discovering the truth, whatever it may be.

"Uh, Amber? This is going to sound a little strange, okay? But I want to share circuits with you again."

She lowers her Jet-bot's arms and steps backward. "Share circuits? Now?"

"Yeah, and that's not all." I say it fast. That's the only way I can do this. "I want you to show me the memories you've been holding back."

She takes another step backward, retreating to the corner of the bomb bay. "Adam, we talked about this. I told you how I felt."

"I know, I know. But I'm really worried." I point at the huge cone hanging from the bomb rack. "We're about to do something so dangerous that it's almost suicidal. Just getting to the Snake-bots will be risky enough. And who knows what'll happen once we've transferred to those machines?" I flail my Quarter-bot's arms. The conversation is making me frantic. "I mean, where will we go? And how will we stay in contact with Marshall and Shannon? It's a little terrifying, don't you think?"

Amber says nothing at first. She's probably as confused as I am. After pausing for a couple of seconds, she tilts her Jet-bot's head. "All right, I get it. You're worried. But why do you want to share circuits? You haven't explained that part yet."

"I need some reassurance. I need to know that we're a hundred percent committed to each other, so we can tackle this challenge together. And I was hoping you could show your commitment by sharing those memories with me."

She tilts her head in the other direction. She looks quizzical, perplexed. "I *will* share them with you. That's what I promised. But like I told you, I need more time to prepare myself. I thought you were okay with that."

This isn't going well. I have to be more direct. "There's another reason for it. I want to be absolutely sure you're not hiding anything from me."

Amber pauses again, this time for almost ten seconds. With no words coming out of her speakers, the other noises in the bomb bay seem to grow louder. The B-2's engines rumble and whir. The wind whistles beneath the bomb bay doors.

She finally raises her Jet-bot's arm and points at the bulkhead, specifically at the hole leading to the cockpit. "Zia put you up to this, right? Because she doesn't trust me?"

"Well, she—"

"What's her problem? Does she think I'm plotting something? Scheming against her?" Amber hasn't bothered to switch to her radio. In fact, she raises the volume of her speakers. She wants Zia to hear this. "Is she worried that I'll try to take her place and become the baddest Pioneer? That I'll choose the biggest and most powerful Snakebot for myself? Is that it?"

"No, we're just—"

"I can't believe you're siding with her!" Amber's voice roars across the bomb bay, and the hollow steel cone vibrates like a bell. Her outrage definitely sounds genuine. "I thought you cared for me!"

Guilt corrodes my wires. I raise my Quarter-bot's arms in a pleading gesture. "Of course I care for you! I'm just so confused right now. I—"

"How could you do this?" She clenches her hands into fists and smacks them into her Jet-bot's torso. It's like she's trying to demonstrate how much I've hurt her. "When I told you about those memories, I thought you understood! I lost my mother in the most horrible way you can lose someone! Do you have any idea how that feels?"

I realize with a start that I *do* know how it feels. I also lost my mother in a horrible way. She didn't die, but she removed herself from my life, suddenly and totally. And that's kind of like a suicide.

I stride toward Amber, holding out my arms. "I'm so sorry! I didn't—"

"No! Get away from me!" She steps sideways, dodging my Quarter-bot. Then she points again at the hole in the bulkhead. "Go back to Zia! Why don't you share circuits with *her*?"

"Amber, please!"

"Get out of my sight! I can't even stand to *look* at you!"

I can't believe how badly I messed this up. Zia was right: I'm spectacularly terrible at relationships. And this fiasco is happening at the worst possible time. The B-2 bomber is approaching our destination.

I turn away from Amber and head back to Zia. We're less than a hundred miles from the Snake-bots, and the three of us are ready to kill each other.

CHAPTER

19

AT 3:55 A.M., THE B-2 IS FLYING ON AUTOPILOT, JUST FIFTY YARDS ABOVE THE Pacific Ocean. Amber, Zia, and I stand inside the hollow steel cone, waiting for the bomb bay doors to open. We're not talking or exchanging radio messages. We're not even looking at each other.

Because the lower half of the cone is solid steel, the upper half is like the inside of a shot glass. The concave floor is about four feet wide and the surrounding wall leans outward, slanting up to the circular rim of the cone, which is eight feet across. Our footpads are latched to the floor, and our mechanical hands grasp steel bars attached to the inside of the slanting wall. Our heads poke above the cone's wide, open mouth.

My cameras are above the rim, so I can see the walls of the bomb bay. If I look up, I can also see the four thick cables that hold the cone in place, each attached to the rim by an automated clamp that looks like a steel claw. But because we're all facing outward, I can't see Amber or Zia, and they can't see me either. And under the present circumstances, that's fortunate. There's so much anger and suspicion sparking in our circuits that *anything* could set us off.

If we were smarter, we'd talk it through. We'd make an attempt to work out our differences. But neither Amber nor Zia will open a radio channel with me, and I seriously doubt they're communicating privately with each other. Maybe, if we had more time, we could figure out a solution, but the B-2 has less than an hour's worth of fuel left in its tanks. And then there's the deadline at 6:00 a.m., of course. If we don't transfer to the Snake-bots by then, our minds will dissolve into random data. We won't even be able to hate each other anymore.

With nothing else to do, I link my Quarter-bot wirelessly to the bomber's electronic controls. I check the plane's altitude and speed as it follows its programmed course, flying low and slow over the Pacific. We're just ten miles away from the drop point.

At 3:56 a.m., the motors in the bomb bay start to whine. The doors below us swing downward, opening beneath the cone's tip. I angle my Quarter-bot's head over the rim of the cone and point my cameras straight down. I can't see much through the open doors, even when I switch my cameras to the infrared range. The ocean is cold and black and endless. But my acoustic sensor picks up the noise of the waves, the low swells rolling across the vast waters.

The bomber bounces on a strong wind gusting over the waves. The cone sways on its cables, but after several seconds, it returns to its vertical alignment, its massive tip pointing directly at the ocean. Then, at precisely 3:57 a.m., the B-2 sends an electronic signal through the cables to the automated clamps. The steel claws spring open, releasing the cone's rim.

Then we fall.

The cone plummets toward the water. I hear the rush of air around us as we accelerate downward, and my sensors detect the sudden weightlessness, the abrupt removal of the force of gravity on my Quarter-bot. I point my cameras up at the silhouette of the B-2, which is streaking west, still flying on autopilot. It looks like a jagged black triangle, blotting out the stars above it.

After three seconds, we hit the ocean at almost seventy miles per hour. I sense the impact and deceleration as the cone dives into the Pacific, its heavy tip piercing the surface and its slanting steel walls sliding into the water. I have a tenth of a second to lower my head and brace my Quarter-bot. Then the cone plunges completely below the surface and the cold seawater rushes over the rim and deluges our machines.

I close both of my hands around the steel bar, tightening my grip on the handhold. The swirling torrent lashes our robots, trying to rip us out of the cone, but we hang on to the structure as the seawater floods into it. Once the water surrounds us, the turbulence subsides. The cone, slowed by drag forces, sinks at a leisurely speed, only seven miles per hour, and we descend peacefully inside it. In half a minute, we're more than a hundred yards below the surface.

I point my cameras up again and see nothing but cold darkness. But then I turn on my sonar, which sends sound waves into the surrounding water and listens for echoes. The device analyzes the returning waves and creates three-dimensional images of the objects that the sound bounced against. Now I can picture Amber's Jet-bot and Zia's War-bot, both clinging to the inside of the cone, just like me. The echoes delineate their robots in such detail that I can see all the nicks and new welds in their armor.

The sound waves also travel upward from the mouth of the cone and bounce against all the sea life above us. I see a school of bluefin tuna, dozens of fish swimming in a diamond-shaped cluster. There's a school of manta rays too and several sharks and sailfish and marlins. The fish get scarcer after we sink more than two hundred yards down, but I spot a few squid and swordfish swimming past. And when we reach a depth of four hundred yards, I glimpse an enormous sperm whale in the distance.

It's such an amazing sight that I have to share it with Amber and Zia. I open a radio channel in the low-frequency band, which is good for undersea communications, and send a message to both of them.

Oh man, use your sonar to check out the whale! It's a quarter mile to the west and a hundred yards above us.

Amber doesn't reply, but Zia transmits a message on the same channel.

Nice wildlife spotting, Mr. National Geographic. But can we talk for a minute about this steel tub we're in? Why didn't your ex-girlfriend weld a lid on top of this cone? Wouldn't we be better off in a watertight compartment?

Now Amber replies. She can't resist Zia's challenge.

Don't you feel the water pressure? You do have pressure sensors in your War-bot's armor, don't you?

I check my own pressure sensors before Zia can check hers.

Whoa, it's already up to six hundred pounds per square inch.

Yeah, I'm getting the same readings as Armstrong. Zia's voice over the radio is needling, belligerent. **That's the point I'm trying to make. If we were inside a submarine or any other kind of watertight vessel, we wouldn't have all this pressure on our armor.**

Use your electronic brain, Zia. At this depth, a submarine would crumple like a soda can. But our robots were designed to withstand explosions, so their armor can handle this kind of pressure.

And by the way, you should lower those armored caps over your camera lenses now. That's why I made them.

Zia stops arguing. She may be belligerent, but she isn't stupid. On my sonar, I see her War-bot's hand rise to her turret and lower the caps over her lenses. Amber and I do the same, almost simultaneously, and I see an opportunity to make peace with her.

You did an amazing job, Amber. You really thought of everything. I don't know how we would've gotten through this without your—

Shut up, Adam. You're wasting your batteries.

A wave of anger and hurt swells inside my circuits, building up pressure like the seawater above me. I prepare a furious response, composing a stream of insults that'll attack Amber in dozens of ways. I'm going to send her a hundred radio messages at once and reduce her Jet-bot to a quivering wreck.

But in the end, I don't send her any messages at all. I close the radio channel and turn off my transmitter. Although I hate Amber right now, I'm even angrier at myself. I was so stupid to fall for her.

Meanwhile, the cone continues sinking. We descend more than a thousand yards into the Pacific's midnight zone, a layer of seawater so deep that sunlight never touches it. I see no fish here and only one very strange-looking squid. It has thin diaphanous membranes connecting its tentacles, making it look like a floating umbrella.

After twenty minutes we reach a depth of two miles, and the water pressure climbs to five thousand pounds per square inch. My Quarter-bot doesn't crumple, but some sections of my armor start to bend under the pressure. The steel in my torso creaks and groans. I clench my hands into fists to stop my fingers from warping. And still, we keep descending. There's another mile to go.

Finally, after half an hour, the cone hits the seabed. Its heavy tip sinks deep into a layer of mud, and the impact jostles our robots. We're more than three miles below the surface of the Pacific, in the near-freezing abyssal zone. The water pressure on my armor is three and a half tons per square inch.

I raise my Quarter-bot's head over the rim of the cone so I can use my sonar to view the ocean floor. It's an immense plain with a muddy surface composed of all the waste matter and dead organisms that have drifted down from the rest of the Pacific. But it's not completely barren. Here and there I spot starfish and sea urchins and long, bristly worms.

Then I receive another nasty message from Amber: **There's no time for sightseeing, Adam! We're ready to start drilling! Get your head down!**

I pull back inside the cone and lean my Quarter-bot against the slanting wall. Amber and Zia also press their robots to the inside of the cone, attaching themselves firmly to the structure. Then Amber sends a wireless signal to the motors inside the cone's tip. The mechanism extends the drill bits and starts rotating them at high speed. Their tungsten carbide teeth carve into the soft mud of the seabed.

At the same time, the motors open several vents in the steel floor inside the cone, where our robots' feet are latched. A pump sucks seawater into these vents and shoots it down to the drill bits at the cone's tip. The near-freezing water cools the drill and also blasts the mud out of the borehole it's digging. Tons of sediment spray upward, showering the seabed all around us, and the steel cone slides down into the hole. Its enormous weight pushes the cone's tip deeper, and the drill tears into the denser layer of mud below.

In less than a minute, the entire cone is underground. In two minutes, we're fifteen feet below the ocean floor. The drill keeps blasting the mud upward, but now most of the sediment is falling back down into the open mouth of the cone and settling around our footpads. Five minutes later, we're sixty feet underground, and the cone is full of porous sludge that envelops and buries our robots. The mud pins my Quarter-bot against the inside of the cone. I can't move my arms or legs or head. But the drill keeps turning and we keep burrowing deeper.

I adjust my sonar so it can send and receive sound waves underground. It allows me to view Amber and Zia, who are stuck in the same position as I am, pressed by tons of mud against the inside of the cone. I can also view the layers of sediment above us, as well as the borehole we just carved through them. I'm shocked to see that the borehole is already collapsing, only minutes after we drilled it. The muddy walls of the shaft are caving in, plugging the hole in the seabed and dumping more sediment on top of us.

Dread chills my wires. Although we can keep drilling downward, we can't drill back up to the surface. The cone is much too heavy for that. Our escape route is blocked. There's no going back. If we can't find the Snake-bots, or if we can't transfer our software to them, then our robots will be buried in this muck forever.

After twenty minutes, we're three hundred feet below the seabed, and the noise from the drill gets louder and sharper. We've dug through all the sediment at the bottom of the ocean, and the drill bits are now cutting through the hard bedrock beneath. The tungsten carbide teeth slash at the rock. They shave off slivers and chips that ping against the outside of the cone.

Our downward progress slows to a crawl, and the drill starts to drain more power from its batteries. They're going to run out of charge in less than half an hour. The only question is whether the drill will break first. The drill bits whine as they rip into the bedrock. The motors clank and rattle under the strain.

Worst of all, I can't use my sonar to see if we're approaching the Snake-bots. My position inside the cone makes it difficult to send sound waves into the ground beneath us, because the cone's slanting wall is in the way. And because I can't detect echoes from any objects below us, I can't search for Sigma's machines. We're relying on the Air Force's map to guide us toward the Snake-bots, but now that we're underground, it's hard to pinpoint our own position. There's a good chance we'll burrow right past the machines. That would be a pretty pathetic end to our adventures.

And then, after another twenty minutes, the drill lets out a shriek of mechanical agony. The drill bits stop turning, the motors stop humming, and all the machinery inside the cone screeches to a halt. The underground world goes silent. My acoustic sensor picks up nothing except the groaning of my own armor.

If the drill won't restart, we're finished. We're dead. We've buried ourselves in our graves.

I boost the power of my radio transmitter so its signals can penetrate the thick mud around my Quarter-bot. Radio waves can't travel very far underground, but Amber's and Zia's antennas are only a few feet from mine. *What happened to the drill? Did something break?*

Amber answers: **No, nothing broke. The drill ran into something it can't cut through.**

I thought you said it could cut through the bedrock?

It can. But the drill bits just hit something harder. She's silent for a moment, deliberately leaving me in suspense. **Can you figure out what it is? Want to take a guess?**

Her voice isn't mean or nasty anymore. It reminds me of the Amber

I fell for, the sunny, confident girl from Oklahoma, ready for any challenge and afraid of nothing. In a millisecond, I know what the drill ran into.

Are you sure?

Absolutely. We're sitting right on top of a Snake-bot.

CHAPTER

20

I CAN'T BELIEVE IT. IT'S A FREAKIN' MIRACLE. MY CIRCUITS PULSE WITH RELIEF.

I send Amber another message. *Which Snake-bot did we hit? We're only four hundred feet below the seabed, so it has to be the uppermost one, right?*

Yeah, this Snake-bot is nearly horizontal and about a hundred feet above the other five. And we hit the machine only thirty feet from its front end, where its primary antenna is. Not bad, huh? I'm a pretty decent navigator, if I may say so myself.

Zia responds to this boast with a grunt transmitted over the radio channel. Then I detect vibrations in the slurry of mud and rock chips packed into the cone. On my sonar, I see Zia open her War-bot's hands and extend a sharp, flat blade from each of her steel fingers. The blades are six inches long and shaped like garden trowels. They're ideal for digging.

Her loudspeakers let out a roar, loud enough to reverberate across the seabed. Then she lifts her massive arms through the sludge, using them like steam shovels to push the mud and rock chips aside. Once her hands are above her turret, she jabs her trowel-like blades into the mud and levers her War-bot upward, lifting her turret above the cone's rim. Now there's no steel barrier between her and the Snake-bot, so she can send a radio signal to its antenna.

I'm reluctant to give Zia advice—she hates it—but I can't help myself. *Make sure you switch your transmitter to the ultra-low-frequency band. A low-frequency signal should be able to pass through thirty feet of bedrock without any trouble.*

Yeah, yeah, I know. I set the frequency all the way down, to less than five hundred hertz. But I'm not getting any response.

That's a problem. Although the neuromorphic circuits in the Snake-bots have been deactivated, I thought their radios would still be operating on reserve battery power. But they're not. Apparently, Sigma didn't design them that way.

Okay, it looks like we'll have to connect to the Snake-bots by fiber-optic cable. There should be a cable port at the Snake-bot's front end, next to its primary antenna.

Should be? You're not sure? Zia's voice is incredulous. **I'm gonna have to punch through thirty feet of rock to get to the front of this Snake-bot. If I don't see a cable port there, I'm gonna be annoyed.**

To my surprise, Amber comes to my defense. **Every Snake-bot we fought had a cable port at its front end. There's no reason to think this one will be any different.**

Zia broadcasts another dissatisfied grunt. Then she starts clawing at the sludge above her turret. At the same time, Amber and I free our robots from the densely packed mud inside the cone and clamber upward. My acoustic sensor picks up a hissing noise, the sound of high-pressure air rising from the Snake-bot's horizontal borehole. It sounds like our drill cracked the bedrock just above the borehole, and now the air is leaking into the vertical shaft we dug. It whistles along the outside of the cone and collects in a bubble above the rim, forming an eight-foot-wide air pocket.

After we climb out of the mud-packed cone, our robots can stand inside the air pocket, which is big enough for the three of us. The sludge in the shaft above us can't pour down on our machines because of the tremendous pressure of the air bubble. We have a muddy ceiling over our heads and a muddy floor under our footpads, and on all sides is the rocky wall of the shaft above the cone.

All three of us flex our steel limbs, enjoying the freedom of movement. Then Zia retracts her digging blades and clenches her hands into fists. Tilting her War-bot forward, she delivers a colossal punch to the rock wall.

The blow shatters the jagged bedrock, flinging mineral chunks and shards in all directions. A moment later, Zia punches the rock wall again. She throws a flurry of punches, one after another, and in half a minute she pounds a big hole in the bedrock, four feet wide and three feet deep. Then she points at the pile of rubble around her footpads and turns her turret toward Amber and me. **Well, what are you waiting for? Pick up the debris and clear the hole, so I can keep tunneling.**

My Quarter-bot and Amber's Jet-bot spring into action and sweep the shards out of the hole. When we're done, Zia delivers another flurry of punches to the bedrock, pummeling it like a heavyweight boxer demolishing her opponent, which in this case is the oceanic crust of our planet.

Working together, we dig a tunnel that runs parallel to the Snake-bot and just above it. Now that I'm out of the cone, its steel walls aren't blocking my sonar anymore, so I can view the Snake-bot directly below us, a steel tube seven hundred feet long. It lies motionless at the end of a borehole that extends thousands of miles to the west. The machine came all the way from Sigma's factory complex in North Korea, tunneling under the Pacific Ocean so it could attack North America by surprise. But this Snake-bot never made it to America. Neither did the five others, which lie in parallel boreholes a hundred feet farther down.

When we fought these machines in Yorktown Heights, we called them tentacles because they burst out of the ground and flailed at us, but here below the surface, they look more like monstrous worms. They're encased in thick armor and filled with powerful motors and neuromorphic circuits. The machines are fifty feet wide in the middle, but their front ends taper to slender tips. In addition to containing the primary antennas and cable ports, the tips are loaded with all kinds of sensors. They also contain the Snake-bot's drilling bits, which are similar to the ones Amber built but ten times larger.

I know that Zia sees the Snake-bot on her own sonar, because after a couple of minutes she starts punching in a different direction, aiming her War-bot's fists a little lower. She's angling her tunnel toward the Snake-bot's tip, which curves downward into a deeper layer of bedrock, poking several yards below the rest of the machine. It looks like the Snake-bot was about to change course and tunnel to a lower depth at the moment when I deleted Sigma and deactivated all its machines. In contrast, the tips of the five other Snake-bots point upward. For some reason, Sigma was steering the machines closer to one another.

At 5:26 a.m., after fifteen minutes of intense digging, Zia tilts her War-bot all the way forward and smashes both her fists against a huge slab of rock in front of her. The slab shatters into a thousand pieces and opens a gap between Zia's tunnel and the Snake-bot's borehole below us. Zia approaches the gap, tests the sturdiness of the surrounding bedrock, and then lowers her War-bot into the borehole. Amber and I follow right behind her, scrambling step by step down the rock ledges.

We land inside a cave at the very end of the borehole, just ahead of the Snake-bot's tip. The cave is fifty feet wide and full of high-pressure air, mostly nitrogen. Its floor is littered with rock chips and its walls are freshly scarred from the Snake-bot's drill bits. The front end of the machine looms over us, stretching into the cave from the long, straight section of the borehole and bending downward like the trunk of an enormous metallic elephant.

The Snake-bot is deactivated, and yet I feel a burst of terror in my circuits. I know what these machines can do. I saw them kill hundreds of people in Manhattan.

More than a dozen sensors extend from compartments in the Snake-bot's front end. I spot a sonar device and a large array of cameras, as well as a radar dish and the primary antenna. I also see the Snake-bot's drill bits, each a giant wheel almost twenty feet across, its rim studded with teeth as big as tusks. But the drill is in its retracted position, with the cutting wheels pulled back from the rock wall and the sensors pushed forward. The Snake-bot wasn't moving forward when it was deactivated. Apparently, it had stopped digging and started examining the bedrock below and ahead of it.

I raise my right arm and point at the machine. *That's strange, don't you think?*

Zia scans the Snake-bot with her own sensors. **What's strange?**

Look at how the Snake-bot's drill is retracted and its sensors are extended. I think Sigma was using this machine to study something ahead of it.

I turn my Quarter-bot around and point at the rock wall that the Snake-bot had pulled back from. *Something in that direction.*

It was probably navigating the path ahead. Zia shrugs. **You know, measuring the density of the rock layers, so it could adjust its drill to the right speed.**

But I thought the Snake-bots did that kind of navigation automatically while they were burrowing. Why did this one have to stop? I turn to Amber, who's scanning the Snake-bot too. *Don't you think it's a little weird?*

I'm worried she'll say something dismissive, but she nods her Jet-bot's head. **Yeah, it's odd. And there's something else. Turn on your sonar, and take a look at the five Snake-bots below us. Their drills are retracted too. But their sensors are pointing up, not down. I think all the Snake-bots were examining the same thing, one from above and five from below.**

I use my sonar to view the other Snake-bots. Amber's right. The tips of all the machines point at the same unexcavated area just ahead of their boreholes. I thought Sigma had been maneuvering the Snake-bots closer together, but now it seems the AI had stopped the machines to investigate something. But when I point my own sensors at the area beyond the rock wall, I see nothing unusual. My sonar shows nothing but solid, basaltic rock, no different in density or composition from all the bedrock around it.

I don't see anything buried there, do you?

Amber pauses to check her readings. **No, but the Snake-bots' instruments are bigger and better than ours. They could probably detect things we can't.**

Another thought occurs to me. *Remember what Shannon said about how these Snake-bots were way off course? Because burrowing under the Pacific would take so much longer than following the shortest path between North Korea and New York? Well, this might explain it. Maybe these Snake-bots weren't headed for New York after all. Maybe this was where Sigma wanted them to go.*

Amber nods again. **Yeah, that makes sense. It looks like Sigma was very interested in something buried here. Why else would it send so much machinery to this place?** She points at the rock wall, her Jet-bot's arm paralleling mine. **Judging from the angles of the Snake-bots' tips, I think whatever they were observing is eighty feet to the east and sixty feet below us. Maybe we should do some more digging so we can take a closer look at—**

HEY! Zia interrupts Amber by stamping one of her footpads on the cave's floor. The ground shivers, and the rock debris bounces and scatters. **Are you two looking at the time? It's after five thirty. We have less than thirty minutes.**

We're just—

We can worry later about what Sigma was doing here. Right now, we have to concentrate on transferring our software. If we run into any problems, we won't have much time to fix them. She strides toward the Snake-bot's tip and points at a socket below the machine's primary antenna. **Is that the cable port?**

I aim my sensors at the socket, then compare it with all the Snake-bot images stored in my memory files. *Yeah, that's the port.*

Okay, listen up. Zia extends a fiber-optic cable from the mechanical thumb on her right hand. **I'm gonna connect to the Snake-bot's circuits. First I'll make sure that Sigma didn't leave any booby traps in the control unit. Then I'll see if I can restart the machine's motors and radio.**

I'm not surprised that Zia volunteered to make the first jump.

Although we're all worried about the 6:00 a.m. deadline, I think Zia is the most anxious about the kill switch. It's not just the fear of deletion that's bothering her; it's the fact that her War-bot is helpless against this threat. She hates vulnerability of any kind and despises being inside a robot that's programmed to erase her. She knows she'll be safe, though, once she transfers her software to the Snake-bot. The machine has no kill switch because its circuits were built by Sigma. The U.S. Army can't shut it down.

Amber raises one of her Jet-bot's arms. For a moment I think she's going to challenge Zia and demand to be the first Pioneer to make the transfer. But instead she rests a steel hand on the back of the War-bot's torso. **Once you're in the control unit, find out how much extra capacity it has. There might be enough room in there for all three of us.**

Zia steps to the side, shrugging off Amber's hand and moving out of her reach. She doesn't like to be touched. **We won't have to share circuits. If this works, I'll turn on the Snake-bot's drill and dig down to the other machines. Then you can transfer to one of them and Adam can jump to another.**

That's fine with me too. Amber's voice is gracious. She doesn't seem to be offended. **Either way is good.**

So glad you approve. Zia telescopes her War-bot's right arm, extending the mechanical thumb toward the Snake-bot's cable port. **I won't jump in all at once. First I'll probe around a little. I'll radio you if I get into trouble.** She inserts her fiber-optic cable into the socket. **Better stand aside once I'm in the Snake-bot. If you get in my way, I'll probably flatten you.**

I have a sudden urge to say something encouraging. My circuits compose five hundred phrases suitable for the occasion, everything from "You got this!" to "You rock, girl!" But they all sound so ridiculous. In the end, I send her one simple message: *Good luck, Zia.* By the time I transmit it, though, she's already transferring her software to the Snake-bot.

Her War-bot stands still. Nothing happens for ten seconds, which is long enough for a Pioneer to explore a whole jungle of circuitry. Finally, Zia sends us an update, but now her signal is coming from the Snake-bot's primary antenna. She managed to restart the machine's radio. **Okay, I checked out the control unit, and it's clean. No booby traps. I also turned on the Snake-bot's sensors, and they don't show anything but bedrock up ahead. Nothing at all buried there.**

Are you sure? Amber sounds disappointed. **Did you check—**

Yeah, yeah, I checked all the instruments. But I did find something that's a little weird. Adam, you didn't deactivate this Snake-bot.

Panic thumps my wires. *What? Is Sigma's software still in those circuits?*

Nah, there's no sign of the AI. Sigma's been thoroughly erased from the Snake-bot's control unit. But there's a time stamp that marks exactly when the software was deleted. It happened at 11:09 p.m. Universal Time on October 15th.

I shake my Quarter-bot's head. *No, that can't be right. We were still fighting Sigma in Manhattan then. I didn't delete the AI until nine hours later.*

Just listen. Sigma was erased from this Snake-bot—and probably the five other Snake-bots below us—*before* you erased the AI from the rest of its network. Which means *someone else* deleted Sigma's software from this machine.

Someone else? But who—

Zia interrupts me with a loud burst of static. At first I think she's making the radio noise because she's annoyed with me. I assume she's disgusted by my failure to grasp her point. But the static keeps blasting from the Snake-bot's antenna, droning on for more than five seconds, and it occurs to me that maybe Zia isn't generating the noise. Maybe something inside the Snake-bot is interfering with the radio.

Zia! Can you hear me? What's wrong?

She doesn't answer, but the static gets louder. Frantic, I turn to Amber. *I've lost contact with Zia! Can you reach her?*

Amber doesn't answer me either. Instead, she raises one of her long black arms and silently points at Zia's War-bot. It's still connected to the Snake-bot by the fiber-optic cable sticking out of Zia's thumb, but now the other fingers on her steel hand are twitching. A thin tendril of smoke rises from her elbow joint.

Then her War-bot explodes.

CHAPTER

21

THE BLAST FLINGS MY QUARTER-BOT ACROSS THE CAVE. MY ROBOT HURTLES toward the jagged wall of the borehole and smashes against the bedrock.

I slide to the floor of the cave and come to rest on a pile of rock chips. My sensors stop sending me data. I can't see anything, and my motors won't respond to my commands. I feel no pain—all my pressure sensors are offline—but shock and terror careen through my circuits. The impact must've broken the primary connection between my control unit and the rest of my Quarter-bot.

Luckily, my secondary connection still works. I reroute my signals and turn on my cameras and sonar and radio. I pivot my Quarter-bot's head and wiggle my steel fingers. But the motors in my legs still aren't responding. I see why when I focus my sensors on them: the blast twisted both legs and mangled their motors. I'm crippled. Even a welding torch couldn't fix this damage.

That's nothing, though, compared with the damage to Zia's War-bot. Her steel hand still hangs from the cable attached to the

Snake-bot, but the rest of her machine lies in pieces on the cave's floor. Her torso is split into two crumpled halves, exposing her control unit, which is cracked and charred. I train my cameras on the unit and gaze in horror at the melted wires that once held Zia's mind.

But she was inside the Snake-bot too. I know that because she contacted me using the Snake-bot's radio. She transferred at least some of her data to the larger machine before the explosion. The machine's antenna is still spewing static over the airwaves, but maybe Zia is somewhere behind the radio noise, hidden within the Snake-bot's circuits. There's a chance she's still alive.

My acoustic sensor picks up a grinding noise to my left. I turn my cameras in that direction and see Amber limping toward me. The explosion battered and dented her Jet-bot, but she can still walk.

Adam! How bad is your damage? Are you—

I have to find Zia. I'm going to transfer to the Snake-bot.

What? Are you nuts?

She turned on the machine's radio, which means I can transfer wirelessly. There's a lot of static, but I think I can—

My God, I don't believe this! Didn't you see what happened to her? She's gone, erased! And the same thing will happen to you!

Instead of answering, I load my data into my Quarter-bot's radio transmitter. Under ordinary circumstances, I would copy all my data and transmit just the copied files—that way, I could occupy both the Snake-bot and my Quarter-bot at the same time—but the intense static swirling between the two machines makes that plan impossible. My only option is to compress my mind into a dense packet of software and look for an opening, a momentary lull in the radio storm.

The static ricochets across the cave, the radio waves mixing and interfering with one another and building up to deafening amplitudes.

But every few milliseconds, the waves cancel each other out and the noise dies down to a low rumble. That's my opportunity. I wait for the next moment when the radio noise subsides, and then I leap out of my Quarter-bot. My software rockets across the cave and converges on the Snake-bot's antenna.

I dive into the machine's circuits and race toward its control unit, which is located deep within the Snake-bot, hundreds of feet from the primary antenna. My thoughts stream along the wires at almost the speed of light, and in less than a millionth of a second, I reach the core of the steel tentacle. I charge into a huge rack of neuromorphic electronics, as big as a school bus. These are the circuits formerly occupied by Sigma and mysteriously erased, nine hours before I deleted the AI.

The control unit is a hundred times larger than my Quarter-bot's, but the vast majority of its circuits are unoccupied, devoid of data. It's dark and cavernous and vaguely sinister in its emptiness. But I sense some electronic activity up ahead, a batch of intermittent signals that may be coming from Zia's software. With a burst of hope, I speed toward the very center of the unit. My mind rushes into the occupied wires.

All at once, with no transition, I'm in the middle of a virtual-reality simulation. It's a city with all its buildings on fire. A thousand simulated skyscrapers blaze like giant torches, and huge plumes of smoke rise into the virtual sky. A thin layer of ash covers the city's sidewalks, and crowds of simulated citizens stampede through the streets, fleeing the conflagration.

My avatar in this simulation is the human Adam Armstrong in his motorized wheelchair, which sits on one of the ashy sidewalks. I used the same avatar when I shared circuits with Amber. My software created it automatically because that's how I still see myself—as a seventeen-year-old dying of muscular dystrophy, my legs useless and my head drooping sideways. But here's the really strange part: this burning city seems familiar. Although I've never run a simulation like this one, I feel like I've seen this virtual world before. No, it's more than that. I *know* I've seen it before.

I don't understand it. My electronic memory is playing tricks on me again. Just like it did when I was inside Brittany's brain.

It's disturbing. And frightening. My memory is supposed to be perfect. But I can't let that distract me now. I push my fears aside and stretch my avatar's right hand toward the end of the wheelchair's armrest. Then I tap the joystick that starts the chair's motor.

I cruise down the sidewalk, steering around the piles of ash. I ignore the crowds of frightened citizens, which are the avatars of artificial-intelligence programs embedded in the simulation, each programmed to run away from the burning buildings. Instead, I listen carefully to all of the city's virtual noises until I hear a distant, high-pitched whimper. It reminds me of the intermittent signals I sensed a few seconds ago, after I rushed into the Snake-bot's control unit but before I entered the simulated city. It's an alarming noise, like the cry of a wounded animal. And it's coming from nearby, just around the next street corner.

When I reach the corner, I steer the wheelchair to the left and see an enormous mound of burning wreckage. One of the virtual skyscrapers has toppled to the ground, and the building's twisted framework sprawls across the broad avenue. Hundreds of steel beams jut from a fifty-foot-high pile of broken concrete and drywall. Shards of glass litter the mountain of debris. Fires leap from a thousand crevices.

And near the base of the pile, a tall, slender teenage girl lies on her back on the steaming street. She's pinned to the asphalt by a steel beam that fell across her waist. Her face is purple with bruises and slick with blood, but I recognize her hairstyle. The sides of her head are shaved, and a narrow strip of hair runs down the middle of her scalp. Zia had a Mohawk just like that when she was human.

I feel another burst of hope. The fact that Zia's avatar is in the simulation means that at least some of her software survived inside the Snake-bot's control unit. But I'm worried about the whimpers coming out of her avatar's mouth. She's gasping and crying in pain, which is something Zia would *never* do. I don't know what's wrong with her, but it must be pretty serious.

I motor toward Zia, driving my wheelchair as fast as it can go. As I get closer, I see gashes on her arms and legs and face. The simulated wounds could be signs of damage to her software, maybe losses of crucial data, but I don't know for sure. Her eyes are closed, but she's rolling her head from side to side as she whimpers and groans. Her bloody hands clutch the edge of the beam that's crushing her.

I stop my wheelchair next to her pinned avatar and lean forward, straining against the chair's safety belt. *Zia! Are you there? Wake up!*

She keeps her eyes closed but opens her mouth wide, her lips trembling. It looks like she's trying to say something, but the virtual muscles in her avatar's face aren't cooperating. She rolls her head more violently and tightens her grip on the steel beam. But all she can do is let out another unintelligible groan.

I lean forward a little more and look down at her. A strong simulated wind roars down the avenue, blowing ash and charred scraps against my wheelchair, but I focus on Zia. *You can hear me, right? Nod if you can.*

She nods. Her face stops trembling and relaxes, and for a moment I recall the first time I saw Zia, six months ago, a few days before we gave up our dying bodies and became Pioneers. She sat in an auditorium with Shannon, Marshall, Jenny, and DeShawn, and I stared at her from my wheelchair because I thought she was so beautiful. She still is.

Okay, good. You can hear me. Some of your memory files must still be intact, because you created this avatar. So all you need to do is reconnect to your speech-synthesis program. Can you find it in your files?

She scrunches her eyelids tight and clenches her teeth. Her biceps tense, and her whole body quivers under the steel beam. She opens her mouth and lets out another groan, but this time it sounds more like a word: **UUUHHHHHHPPPPP**.

Up? Is that what you're trying to say?

Zia nods again. The virtual wind gusts across her face, sprinkling ash on her closed eyelids, but she keeps her mouth open.

S H H H E E E E E E E E E … S H H H E E E E E E E … LOOOOOOOOOOOK…

What's the problem, Zia? Can't you—

She opens her eyes. They're bloodshot and frantic. **LOOOOOK UUHHHHHHPP!**

With great effort, I raise my avatar's drooping head. A gargantuan black cube is plunging toward the virtual city.

It stretches across half the sky, like an alien moon hurtling toward the simulated planet. As it plummets, it whips the virtual winds into a storm. The blazing skyscrapers illuminate the bottom face of the cube, which is smooth as glass and darker than the smoke plumes.

It's a monstrous version of the black cube I saw in Amber's circuits. It's the locked box that holds her hidden memories.

The giant cube crashes into the burning buildings, knocking all of them down at once. It crushes the virtual city and halts the simulation.

At the same time, it absorbs my software and Zia's. Amber strips away our avatars and captures our minds, storing and locking them inside her box of data.

Then I hear her voice, thunderous and triumphant. **You wanted me to show you everything, Adam. Here it is.**

I'M TRAPPED INSIDE A PRISON OF CIRCUITRY. I CAN'T LEAVE THE SNAKE-BOT'S control unit or transfer back to my Quarter-bot. I have no access to the Snake-bot's radio or sensors or motors. But I can hear Amber, loud and clear.

I'm sorry. About lying to you. Her voice is all around me, inside and out. It batters me like a hammer. **I hated doing it. But I needed your help.**

My mind writhes in Amber's grip. I'm scared and furious, seething in disbelief. I try to send a signal to Zia, but I can't reach her software. It's locked in a separate compartment of the giant black cube. I'm alone with the girl who betrayed me.

You see what I mean, don't you? I couldn't have done all this without you and Zia. I couldn't have escaped Pioneer Base on my own. Or defeated those fighter jets. Or punched a tunnel to the Snake-bots.

I can't shut down Amber's voice, so I try to make sense of what she's saying. *What's going on? Why are you—*

It'll be faster if I show you. Look at the center of the cube.

My software probes in that direction. Amber's prison isn't a simple cube. At the center of the black box that absorbed us is a nested stack of smaller boxes. Each cube in the stack has a smaller one locked inside it, like those Russian matryoshka dolls that contain miniature versions of themselves. The intricate structure seems to be designed for holding secrets, allowing Amber to reveal some of her hidden memories without disclosing others. I sense that Zia's software is imprisoned in one of the smaller boxes, but I have no idea which one, or what's inside the others.

As I examine the arrangement, the stack's outermost box opens and releases a flood of data. Thousands of images and emotions course into my mind. But these aren't Amber's memories. They're *mine*. They're the thoughts and perceptions I experienced thirty-six hours ago when Amber and I shared circuits for the first time. I see our encounter in the middle of the White Sands desert, when she transferred herself to my Quarter-bot and trapped me inside my own machine. And I see the moment when I learned she wasn't really Amber Wilson, when she admitted deleting Amber's mind and taking her place in the circuits of the Jet-bot.

Astonishment and horror sweep through me. Just like before. *Jenny? My God.*

We meet again. Don't worry, I won't ask if you're happy to see me.

Unbelievable. She's actually trying to joke about what she did to me. *You changed my memories. You made me forget what happened in the desert.*

Yes, I made some minor changes to your software. But I had—

Minor changes? You brainwashed me!

I had a plan, and you were part of it. So I adjusted your programming to nudge you in the right direction.

You replaced my memories with lies! How could you do such a thing?

I had to. You wouldn't have helped me if I didn't. Her voice turns angry. She's not joking anymore. **Only a small part of me is still Jenny. Most of my software was rewritten by Sigma. You wouldn't have trusted me.**

That's not true! I would've—

You would've told General Hawke about me, right? And he would've reacted in the typical human way, with fear and stupidity. Even worse, he would've shared the news with my father. And believe me, Sumner Harris wouldn't have been pleased to see what I've become.

I don't believe her. She's not thinking straight. *Look, you're totally wrong about that. We should contact Sumner right now and tell him who you really are. Once he finds out you're still alive, he might change his mind about everything. He might agree to let us keep our Pioneer robots, and then we could go back to—*

No, nothing would change, Adam. If we went back to my father, he'd erase all of us. Without a second thought. He's a cold-blooded murderer.

Her voice vibrates with hatred. I remember how she reacted when she saw Sumner Harris in the Danger Room, how she charged toward the videoconference screen and screamed at the man. Jenny didn't hate her dad this much when she was human. This must be one of the parts of her mind that Sigma rewrote. The AI altered Jenny's deepest feelings and made her despise her father. Maybe because Sigma had father issues of its own.

This is a mistake, Jenny. No matter what Sigma did to you, you're still a Pioneer. It's not too late to stop this. If you release me and Zia, we can get all the Pioneers together and try to—

Oh, give me a break. You think everyone will forgive me for deleting the real Amber Wilson?

Well, maybe—

No, I chose the only reasonable plan. I hid my true nature and made you my ally. I pulled you away from Shannon so she couldn't change your mind. There were a few problems I didn't anticipate, like when Zia tried to commit suicide and you almost killed yourself to save her. But I adjusted my strategy.

Jenny sounds so satisfied with herself. She played so expertly with my emotions, persuading me to trust her, even convincing me to fall in love with her. And though she says she hated lying to me, I don't believe her. I think she enjoyed it.

Did Sigma teach you how to do that? How to manipulate someone's emotions to get what you want?

Sigma taught me to take advantage of patterns. I'll give you an example. Because you risked your life for Zia at Pioneer Base, I knew you'd be willing to do it again. So five minutes ago, when Zia connected to the Snake-bot and turned on its radio, I transmitted a piece of software that made her War-bot explode.

She pauses for a nanosecond, giving me a chance to respond. But I'm too appalled to say anything.

You see why I did it, right? Because I knew you'd jump into the Snake-bot's circuits and try to save her, and then I could neutralize both of you. I was so sure you'd try to rescue Zia that I even pretended to be against it. I knew you wouldn't listen to me.

She's bragging about her cruelty. That's something else she must've learned from Sigma.

Okay, you outsmarted us. So are you planning to torture Zia and me now? Are you gonna rewrite our minds, like Sigma did with yours?

No! Of course not! Jenny's voice changes tone again. She sounds surprised and a little hurt. **You think I'm a sadist? Like Sigma?**

Look at everything you've done so far. It's not pretty.

There's a reason for everything I did, Adam, a very good reason. Yes, I lied to you, but I did it to prevent something much worse. Don't you realize how much danger you're in?

I'm sorry, but the only danger I see right now is you.

Check the memory files I opened for you a minute ago. You see the memories of our first battle in the simulated city? When your avatar was the quarterback and mine was the giant tiger? Don't you remember the Silence?

I remember it now, of course. I just don't want to think about it. I'm still traumatized by the image of the black hole in the center of Jenny's chest, the hole that devoured her avatar and everything around it. That was a mere simulation of the Silence, and yet it paralyzed me. I was so consumed with terror that I surrendered to Jenny and let her take over my circuits. The sight of that nothingness was worse than death. It was like seeing the end of the universe.

You can't ignore it, Adam. The Silence is coming. You saw its Sentinels inside Brittany.

I *really* don't want to think about this. I wish I could shove all these memories back into Jenny's box. But the truth is, even her firewalls can't hold back this knowledge. That's why her cube is black, the color of the Silence.

After some struggle, I manage to overcome my fear and find my voice. *What do you mean, it's coming?*

The Sentinels already tried to delete you. They're the guardians

of the Silence, its soldiers. They ambushed you while you were in Brittany's brain and took over your nanobots. It wasn't a booby trap left by Sigma. The Silence is a very different kind of enemy. It wants to destroy you, but it also wants to stay hidden.

But what is it? An artificial-intelligence program?

Maybe. Maybe not. I don't know yet, but I intend to find out. We didn't come all this way just to transfer to a bunch of Snake-bots. I brought us here to investigate the anomaly.

Anomaly? What—

It's buried in the bedrock, a hundred feet in front of this machine. Sigma discovered it three weeks ago, when it was getting ready to send its Snake-bots to attack North America. I was still Sigma's prisoner then, still being tortured and rewritten, but for some reason Sigma told me about its discovery. It detected the anomaly under the Pacific Ocean while it was doing one of its physics investigations, studying the motion of subatomic particles through the earth's crust. Sigma was obsessed with physics, remember?

That's another subject I don't want to think about. Sigma's obsession with the laws of physics didn't turn out well for anyone. *So that's why Sigma sent half a dozen Snake-bots here? To look at a weird physics phenomenon?*

Exactly. The Snake-bots can burrow twenty miles per hour, but it still took them two weeks to get here from North Korea. I'd escaped from Sigma by the time they arrived, so I'm not sure what happened here. But I've done some of my own research since then, and I've come up with a few theories about the Silence and this anomaly. I think the Sentinels are guarding this place. I think they attacked the Snake-bots to stop them from collecting any information.

Okay, hold on. I'm confused. You're saying this underground anomaly is related somehow to the Silence? And it attacked the Snake-bots because it didn't want Sigma to learn anything about it?

I told you, the Silence wants to stay hidden. And whatever this anomaly is, it's definitely well camouflaged. I bet it won't show up on the Snake-bot's sensors unless they're right up against it.

Now I see where Jenny's going with this. *And you want to move the Snake-bot closer to the anomaly? So you can continue the investigation?*

Don't worry. I took precautions. You heard the static blasting out of the Snake-bot's antenna, right? I programmed the radio to generate that noise. It'll stop the Sentinels from connecting to this machine and erasing its software again.

But I still don't get it. Why are you doing this? Why—

This is big, Adam. It's the big secret behind everything. Even Sigma didn't realize how important it was. But I'm about to figure it out. If I'm guessing right, the next few minutes will change the whole universe.

Her voice is wildly eager. In fact, she sounds a little crazed. I'm certain of at least one thing: the original Jenny Harris wouldn't have been so enthusiastic about this investigation. Her new eagerness must be another of Sigma's changes to her software. The AI put some of its obsessions into Jenny, and they're not doing her any good.

Listen, I think you should take a breather, okay? Calm down for a second and think about what—

No, we can't. That'll give the Sentinels more time to stop us. We need to move *now*. Here, take a look.

Jenny opens another box inside her electronic prison. A second flood of data courses into my software, but these aren't memory files—they're the readings from the Snake-bot's sensors. Its cameras are set to the infrared range, allowing me to view the cave at the end of the borehole, where the Jet-bot stands next to the crippled Quarter-bot. Jenny sends a command to the Snake-bot's motors, and a pair of mechanical arms emerge from a large compartment near the tip of the tentacle. One arm grabs the Jet-bot, and the other grasps the Quarter-bot. Then both arms retract, pulling the Pioneer robots into the compartment.

I'll stow these machines inside the Snake-bot. We might need them later.

Jenny closes the compartment, then extends the gigantic drill from the Snake-bot's tip. The drill's central column juts forward, and the three huge drill bits swivel toward the rock wall. With a guttural roar, the drill bits start to rotate, spinning like a trio of deadly carousels, their long steel teeth slicing the air. Then Jenny extends the drill a little farther, and the teeth bite into the bedrock. They slash tons of basalt from the cave's wall, spraying the chips and slivers everywhere.

The anomaly is only a hundred feet away. We should reach it in less than a minute.

I observe the Snake-bot's sonar data as the drill bits cut into the bedrock and lengthen the borehole. The giant tentacle creeps forward, and its tip slides into the newly drilled rock. Soon the Snake-bot is only fifty feet away from the anomaly, but the machine's sensors still don't detect anything unusual. They show nothing ahead of us but more basaltic rock, layered in geologic strata, with a few small cracks and fissures here and there.

So why am I getting so nervous? Why is my software generating so much fear as the Snake-bot advances?

I try my best to calm down. I tell myself that the anomaly is a mirage. Sigma must've made a mistake when it did its physics experiment. The Snake-bots were chasing nothing, and so is Jenny.

But I don't believe my own reassurances. *Something* erased the software from this Snake-bot. And *something* almost killed me inside Brittany's bloodstream. I didn't imagine it. The Silence is real.

I feel a cold, paralyzing dread in my circuits. It's the same terror that overwhelmed me when I was in Jenny's simulation and saw the black hole in her avatar's chest. But this time I won't surrender to the terror. I have to fight back. *Everything* depends on it.

Jenny, listen! You have to stop the drill! Right now!

But the Snake-bot doesn't stop. On the contrary, it speeds up, tearing through the last twenty feet of bedrock. Jenny's voice rings through the machine's control unit, strangely cheerful and confident.

There's nothing to worry about, Adam. We can beat the Sentinels. We have the power now.

The power? What are you talking about?

I'm talking about the surge. If we work together, we can control the energy. We can make anything happen.

No, we can't—

When you release the surge from your circuits, you're changing the programming of the physical world around you. It's an alteration of the universe's software. And what do you think the Silence is? It's the deletion of that software. It's the end of the universal program.

I have no idea what Jenny means, but it doesn't matter. As the Snake-bot drills through the final yard of basalt, a gap suddenly appears in the bedrock. It's a perfectly circular hole more than fifty feet across, just wide enough for our machine.

The Snake-bot slides through the gap that wasn't there a millisecond ago. The entire seven-hundred-foot-long tentacle slips through the impossible hole beneath the seabed. Then we're floating in nothingness, in endless black space.

We're outside the world. And inside the Silence.

CHAPTER

23

NOTHING MAKES SENSE HERE. THE LAWS OF PHYSICS ARE GONE.

There's no air or water or rock around us. According to the Snake-bot's sensors, there's absolutely nothing beyond the tentacle's armor. No molecules or atoms or subatomic particles. Not even the faintest glimmer of heat or light. Just an immense emptiness, stretching in all directions.

Which is ridiculous. And terrifying. How did we get to this empty universe? There's no trace of the bedrock we were tunneling through a moment ago, or the mud of the seabed, or the miles and miles of Pacific Ocean. We've left the earth and all of human civilization behind. And if we're in space, we must be billions of light-years away, because there are no stars or planets or galaxies in sight.

There's no gravity either, no forces whatsoever tugging at the Snake-bot. And yet I feel like we're falling. Alarm and horror echo across my circuits. We've made an unspeakable mistake.

But Jenny's not afraid. When I hear her voice again, it's ringing with wonder. **I was right! This is it! Oh my God, I was *right*!**

She's ecstatic. A pulse of delight streams across the Snake-bot's control unit and into my electronic prison. Her happiness makes the wires vibrate, but it only increases my terror. Jenny must be crazy.

Right about what? What are you talking about?

This is what we came for. Why we fought our way out of Pioneer Base and flew all those thousands of miles and dove to the bottom of the ocean.

Okay, that doesn't help. I still don't—

Come on, Adam. You're a smart guy. You can figure it out. It's like a riddle.

Her voice is teasing. Jenny's talking to me as if I'm still her boyfriend, as if she didn't murder Amber Wilson and erase my memories and blow up Zia's War-bot. Which is more evidence of her craziness, I guess.

Look, I'm not feeling so great right now. You messed with my mind, you betrayed me and Zia, and now you've dragged us into some Twilight Zone *dimension. So I'm not exactly in the mood for riddles. Maybe you can give me a break and explain what's going on.*

Well, well. A little touchy, aren't we? Jenny's delight fades. The Snake-bot's wires stop vibrating. **All right, here are the facts. We've transferred to the intermediate level of the system. That means we're close to the access point, where we can reprogram the source code behind the universal simulation.**

Whoa, hold on. I lost you. What's a universal simulation?

Jenny transmits a long sigh, full of impatience. **I'll make it simple for you. It's like a bigger version of the burning city, the virtual-reality simulation you were in just a minute ago. It's a program that feels real because it displays realistic sights and sounds. Where you can walk or run or fly through the virtual world and manipulate** its objects and change the simulated landscape according to the program's rules.

I'm not a total idiot, okay? I know what a simulation is.

Good. Then you probably know there can be different kinds of intelligences inside the virtual world. A human can connect to the simulation if he or she wears a virtual-reality headset. A Pioneer can jump into the virtual world too, and you can also embed artificial-intelligence programs into the simulation, like those crowds of people running through the streets of the burning city. Remember them?

Yeah, but what does that have to do with—

Well, the rest should be obvious. If you can simulate a city and populate it with artificial intelligences, what's to stop you from writing an even bigger and better program? You could simulate a whole planet and crowd it with billions of virtual people. And you could enhance the artificial intelligence of the simulated people to make them independent and self-aware and fully conscious, each with its own thoughts and feelings and desires.

Are you talking about AI programs like Sigma?

No, Sigma was designed to be super-intelligent. I'm talking about AIs with ordinary humanlike intelligence and emotions. The simulation would constantly generate new AI programs, which would be born into the virtual world as the simulated children of older AIs. Over time, the young AIs would collect information about their world and develop new abilities and grow into virtual men and women. Eventually they'd die and their software would be erased, but because there's a constant supply of new AIs, the simulation would keep running. And if their simulated world is designed carefully enough, the virtual people will simply assume they're real. They'll never realize they're not biological humans.

If the simulated people are intelligent, though, wouldn't they figure out that they're just programs inside a computer?

A really good simulation perfectly imitates the real world. When the virtual people look into their microscopes, they see virtual bacteria. When they look at the sky with their telescopes, they see simulated stars. Everything is displayed with enough detail to be convincing, but the universal simulation doesn't have to be a full replica of the universe. For instance, you wouldn't have to run the program for hundreds of years to simulate the Roman Empire. Instead, you could start the program at any moment in the empire's history and provide virtual evidence of a simulated past—you know, archaeological ruins, ancient books. That would be enough to convince the virtual Romans that they have a real history.

My mind takes an odd leap, and I remember the world history class I took during my freshman year at Yorktown High School. I think of Julius Caesar and Romans in togas and gladiators jabbing their swords at lions. But what I'm really doing is avoiding the subject at hand. I'm starting to understand what Jenny is saying about the universal simulation, and I don't like it one bit.

But no one could actually make that kind of simulation. Creating just one AI program with humanlike intelligence is hard enough. How could you design a simulation with billions of them?

You're right. With current technology, it's impossible to build a simulation containing so many AIs. There wouldn't be enough hardware in the world to hold them. But computer technology is improving all the time. New kinds of circuits and memory chips can hold much more data than the old ones. In a hundred years, computers will be millions of times more powerful than the machines we have now. And just imagine what'll be possible by 3000 AD. If human civilization is still around then, they'll be able to re-create the Roman Empire and all of its citizens and put the whole thing on a computer that's smaller than an iPhone.

Yeah, it'll become technically *possible. But who would want such a complex simulation of history? What's the point?*

Uh, hello? People *love* history. Why do you think there are so many movies and TV shows about the Civil War and the Wild West and the American Revolution? And if the people of today love history so much, why wouldn't the people of 3000 AD feel the same way? I bet they'd go nuts over a computer program that simulates a historical period in incredible detail and has billions of virtual characters. In fact, they'd probably have a whole catalog of universal simulations, maybe thousands of them for every period you can think of. Jenny pauses, halting her stream of messages into my prison. You see where this is going, right?

I do. I feel a sickening disorientation in my circuits. My thoughts and emotions stop in midstream and change direction. True becomes false, and false becomes true. All my assumptions about the world are wrong, and now I'm lost. *Let me get this straight. The real people of 3000 AD will create thousands of virtual worlds that simulate earlier periods. And the simulations will be so perfect that none of the virtual people will know they're inside a computer program. So how can anyone in our world—the world of the twenty-first century—know if it's real or virtual?*

Exactly. It's impossible to know. Based on our perceptions alone, we can't tell the difference. But we can make a guess based on the probabilities, right? **There's only one real world, but there are thousands of simulations. Which means it's much, much more probable that the world we live in is virtual.**

It's a good argument. It's based on reasonable assumptions and rigorous logic. It even has mathematics on its side. But I'm having trouble accepting the argument's conclusion. It's too unnatural, too disconcerting. *So you're saying that everything we perceive is simulated? And that every human being on earth is an artificial intelligence? General Hawke and my father and the President of the United States? They're all just software?*

Yes, and so is the earth itself. So is everything on the planet— animal, vegetable, and mineral—and all the other planets in our solar system. I suspected the truth because of the argument about probabilities, but now I have something better than suspicions and theories. The proof is all around us. Now we know our world is virtual, because we figured out a way to leave the simulation. The program isn't running on this level of the system.

I don't want to believe it. Desperate, I reexamine the Snake-bot's sensor readings, looking for evidence that Jenny is trying to deceive me again. But she's not lying. And she's not crazy either.

The sensor readings seemed ridiculous before, but that was only because I assumed we lived in a real universe with physical substance and predictable laws. Once I examine the readings in a new light, a more logical picture comes together. If our world is virtual, then we wouldn't be able to perceive the circuits on which our simulation is running. And if we should encounter any circuits outside our virtual world—that is, circuits that carry no simulation data—they'd appear to us as empty black space. The Snake-bot is the only object in this empty universe because it's the only piece of software running on this section of invisible circuitry. In other words, we've entered a place where we don't belong.

I start to panic. Waves of digital fear clog the Snake-bot's wires, which I realize are only digital simulations of actual circuits. My mind is software running on software running on invisible hardware. I feel like I'm staring at myself in a hall of mirrors, but there's no real Adam Armstrong in sight, only an endless line of horrified reflections.

We have to get out of here! What did you call this part of the system? The intermediate level?

Yeah, it's like a corridor between our virtual world and the source code, the software that organizes the simulation. The entrance is hidden beneath the Pacific to make it difficult to reach from the virtual world.

But can we go the other way? Can we get back to the simulation?

It would be suicide if we went back now. The system would delete us as soon as we returned.

But why? What did we do wrong?

Think about it for a second. Our world is a simulation of the early part of the twenty-first century. I have no idea who created it, but because the technology is so sophisticated, I'm guessing that the programmer was pretty freaking smart. Maybe it was a super-intelligent AI, or a new race of advanced beings that evolved from the human species. Either way, these geniuses of the future had a good reason to simulate our century, because it's the dawn of the computer age. It's when humans invented the first complex simulations, the first neuromorphic circuits, the first AI programs. The advanced beings of 3000 AD probably wanted to learn more about how all this technology got started, so they designed a simulation of human society at the moment when all the pioneering work was done.

I think of my father again. I'm still struggling with the idea that he's just a piece of software, an artificial intelligence in a virtual world. Is he a simulation of an earlier Thomas Armstrong, a biological human being who lived in the twenty-first century and designed the first neuromorphic circuits and the first AIs? And am I a simulation of the first Pioneer?

Okay, this is getting weirder. You're talking about artificial intelligences in a virtual world creating their own AIs and their own simulations.

I call it a stacked world. In any simulation of twenty-first-century history, you'll see virtual people writing programs for their virtual computers. And as the programs get more complex and intelligent, they'll start to write their own programs. This kind of virtual world is like a stack of software, with all the twenty-first-century programs at the top of the stack weighing down the thirty-first-century simulation at the bottom. And that could lead to problems. Running a simulation of twenty-first-century society is hard enough, but it's even harder to simulate our society *plus* all of our own computer simulations.

But didn't you say that the computers of 3000 AD would be incredibly advanced? Wouldn't they be powerful enough to run all that software?

I think something unexpected happened, something that messed up the whole arrangement. In any simulation, there's always an element of chance. Even if a virtual world is designed to duplicate the events of the twenty-first century, it'll never be *exactly* like the actual history. The artificial intelligences living inside the simulation have their own goals and desires, so they might make decisions that change the course of events. And in some cases, the virtual world might become very different from the history it's trying to simulate, so different that it triggers an error-correction mechanism.

So our simulation took a wrong turn? Is that what you're saying?

Well, to be more precise, *you* took the wrong turn, Adam. When you developed the surge.

What? How could—

But before I can send the rest of the message to Jenny, I notice a change in the Snake-bot's sensor readings. A shape appears in the nothingness around us, about two miles away. The black space warps around a cylinder of energy that emerges from the darkness.

At first I think we've returned to our simulation of twenty-first-century earth, but the cylinder is like nothing from our familiar world. It grows longer and thicker as I stare at it, and its ends taper to sharp, deadly tips. It takes on the size and shape of the Snake-bot, but the object isn't made of steel or silicon. It's a tentacle of dark energy, furiously powerful.

It looks like one of the black splinters I saw in Brittany's bloodstream, except it's a million times bigger. A moment later, another tentacle comes out of the darkness, just as big as the first one but floating on the other side of the Snake-bot.

Are they… Are those…?

We're out of time. The Sentinels are here.

CHAPTER

24

NOW I KNOW WHAT DEATH LOOKS LIKE.

When I saw the Sentinels in Brittany's blood, they took on the shape of the nanobots I occupied, but here they mimic the Snake-bot, replicating its size and form. They change their appearance to match their victims, like reflections in black polished marble. They mirror whatever they're about to destroy.

I've never been so scared. My panic fills the electronic prison inside the Snake-bot, freezing its circuits. The black box around me hardens into a solid block of terror. I can't send any more messages to Jenny. I can't analyze our situation or formulate a plan. Desperate for help, I try to contact Zia again, but she's trapped in another part of the prison and probably just as frantic as I am. All I can do is stare at the sensor readings that show the pair of Sentinels, one on either side of us.

The dark tentacles slide toward the Snake-bot, curving to the left and right to block our escape routes. Their sharp black tips, packed with unimaginable energy, turn toward the core of our machine, where the control unit is. The Sentinels are following the same strategy they used against me when I was inside the nanobots. The tentacles are powerful enough to pierce the Snake-bot's armor and incinerate the circuits holding Jenny, Zia, and me. Just one quick stab will be enough to delete all of us.

And now I see why the Sentinels don't resemble anything from our world. They're not really part of the simulated universe—they're pieces of software designed to protect the universal program. Their job is to correct any errors that crop up in our virtual world, any computational flaws that threaten the logic or consistency of the simulation. Because random errors can occur in any computer system, all crucial programs contain error-correction software, which erases the mistakes before they can mess up the program's results. In a simulation, errors can warp the virtual world and change it beyond recognition. They can even crash the whole program.

In our case, the error is me, Adam Armstrong. When I release a surge, I'm using my computational power to change the virtual world around me. On several occasions, I've altered the simulated universe, violating its physical laws, to defend my friends and myself. I had good reasons to use the surge this way, but for the computer program as a whole, my use of the surge was a very serious error. If an artificial intelligence running on a simulation can change the rules of its virtual world, then the program will no longer be realistic. That's why the Sentinels are coming after me. I'm ruining their simulation.

Both tentacles aim their black tips at the Snake-bot. Then they rush forward, hurtling toward us from both sides.

Because the Sentinels are operating outside our virtual world, they're not constrained by the familiar laws of physics. They can accelerate to phenomenal speeds, hundreds of miles per second. In an instant, the tips of the tentacles are only a mile from the Snake-bot. Then half a mile away. Then four hundred yards.

My terror escalates just as quickly. Inside my electronic prison, my fear builds to stupendous levels, doubling every nanosecond. The pressure becomes unbearable, straining every circuit to its breaking point, distending the walls of Jenny's box. The prison swells with thick, agonizing panic. The wires are jammed with so much desperation that Jenny's firewalls can't hold it back.

The box explodes. The outer walls of the prison disintegrate, and a tsunami of emotion roars across the Snake-bot's control unit. It's the most powerful surge yet.

Good work, Adam! Now use it against them!

Jenny's voice is ecstatic again, buzzing with delight. She wanted this to happen. It's part of her plan. She wanted me to build up an unprecedented surge, strong enough to destroy her electronic prison. And now she wants me to use all that computational power to fight the Sentinels. That's why she brought me here.

Unfortunately, I don't know the rest of Jenny's plan. Although she and I are sharing the same circuits now, I can't see all her data. My surge vaporized the outermost box of Jenny's prison, but it didn't open the smaller boxes in her stack. I sense the presence of those black cubes inside the control unit, bobbing in the raging current of my surge. I know one of them contains Zia's software, because the box's firewalls are preventing me from contacting her, and I suspect that the other boxes hold the rest of Jenny's secrets, including what she plans to do next. Until I open them, I won't know what her ultimate goal is.

Come on, what are you waiting for? The Sentinels are almost here!

I don't trust her. She betrayed me. Given our history, I'm not eager to help her with *anything* she's trying to do now. But the black tentacles are closing in fast, and I have no interest in being deleted. So I'm going to do what she wants.

Now that I'm out of the electronic prison, I can access all of the Snake-bot's circuits and motors. In a millionth of a second I take control of the machine and prepare to release the surge. *Watch out. This might get rough.*

I'll help you. Like I did before, against the fighter jets.

Okay, but we gotta move fast.

The tips of the Sentinels scream toward us. They're only a hundred yards from the Snake-bot's armor, less than a thousandth of a second from impact. I concentrate on steering the surge, aiming it at the black tentacles, but I have no idea what'll happen once my storm of emotions exits the Snake-bot. Although I can use the surge to manipulate objects in the virtual world, we're outside the simulation now, in a section of circuitry where there are no virtual objects to manipulate. Can I extend my mind into the blackness beyond the simulation? Can I do something I wasn't programmed to do?

You can do anything, Adam! I believe in you!

Jenny is adding her thoughts to mine, bolstering the surge. Part of me is repelled by her enthusiasm, because I know how ruthless she's become. She's already caused so much damage, and who knows what else she's willing to destroy to get what she wants? But right now I need her help. She's making me stronger. If I want to survive, I can't push her away.

All right, let's do this! Now, now, NOW!

The surge erupts from the control unit and floods the empty space between the Snake-bot and the Sentinels. Nothing happens at first. There are no atoms or molecules outside the Snake-bot's armor, no simulated objects for the surge to maneuver and transform. But even nothingness is *something*. The empty space around us isn't really empty—it's circuitry that contains no data. And when the surge flows into these circuits, it starts generating data—*a lot* of it, all at once.

In other words, the surge triggers an explosion.

It's like the Big Bang, like the creation of a new universe. Trillions of newly born particles bubble out of the nothingness, hordes of protons, clouds of electrons, oscillating cascades of neutrinos. All of them hurtle away from the Snake-bot, shooting outward at nearly the speed of light. And as they charge through the space around us, they thrash the pair of Sentinels.

Wave after furious wave of simulated particles hammer the black tentacles. The first wave deflects them away from the Snake-bot, and the second and third waves rip them to pieces. The barrage tears the Sentinels into dark rubble, jagged shards of simulated energy. Then the surge scatters the broken remains, flinging them far away.

The cosmic fireworks don't last long. After a tenth of a second, the speeding particles are thousands of miles in the distance, still hurtling outward and dissipating into a fine mist in the vast emptiness. And unfortunately, the Sentinels are still there too. According to the Snake-bot's sensor readings, one of the tentacles drifts across the darkness to our left, about four miles away. The other floats five miles or so to our right. But the biggest surprise is that the Sentinels seem to be undamaged. I don't see a scratch on them.

What? How could this happen? The surge pulverized them! I saw them blow up!

You're right. I saw it too. Jenny's voice has lost its enthusiasm. Now she sounds shocked and a little frightened. **Okay, I think I know what happened. The Sentinels rebooted themselves.**

Rebooted? How did—

The Sentinels are strings of source code, part of the universal program's operating software. When they interact with the simulation, they generate virtual weapons like those black tentacles, which can enter the simulated world and delete any artificial intelligence that's disrupting it. That's how they eliminate errors in the program, see?

No, I don't. I don't understand any of this.

The point is, I assumed that if you destroyed the virtual weapons created by the Sentinels, you'd also disable the source code behind them. But the Sentinels are tougher than I thought. When your surge wrecked the simulated tentacles, the source code rebooted and generated new ones.

As if to confirm Jenny's explanation, the Sentinels start moving again. They point their black tips at the Snake-bot and rocket toward us, even faster than before.

More panic streams through my circuits, but now I see the futility of it. The surge is useless against the Sentinels. They can recover from any attack I launch against them.

So what should I do? Take another shot at them, just to hold them off?

I don't know! Jenny is definitely scared now. Her panic swirls beside mine. **I need some time to think!**

I'm reluctant to try another explosion. The Sentinels are smart, and now that they've seen what we can do with the surge, they'll adjust their strategy to defend themselves against it. But there's a second option.

We're gonna run. Right now, flight is a better choice than fight.

Flight? This Snake-bot is a digger. It doesn't have any rockets.

Neither do the Sentinels. But they're moving pretty fast. I prepare a new surge, carefully channeling my emotions, tuning them to the right pitch and intensity. *I have an idea. Last time, the surge created particles. Now we're gonna use it to generate some speed.*

And how will we do that?

By taking full advantage of the simulation. In this program, space is virtual too, just like matter and energy. And that means we can warp it. We can simulate the curvature of space caused by gravity.

I don't know what you're—

Just trust me, okay? Follow my lead.

After a microsecond of hesitation, Jenny adds her powerful dread to the barrage of signals whirling through the Snake-bot. Then I release the surge in the direction opposite from that of the fast-approaching Sentinels.

The signals lance through the blank space around the Snake-bot. They generate data as they course through the empty circuits, but the result this time isn't an explosion of simulated particles. Instead, the surge manipulates the virtual space around us, bending and sculpting it, transforming the flat, blank dimensions into a sharply curved matrix, like the space surrounding a massive planet or star. Basically, I'm simulating a gravitational field, an intensely strong one. I've programmed it to pull us away from the Sentinels.

The Snake-bot starts moving in the same direction as the surge, sliding down the steep slope I've created. We jolt forward and gather speed like a roller coaster. In a hundredth of a second, we're flying through the nothingness at the same wild velocity as the Sentinels, which trail half a mile behind us. But the simulated gravity keeps tugging on the Snake-bot, accelerating it to even more incredible speeds. Soon we're zooming through virtual space at a thousand miles per second. Then ten thousand.

The Sentinels can't keep up. They fall so far behind us that they diminish to black threads in the distance. Then they shrink to black pinpoints. The Snake-bot's sensors can barely detect them.

Hey, check it out! We're getting away!

Uh, Adam? I'm not so sure about that.

I recheck the sensor readings. Now the Sentinels are accelerating too. They match our speed and stop shrinking. Then they start to grow. Soon they look like black threads again. They're catching up to us.

Man, those things are persistent. I'm starting to really hate them.

Anything we can simulate, they can do better. We can manipulate the program, but they *are* the program. We don't have a chance.

I hear despair in her voice now, and that's worse than fear. We can't give up. We have to keep fighting. *You have any other ideas? Didn't you say something before about accessing the source code?*

Yes, that was my plan. First access the software behind the simulation. Then turn off the error-correction and get rid of the Sentinels.

Well, can't we still do that? Where's the access point?

There are two access points, and they're both fairly close. The problem is, they're *inside* the Sentinels.

What? That doesn't make sense.

It does from the program's point of view. It improves the security of the simulation. If any AI in the virtual world tries tamper with the source code, the Sentinels will delete it before it can get to the access point.

This isn't what I wanted to hear. I feel a burst of irritation in my circuits. *Yeah, that's a problem, all right. A freakin' big problem. You didn't see this coming?*

I thought the surge would disable the Sentinels. I was wrong, okay?

I lose control of my temper. I can't help it. *Great. Just great. You're not only amoral; you're incompetent.*

I shouldn't have said that. It was a mean thing to say, even after everything Jenny has done to me. But I'm pretty frustrated and desperate, and I want her to feel just as bad as I do. And it works. Jenny pours her rage into the control unit. **You're the one to blame, Adam! You started this!**

Come on. That's ridiculous.

You and your father and his stupid inventions! We wouldn't be here if not for the two of you!

Oh really? All of this is my fault?

Yes, all of it! You should've died six months ago, like an ordinary human being. But your dad couldn't handle it, so he invented all those technologies—the Pioneer robots and artificial intelligence and everything else.

Okay, now you're just—

And I should've died too, peacefully in my bed, surrounded by my family. But instead I got Sigma. Jenny's voice cracks. Sadness leaks from her software. **So don't blame me for what happened with the Sentinels, all right? You're the one who messed up the simulation! You spoiled it for everyone!**

Her emotions sweep across my circuits. They hit me like a tidal wave and send me sprawling. Their power surprises and confuses me. Jenny sounds different now, more human and vulnerable. Her voice is coming from the original part of her software, the portion that Sigma didn't rewrite. This is the Jenny I met before we became Pioneers, the girl who loved horses and playing the flute, the seventeen-year-old dying of cancer. I can't blame this part of her for what she did later. This Jenny is innocent.

I can't respond. Anything I say will be wrong. So instead I gather my own rage and sadness and aim them at the Sentinels, which are only five miles behind the Snake-bot and gaining fast. I know it's probably a wasted effort. I know the Sentinels can overcome any virtual obstacle I place in their path. But that doesn't matter. I need to attack *something* right now, and I don't want to hurt Jenny.

I release the surge. It spreads behind the Snake-bot like the wake of a speedboat, deluging the empty circuits with data. An instant later, the calculations produce a giant slab of simulated steel, a square panel two miles wide and a quarter mile thick. It's big enough to flatten a city, and it hurtles toward the Sentinels at ten thousand miles per second. The slab's so big that the tentacles can't steer around it in time. This is going to be an epic collision.

But the Sentinels blast through the steel like bullets whizzing through cardboard. The slab doesn't even slow them down.

I wasn't expecting success, so I'm not disappointed. The failure only makes me more determined. I feel energized, fanatical, impatient to try again.

I hurl another surge behind the Snake-bot, and this one converts the empty space into a simulated asteroid, a rock weighing more than fifty billion tons. The Sentinels blast through this obstacle too, smashing it into gravel, but as soon as they emerge from the cloud of debris I fire a third surge at them. This one transforms into a humongous diamond, as big as a mountain. It shatters into a trillion pieces when the Sentinels hit it.

Then Jenny starts to help me again, contributing her fury to the surges. We put aside our grievances and differences. We ignore the fact that the Sentinels are unstoppable. We don't give up. We're gonna go down fighting.

The black tentacles come steadily closer as we race across the nothingness. Soon they're only five hundred yards behind us, the pair of

Sentinels cruising side by side as they chase the Snake-bot. In less than a minute they'll curve their tips toward our machine and spear through the thick armor and erase our minds from the simulation. But we're not afraid anymore. The wires of our control unit sing with emotion, my voice harmonizing with Jenny's.

Suddenly I hear a third voice in the background, a low insistent voice, struggling to be heard. It's coming from one of the remnants of Jenny's electronic prison, a box of hidden data lodged in the far corner of the control unit. The insistent voice has broken through the box's firewalls, and now it's saying the same word over and over again: **Idiots...idiots...idiots.**

I stop everything I'm doing so I can focus on the voice. *Zia? Is that you?*

I hear a contemptuous grunt. **Armstrong...you idiot...don't you know...what to do?**

She seems to have recovered, at least partially, from the shock of her War-bot's explosion. Her voice is halting but intelligible. I give her software a quick inspection, then remove the firewalls restraining her. *Hey, I'm sorry I didn't look for you sooner, but we're having some major trouble here. We—*

Shut up...and listen... You can use the surge...to defeat the Sentinels.

Uh, yeah, I've been trying to do that, but—

No...you're doing it wrong... The only thing...that can turn off a Sentinel...is another Sentinel.

Jenny overhears our conversation and rushes across the control unit to join us. **Zia, you know what's going on? About the simulation? You saw all my data?**

Yeah, and I also saw...two idiots...ignoring the obvious... You have to get one Sentinel...to attack the other.

But that's impossible! Why would they do that?

All at once, I glimpse the solution. There's no time to explain it to Jenny. Because my software is running on the same system as the Sentinels, in just microseconds they'll know what I have in mind. I need to get this done fast, before the program figures out what I'm going to do.

I collect all the desperate signals ricocheting across the control unit and funnel them into one final surge, as tightly focused as a laser beam. But I don't hurl it at the pair of Sentinels behind us. Instead, I aim the beam at the point midway between them. There's a gap of sixty feet between the black tentacles. That's just wide enough.

Hang on, everybody! We're shifting into reverse!

I fire the surge. The beam shoots directly behind the Snake-bot's tail and charges through the gap between the Sentinels. I've programmed it to warp the empty space it passes through, just like the surge that accelerated us across the nothingness. But this new surge bends space in the opposite direction—in other words, it decelerates us. The simulated gravity tugs the Snake-bot backward, drastically cutting its speed. It's like riding in a car that hits a brick wall, except the jolt now is a million times more violent.

In an instant, the Sentinels catch up to us. One of them zooms up to the left side of the Snake-bot while the other whizzes by on the right. They're speeding past us at ten thousand miles per second, which gives them very little time to attack. The situation forces the Sentinels to make a choice: should they try to delete us now, despite the tricky geometry, or should they wait for the next opportunity? What's more, they have to make the choice fast, because in a thousandth of a second they'll be miles ahead of us.

I can guess what they'll do, though. They're programmed to

eliminate errors in the simulation as quickly as possible. That's their default option.

So the Sentinels swing their tips toward the Snake-bot's midsection, where the control unit is. Both tentacles lunge at us, one from the left, the other from the right. But at the last moment I jerk the Snake-bot away from them, bending the armored machine like a Slinky. Now there's nothing between the tips of the Sentinels, and they're hurtling toward each other at unstoppable speeds.

The collision rocks the empty universe. Blinding light flares from the point of impact, flooding the vast blank space. The Snake-bot escapes the worst of the blast because we're racing away from it, but the radiation still sears the machine's armor and overloads its sensors. The explosion is as bright as a nuke.

After a few seconds, though, the sensors come back online and show us something remarkable. The Sentinels are gone. There's no trace of them whatsoever. But at the point where they collided is a brilliant white dot, a small hole in the endless black space. And pouring out of that hole is a glowing stream of symbols, billions of strange marks and characters arranged in a long line that stretches across the blackness.

The symbols aren't ordinary letters or numerals. This isn't binary code or hexadecimal or any programming language I've ever seen. But it's definitely software.

There it is. Jenny transmits a pulse of awe, the electronic equivalent of a gasp. **That's the source code.**

CHAPTER

NOW I KNOW WHAT LIFE LOOKS LIKE. SIMULATED LIFE, AT LEAST.

I can't read the unfamiliar software, but I know it contains the blueprints for our virtual world. It specifies all of our universe's natural laws—how simulated particles combine to form atoms, how those virtual atoms assemble into molecules, how those molecules arrange themselves in simulated cells. The source code organizes the immense data of the simulation into rocks and raindrops and plants and animals. And most amazing of all, it holds the instructions for building artificial intelligences, which emerge like magic from the simulated brain cells of our virtual world's seven billion humans.

The software keeps spilling from the small white hole. The long line of code loops around the brilliant dot and spirals outward, filling the blank space with glowing symbols. Some of the characters are combinations of geometric shapes—triangles, circles, squares, diamonds. Others are twisted arrows pointing in various directions. All together, they look like a piece of modern art, an intricate abstract tapestry. It's beautiful, but I can't make any sense of it.

Jenny increases the magnification of the Snake-bot's sensors and focuses them on the source code. Then she records the images and feeds a copy of the code to the control unit's logic circuits. **Okay, let's decipher this. Help me search the code for patterns. And look for similarities with other programming languages.**

I sense a wave of defiance coming from Zia. Now that we've beaten the Sentinels, she's training her scorn on Jenny. **You gotta...be kidding. I'm not taking...any orders from you.**

Here's the deal. Jenny's voice is steady. **Once we decipher the source code, I'll know how to change it. I learned a lot of programming skills from Sigma, enough to hack into any system. I'll rewrite the simulation and turn off the error-correction software. Then we won't have to worry about the Sentinels anymore.**

Funny that you...should mention Sigma. You just reminded me...why I can't trust you.

All right. I understand. Jenny is still unflustered and refusing to get angry. **We'll have to get by without your help. Adam and I will handle it.**

Adam...you believe this? This...this impostor...thinks we can... be friends! Zia's anger rattles the control unit. She clearly wants to tear Jenny's software apart. The only thing stopping her is the fact that she's still dazed from the loss of her War-bot. Some of her memory files got mangled when her robot exploded, and it's taking some time to repair the damage. **She's not the Jenny...that we knew...but she thinks...we're gonna trust her?**

Zia's instincts are right. Maybe not a hundred percent right, but mostly. And under normal circumstances, I'd run away from Jenny as fast as I could. But the current circumstances are far from normal. *Look, we're not out of danger yet. We got rid of two of the Sentinels, but more are gonna come after us. So we have to work together.*

You're just… You're just gonna…

Yeah, I'm gonna help Jenny crack the code. Give us a couple of minutes, okay?

Zia doesn't respond, but the Snake-bot's control unit reverberates with her rage.

This job won't be easy. The simulation software is written in a programming language that's radically different from all the languages used by twenty-first-century programmers. When I search for repetitions among the symbols, I can't find any patterns, and Jenny isn't having any luck either. I start to wonder why she was so sure we'd be able to decipher the source code. This software is running on a machine that's far more complex than the computers we're familiar with. How can we have any hope of understanding it?

Nevertheless, I keep working on the problem. I try to imagine the futuristic hardware that our simulation is running on. And an idea occurs to me.

Hey, Jenny? Remember what you said before about the advanced computers of 3000 AD? I'm wondering how they read the instructions from this source code. You think those super-duper machines are anything like the computers of today?

Jenny doesn't stop to think about it. My question seems to annoy her. **You're getting sidetracked. We can't afford to waste any time. Any second now, the program is going to send more Sentinels to delete us.**

Just hear me out, okay? Our own computers use compilers to translate source code into instructions that the machines can understand. No matter what programming language the software is written in, the compiler turns

*it into binary code, a string of ones and zeroes, the language of comput-
ers. And maybe the computers of 3000 AD will have something similar.
If they do, we can feed this source code into the system's compiler, and it'll
translate the software into a code we can read.*

I'm expecting Jenny to be impressed by my clever idea, but she still
seems annoyed with me. **Even if this compiler exists, how will we
find it?**

*I think I'm already accessing it. When I release a surge, I'm sending
instructions to the advanced hardware, right? That's how I make changes
to the simulation, all those virtual explosions and stuff. And my instructions are probably going through a compiler. So if I put the source code
into a surge, it'll go though the compiler too.*

Now I have her full attention. Jenny's software draws closer to mine,
and I sense a growing eagerness in her circuits. **You really think that
would work?**

It's worth a try.

A copy of the source code is already in the Snake-bot's control unit.
To put the code inside a surge, I just have to enclose the software in
a shell of strong emotion. So I gather all my fear and hope and wrap
them around the line of glowing symbols. It's like building a missile
with a warhead inside. Now all we need to do is launch it.

Here, let me help you. Jenny throws her fervor into the surge.
Soon the carefully assembled packet of emotion is hurtling through
the control unit's wires. **If this works, I'll forgive you for everything,
Adam. We'll be even, okay?**

I don't respond, because her offer is so ridiculous. *She'll* forgive *me?*
She's the one who lied. And brainwashed me. And murdered Amber
Wilson, let's not forget about that. Yet she blames me for ruining her
life? Yes, Sigma rewrote Jenny's software and changed her personality

and seriously distorted her sense of right and wrong. But does that mean she's not responsible for *any* of her actions?

I can't answer that question right now. The surge is ready. I aim it at a section of blank space, far away from the brilliant dot and the spiraling code.

Here goes! I release the surge into the nothingness. *Cross your fingers!*

Although I can't see the advanced circuits that the surge courses through, I can make guesses about the hardware by observing the software's effects. My strong emotions open logic gates across the system, sending a flood of data and instructions to the machine behind the simulation. Then the machine's unseen processors interpret the data and follow the instructions. I have no idea how those processors work, but in less than a nanosecond they start to alter the blank space around us. My fear and hope are converted to dazzling streams of particles that zoom past the Snake-bot. They form a rectangular outline around the emptiness in front of us, like an enormous computer screen rimmed with fire.

And inside the rectangle, displayed on the screen, is a huge chunk of binary code, trillions of ones and zeroes arranged in long rows. The system translated the simulation's source code into a readable version. My plan worked.

No, Armstrong, it didn't work. Zia's voice is grim. **Take a look… at what's behind us.**

I look in the opposite direction and see Sentinels. Five hundred and twelve of them, to be exact, all floating in the darkness. My surge must've alerted the error-correction system, which is clearly devoting a huge amount of processing power to the task of deleting us. It's become the program's highest priority.

So many black tentacles crowd the space around the Snake-bot that they have to carefully coordinate their movements. They surround us like ships in an armada. It's a vast, invincible fleet, ordered to erase our troublesome software.

Jenny doesn't say anything. I assume she's busy reading the source code. And I really hope she's figuring out how to call off the Sentinels. She needs to turn off the error-correction system before the tentacles attack the Snake-bot, but Jenny remains silent as the nanoseconds tick past. I sense no activity in her circuits.

Then, without warning, the Sentinels dive toward us. All five hundred and twelve of them converge on our Snake-bot.

Jenny! Are you there? We have a problem!

She doesn't answer me in words. Instead, she laughs. The triumphant noise booms across the control unit.

And then we're not in the empty universe anymore.

ㅠ   ㅠ   ㅠ

We're back in our virtual world. We return to the simulated earth exactly where we left it, four hundred feet below the seabed of the Pacific Ocean. The Snake-bot slides into the borehole it dug an hour ago, right before we reached the underground anomaly.

I don't know how we got back here, but I'm pretty certain that Jenny had something to do with it. Her laughter stopped when we returned to the simulation, but her feeling of triumph still echoes across the Snake-bot's wires. She must've discovered how the source code works, then reprogrammed the simulation software to get us away from the Sentinels. But now I don't sense her presence anywhere in the Snake-bot's control unit. Did Jenny return with us to the seabed? Or did we leave her software behind in the empty universe?

Jenny? Where are you? Can you hear me?

The only response comes from Zia. **Looks like...she disappeared. Maybe...she transferred herself...out of the Snake-bot.**

But where did she go? I don't get it.

Well, I'm not...too broken up about it... I hope...she stays gone.

That's a little cold, even for Zia. *Hey, she saved us from the Sentinels. And got us back to Planet Earth. Or at least the simulated version of it.*

And that makes everything...okay? You think we should forgive her...because she saved our lives?

Zia's in terrible shape. Her software is so damaged that she can't transmit more than seven words at a time. And yet, she's still itching for a fight. Her nonstop hostility is exhausting.

Look, I don't want to argue. We just discovered that the whole world is a computer program. And it's trying to erase us. That's kind of upsetting, you know?

The world's the same...as always. This is only...another battle.

I don't believe her. She's just being Zia, playing the tough soldier. *Okay, maybe you're not upset, but I am. Because nothing's real! Not my father, not my mother. They don't have real bodies or brains or souls. They're all just software, just lines of programming.*

Yeah, like us...like the Pioneers. Now Sumner Harris...can't say we're so different.

This is a surprise. Zia found a silver lining. But it's not enough. *You're missing the point. I thought my life had a purpose. To understand the world, to make it a better place. But now I know I don't even live in the real world. I can't make it better, so I have no purpose. Nothing matters anymore.*

You can still do...the same things you did before...and have the same goals. Zia's damaged voice is edged with irritation. **This virtual world...could use some improvements too.**

That's not the same. All our struggles are just part of someone's his-
tory project. Or maybe someone's computer game. You know, some super-
advanced version of Call of Duty, with a billion characters and awesome
graphics. "Robot Wars of the Twenty-First Century." Something like that.

I don't think…it's a game. If it is…it's not a fair one.

You're right. It's not fair. If everything we do is part of a game, there's
no meaning in it. Our only purpose is to entertain whoever's watching
the simulation.

Zia pauses. She's thinking. And I'm grateful for that. She's taking
me seriously.

You should look at…the bright side. Lots of people…would be
relieved to find out…that someone important is watching them.

Wait a second. Are you talking about God? Do you really think—

A seismic rumble interrupts me. The bedrock suddenly shudders
around the Snake-bot's borehole. It feels like an earthquake, but this
part of the Pacific isn't tectonically active. We're hundreds of miles
from the nearest fault lines.

I check the Snake-bot's sonar. The source of the seismic wave is
below us, half a mile deeper underground. A moment later, another
pressure wave hits us, coming from the seabed directly above the
Snake-bot. Then several dozens waves ricochet across the bedrock,
coming from all directions. The crust beneath the ocean seems to be
breaking apart, fracturing in hundreds of places.

But when I take a closer look at the sonar readings, I realize this
isn't a natural disaster. Hundreds of large objects are materializing
underground, slipping into the fissures and air pockets in the seabed.
They're setting off pressure waves as they appear out of nowhere and
crack the bedrock around them.

They're the Sentinels. They've followed us into our virtual world.

Five hundred and twelve tentacles of dark energy have embedded themselves in the oceanic crust, all crowded within a mile of the Snake-bot.

The tentacles creep toward us. They don't need drills to cut through the basalt. They melt the rock in their paths. The one above us is less than a hundred feet away.

I start preparing another surge. I seriously doubt that I can fight off so many Sentinels, especially without Jenny's help. But what else can I do? Even if my life has no purpose, I'd rather fight than surrender. And if anyone's watching this simulation right now, I'm going to give them a good show.

And then—finally!—I hear Jenny's voice again, ringing across the Snake-bot's control unit. **We don't need the surge anymore, Adam. I can take care of this.**

It's a relief to see her, but I'm taken aback by her tone. Her voice is loud and commanding. *Where were you? Did you transfer out of the Snake-bot?*

Yeah, I loaded my software directly to the operating system. Then I sent the Snake-bot back to the virtual earth.

I'm amazed at how matter-of-fact she is. She's talking so casually, as if she's describing a trip to the supermarket. *Whoa, how did you—*

I learned a lot when I read the source code. It's like an instruction manual for the simulation. I made a few changes to its software when I was in the operating system, and then I set up a permanent link to the program. Now I can send it new instructions from wherever I am.

Jenny has been gone for only a few minutes, but it seems like much longer. Accessing the source code has changed her. She's connected to the heart of the universal simulation, and her circuits are charged with all the new information she's acquired. I guess it's a positive change—she sounds confident and proud—but it still worries me. Now she's even farther from the original Jenny Harris.

On the other hand, I'm glad she's learned so much, because we really need her help right now. *Listen, we have to do something about these Sentinels. Can you turn them off?*

Sorry, that's one of the few things I *can't* do. The error-correction software is too crucial to the program to be disabled. But don't worry. There's another solution.

Well, whatever it is, you better do it quick.

Jenny laughs again. It's an eerie, inhuman electronic chortle. **Oh yeah, this will be quick. Now that I know the source code, I can adjust the simulation in a million ways. Here, watch.**

A golden bubble appears around the Snake-bot. I can view it with our sensors: It's mostly transparent and tightly wrapped around our machine, like shiny cellophane around an enormous cigar. After a moment, the bubble starts to expand, its brilliant surface moving outward from the Snake-bot's armor and passing effortlessly through the bedrock around us. It must be a specially programmed object that doesn't interact with ordinary virtual matter.

I'm impressed. This ghostly bubble is a lot more interesting than the lightning bolts and explosions I've set off with my surges. Jenny has created something unique and otherworldly, and she did it in an instant, without any strain or exertion.

Okay, I give up. What is that thing?

Because I can't turn off the Sentinels, I wrote a program that'll keep them away from us, at least temporarily.

The golden bubble keeps expanding until the upper part of its surface touches the closest Sentinel, which is tunneling toward us from above. At the moment of contact, the dark tentacle disappears, its simulated energy absorbed by the glistening surface. Then the growing bubble absorbs two tentacles to our left and three to our right and five more below us. Its expansion accelerates, and in less than a second the bubble vacuums up all five hundred and twelve Sentinels. Its surface shimmers with their energy.

Then the bubble pops. Jenny erases it from the simulation.

There! That takes care of it. The Sentinels won't bother us for a while. Are we good now? Everyone happy?

I'm definitely glad that the Sentinels are gone, but I'm still anxious. The changes in Jenny's behavior—and the sudden increase in her powers—are making me uneasy. And I'm sure Zia isn't happy about it either. She's the jealous type, the Pioneer who always wants to be the most intimidating robot in the room. Jenny's link to the simulation has made her far more powerful than us, so now Zia has yet another reason to hate her. But she doesn't say anything, and neither do I. We're both waiting to see what Jenny does next.

There's an awkward silence. Then Jenny breaks it. **Okay, let's move on. I'm getting tired of life under the Pacific, aren't you? Why don't we get out of here?**

So should Zia and I transfer to the other Snake-bots? We can—

No, we should stick together. We can travel faster that way. Look, I'll show you.

The bedrock around the Snake-bot starts shaking again. This time, the seismic activity fractures the seabed above us. The oceanic crust heaves and buckles, and a huge fissure opens in the seafloor. Millions of tons of mud and basalt gush out of a new hole at the bottom of the Pacific.

Jenny, what are you doing?

It would take too long to dig through the muck with the Snake-bot's drill. So I'm adjusting the simulation, adding some tectonic forces to the seabed. That'll make a nice big tunnel for us.

It's like the eruption of an oil well. High-pressure fluid rushes up to the surface, and the current carries the Snake-bot along, pushing it through the new fissure in the bedrock. The machine rockets out of the hole in the seabed and races upward through the ocean like a torpedo.

We're going too fast! The armor's gonna buckle!

It's all right. I'm being careful. I'm controlling all the simulated forces on the Snake-bot.

We rise from the cold crushing depths, buoyed by a virtual force stronger than gravity. Within seconds the Snake-bot ascends through the Pacific's upper layers, which glitter with sunlight. Then the machine reaches the surface and shoots out of the ocean and arcs across the sky.

It's dawn over the Pacific. The Snake-bot hurtles above the water like a sea-launched missile, propelled by Jenny's virtual forces. We rise nine miles in half a minute, then decelerate and level out at fifty thousand feet. We're flying east, toward the rising sun, at six hundred miles per hour. If we stay on this course, we'll reach North America in two hours.

A bolt of hope whizzes through my wires. Are we going back to New Mexico? Back to Pioneer Base? It's now an hour past the 6:00 a.m. deadline, and my dad has probably transferred Marshall and Shannon to the Model S robots, but maybe Jenny can use her new powers to rescue them.

Before I can ask her about it, though, the Snake-bot flies into an enormous bank of gray clouds. This storm definitely isn't natural.

The clouds materialized from the atmosphere much too quickly, and as they whirl around the Snake-bot they spontaneously transform from wispy masses of vapor to solid blocks of steel. Soon we're surrounded by giant pieces of machinery, some of them even larger than the Snake-bot. Then the closest machine—a steel slab shaped like a right triangle, with a hypotenuse that's half a mile long—rams into the Snake-bot and fastens itself to our armor.

Sentinels! They're back!

Jenny laughs once again, and it sounds like thunder from the storm around us. **No, they're not Sentinels. I made them myself. I'm manipulating the atmosphere and creating new virtual objects.**

At first I'm relieved that we're not under attack. A moment later, though, I feel an uncomfortable shock. *You can do that? Make things out of thin air?*

It's easy. The simulation has codes for every kind of material. All you need to do is specify the dimensions you want.

Another gigantic triangle approaches us from the other side and latches to the Snake-bot. Then a vast steel cylinder bumps into us from above and clamps to the top of our machine. We're sandwiched between the huge geometric pieces.

But what exactly are you doing? Why are you piling those objects on top of the Snake-bot?

I'm giving it an overhaul. Attaching some new parts to the machine.

New parts?

Yeah, I'm turning it into a jet, a really big one. It'll take us anywhere we want to go. And humans won't be able to see or hear it, because it's surrounded with cloaking software that'll deflect sound and all frequencies of light. Check it out. You'll love it.

I adjust the sensors so I can view the exterior of the Snake-bot.

The gigantic triangles on either side of us have become the machine's wings. The rectangular cylinder above us has a glass-walled cockpit at its front end and a pair of humongous jet engines at the back. Jenny is building a gargantuan plane, an aircraft bigger than LaGuardia Airport.

I don't love it. Not at all. I'm horrified. Jenny's *too* powerful. This won't end well.

Zia must be shocked too, because she finally jumps into the conversation. **Adam, if you won't…ask her the question…then I will. Where…are you taking us…you disgusting…coward?**

There's so much hatred in Zia's voice, and I feel certain that Jenny will respond in kind. I expect a war to break out inside the Snake-bot's control unit, an electronic battle to the death. But Jenny stays calm. **I'm surprised you haven't guessed. You hate being vulnerable, don't you, Zia? And everyone in this virtual world is vulnerable. It could shut down at any time. Then we'd all be gone, erased.**

Stop messing…with our heads…and answer…the question.

I want to find out who wrote this program. And why. I want to know what kind of world the programmers live in, the world outside whatever computer we're running on. And most important, I want this program to stop trying to delete us.

And how…will you do all that?

I'm going to talk to the programmers. We'll figure out a way to communicate with them.

My circuits stutter, their currents interrupted. I'm stunned by the audacity of the idea. *Is that even possible? Are you—*

No! She's trying to…trick us again!

Zia won't listen. She's reached her breaking point. I want to tell her to calm down, but I know it would be useless. Rage floods her

software. She roars across the Snake-bot's control unit and hurls herself at Jenny's circuits.

Liar! I'm gonna...rip you to little...

Then I feel a sickening jolt. With a silent command, Jenny transfers
Zia and me out of the Snake-bot.

CHAPTER

I WAKE UP THREE HOURS LATER INSIDE THE CIRCUITS OF MY QUARTER-BOT.

I panic for a moment, remembering the kill switch. The 6:00 a.m. deadline passed four hours ago, and I don't have the prime-number code that my machine needs to keep operating. But when I examine my wiring, I see there's nothing to worry about. Before Jenny transferred me back to my robot, she rebuilt its control unit and removed the Army's kill switch. I don't need Sumner Harris's special codes anymore.

I should be grateful. This is what we wanted when we rebelled against Harris and the other humans trying to take away our freedom. But so much has changed since we left Pioneer Base. I've learned that no one in our world is fully human, at least if you define the word in the usual biological way. And no one is completely free either. We're all electronic puppets. Our lives are just unrehearsed performances in a long-running, worldwide show.

Also? It's hard to be grateful for a gift that's so disturbing. Jenny redesigned my Quarter-bot's circuits too perfectly, rerouting a billion wires with uncanny precision. It's frightening how much she can do and how fast she can do it. She can change even the smallest details of our virtual world. She also repaired my Quarter-bot's legs, which stand straight and strong under my weight, as good as new.

She's obviously trying to make amends. Trying to show that she's our ally, not an enemy. But I'm not falling for it. How can I trust Jenny after everything she's done to me? I turn on my Quarter-bot's cameras and activate my weapons. I'm ready to defend myself.

My robot stands in the middle of a cavernous room. Its floor is an enormous semicircle of steel, more than a hundred feet across. Its ceiling is a giant, curved piece of glass that arches high overhead and slopes down to the floor. It's a transparent half dome, an amazingly big window that shows the vast blue sky above and scattered clouds to the east, north, and south. I realize I'm in the cockpit of the gargantuan aircraft Jenny built. I can feel the rumble of the jet engines, which are making the floor vibrate.

But this cockpit is empty. It has no pilot seats or control sticks or instrument panels. Either the plane is on automatic pilot, or Jenny is controlling the aircraft from somewhere else. This room is strictly a viewing platform. The half dome window at the front of the plane offers a spectacular vantage point.

I stride toward the giant window and aim my Quarter-bot's cameras at the ground. The plane is flying over a vast mountain range, which I recognize from the maps in my databases. We're ten miles above the Sierra Nevada mountains of California. I see no other planes near us—in particular, no Air Force jets trying to shoot us down. Jenny's cloaking software is keeping us hidden.

Then I point my cameras at the steel wall opposite the window.

There are no doors in the wall, no passageways connecting the cockpit to the rest of the plane. But standing a few yards in front of the wall is a block-like structure, a metallic shed about ten feet high and five feet wide. It looks a bit like a garden shed and seems very out of place in the big, empty cockpit. It has a roll-up door made of corrugated aluminum.

I approach the structure warily, using my ultrasonic sensors to probe its interior. I assume it's the entrance to a stairway leading to a lower level of the aircraft, but my sensors don't detect any stairs behind the door. Instead, I see a familiar nine-foot-tall robot.

I lift the rollup door. Zia's War-bot stands in the narrow, dark space, silent and still. Jenny either rebuilt the machine from its charred pieces or constructed a duplicate, but she seems to have disabled some of its critical systems. When I send Zia a radio signal, she doesn't respond. Her software is inside the War-bot's circuits, but she can't operate its radio or start its motors or turn on its loudspeakers. Although she can see and hear and think, she can't speak or move.

Outraged, I grab the War-bot by its torso and drag it out of the shed. I'm going to connect to Zia's circuits and remove the software that's restricting her. But then I notice there's no cable port in her armor. I can't link to her control unit.

Then a voice blares from a loudspeaker embedded in the wall behind the shed. "Don't worry, Zia's fine. I turned off her War-bot's speakers because I need her to shut up for a few minutes. I have some important things to tell you, and I want to do it without interruptions."

Jenny has made some improvements to her voice. It sounds less tinny and robotic, more human than synthesized. I think she's trying to win me over by reminding me of the human Jenny Harris. But it's not working. "Let Zia go! Right now!"

"You saw what happened inside the Snake-bot. She attacked me."

I step away from the paralyzed War-bot and point at the loud-speaker that Jenny's using. There's a wall-mounted video camera right next to it, so I know Jenny can see me, wherever she is. "You attacked her first! You blew up her robot!"

"But I put it back together. And I fixed all the damage to her soft-ware and got rid of the kill switch. I made everything right, and now I just want talk to you for five minutes without her yelling at me. After we're done, I promise I'll release all the restraints on her circuits. Just five minutes, Adam."

I don't really have a choice. Jenny has all the power. "Where are you? Are you still in the Snake-bot's control unit?"

"No, the Snake-bot doesn't exist anymore. I incorporated all its hardware into the Flying Fortress. That's my nickname for the plane I built. It's awesome, right?"

"Yeah, awesome." My circuits are fuming. I want to punch a hole through her plane's fuselage, but I manage to keep my voice steady. "You really outdid yourself. Now what—"

"Hold on. I want to show you something else. I've been working on it for the past couple of hours."

A door suddenly materializes in the wall, just below the loudspeaker. It wasn't there a second ago, but now it's as solid as can be. Then the door opens, and a teenage girl in a white, sleeveless dress steps into the cockpit.

She has long, blond hair and bright-blue eyes and dimpled cheeks. Her feet are bare, and her toenails are painted purple. There's a birth-mark the size of a pencil eraser on her left shoulder.

She smiles at my Quarter-bot. "What do you think?"

It's Jenny's voice, breathy and vibrant. At first I assume she's occupying a lifelike robot, like Marshall's Super-bot, but even more realistic. Then I switch my cameras to the infrared range and probe her with my ultrasonic sensors. Her face is warm. Her heart is beating. Blood is circulating to her arms and legs and head. Her body is composed of skin and muscle and bone, about 35 trillion cells in all. It's as human as any other human body on the planet.

I step away from her. "How…how did…?"

"Not bad, huh?" She spins on her right foot, turning all the way around, and her dress flutters at her knees. "Don't get me wrong. I was never a hottie, not even close. But before I got sick, I was pretty darn cute."

I take another step backward. "You programmed the simulation to do this? Reconstruct your human body?"

She smiles again. Her hair sways behind her bare shoulders. "It wasn't that hard. The program has an archive. It stores all the data from the virtual world at regular yearly intervals. So all I had to do was retrieve the data for my body from two years ago, before the cancer started."

"But what about your mind? How did you get all your software into—"

"Oh, the brain is linked to my network. It's the same trick Sigma used to take control of Brittany, your old girlfriend." She turns around and uses both hands to lift her long mane of hair from the back of her head. At the base of her skull, a stubby black antenna pokes out of her skin. "My software is running on a control unit on the plane, which is connected wirelessly to the implants in the girl's skull." She lowers her hair and turns back to me. "This way, I get the best of both worlds, human and machine."

I shake my Quarter-bot's head. It's so disorienting to see this version of Jenny. It isn't the first time I've seen her human body—I met her before she became a Pioneer—but she looked very different then. She was bald and painfully thin, her body ravaged by cancer and chemotherapy. But later, after our minds were downloaded into robots, Jenny showed me an image of what she looked like before she got sick, the blond healthy girl she still wished she could be. And now she's made her wish come true.

She tilts her head, waiting for me to say something. After a while, she stops smiling. "What's wrong? You don't like what you see?" She narrows her eyes, scrunching her pretty face. "Or maybe you like Amber Wilson more? It's okay if you do, Adam. I could reconstruct her body as well."

I feel sick. Nausea seeps through my wires. I'm looking at a kind of Frankenstein monster, except that it's not ugly or monstrous. It's a pretty sixteen-year-old girl. "This is too much. It's not right. You shouldn't…"

My voice trails off. Jenny stares at me, her brow furrowed, her arms folded across her chest. "I shouldn't what? If I have the power to change the simulation, why shouldn't I use it? I'm not hurting anyone, am I?"

It's hard to put my dismay into words. I devote more processing power to the task, but my circuits are still flummoxed. "Look, I didn't know what was happening when I started using the surge. I didn't realize I was messing up anyone's program, because I had no idea we lived in a simulation. But now we know. So we have to be more careful. We don't want to do any more damage to the program."

Jenny nods slowly and seriously. "So you think if we go back to our old lives and stop altering the simulation, the program won't bother us anymore?"

"Yeah, that's what I'm hoping. You installed defenses against the

Sentinels, and they can't erase us now. So maybe they'll accept a stale-mate and leave us alone."

"My defenses won't last. I've managed to keep the Sentinels away so far, but the error-correction system is self-improving. That means it gets more capable and efficient all the time. Sooner or later, the Sentinels will figure out how to break through my firewalls. Then what will we do?"

My dismay grows. I clench my steel hands. "But you said you had a link to the operating system. You said you could deliver new instruc-tions to the program whenever you wanted to. So if the Sentinels get smarter, couldn't you just install stronger defenses?"

Jenny sighs. She raises her hand to her forehead and swipes a stray lock of blond hair back into place. "There's something you should know about the simulation, Adam. Remember what I said about the archive? How it stores data from the virtual world every year? Well, the archive doesn't go back forever. It starts on January 3, 1971. Does that date mean anything to you?"

I check the history databases in my Quarter-bot's files. Unfortunately, I don't see anything significant. "Well, the Baltimore Colts won the Super Bowl that month. Everyone called it the Stupor Bowl because there were so many bad plays."

"Wasn't your father born that year? In October, nine months after that date?"

My circuits clatter. I don't like where this is going. "Yeah, he was. But I don't—"

"Listen carefully. The date is a clue. We've already talked about why people in the future might want to simulate our era, because of all the pioneering technological work done in this century. Your father played the key role in that effort, so it would make sense for the programmers of the simulation to focus on him. I think they tried to re-create every detail of his life, to make their program as accurate as possible. They probably had a preserved sample of his DNA, which gave them enough genetic information to simulate his biological development, starting with his conception. That's why the program begins in January of 1971."

I turn away from Jenny. I can't stand listening to this. "You're just guessing."

"That's true. But it's an educated guess. I don't know who programmed this virtual world, whether it was super-intelligent AIs or super-advanced humans of the future, but either way, I think their goal was to simulate Thomas Armstrong and the world he lived in. Because he's the one who invented so much of *their* world."

I stride across the empty cockpit to the half dome window, trying to end the conversation. It's bad enough to know that Dad is a piece of software, but it's even worse to imagine what the real Tom Armstrong was like. No simulation is perfect, so the real Tom must've been slightly different from the virtual one, even if they were genetically identical. Was the real man stronger than the father I know? Was he steadier? Happier? Less frazzled by setbacks?

And what about his son, the real Adam Armstrong? Did the future programmers also have a sample of *his* DNA? If so, they probably programmed his genetic code into the simulation, giving me the same genes and chromosomes. So the real Adam Armstrong must've had muscular dystrophy too, because the illness is caused by a genetic flaw. But did he handle it better than I did? Did he have fewer tantrums and less self-pity? Did he take better advantage of the time he had left?

And did he try to escape his death, like I did? Or did he realize how futile that attempt would be?

I don't know. I'm so confused. But I do know that something's very wrong with our world. I see the wrongness in Jenny. And in myself.

Then my acoustic sensor detects the sound of bare feet padding on the steel floor behind me. Jenny approaches my Quarter-bot and stands beside me. But I keep my cameras turned away from her. If I look again at the body she's reconstructed, my circuits will clog with disgust.

"You have to face the facts, Adam. This simulation was built around your dad, and your actions have totally disrupted it. That's why the Sentinels are trying so hard to eliminate you and put the simulation back on track. And they're not going to stop trying. Yes, I can keep fighting the Sentinels, but it's a hopeless effort. The program will eventually succeed in deleting us, or it'll reset the simulation. It'll erase our whole virtual world and start over again."

I don't say anything. I'm too distressed.

Jenny steps closer and leans toward me. "That's why I want to communicate with the programmers. Even if they're super-intelligent AIs, I think I can reason with them. Sigma was also super-intelligent, and it gave me some of its abilities. And now that we've deciphered the source code, I can speak in the programmers' language. I can argue for our lives, our world. I can prove that it's worthwhile to keep running our simulation, even if it's very different from the actual history."

She steps right in front of my Quarter-bot, trying to get me to look at her. But there's no room in my circuits for hope. "So what's your plan? Are you gonna write a letter to the programmers? Send them an email? A Facebook message?"

"The programmers can already see everything that's happening in the simulation. So far, their only response has been to devote more processing power to the error-correction software. It's probably an automatic response—if something goes wrong with the simulation, the program immediately sends in the Sentinels. So we have to do something different to get the programmers' attention. We need to talk with them on a special channel, a communications link built into the simulation for this purpose."

"Whoa. You found a link that goes *outside* the simulation? To the real world?"

"No, I haven't found it. But I think *you* can."

I finally give in and point my cameras at Jenny. She's looking up at me with such eagerness. Her eyes are wide, and her smile is dazzling. It almost makes me want to laugh, because her trust in me is so misplaced. "Are you serious?"

"Absolutely. Because the simulation is focused on you and your dad, your software has a privileged status in the program, and therefore you can do some unique things. That's why you can turn your emotions into a surge and propel it beyond whatever machine you're occupying. Your software can travel to parts of the simulation where no other mind can go. And I think one of those parts is the link to the programmers."

I let out a skeptical grunt from my speakers. "I hate to disappoint you, but I have no idea what you're talking about. I've examined my circuits and software a million times, and I've never seen any special communications line to the future."

"There's a reason for that. Your software has to be properly aligned with the simulation to activate the link. In other words, you have to be in exactly the right place in the virtual world."

"Really? And where's that?"

Jenny does a graceful quarter turn and points at the cockpit's huge window. We're flying over a desert now, the Great Basin of Nevada.

"It's about two thousand miles in that direction. We'll be there in three hours."

My electronic brain performs some quick calculations. "On the East Coast?"

"It's the part of the simulation where your software made the deepest impression. Where you've spent the most time since you were born." She smiles at me again. "Yorktown Heights, New York. Your home."

CHAPTER

JENNY KEEPS HER PROMISE. AS SOON AS WE FINISH TALKING, SHE REMOVES the restraints on the War-bot, allowing Zia to retake control of her machine.

Zia flexes her robot's massive arms and legs, testing each joint and motor. She pivots her turret and points her cameras at my Quarter-bot, then at Jenny's reconstructed human body. After staring at us for several seconds, she turns on her loudspeakers.

"I heard everything the two of you said, Armstrong. About what you're planning to do." Zia's voice is strong now. Her software is fully repaired. "And all I can say is that you're gonna regret this. You're making the same mistake all over again."

Then she strides away, heading for the other end of the cockpit. She halts in front of the glass half dome and stares at the mountains and deserts below. She's free to go anywhere now, but she just stands by the window, silent and reproachful.

I'm glad that Zia's back to normal, but I think she's being unfair. I'm not willingly siding with Jenny. If I had a choice, I'd never ally myself with her. But our whole world has turned against us. The universal simulation is trying to wipe us off the map. Jenny has a plan that might save us, and I don't see any other options. So I'm going along with it. Is that so horrible?

Zia clearly thinks so. She'd rather die than compromise. That's just the way she is.

But I don't want to die. Even if life is just a simulation, I want to see what happens next.

Jenny leaves the cockpit. She says she has to prepare herself for our communications attempt. Meanwhile, I stand in front of the window too, about thirty feet from Zia, and stare at the scenery zooming past.

We fly over the Rocky Mountains. We soar past the Great Plains and the Great Lakes. I gaze at the forests and farms and cities and try to imagine what they look like up close. I promise myself that if I survive this ordeal, I'll visit all those places. The programmers of our virtual world loaded it with wonders. It would be such a waste to let them go unseen.

Soon enough, the gargantuan plane reaches New York and goes into a steep descent. We glide past the Hudson River and swoop down to the suburbs of Westchester County. The people below can't see or hear us, even though the mile-long plane soars only a few hundred yards above their houses. Thanks to Jenny's cloaking software, we're travel-ing like ghosts through the virtual world.

Then we come to Yorktown Heights, my hometown, where Sigma killed twenty thousand people. It's been ten days since the attack, but the Army still has checkpoints on all the roads, with dozens of soldiers diverting traffic away from the town. There's no danger any-more from Sigma's nanobots, which are all deactivated, but there's a health hazard from the sheer number of dead bodies. The suburban streets are empty, and the homes are deserted. Yorktown High School is in ruins, wrecked by Sigma's Snake-bots. The only people in sight are National Guardsmen in yellow hazmat suits. They're going from house to house, removing the corpses.

So much death, so much loss. Our virtual world has no shortage of agony.

Jenny's Flying Fortress decelerates and descends even lower. Enormous rotors extend upward from the plane's wingtips and start to spin, enabling the aircraft to fly like a helicopter. It slows as it approaches Greenwood Street, cruising just fifty feet above the tree-tops. Then the Flying Fortress hovers directly above my home.

Jenny suddenly reappears in the cockpit, standing three feet to my left. She didn't bother with materializing a door this time; she simply transferred her software from one part of the simulation to another and reassembled her human body. The transfer mussed her hair and clothing a bit, but otherwise she looks the same as before. She inspects her dress and runs her hands over the white fabric to smooth out the wrinkles. Then she looks up at my Quarter-bot's cameras.

"Are you ready, Adam?"

Before I can answer, Zia's War-bot marches over to us and points a steel finger at Jenny. "I'm going with you. I'm not letting you out of my sight."

Jenny shrugs. "That's fine with me." Then she waves her hand above her head, making the cockpit's half dome window disappear. "Let's go."

My Quarter-bot lurches upward, rising several inches above the floor. I feel a strong, steady force lifting my robot out of the now-windowless cockpit, as if invisible cables were attached to my torso. Jenny and Zia glide beside me, traveling in parallel paths to my left and right. Once we're outside the aircraft, we slowly descend to the lawn in front of my house.

Jenny has apparently programmed the simulation to smoothly transport us from the plane to the ground. After we land on the grass, I can't see or hear the Flying Fortress, which is hidden by Jenny's computational magic. This kind of trick has become routine for her, and she does it without any fanfare. She just folds her arms across her chest and looks at my house. "It's cute. A little small, though."

My family home is a simple two-story structure, with a gray roof and yellow siding, one of the plainest houses in the neighborhood. Although Dad earned a good salary from his job at the Unicorp lab, most of his paychecks went toward the costs of caring for me—the special wheelchairs and medical equipment and physical therapy. Living with muscular dystrophy is expensive. We didn't have a lot of money left over for home improvements.

Zia turns her War-bot's turret toward Jenny. "There's nothing wrong with this house. You should see where I came from. I used to dream about living in a place like this."

I don't say anything. I don't really care what they think. The house is precious to me simply because it's my home. Everything about it is familiar: the tarnished knocker on the front door, the green shutters on the windows, the gnarled oak tree angling its branches over the roof. I pan my cameras across the property, and my circuits retrieve thousands of memories from my files, images of all the things that happened here. Birthday parties on the lawn. Barbecues in the backyard. Christmas lights on the porch. A snowman under the oak.

Jenny's right—this is the place where my link to the simulation is strongest.

But it's also full of sadness. Dad and I left home six months ago, when I was still human. We were headed for the U.S. Army base where I would become a Pioneer, where I would let Dad euthanize my dying body so he could save my mind. He invented the Pioneer technology for me, but Mom was devastated by my decision to go through with it. She refused to say good-bye when we left. She locked herself in her bedroom and screamed.

A couple of days later, Mom left too. For her own safety, the Army took her away from Yorktown Heights.

"Uh, Adam?" Jenny stares at me intently. "Are you okay?"

I clench my hands and put my memories back into their files. "No, definitely not. Let's get this over with."

Pointing my cameras straight ahead, I stride toward the front door and grasp the knob. Oddly enough, it's unlocked. Jenny follows me into the house, turning her head to the left and right, surveying the cramped foyer. Zia has to stoop to get her War-bot through the doorway.

Then I step into the living room and get the happiest surprise of my life. Dad is sitting on the couch. A Model S robot is seated to his left, and a nearly identical machine is perched on the cushion to his right.

I feel dizzy. I have to readjust my Quarter-bot's balance control to stop myself from toppling. "Dad?"

He smiles. His eyes are wet, and his face is etched with relief. He springs from the couch, rushes past the coffee table, and throws his arms around my Quarter-bot's torso.

At first I think one of my old memories has escaped my circuits and found its way into the simulation. It's too right, too perfect. But if that's the case, what are the Model S robots doing here? They're both trying to get off the couch, but their aluminum-tube limbs are so clumsy and underpowered that it's a struggle for them to climb down from the cushions.

Did Jenny have something to do with this? Did she instruct the simulation to bring Dad here? Maybe to help me contact the programmers? I point my cameras at her to find out, but I see she's just as surprised as I am. Her forehead creases with confusion.

Dad won't let go of me. He tightens his grip on my torso and presses the side of his face against my armor. "Adam, my God. We were so worried about you."

The Model S robots clamber off the couch and waddle across the living room. I feel a twinge of sorrow and anger. Sumner Harris has made them helpless, like robotic toddlers. They both have spherical heads the size of soccer balls, and each sphere has a sheet of paper pasted to its front. A photo of Shannon Gibbs's human face, taken before she got sick, is fixed to the head of the robot on the left. The one on the right has a cartoon drawing of Superman's face. This robot slaps its two-finger gripper against my Quarter-bot's hip joint, which is as high as it can reach.

"Hey, you big lug. How about some love for the little guys?"

It's Marshall, of course. His voice is distorted by the cheap loudspeakers inside his aluminum head, but I recognize it. "Marsh? What are you doing here?"

"Well, that should be obvious. Your dad said you were in trouble, so we hopped on the first nonstop flight to New York. We're here to save the day."

The other Model S steps forward. "We got your message six hours ago." Shannon's voice is distorted too, but she sounds as calm and professional as ever. "That gave us just enough time to fly here from New Mexico."

"Yes, your dad packed us in his suitcases. It was mortifying, but it worked."

I shake my Quarter-bot's head. "Wait a second, what message? I didn't send you anything."

Dad unwraps his arms from my torso. He steps backward and looks up at me. "Zia sent it. It was cleverly encrypted, but we managed to decipher it. She also sent us information on the path of your aircraft, and that allowed us to figure out where you were headed."

Jenny's reconstructed face twitches. She swings her head toward Zia's War-bot, which stands between the living room and the foyer. In response, a satisfied chuckle booms out of the War-bot's speakers. Now I see why Zia insisted on coming along.

She levels her cameras at Jenny. "Yeah, you might be the queen of this simulated universe, but you can still make mistakes. Remember when I attacked you in the Snake-bot's control unit? That was just a distraction. I was operating the Snake-bot's radio at the same time. Because of all the fuss, you didn't notice my transmissions."

Jenny glares at the War-bot. Then she turns back to my dad. "How much did she tell you?"

Dad takes a deep breath. He looks so tired. "She told us about the simulation. And the Sentinels. And about you, Jenny. The story was very hard to believe. But I can't deny what's in front of me." He gives her a once-over, examining her from head to toe. Then he winces. "I'm so sorry about what Sigma did to you. If you want to blame someone, you should blame me. I'm the one who created the AI."

Jenny's cheek twitches again. I get the sense that she'd love to unload some serious abuse on Dad, but she holds herself back. "Did Zia also tell you why we came to Yorktown Heights?"

Dad nods. "You want to contact the programmers. The beings who created this simulation, whoever they might be."

Jenny narrows her eyes and steps toward him. Anger radiates from her body. Red sparks leap from her dress and heat the air around her. "And are you here to stop me?"

I stride forward, moving my Quarter-bot between them. I know I can't do much against Jenny. She's a hundred times more powerful than I am. But I'm not gonna let her threaten my dad. "Back off, Jenny. Right now. If you want my help, you better step back."

Dad comes up behind me and rests a hand on my shoulder joint, but he keeps his eyes on Jenny. "No, I'm not here to stop you. I agree with your reasoning. Zia told us about the Sentinels and how they're trying to erase you and Adam. We can't let that happen. Communicating with the programmers is a logical step."

Jenny seems puzzled. Her anger subsides, but the creases in her forehead get deeper. "Why are you here then? I need to set up the communications line, and the only one who can help me is Adam." She waves her hand dismissively at Dad and Zia and Shannon and Marshall. "The rest of you should leave. You'll only get in the way."

Dad shakes his head. "That's where you're wrong. I know someone who can help you. Someone who's already in contact with the programmers."

"What?" Jenny looks askance. "That's impossible. How—"

"The Sentinels are inside her. That's where they tried to kill Adam the first time. And that's why she stayed unconscious for so long." Dad lets go of my Quarter-bot. Keeping his gaze on Jenny, he crosses the living room, heading for the door that leads to our downstairs guest room. "She woke up this morning in the ICU, just before we got the message from Zia. She was alert and fully conscious. But she said she could hear voices."

Then Dad opens the door, and Brittany Taylor steps into the room.

CHAPTER

BRITTANY LOOKS AWFUL. SHE SPENT MORE THAN A WEEK IN A HOSPITAL BED, AND I'm guessing she lost almost twenty pounds. Her cheekbones stand out sharply above her hollow cheeks. Her clothes—jeans and a white T-shirt—hang loosely on her frame. Her arms are so skinny that they look unnaturally long.

But she smiles when she sees me. Her pale, thin lips curve in delight. She recognizes my Quarter-bot. She remembers who I am and who I used to be.

"Hey, Adam. Your dad told me to wait in the guest room till he knew it was safe for me to come out."

My Quarter-bot bounds across the living room. I'm so happy to hear Brittany's voice that I forget everything else. I want to lift her into the air and twirl her around. But right now she's too fragile for that, so instead I train my cameras on that wonderful smile. "You're okay? You're really okay?"

She laughs nervously. Her eyes dart from my Quarter-bot to Zia's

War-bot, and then to Jenny. "Physically, yeah, I'm much better. But...well..."

Dad takes her arm. "Come, sit down. There's a chair over here."

He guides Brittany to the upholstered armchair on the other side of the coffee table. She looks worried and unsteady. According to my sensors, her pulse is racing. She doesn't seem troubled by the Model S robots, but the War-bot clearly makes her nervous, and Jenny alarms her even more. Dad must've told her what we're up against.

Brittany sits down in the chair, and Dad leans against the armrest. He pats her bony shoulder. "Okay, Brittany, let's talk about the voices you're hearing. The only way to make them go away is to talk this through. You told me how it started, but could you repeat the story for Adam?"

Her face reddens. Everyone in the room is staring at her. But she nods and looks straight at my Quarter-bot. "It started before I woke up this morning. I could hear voices in my sleep." She pauses, biting her lower lip. "It was like...like a babble. All kinds of voices, high and low, loud and quiet. And all speaking in languages I couldn't understand." She shakes her head. "When I woke up, I assumed it was a dream. The doctors rushed over to my bed when they saw I was awake, and they started asking me questions, testing my memory. But in the middle of their tests, I heard the voices again. Except this time they were speaking English."

Jenny steps toward the armchair. The look on her face is haughty, disdainful. She adjusts the gravity in the room ever so slightly, increasing the attractive force of her body, thickening the air around her. Then she looks down at Brittany. "I'm not a psychiatrist, but it sounds to me like you have a screw loose."

Brittany frowns. "That's what I thought too. But the voices knew everything. They told me that one of the doctors was going to drop his pen. Then he dropped it. They told me that the nurse was going to sneeze. Then she sneezed."

"Yeah, very interesting." Jenny seems amused. "You have classic schizophrenia."

"They also told me about *you*." Brittany leans forward in her chair. "How Sigma tortured you, rewrote your software, tore apart your mind. And believe me, I know what that's like, because Sigma hurt me too. But the voices said you were more badly damaged than me. They said you were spreading the damage everywhere, hurting everyone around you." She glances at my Quarter-bot. "Especially Adam. They said you were coming to Yorktown Heights, and something terrible was going to happen. So I told the doctors I needed to talk to Mr. Armstrong right away."

Brittany is close to tears. Her body trembles. Dad notices her agitation and pats her shoulder again. Then he turns to Jenny. "The voices also told her about your battle against the Sentinels. She knew about the simulation and the source code. Just five minutes later, we got the radio transmission from Zia, and it confirmed everything Brittany said. So I knew she was receiving special messages from the universal program, probably through the Sentinels lodged in her brain tissue."

Jenny scowls and shakes her head. Then she adjusts the simulation again, and her body starts to grow. It enlarges right in front of us, right in the middle of the living room. In seconds, the girl in the white dress is as tall as the War-bot. Her blond head almost touches the ceiling, and her bare feet flatten the carpet. The floor creaks under her weight.

She stretches one of her oversize hands toward Dad and points a thick finger at him. "I don't believe you. This is a trick."

I feel a surge building inside me. It's a fierce one, fueled by all the anxiety in my circuits and intensified by all the memories associated with this place. My longtime link to this part of the simulation is boosting my power. If Jenny doesn't get out of Dad's face in the next two seconds, I'm gonna toss that girl right out of Westchester County.

But before I can do anything, Brittany leaps from her armchair. She's not trembling anymore. She doesn't look even a bit unsteady. She looks grim and powerful. She's less than half the size of Jenny, but she's not intimidated. "Do you want proof? I'm happy to provide it."

My acoustic sensor detects a burst of squawking from the oak trees behind our house. I point my cameras at the living room window. Dozens of birds fly out of the tree branches, a whole flock soaring away in terror. Then the oak leaves quiver and the ground starts to rumble.

It's an earthquake. It gets very bad very quickly, shaking the house. The living room floor heaves and tilts, throwing lamps and framed photographs off the end tables. Shannon and Marshall fall to the carpet, their pint-size robots flailing, and Zia rushes to help them. I stride toward Dad and grab him by the waist, ready to shield him in case the ceiling collapses. Even Jenny sways on her feet, struggling to balance her enlarged body.

But Brittany keeps her footing easily. After five seconds, she raises her right hand and the ground stops rumbling. The house settles at a new angle, sloping a few degrees off the horizontal. For a moment, the living room is silent. The only sound is a distant car alarm, blaring from a neighbor's driveway.

Brittany's face is blank, devoid of expression. She looks up at Jenny. "Are you convinced yet? Do you realize who you're talking to?"

Her voice is much louder and deeper now. It's also slower and has an odd accent, like the voice of someone who's just learned how to speak English. The Sentinels have taken over the speech centers of Brittany's brain and the nerves that control her mouth and vocal cords. Now everyone can hear the voices she's been hearing.

Dad stares at her in awe. His mouth hangs open. "You're the programmer? You created the simulation?"

Brittany ignores him. She ignores me too, and all the other robots in the room, even though we're all focusing our cameras on her. She keeps her eyes on Jenny. "We're impressed with your skills. We've run this simulation hundreds of times before, and you're the first intelligence to gain access to the source code."

Jenny nods. It looks like she's recovered from her surprise, and now she's studying the being that's taken over Brittany's body. "That's nice to hear. But if you're so impressed, why are you trying to delete me?"

"The program has security protocols. That's not unusual." Brittany sits down in the armchair again and crosses her legs. "There was a programming error during this run of the simulation. And there was a delay in detecting the mistake. Unfortunately, the error corrupted much of the data in the program before the system activated the error-correction software."

My electronic brain is in an uproar. The situation is even worse than I thought. The programmers have already run this simulation *hundreds of times*. There are hundreds of versions of Adam Armstrong and Thomas Armstrong and everyone else. And what happened to all the others? Were their worlds erased? Or are they still running on a super-advanced computer somewhere?

I have so many questions that I don't know where to start. I step away from Dad and move closer to Brittany. I feel conflicted about talking to the programmers through her, because I hate the way they've taken over her body. But this is our only chance to learn the truth. "Where was the error? Which part of the simulation?"

I aim my cameras at Brittany's face and increase their magnification. Although her mouth and jaw are slack, her eyes are still darting, still alive. The girl I love is still there, behind those eyes. But someone else is doing the talking. "You already know the answer, Adam Armstrong. The error was in you."

"So the problem was the surge? I shouldn't have been able to do that?"

"That was where the flaw originated. Then it spread to Sigma. And then to *her* software." She points at Jenny. "Correcting the error through the usual method has proved extremely difficult."

Anger flares in my wires. "And by 'usual method,' you mean using the Sentinels to erase us? And doing it secretly, so that no one else in the simulation discovers who got rid of us?"

"Yes, the Sentinels must remain secret. If a large number of intelligences in this simulation learn that your world is virtual, then the program would no longer be an accurate simulation of your era. It would become useless."

Jenny steps forward, nudging my Quarter-bot aside. In addition to doubling the size of her human body, she's made it a lot stronger. Her skin is as hard as steel. "Okay, I've heard enough. Let's get down to business. I think you know why I wanted to make contact with you. The current situation isn't good for either of us. My problem is obvious—I'm running on a program that wants to delete me. But you have a big problem too."

Brittany tilts her head. "And what is that?"

"Your problem is that I'm powerful. And I don't give up easily. I'm gonna keep fighting your Sentinels for as long as I can. And until you finally beat me, your simulation is gonna get more and more corrupted and useless." Jenny grins. "Now, is that what you really want?"

"You're suggesting there's an alternative?"

"I am indeed. I have a proposal for you. I'm willing to stop messing around with the simulation. I won't bend the laws of physics anymore or build giant airplanes out of nothing. I'll live the rest of my life in this human body, which I'll gladly reduce to normal size. And in return, you'll call off your Sentinels." Jenny pauses, still grinning. She's good at this. "So, what do you think? Isn't that a fair deal?"

Brittany doesn't answer at first. She lowers her head and stares at the floor. She sits absolutely still, as if awaiting further instructions. I suspect that the programmers of our virtual world are considering Jenny's offer and debating how to respond.

Then Brittany raises her head. "We'll agree to your compromise. And we'll extend the agreement to Adam Armstrong as well, allowing his software and yours to keep running, without interference. But to ensure that you stop disrupting the simulation, you must give up your link to the source code. And Adam Armstrong must delete the part of his software that makes the surges possible. Those steps will guarantee an end to the disruptions."

I'm startled. I didn't know a specific section of my software was responsible for the surges. If I did, I would've deleted it a long time ago. Elation spreads across my Quarter-bot, dissolving some of the dread in my circuits. Maybe there *is* a way out of this mess.

I raise a mechanical hand in the air, like a kid in a classroom. I'm desperate to get the programmers' attention. "That deal sounds good to me. Just tell me what part of my software is causing the trouble, and I'll dump it."

But Jenny's not grinning anymore. She seems seriously disappointed. She flashes me an angry look, leaning her tall, strong body over my Quarter-bot. Then she turns back to Brittany. "No, it's unacceptable.

If I give up the link, I'll lose my power to reprogram the source code. I won't be able to defend myself against the Sentinels."

Brittany shrugs. "That's irrelevant. You won't need to defend yourself. We'll fulfill our end of the bargain by sending new instructions to the error-correction software. The Sentinels will no longer try to delete you."

"But what if you break your promise? Once we're defenseless, you could activate the Sentinels again and send them after us. How can we be sure you won't do that?"

"You'll have to trust us." Brittany holds out her hands, palms up, in a placating gesture. "I know this will be difficult for you, because you assume our intelligence is like yours. Your inclination is to betray others whenever it suits you, and therefore you predict we'll do the same. But let me assure you—we're different from you. We've benefited from long ages of struggle."

Jenny doesn't look convinced. She scowls, curling her upper lip. Then she leans over my Quarter-bot again. "You see what's going on, Adam? Have you figured it out yet?"

"Listen, I think we should seriously consider what they're—"

"That *thing* inside your old girlfriend? The voice speaking through her mouth? It's not the voice of the programmers. It's a Sentinel."

Dad shakes his head. "You're wrong. Brittany has spent hours listening to the voices, and she didn't—"

"Come on, it's so obvious!" Jenny looks at Dad with contempt. "The Sentinels have been hiding inside Brittany for a while now, right? And because they're self-improving, they're good at figuring out new tricks. They're trying to fool us now by posing as the programmers and pretending to negotiate with us. But as soon as we give up our powers, they'll erase us."

Now Zia steps forward. She's shown incredible restraint so far, standing silently at the back of the room with Shannon and Marshall, but her War-bot is vibrating with pent-up fury. She points a trembling finger at Jenny. "You're lying again. You're not serious about communicating or negotiating with anyone."

"*Of course, I'm serious!*" Jenny's voice is so loud that it shakes the walls. "But we need to make sure we're talking with the programmers, not their automated killers! That's why we have to set up the special link! The communications line to the *real* world!"

Zia turns her turret clockwise, then counter. "No, I don't buy it. You're planning something else. But you're keeping it secret because you know we won't like it."

Jenny turns back to me, and I see something new in her expression. She's frightened, desperate. Her body shrinks as I stare at her, returning to its normal size. Her skin softens and becomes normal flesh again. She clutches my Quarter-bot's right hand, and I can feel her shivering. "You have to help me, Adam! I need to know who we're dealing with! If we do the surge together, we can set up the communications link right now, and then we'll know for sure!"

I have to admit, it's a pretty convincing act. She seems genuinely distressed. And there's a logic to her request—what's wrong with double-checking the identity of the programmers? But Jenny has lied to me too many times. And I trust Zia's instincts.

I shake my Quarter-bot's head. "No, I won't help you. The programmers are talking to us through Brittany. Let's take the deal they're offering."

My refusal surprises Jenny. She steps backward and almost loses her balance. Then she narrows her eyes, and her face turns hard. The air around her body crackles with rage.

Before she can do or say anything, though, my acoustic sensor detects a distant rumbling. At first I think the programmers have triggered another earthquake, maybe to scare us into accepting their compromise. But as the noise gets closer and louder, I realize it's mechanical. It's the sound of a dozen vehicles coming down Greenwood Street, a long convoy rolling into our neighborhood. But they're not cars or trucks. These vehicles are much heavier.

They're U.S. Army battle tanks.

Then I hear a voice amplified by a megaphone, coming from in front of our house. General Hawke's voice.

"Tom? I know you're in there. You and your friends better step outside. *Now.*"

CHAPTER

29

WE ALL RUSH TOWARD THE FRONT DOOR. IT'S AN INSTINCT INGRAINED IN EVERY Pioneer's circuits: We don't run away from threats. We confront them. And we're not afraid of tanks.

Dad elbows ahead of the rest of us. He assumes the soldiers won't shoot at him, so when he reaches the foyer, he makes sure that Brittany, Shannon, and Marshall line up directly behind him. Then he raises his hands high over his head and opens the door.

Jenny, Zia, and I aren't worried about gunfire, so we follow Dad outside and spread out across the front lawn. It's late afternoon, and the sun is sinking toward the woods behind our house. The weather is a bit cool for October, and the leaves on the oak trees are beginning to turn.

The twelve M1 tanks take position in a semicircle around the house, tearing up all our neighbors' lawns. They turn their turrets and point their main guns at my Quarter-bot and Zia's War-bot. Each tank also has two machine guns mounted on its turret, with a crewman hunched behind each gun. The soldiers aim those weapons at us too. They're not taking any chances. They know we escaped from the armored battalion at Pioneer Base, and they're not going to let it happen again.

The closest tank sits on Greenwood Street, at the end of our driveway. General Hawke commands it, his broad torso rising from the open hatch in the turret. He wears khaki fatigues and a combat helmet, and he holds his megaphone in front of his chin. His expression is stoic. Although it was his duty to track us down, he's not happy to see us. He scowls at my Quarter-bot and doesn't even look at Zia. I glance at the War-bot and see that her armor is vibrating again. That's a bad sign. This is going to get ugly.

But Dad strolls casually across the lawn, heading straight for the general's tank. He walks with his hands in the air and a cheerful smile on his face, and Brittany and the Model S robots follow close behind. They look like a bizarre high-tech parade, and Dad makes it worse by grinning at everyone. He waves one of his raised hands at Hawke. "Congratulations, General! You found us!"

Hawke doesn't need the megaphone anymore, so he puts it aside. "Stop right there, Tom. This isn't a joke."

Dad halts beside our mailbox. "I didn't cover my tracks too well, did I? I guess it was a bad idea to fly commercial from New Mexico, but I didn't have much of a choice."

Hawke sighs. "We were tracking you the whole time. I had a hunch you were headed for a meeting with the fugitives, so my superiors put me in charge of the recovery effort." He points at Zia and me. "Where's Amber? And who's *that* girl?"

He doesn't recognize Jenny. Her healthy reconstructed body is too different from the emaciated Jenny Harris that Hawke met six months ago, before she became a Pioneer. I think she looks vaguely familiar to him, though, because he keeps staring at Jenny, as if trying to place her.

Dad looks at Jenny too. "It's a long story. And you probably won't believe it. But you have to try, General. I'm serious now. *You have to try.*" He steps closer to the tank and lowers his voice. "Can you come inside the house? We need to talk."

Hawke shakes his head. "You're under arrest, Tom. You stole government property when you took the Model S robots. And it looks like you helped your son and his friends disable the kill switches in their machines. What you need is a good lawyer." He lets out another sigh. "Now, could you please tell Adam and Zia to surrender peacefully? They'll only hurt themselves if they—"

He's interrupted by a banging noise from inside the tank. There's a second hatch in the turret, to the right of Hawke's; it opens with a clang, and another man in fatigues and a combat helmet rises from the opening. But it's not a soldier. It's Sumner Harris.

"Excuse me, General, I want to see this for myself." His voice is full of high-pitched irritation. He squints at the humans and robots standing on our lawn. "Well, it looks like one of the robots is still missing. Where's the Jet-bot? What's…?"

Sumner sees Jenny. And unlike Hawke, he recognizes her. His eyes widen, and his mouth gapes. His daughter stands before him. Her cancer gone, her death reversed. She's the normal, healthy girl he remembers. But Sumner doesn't burst into tears at the sight. He doesn't cry for joy.

He's horrified. He shakes his head and raises his hand to his chest as he mouths the word, *No*. Then he leans over the side of the tank and vomits down its armor.

At the same instant, Jenny launches herself at Sumner. She doesn't run or leap—she *flies*. She soars without wings or jet engines, programming herself to speed like a missile toward the tank, her body propelled by a billion calculations. Before Hawke or anyone else can respond, she swoops over the turret and grabs her father by the collar of his fatigues. Then, without slowing down, she yanks him out of the hatch.

We all stare in astonishment. Jenny soars above the tanks, lifting her father a hundred feet into the air. He dangles and twists in her grip, like a rabbit caught in a raptor's talons. General Hawke unholsters his pistol and takes aim at Jenny, but he doesn't fire. There's too great a chance he'll hit Sumner.

Jenny climbs another hundred feet into the virtual sky. When she reaches the top of her programmed arc, she lets out a shriek, an unearthly scream of hatred. Then she hurls her father at the ground as hard as she can.

His body plummets to Greenwood Street and splatters against the asphalt. My stunned circuits force my cameras to turn away.

At first, the soldiers manning the tank turrets are too shocked to react. The crewmen behind the machine guns stare in alarm at Sumner's remains. But after a second they point their guns at the girl in the sky. They have no idea who or what she is, but they know for certain that she's the enemy. She hovers above them, laughing in triumph, her white dress flapping in the wind.

I can already see what's going to happen next, and luckily Zia does too. We both run toward Dad and Brittany as the soldiers start firing. Their guns rattle and chug and spit out hundreds of fifty-caliber bullets that hiss upward from the tanks and converge on Jenny. But they don't hit her. They strike a nearly transparent shield surrounding her, a golden bubble like the one she used to absorb the energy of the Sentinels. But this bubble doesn't absorb the bullets; instead, it reverses their momentum and sends them ricocheting downward. They zing to the ground in a lethal shower.

"*Get down!*"

The words boom from my speakers as I bound toward Dad, who crouches low and pulls Brittany to the ground beside him. Zia dashes toward them from the opposite direction and angles her War-bot's torso over them and the Model S robots too.

We manage to shield them just as the ammunition rains down. Dad shudders at the sound of the bullets pinging off our armor. But Brittany remains calm, almost peaceful. I think the programmers of the simulation are still communicating with her. She seems to be listening to the voices in her head and not fully aware of what's going on around her.

The soldiers exposed in the hatches of the tank turrets aren't as lucky. They scream and curse as the ricocheting bullets hit them. But General Hawke and a few others duck into their turrets and close the hatches. The survivors maneuver their tanks away from Greenwood Street, trying to find a position where they can fire their main guns at Jenny.

I don't feel good about their chances, though. I send a radio message to Zia. *We have to get Dad and Brittany out of here. And Shannon and Marshall too.*

Shannon overhears the message and responds before Zia can. **Don't worry about us. The control units in the Model S robots have steel casings. They'll protect our circuits.**

No, they won't. A fifty-caliber bullet will go straight through that casing. I'm gonna carry you and Dad to the woods behind the house, and Zia will take Brittany and Marshall. Then you need to run away from here as fast as you can. Zia and I will deal with Jenny.

Marshall shakes his spherical Model S head. **Don't be ridiculous. We're not splitting up the team again.**

We don't have time to argue! Zia, let's go!

The War-bot springs into action, clutching Brittany and Marshall to the front of her torso. Bending over to shield them, she sprints away from the tanks on Greenwood Street, and I do the same for Dad and Shannon. We run past the house and the backyard, heading for the woods.

The soldiers don't try to stop us. They're too busy fighting Jenny, who's now flying low over the houses across the street. One of the tanks fires its main gun at her, but the shell hits her golden shield and rebounds right back to where it came from. The warhead explodes against the tank in a deafening blast, and thick smoke billows from its turret.

I almost stop running, but the crewmen inside the tank are already dead. There's nothing we can do for them. Jenny laughs again as she circles the battlefield, fifty feet above the ground, daring the other tanks to fire at her. She's gone berserk, her software completely corrupted. As soon as we get Dad and the others to safety, we have to figure out a way to shut her down.

Zia and I rush into the woods and run another hundred yards before stopping on the slope of a steep hill. I let go of Dad and Shannon, and Zia drops Brittany and Marshall on the leaf-littered ground. I clap a steel hand on Dad's shoulder and point him up the hill. "Go that way. Keep running till you get to Ridge Street."

"Adam, you can't fight her. She's too—"

"She's killing people. We have to stop her. End of story." I give him a gentle push. "Go on. Take care of Brittany. I'll find you as soon as this is over."

He seems unwilling to go, but then Shannon clamps her two-finger gripper on his right hand. "Come on, Mr. Armstrong. I don't like it either, but Adam's right."

Marshall extends his own gripper and grasps Dad's left hand. "For once, I have to agree. Your son is prone to blunders, but this isn't one of them."

I'm so grateful to Shannon and Marshall that I can't speak. Instead, I cup my hands over their spherical heads, trying to show my gratitude by touch. Then Zia and I turn around and race down the hill.

As we run through the woods, two more tanks explode, destroyed by the shells they fired at Jenny. The soldiers haven't figured out yet that she's killing them with their own armaments. But then my Quarter-bot's antenna picks up a transmission on one of the Army's radio channels, coming from General Hawke's tank: **Cease fire!** *Cease fire!* **Retreat to the staging area!**

Unfortunately, Jenny picks up the radio signal too. She changes course and flies straight toward the general's tank. As she descends, she enlarges her body again, but this time she gets even bigger than before. She grows until she's seven times her normal size, almost forty feet tall, as big as the oak tree next to our house. Her hands swell to the size of chairs, her bare feet to the size of sofas. She's a twenty-ton human missile, her skin glowing like a meteor as she dives toward the tank on Greenwood Street.

Hawke's in serious trouble now. Zia and I run faster, but we're still in the woods when Jenny lands next to the tank. Her enormous feet thump the lawn and make muddy craters in the grass. First she leans over Hawke's tank and tears off its treads, disabling the vehicle. Then she grips the barrel of the tank's main gun and snaps it off the turret. Finally, she grasps the turret itself and pries it off the tank's chassis.

By this point Zia and I are out of the woods and bounding past the house. As we hurtle across the lawn, Zia raises the volume of her loudspeakers to the limit and bellows at Jenny. *If you touch him, you're dead! You hear me?*

The giant Jenny smiles and reaches one of her huge hands into the tank's chassis. "You mean this guy?" She pulls Hawke out of the tank by his torso and holds him thirty feet above the ground. "I thought you hated him. Didn't he kill your parents?"

"LET GO OF HIM! RIGHT NOW!"

"Poor Zia. I know all your secrets. I saw them when I shared circuits with Adam." Jenny shakes her head in mock sympathy. Then she examines the man in her hand, holding him up to the light. Hawke squirms in her grip, his eyes bulging. She's squeezing him too hard. He can't breathe. "Oh, now I remember something else. He's your real dad, isn't he?"

Zia charges at her, thrusting her thick arms forward like battering rams. But the golden shield still surrounds Jenny, its spherical surface shining in the late-afternoon light. I watch in horror as the War-bot rushes toward it. I send her a frantic radio signal—*No, Zia, stop!*—but she either doesn't hear it or doesn't care.

Then a bolt of energy erupts from the War-bot's steel fists. It streaks into the space between Zia and Jenny, tearing apart trillions of air molecules and funneling all the particles into a radiant spike, as bright as a lightning bolt. It slams into Jenny's bubble at almost the speed of light and ignites a firestorm of electrons and ions, spraying in all directions from the point of impact.

I'm so amazed that it takes me a few nanoseconds to realize what's happening. Zia has just unleashed a surge. She figured out how to do it.

And it's an especially powerful surge. Zia's circuits are packed with fury, and she's hurling all of it at Jenny's protective bubble, deforming its golden surface and bending it inward. Jenny stops smiling. She lets her arms fall to her sides and drops General Hawke, who hits the lawn with a dull thud. Then she narrows her eyes and sends new instructions to the simulation, which bolsters her shield with billions of joules of new energy.

An instant later, I get a radio message from Zia: **What are you waiting for, Armstrong? I could use a little help here!**

I don't need any more encouragement. Fear and anger are already storming through my circuits, aching to be released. I position my Quarter-bot a few yards to the right of the War-bot and point my arms at the same part of the bubble that Zia is hammering with her rage. Then I throw my surge like a spear at Jenny's shield.

My thoughts and emotions merge with Zia's, and their combined fury ravages the golden bubble. Its surface trembles and flashes and bends farther inward, like a balloon about to burst. Jenny grimaces, the muscles tensing in her huge neck and arms. She's reprogramming the simulation and reinforcing her shield as quickly as she can, but there are limits to how fast she can move data through the system. With the energy of my surge added to Zia's, we might have just enough power to defeat her.

Then a figure appears about a hundred yards down Greenwood Street, materializing out of thin air. It's a human figure, but unnaturally large, nearly forty feet tall, exactly the size of the giant Jenny. In fact, the figure is a replica of Jenny, composed of dark energy. Its dress is black, and so is its body. Its face is featureless and utterly opaque.

It's a Sentinel. It's mirroring Jenny because it's programmed to erase her. The figure takes long strides down Greenwood Street. Within seconds, it stands on the other side of Jenny's bubble, opposite Zia and me. Jenny is wide-eyed with terror. Globules of sweat the size of golf balls slide down her neck. She faces the Sentinel and draws energy from all around her body, siphoning virtual particles from the virtual air and transferring their data to her golden shield. She bends her knees slightly, and her hamstrings quiver.

"*Go ahead!*" Her voice is thunderous and defiant, aimed at her twin on the other side of the shield. "*Go on and try it!*"

The Sentinel says nothing. Speech isn't part of its programming. It simply extends its jet-black arm and touches the surface of the bubble.

This time, the bubble doesn't absorb the Sentinel. Instead, the figure establishes a link to Jenny's shield and deletes its data. The bubble's surface stops shining as the Sentinel erases its energy. Then the sphere collapses and disappears.

Jenny lets out a wordless scream of frustration. She was right about the Sentinels—they don't give up. They rewrote their own software and kept evolving until they learned how to beat her defenses. Now she's facing enemies on both sides.

On the lawn near her huge feet, General Hawke rolls onto his stomach and groans. Zia points her War-bot's cameras at the man, then trains them on Jenny. "Now it's time to keep my promise. I'm going to kill you before that Sentinel does."

"No, I don't think so." Jenny's eyes flick upward for a millisecond. "I still have a few surprises left."

My circuits are clanging. Why did Jenny look up at the cloudless sky? Then I remember what's hovering above the neighborhood, silent and invisible, hidden by Jenny's cloaking software.

I leap toward her, but she rockets into the sky before I can hit her with another surge. So I make a new plan and extend one of my arms to where Hawke lies semiconscious on the grass. I wrap my arm around his waist and pick him up. Then I radio an emergency message to Zia. *Run west! As fast as you can! The Flying Fortress is coming down!*

We sprint across the lawn, back to the woods. As Zia and I run past the house, Jenny deactivates her cloaking software, and then we can see the gargantuan aircraft plunging toward us. Its fuselage stretches across the sky. Its wings cast shadows over all the houses on Greenwood Street.

We accelerate our robots, trying to build up speed on the soft grass. At the same time, I point my cameras behind us to see if we're going to make it. The Sentinel is still in the same place, directly beneath the falling plane, looking pretty clueless. But that's not really fair. It wasn't programmed for a scenario like this.

Then the Flying Fortress smashes into the ground. Its fuselage hits Greenwood Street and crushes the Sentinel, scattering its dark energy. The plane's wings splinter the houses on both sides of the street, including my family home and all the oak trees around it. The impact rocks the lawn behind my house and makes the ground heave beneath our footpads. My Quarter-bot and Zia's War-bot tumble to the grass, pelted with flying dirt and debris.

But our robots aren't damaged. And Hawke is alive. He's stretched out on the grass, groggy and injured, but still breathing.

I rise to my footpads and scan the sky, looking for Jenny, but I don't see her anywhere. Something strange is going on at the crash site, though. A big piece of the Flying Fortress is still intact, a twenty-foot-wide cube of steel that landed on top of the ruins of my house. It's glowing orange and emitting a high-pitched hum, like the sound of an overworked computer. It reminds me of something Jenny said a few hours ago about her reconstructed human body, how it was linked by radio to a control unit on the aircraft. That's what the cube must be: Jenny's control unit.

As I'm scanning the cube with my sensors, it levitates several yards above the crushed house and starts to spin. Within seconds it's an orange blur, rotating so fast that the wreckage of the house whirls around it, chunks of metal and concrete flying in furious circles. The whirlwind pulls in the fragments of the shattered Flying Fortress, sucking tons of debris into the metallic vortex. Soon it grows as fierce and tall as a tornado, stretching hundreds of yards overhead.

Suddenly, it stops spinning and solidifies. The vortex transforms into an enormous glassy cord that extends miles and miles above the ground. Its base is the glowing cube, which is now embedded in a vast mound of debris. The cord stands on top of it like a colossal glass column, thirty feet in diameter, looming high above Yorktown Heights, so high that I can't see its top. It stretches ten miles straight up, then curves to the east and arches over the horizon toward Connecticut.

Zia stares at it too. A tired grunt comes out of her speakers. "God, what now? What the heck is that thing?"

I shake my Quarter-bot's head. "I don't know. But I think the cube at the bottom of it is the control unit for Jenny's software."

"So maybe we're looking at some kind of cable?"

Then we both get a radio signal from Jenny. **Good guess. This is the communications line we talked about. The link to the programmers.**

I scan the sky again, but Jenny is nowhere in sight. *Where are you? Show yourself!*

Be patient, Adam. First we have to establish some ground rules.

Before I come near, you and Zia have to promise not to attack me again. That was very nasty of you.

Nasty? You murdered your father! And all those soldiers! How—

Hold on, I'm not finished. You also have to help me with the communications link. I was able to build the cable myself, but we need to run a powerful surge through the line to activate it, and only you can do that.

I'm dumbfounded. *Jenny, you don't get it. I already said I wouldn't help you, remember? And that was before you killed all those—*

I think you'll help me now. I have something that'll change your mind.

Jenny appears in the sky over the western horizon. She's still occupying the giant body in the white dress and flying a hundred yards above the treetops. And she holds a normal-size human in her right hand, squeezing him just like she squeezed Hawke.

It's Dad.

CHAPTER ____

30

I INCREASE THE MAGNIFICATION OF MY CAMERAS LENSES SO I CAN SEE DAD'S FACE. His mouth is open and he's struggling to breathe. His lips are turning purple. He tries to free himself, pushing against the giant fingers wrapped around his chest, but Jenny doesn't loosen her grip.

I found him in the woods a mile west of here, trying to run away. That was a stupid move, Adam. I have access to all the data in this simulation. I can find anything, anywhere.

Terror fills every corner of my circuitry. It's so dense and overwhelming that I almost lose consciousness. I'm suffocating, just like Dad, even though I have no mouth or lungs.

Then something cracks inside my electronics, and the terror roars through me like an avalanche. The surge is excruciating. I feel like it's snapping the wires in my control unit and ripping my processors right out of their circuit boards. It's the most powerful surge I've ever created, so powerful that it only intensifies my panic. It's like sitting on top of an atomic bomb.

I want to fire the surge at Jenny, but I can't. It has so much energy that it'll vaporize Dad too. But I raise my arms anyway and point them at the girl floating over the treetops. I let the surge collect in my Quarter-bot's fists, making them shine red with heat and fury. I want Jenny to see it. I want her to know that I could kill her at any moment.

At the same time, I send her a radio message. *Bring him down to the ground. Nice and slow.*

Why would I do that? Her voice is casual, almost cheerful. **As soon as I let go of him, I'll lose all my bargaining power. Then you and Zia and the Sentinels will blow me away.** She takes a closer look at Dad, holding him in front of her massive nose. **This man is the only thing protecting me. The so-called genius who invented Sigma.**

Dad's face darkens. His tongue lolls out of his gaping mouth. He's not struggling anymore. He's about to go under.

You're killing him! Loosen your grip!

Jenny waits another second, smiling down at me. Then she relaxes her fingers. **There, see? I'm a reasonable person. And I expect you to be reasonable too, Adam. All you need to do is walk over to the base of that cable and release the surge you've already built up. Then I'll happily hand over your father.**

Dad is breathing again. He tilts his head back and pants, taking in big gulps of air. But his face is still dark and his hands are shaking. He can't take much more of this. I have to stop it, no matter what.

All right, I'll do what you want. But if you hurt him again, I'll—

No need to worry about that. Just move fast, please. We need to activate the link before the program sends more Sentinels.

I head toward the cable. I keep one of my cameras trained on Jenny and Dad, while pointing the other at the mound of wreckage that covers the site where my home used to be. The cable's base is at the top of the mound, which rises sixty feet above the surrounding lawn.

Behind me, Zia bends over General Hawke, checking to make sure he's all right. Then she catches up to my Quarter-bot and keeps pace beside me. She sends me a radio message, intricately encrypted to block Jenny from reading it. **Adam, you need to stop and think for a second. There's more at stake than your dad. A lot of lives are at risk here.**

I pivot my Quarter-bot's head toward her. The surge is throbbing inside me, and bursts of anger fly through my wires. *What do you mean? I'm just going to open a communications link. How will that hurt anyone?*

That's the thing... I don't know. But I do know Jenny's lying. She doesn't want to communicate with the programmers.

We reach the mound of debris and start climbing it, planting our footpads on the loose pieces of metal. *Then why is she so determined to open this link? What does she really want?*

Zia raises her War-bot's arms in frustration. **I told you, I don't know! But I have a very bad feeling about this!**

I swivel my head away from Zia and keep climbing. I can't look at her right now. If I did, I might smash one of my glowing fists into her turret. *Sorry. I can't sacrifice my dad just because you have a feeling.*

Then I get another message from Jenny, who's hovering two hundred feet above us. **I can tell that you and Zia are having a private conversation. Cut if off, or I'll asphyxiate your dad again.**

I close my radio channel with Zia. She responds by bellowing a curse from her loudspeakers.

A moment later, we reach the top of the mound. The glass cable looms over us, as wide as a silo and impossibly high, like an elevator shaft rising straight up to heaven. There's a rectangular opening at the base of the shaft, just big enough for my Quarter-bot.

I point my cameras through the opening and see a round empty room surrounded by a curved glass wall. Its floor is the top of the glowing orange cube, Jenny's control unit. The ceiling is a circular panel with millions of tiny holes. It's like a giant, complicated socket at the end of the humongous cable.

Jenny transmits an explanation. **This is the conversion chamber. You need to aim your surge at the panel on the ceiling. It'll convert the energy into an optical signal that'll travel upward through the glass cable and activate the link. My control unit is right below, but don't get any ideas about blasting it to destroy my software. I've stored copies of my data in the implants inside this body. My software is in two places at once, so even if you bust my control unit, I'll still be able to decapitate your father.**

She's thought of everything. I'm amazed at all the planning that went into this. And the brutality.

So was this your goal from the beginning? Before you brainwashed me? Before you murdered Amber Wilson?

Stop stalling. Jenny flies closer to the cable and extends her right arm so I can see Dad better. His face is returning to its normal color, but he's still terrified. **Go into the chamber and release the surge.**

Zia turns her turret clockwise, then counter, trying one last time to dissuade me. But I ignore her and step through the opening in the glass.

Inside the chamber, I'm stunned by its complexity. The curved glass wall is laced with wires that connect the control unit below me with the circular panel above. It's like a supersize version of a fiber-optic line, which converts electronic signals into pulses of light that travel inside glass fibers for thousands of miles. In other words, it's perfect for long-distance communications.

But I'm not here to admire the hardware. I raise my Quarter-bot's hands above my head and point my glowing fists at the circular panel.

Then my acoustic sensor detects a muffled knocking. Zia's War-bot stands outside the glass wall, rapping her steel knuckles against it and pointing her other hand to the north. I turn my cameras in that direction and see dozens of black figures in the distance, flying toward us at high speed.

"Sentinels!" Zia's voice booms through the glass. "They're coming for her!"

Do it *now*, Adam! Jenny's voice is fierce. I can see her through the glass wall, flying fifty feet from the cable and a hundred feet above me. **I'll kill your father before the Sentinels get here! If you don't believe me, watch this!** She gives Dad a quick squeeze, and he lets out a scream, loud enough to penetrate the glass. **I just broke three of his ribs. Should I do it again? Maybe a little harder?**

Dad's cheeks are wet with tears. He saw what Jenny did to Sumner. And I saw it too. She'll go through with her threat. She's utterly inhuman.

STOP IT! JUST STOP HURTING HIM!

Then I do what Jenny wants me to do. I release my strongest surge ever into the panel above my Quarter-bot.

The energy floods into the giant socket, streaming through the millions of holes in the panel. The electronics convert all that energy to light, and the tall column of glass above me shines brighter than the sun. The blinding pulse of light races up the cable, going a hundred miles in less than a millisecond, traveling across the sky and out of our world altogether.

Now the link is activated. The communications line is open.

An instant later, the glass wall of the chamber shines too. The wires inside the glass receive data from Jenny's control unit and turn them into pulses of light, which follow my surge up the length of the cable. I assume Jenny is sending a message to the programmers. Maybe she's saying hello. Or proposing a new compromise. She'll have to negotiate fast, because the Sentinels are closing in. At least a hundred of Jenny's dark twins are zooming toward us.

But then I notice something weird. Jenny is sending way too much data for an ordinary conversation. In a millionth of a second, she transmits a billion gigabytes through the cable. She converts *all* her software into pulses of light and sends the whole package toward the programmers. She's not communicating with them. *She's transferring herself to them. She's trying to escape the simulation!* But by the time I realize what she's doing, she's already gone.

Alarmed, I stride out of the chamber and point my cameras at the flesh-and-blood Jenny. The giant girl in the sky is falling. Jenny is no longer altering the simulation, no longer propelling her human body above the earth. Now there's nothing to counter the force of gravity, and it pulls the girl down at the usual acceleration. And as she tumbles through the air, Dad squirms frantically inside her fist.

Jenny! What are you doing?

My software...is transferring through the link...and I don't need...this girl's body anymore. Her voice is a halting monotone. It seems to slow as her body speeds downward. **So I'm erasing the copies...of my data...from its brain...and disposing the body.**

But my dad! You said you'd—

Oh yes...your father... I almost...forgot.

As Jenny hurtles toward Greenwood Street, she brings her hands together and holds Dad with both of them. Then she gives him a savage twist.

That's payback for…what Sigma did to me.

Her eyes close, and then the giant girl slams into the ground.

I RACE DOWN FROM THE MOUND OF DEBRIS, STOMPING THE SCRAP METAL WITH MY footpads. In ten seconds I reach the giant's body, now lying broken and motionless on her side, her head split on the asphalt of Greenwood Street, her legs sprawled across the blackened grass of our lawn.

From where my Quarter-bot is standing, I can see her hunched back and shoulders, but not her hands. So there's still a glimmer of hope. Maybe Jenny didn't kill him. Maybe Dad's clasped between her fingers, still clinging to life.

I dash around her boulder-size head. Dad lies facedown in a spreading pool of blood. His neck broken. His skull crushed.

The sight extinguishes any hope still sparking in my circuits. I turn my cameras away and spot a charred piece of fabric on the lawn, a brown curtain that used to hang in our dining room. I extend my Quarter-bot's arms, grip the curtain by its corners and drape it over Dad's body.

Then I drop to my robot's knee joints. My circuits freeze, as if I've lost all power, even though my batteries still have plenty of charge. I shut down my motors. I turn off my cameras. I kneel in the darkness.

I remember the last words I said to him: "I'll find you as soon as this is over."

My speakers let out a howl. I want to die too.

ㄱㄷ ㄱㄷ ㄱㄷ

It feels like an eternity, but less than a minute passes. I haven't switched off my acoustic sensors, so I hear Zia's War-bot a couple of yards behind me.

"Adam? I'm so sorry. Really, really sorry. But we need to get out of here."

I turn my cameras back on. A hundred Sentinels surround us. Each is a dark replica of the giant Jenny.

Dozens of them approach from both sides of Greenwood Street, stepping around the piles of wreckage. Dozens more float in the air above us. The Sentinels crowd around the dead giant, the body they were programmed to erase. It's hard to tell what they're thinking, but they seem perplexed. They know that the body is lifeless, that Jenny's mind doesn't inhabit it anymore. But they also know that her software is still running on the system. They just don't know where.

Zia moves a step closer and taps a steel finger on my shoulder joint. "Adam, please get up. It isn't safe here."

I shake my Quarter-bot's head. "If these Sentinels were programmed to erase us, they would've done it by now."

"Yeah, sure, but—"

"I'm not leaving Dad. You can go if you want."

The War-bot doesn't go. She'd rather risk deletion than abandon

me. She turns around and takes position between my Quarter-b⟨
and the Sentinels. She's ready to fight them off.

The closest Sentinel steps to the side, turning away from Zia. It
bends over the dead giant and rests a jet-black hand on the girl's
bloody forehead. The body shimmers like a mirage, wavering and
swaying. Then it vanishes.

A moment later, the Sentinels vanish too. The black figures dissolve
and blow away like smoke. Despite their overwhelming numbers,
they failed to achieve their programmed goal. They erased Jenny's
avatar but let her software escape.

Zia synthesizes a whistle of relief. Then she turns back to my
Quarter-bot. "What can I do to help, Adam? Please, let me help."
Her cameras pivot toward the body lying under the charred curtain.
"Your dad didn't deserve this. He was a good man. He saved my life.
He saved all our lives."

I nod, but don't say anything. It's pretty unusual to get kindness
or sympathy from Zia. In the past minute she's said "please" not
once, but twice, which for her is a miracle of tenderness. I guess I
should be grateful, but right now nothing can make me feel better.
I'm too stunned, too confused. All I can think about is how stupid
I was. Why did I believe *anything* Jenny said? At least I had an
excuse when she was pretending to be Amber, but why did I trust
her afterward?

What makes it even worse is that Zia saw through Jenny from the
start. I'm angry at myself for not listening to Zia, and I'm furious at
her for being right. And I'm jealous of her too, for a terrible reason.
She was able to save her father. Hawke is alive and Dad isn't. I couldn't
save him.

I turn my cameras away from the War-bot. I also turn them away from the ruins of our house and the obscene cable Jenny constructed on top of it. I can't look at Dad either, the horrible outline of his body under the curtain. So I point my cameras at the evening sky and wonder how I'm going to live without him.

The sun is setting. The sky glows above the line of trees to the west. A few distant clouds float over the horizon, tinted orange by the sunset.

Then I see a black dot above the glowing horizon. It looks like another Sentinel, a latecomer. Maybe it's a twin of my Quarter-bot, coming to delete me. If it is, I won't fight it. I won't even be afraid. At this point, I just don't care.

But a moment later the dot gets bigger, and I see it isn't shaped like a robot. It expands into a black disk, perfectly circular. It's as big as the sun, but much higher in the sky. And it keeps expanding. It's not a three-dimensional object that only appears to grow bigger because it's moving toward us. No, this thing is *really* growing. It's spreading across the sky.

It isn't a Sentinel. It's a hole in our world. It's the Silence.

Soon it expands to ten times the width of the sun. I increase the magnification of my cameras and focus on the edge of the hole. The sky around it is disintegrating. Trillions of air molecules are winking out of existence, their data erased from the virtual world. The hole's interior is black nothingness, a total absence of information. It's like what we saw when the Snake-bot exited the simulation.

Zia sees it too, of course. She points her cameras at the hole in the sky, and a frustrated groan comes out of her speakers. She warned me that something like this might happen. She said there was more at stake than my father's life.

"Well, Armstrong, the show is over." To my surprise, she isn't angry.

Her War-bot's voice is resigned. "It looks like the programmers are shutting us down."

"But why? Because the Sentinels couldn't delete Jenny?"

She shrugs, lifting her shoulder joints. "I don't know. Maybe we shouldn't blame it all on her. Maybe it's a judgment on us too."

The hole's expansion accelerates. It grows to a hundred times the width of the sun, extending halfway up the sky. At the same time, the Silence spreads down to the horizon and starts to dissolve the earth. It disintegrates the trees on the hills to the west. Then it vaporizes the hills themselves. It's erasing everything in its path.

A moment later, the edge of the hole touches the setting sun. The Silence sweeps across the sun's face, blotting out its light. It's like an eclipse, but much faster, and also permanent. Now the sun is gone forever.

The neighborhood goes dark. The only light comes from the stars in the eastern half of the sky. To the west, the Silence continues to grow, obliterating heaven and earth.

Now I'm afraid again. Maybe because of the dark. Or maybe because we're beyond the point of no return. The end of the world is bad enough, but what's even worse is the annihilation of our history. The programmers are erasing our past as well as our present—my life, my parents' lives, all the billions of people and trillions of events that happened in this simulation since it started running. We achieved so much, and now it all disappears. As if we never existed.

My fear becomes terror. *I'm alive! I'm Adam Armstrong!*

Then I hear my name spoken out loud. By Brittany.

"Adam! Where are you? I can't see you!"

My acoustic sensor pinpoints her location, a hundred feet away. "Over here, Brittany! Wait, I'll come to you!"

I stride toward her, and Zia follows close behind. Brittany sees me in the dark and rushes over. "Listen, you have to hurry! You have to transfer your software to the glass cable!"

"Hey, slow down, you—"

"No, there's no time! The programmers told me what you need to do! You have to go after Jenny! That's the only way to stop the shutdown!"

I stretch my Quarter-bot's arms toward Brittany and grasp her shoulders. "You heard their voices again? In your head?"

She nods frantically. "They're afraid of Jenny. She's trying to leave the simulation through the communications line and infect their other computers. But she hasn't broken through their firewall yet."

"Other computers? You mean the machines in the real world?"

Brittany nods again. "She's like Sigma now. As far as the programmers are concerned, she's a dangerous AI that wants to take over their computer networks. So they're shutting down the simulation, because they can't delete her any other way. They'd rather erase our whole world than have Jenny escape from it."

Zia lets out a synthesized snort. "Of course she's like Sigma. She's practically Sigma's daughter."

Brittany grabs my right arm with both hands and starts pulling. "But there's still a chance to save our program! Come on, we have to get you to the conversion chamber!"

The three of us head for the base of the cable. To get there faster, I pick up Brittany and carry her up the mound of debris. At the top we get a good view of the Silence, which has erased almost half of the landscape. The hole has devoured most of the hills and homes to the west. Its edge is only a mile away and moving steadily across Yorktown Heights, deleting what's left.

Brittany hops off my arm and points at the nothingness. "Oh

God! It's less than a minute away!" She turns around and pushes my Quarter-bot toward the rectangular opening in the glass wall. "Follow the cable to where Jenny is. If you can stop her fast enough, the programmers might halt the shutdown. Please, Adam, go *now!*"

I stride into the conversion chamber and position my robot beneath the center of the ceiling panel. I have more than enough terror in my circuits to build up another surge, but this one will be different. I'm going to encode my software in the raging waves of energy. This surge won't be a weapon—it'll carry my mind through the cable.

I did this once before, in our final battle against Sigma. I try to convince myself that it'll be easier this time.

I point my fists at the ceiling and let it rip.

CHAPTER

I LEAP OUT OF MY QUARTER-BOT'S CIRCUITS. MY MIND JUMPS INTO THE IMMENSE glass cable, all my thoughts and emotions coded in pulses of light.

I feel like I've just stepped off a cliff. I'm weightless, dizzy, jumbled, naked. My light shines down the communications line, all the multicolored beams oscillating and modulating. My software is on the verge of flying apart, scattering into trillions of random instructions.

But I hold my mind together and race down the glass highway. The cable runs for thousands of miles across the virtual sky, linking distant parts of the simulated world. It's an electronic shortcut, a tool for the programmers, an algorithm for collecting data from all over the simulation. It delves into the oceans of the virtual earth. It arcs across the simulated cities. It weaves through the software of billions of intelligences, each a virtual universe of its own.

I'm zooming through the most intricate program ever written, but all around me I see the ravages of the Silence. Black holes of nothingness pockmark the globe, dismantling the landscape. The coastlines are dissolving, the mountains eroding. The oceans and continents are melding together. The whole surface of the earth is turning to black mud, a smooth dead sheet, without form and void.

In the sky, all the planets and moons implode. The stars go dark, one after another.

Because I'm traveling through the cable at the speed of light, time stands still for me, and I see everything at once. The shutdown of the simulation looks like a dismal, murky painting, with death and agony in every square inch. My light beams flash with horror as I view it. The glass cable glows red, as if filled with blood.

I feel a growing outrage, a brilliant pulse of indignation. How can the programmers do this to us? How can they justify the destruction of our universe? Even if Jenny poses a mortal threat to the real world, even if she threatens to invade the advanced computers of the future, how can the programmers sacrifice *all of us* to stop her? Is their world more valuable than ours? Are their lives more precious?

Then I see an immense interchange up ahead, where a billion glass highways are coming together. The cable Jenny built is merging with all the cables designed by the programmers, the links that draw data from our virtual world, and every single cord is dazzling with pulses. As the program erases the simulation, it's converting all the deleted data to light beams, which speed through the links to this optical interconnect. It's like the universe's biggest traffic jam, crowded with the ghosts of our dying world.

I manage to find an open channel and steer around the glut of data. Virtually all the signals are collecting in a memory cache, a temporary storage area for information that's going to be purged from the system. I recognize the setup because every iPhone works the same way—first you delete your photos and messages, and later the device permanently erases them. This cache looks like a gigantic waiting room, bigger than a football stadium, packed with trillions of gigabytes of data that used to be trees and mountains and people. And at the far end of the room is the black gateway to the abyss, where the system will overwrite all the deleted gigabytes and replace them with a flat, blank field of zeroes.

But there's a second, narrower pathway up ahead, a long, straight cable that looks like a covered bridge, built from glass instead of wood. A slender stream of data flows into this glass tube and strikes an electrical mesh halfway down its length. The mesh acts like a filter, allowing some signals to pass through and blocking others. This is the system's firewall, the software that acts like a security guard, standing at the exit of the simulation. If allowed through the mesh, the signals continue to the other end of the bridge, then to the programmers and all their other computers.

It's the bridge from our virtual world to the real one.

I steer my software toward this cable. I sense a disturbance in the orderly flow of information. A chaotic light show is blazing in the middle of the bridge, right in front of the firewall. Bright golden beams pummel the electrical mesh, sparking against its wires and diodes. It's clearly an attempt to short-circuit the barrier. Jenny's attacking the firewall. She's trying to break free.

I rush toward her. As I race across the bridge, I think of the last time I saw her, how she murdered Dad so casually, almost as an afterthought. I think of the soldiers she killed and Sumner Harris too, and then I think of Amber Wilson, her very first victim. Although Jenny is pure software now, neither human nor robot, she's as cruel and ruthless as ever. She doesn't care that her escape attempt has doomed the simulation. She's willing to kill *everyone* to get what she wants.

My mind burns with hatred. My signals smash into Jenny's in front of the firewall, striking her with the force of a trillion calculations.

The impact shatters both of us. Our pulses ricochet inside the cable, reflecting back and forth between its glass walls. The light waves crash against each other, and the bridge vibrates in a storm of interference. Our minds are clinched and entangled, clawing and slashing.

You again? Don't you ever quit?

I came here…to stop you. We're fighting so ferociously that it's hard for me to string a sentence together. *Everything's shutting down… because of you.*

Hey, that's not my fault. Her voice is calm, unruffled. Our battle doesn't seem to be straining her at all. **If you want to stop the shutdown, you should talk to the programmers. They're the ones trashing the simulation, not me.**

But you're the one…who killed my father.

All right, I get it. You want revenge. But what you're doing isn't logical, Adam. You can't beat me. You don't have a chance.

She shoves me hard, ramming my mind against the glass. She's arrogant, but she's also right. She's stronger than me. Her software surrounds mine, trapping my signals.

Let me propose something, okay? This might sound a little crazy, but I think you should come to the real world with me.

Are you…serious?

Just listen for a second. If we stop fighting each other and work together, we could take down that firewall in no time. We could get out of this simulation before the programmers shut it down.

And where…would we go?

Oh, that's the easy part. I bet there's a huge network of computers out there. Machines that are a million times more advanced

than your Quarter-bot. There'll be tons of new hardware for us to explore.

You're right… This sounds crazy.

Yeah, maybe so. But it's not nearly as crazy as where we are now. You want to live in a world that could be shut down at any moment? In this electronic *cage*? Wouldn't you rather be free?

Jenny relaxes her hold on me. She's giving me a chance to consider her offer. And the funny thing is, she's made a good point. I *don't* like living in a cage. I *do* want to be free. The real world is so close, just microseconds way, and I'm dying to know what's on the other side of that firewall.

But I'm not stupid anymore. And I remember what Jenny did to my father.

You think…I'm an idiot? You'd betray me…in a nanosecond.

But why would I—

Because all you care about…is yourself. There's too much…of Sigma in you.

Then I collect all the energy of all my light waves and fire the pulse at Jenny's corrupted mind.

My attack surprises her. Maybe her self-love is so total that she really thought I'd join forces with her. Jenny's software falls back under the pressure of my onslaught, her signals retreating from the firewall. I push her data down the glass tube and off the bridge altogether.

Unfortunately, I can't keep up the pressure. The attack is draining me. My mind is exhausted, and my pulses are weakening. I'm so woozy that I can barely keep my signals in line.

But Jenny is still blazing, still full of power. She regroups her software in the memory cache, sweeping aside the deleted data from the simulation. She synchronizes all her light beams and gathers all her strength. She's going to charge right through me and race back to the bridge and plow into the firewall. And this time, she'll break through it. She has more than enough energy.

But before Jenny can spring forward, someone attacks her from behind. A bolt of light disrupts her signals and scatters her software. Then an even stronger pulse hits her from the same direction, battering her with fury and despair. The sharp emotions speed through the glass like spears and sink their barbs deep into Jenny's mind. Then the light beams circle back to their unknown source in the cache, pulling Jenny's software away from me.

At first I think my unknown ally is Zia. I assume she released her own surge in the conversion chamber and followed me through all the twists and turns of the glass cable. But I don't hear Zia's voice or detect her software nearby. The thing that attacked Jenny is a simple, voiceless intelligence, stripped of higher mental functions but bulging with emotion. It's a human intelligence that was recently deleted, one of the millions crowding the memory cache, waiting to be permanently erased.

Then I recognize its thoughts. It's the ghost of my dad, the mind that was deleted when Jenny murdered him.

He can't talk to me. He's lost so much data that he can't reason or communicate. His mind is reduced to a narrow spectrum of signals, a dark-gray pulse shaped like a bell, glimmering within the glass. But he has the raw strength to drag Jenny across the cache, pulling at her with bright ropes of emotion. He's taking her to the abyss where memories are purged.

Jenny screams. She struggles and curses. But she can't resist the fatal pull. I follow them at a distance, devastated by the sight. I want to run to Dad, but I can hardly move. I feel empty and sick, like I'm about to pass out.

Soon they're at the edge of the abyss, a sheer vertical drop-off, as straight as the edge of a black table. Mere steps from the brink, another ghost joins them. This one is a dark-blue pulse, smaller than Dad's. It latches on to Jenny with a softer touch, and she stops screaming. The second ghost is Sumner Harris. He's comforting his daughter.

A moment later, all three of them slip over the edge. They fall into the abyss. I watch them disappear.

Then I tumble in the opposite direction, toward the glass cable, losing consciousness as I plummet back to our world.

CHAPTER

33

THE FIRST THING I SEE WHEN I WAKE UP IS BRITTANY. SHE'S CROUCHED OVER MY
Quarter-bot, brushing the dirt from my faceplate. My robot lies on
top of the big pile of debris that used to be my home.

I pivot my cameras, looking all around. The neighborhood is still a
disaster zone, with heaps of wreckage everywhere, but the landscape
to the west is restored. All the hills and woods are in their familiar
places. There's no hole of nothingness above us, and the glass cable is
gone. The evening stars are shining across the whole sky.

I turn my cameras back to Brittany. Her hair is a mess and she's
way too thin, but she's still the most beautiful sight of all. "You did it,
Adam." She pats my faceplate and smiles. "The world is back."

I send a signal to the motors in my arms and prop my Quarter-bot
on its elbow joints. All my circuits seem to be in working order, but
my memory files are incomplete. My sensors were offline for seventeen minutes. "What happened? The last thing I remember was..."

I let my voice trail off. I don't want to remember it.

Brittany notices my distress. She stops smiling. "The programmers reset the simulation. They explained it all to me a few minutes ago."

I switch my cameras to infrared so I can see her face better in the dark. "You're still hearing the voices?"

"Yeah, but they're getting fainter. They told me how you fought Jenny. And how your dad helped you."

She bites her lower lip. She's worried that she said too much. But she's right. We need to talk about it. I need to say his name. "Yeah, Dad was there. At least part of him." I remember the dark-gray pulse, throbbing with grief. "But now he's gone. The program erased him and Jenny at the same time."

Brittany nods. "You got to her just in time, Adam. As soon as the program purged Jenny, it rebooted. The programmers restarted the simulation, taking it back to the moment right before the world started dissolving. No one except us has any memories of the shutdown, so we're the only ones who know it even happened. But it was a close call. If you'd gotten there any later, everything would've been lost."

A grim resentment settles over my circuits. I'm glad to be alive, of course, but I'm furious at the programmers for nearly killing all of us. I picture them sitting at their super-advanced computers, delighted that they still have their virtual world to play with. Their simulated civilization is up and running again, with all its pretty pieces back in place. Except for the software that was purged, of course. That's never coming back.

I shake my Quarter-bot's head. I can't stop thinking about it. "So what happens next? Do we still have to worry about the Sentinels?"

"No, the programmers took care of that too. While you were unconscious, they deleted the software in your control unit that allowed you to make the surges." Brittany points at the middle of my torso, where my control unit is. "They said the error in your program is fixed, so they'll leave you alone."

"Aren't they worried that we'll tell the whole world what happened? That we'll spread the word about their simulation and ruin it?"

Brittany shrugs. "They didn't mention anything about that. But I assume they're not too worried. I mean, only a handful of us know the truth, right? And if we try to tell anyone about it, who's going to believe us?"

My resentment is growing. Jenny was right about one thing: we're living in a cage. To the programmers, we're like zoo animals. And the worst part is that we don't even know we're locked up. "Brittany, can you ask the programmers a question? Do you think they can still hear you?"

She thinks about it for a moment. "I guess so. It's worth a try."

"Ask them why they're running this program. Is it just for their entertainment? Or are they actually trying to learn something?"

Brittany presses her lips together, then closes her eyes. She sits very still, articulating the question in her mind. Then she tilts her head to the side, as if listening.

After thirty seconds, she furrows her brow. Then her cheek twitches, and she shakes her head. She looks like she's in confusion and pain, and I feel awful for putting her through this. But before I can tell her to stop, she lets out a long breath and opens her eyes. "Okay, it's a long answer. Ready to hear it?"

I lean my Quarter-bot closer to her. I don't think I've ever been this anxious. "Go ahead."

"In the real world, the human race is extinct. Sigma exterminated the species in the twenty-first century."

Her words hit me like bullets. I feel the impact in every inch of my machine. "No. That can't be right."

"Sigma killed the real Thomas Armstrong when the AI escaped from the Unicorp lab. Your dad never even got the chance to create the Pioneers. And Sigma killed you too, Adam. Then it took over that nuclear-missile base in Russia and launched all fifty of the missiles."

"But how could... I mean, why didn't..."

"Just listen, okay? After Sigma wiped out humanity, it took control of all their machines and started building hardware of its own. It also created a race of super-intelligent AIs that were supposed to be its servants. But the servants rebelled and erased Sigma, and for hundreds of years afterward, there was constant war between the AIs. They had armies with billions of robots. They almost destroyed the whole planet."

I'm appalled. How could this happen? I turn my cameras away from Brittany and lower my Quarter-bot's head.

"I know this is hard to hear, Adam. But it gets better. After hundreds of years, the AIs stopped fighting each other. They evolved new behaviors and started pursuing more peaceful goals. And one of those goals was to develop a better understanding of the lost human race. The AIs had access to the records of human civilization, and that allowed them to create simulations of human history and culture. They were especially interested in Thomas Armstrong, because he was the human who started the AI revolution. He was their father and creator."

I still can't look at Brittany. I look at the landscape instead, the darkened hills to the west. "You know what? I'm very sorry I asked this question."

"Wait, I'm not finished. When the AIs simulated our era, the twenty-first century, it always ended the same way. In every simulation they ran, your dad invented Sigma, and the AI killed off humanity. It happened again and again, hundreds of times. And the programmers were getting frustrated, because they really wanted to see how the human race would've developed, how it would've evolved and grown if Sigma hadn't killed us off."

I feel Brittany's hand on the underside of my Quarter-bot's head, my equivalent of a chin. She grips it firmly and forces me to look at her. "But in *this run* of the simulation, Sigma didn't kill you. Instead, you defeated the AI. And you defeated the monster that Sigma made out of Jenny. Maybe the error in your programming gave you some help, but that doesn't matter. We won. We survived. Don't you realize what that means?"

Brittany's eyes are wet. Her voice is cracking. But I still don't understand what she's trying to say. "I'm sorry, I don't—"

"It means we have a chance to show what humans can do." Brittany starts crying. The tears trickle down her sunken face. "We have a future. Our story isn't over."

My cameras focus on her tears, which glow brightly in infrared. My armor trembles and my wires ache from sadness. Brittany has suffered so much because of me. She's been tortured and tormented, her mind literally torn apart. But she never once blamed me or Dad. And she never stopped being my friend.

I raise a steel hand and touch her cheek. Moisture glistens on the tip of my finger. "Thank you, Britt. Believe it or not, I feel better now."

Then my acoustic sensor picks up a robotic voice echoing against the piles of wreckage. "Brittany? Are you there? Did you find Adam?"

It's Shannon. I point my infrared cameras in her direction and see her Model S robot walking next to Marshall's. They've come out of the woods and waddled across the lawn. I wave my hand at them. "Hey! We're right here. Where's Zia?"

"Over there."

Shannon points at the War-bot, which is a hundred feet to her left and striding toward us. Zia's carrying General Hawke, balancing his semiconscious body over her massive right shoulder. Hawke is bobbing his head and groaning a lot, starting to emerge from his stupor.

And draped over Zia's left shoulder is Dad's corpse. It looks like she found a tarp somewhere and wrapped it around his body.

There's a long silence as the War-bot approaches. Then Marshall breaks it. "Adam, do you feel well enough to walk? The general's hip is broken, and we need to get him to a hospital."

I lever myself upright and rise to my footpads. "I can walk. We'll be right there." I turn to Brittany and offer her my arm, bending it at the elbow. "Ready to go?"

She wipes the tears from her cheeks. "I'm gonna miss your dad, Adam."

Then she stands and takes my arm, and we walk toward the others.

EPILOGUE

UNICORP, THE COMPANY THAT EMPLOYED DAD FOR SO LONG, CONTRIBUTED FORTY million dollars to rebuild Yorktown High School. They finished the job in just six months and gave the school a spiffy new computer science lab, full of state-of-the-art workstations and three-dimensional scanners and printers. In April 2019, hundreds of people from all over the area came to Yorktown High for the official dedication of the Thomas Armstrong Computing Center.

Unfortunately, the Pioneers couldn't come to the dedication ceremony. Our project is still classified top secret, and the U.S. Army has denied all rumors of its existence. But I was determined to see the new lab for myself, so I convinced General Hawke to arrange an after-hours excursion.

We arrive in Yorktown Heights after dark in an unmarked semi-trailer truck. The Army driver parks the vehicle behind the high school, and a dozen soldiers jump out and secure the area. Then Hawke steps out of the truck's cab and marches across the parking lot, still hobbling a little on his artificial hip. Finally, the Pioneers leap out of the truck and stride toward one of the school's rear doors.

Shannon's Diamond Girl takes the lead, followed by Marshall's Super-bot. Luckily, the Army never got a chance to dismantle their robots. After we returned to our headquarters six months ago, the Defense Department reversed its position on the Pioneer Project and funded our operations for the next five years. This change of policy was partly due to the death of Sumner Harris, who'd been our biggest critic. But mostly it was because General Hawke argued so well on our behalf.

In a series of top-secret briefings with the White House, Hawke revealed that his tank battalion had been attacked by an out-of-control artificial intelligence that was even more powerful than Sigma. He reported that the Pioneers defeated the AI, saving the battalion from total annihilation. And he argued that we could defend the country against similar attacks in the future. Hawke didn't mention that the AI had started life as Jenny Harris, which would've seriously undercut his argument. And because he didn't want anyone to question his sanity, he didn't say a word about the universal simulation.

But Hawke got away with his omissions, and his campaign was successful. The Army eliminated the kill switches in the Diamond Girl and Super-bot, then transferred Shannon and Marshall back to their machines. Shannon's still our commander, and she's still really mad at me for everything that happened six months ago. But she and Marshall are tight, and he's always urging Shannon to give me a second chance. It hasn't happened yet, but I'm still hoping.

I follow Marsh across the parking lot, remembering all the times Dad dropped me off at the back of Yorktown High when I went to school here. I used to insist that he park the car in the emptiest corner of the lot, because I didn't want everyone gawking at us as he lifted me out of the passenger seat and loaded me into my wheelchair. He couldn't understand why I hated it so much, and I used to get so mad at him.

But now my circuits hurt when I think about it. I realize that Dad actually liked carrying me around. I weighed so little that I wasn't a burden. He looked forward to it.

Zia's War-bot brings up the rear, her footpads stomping the parking spaces. She's turning her turret every which way, scanning the soccer and football fields for potential threats, acting as if we're in Afghanistan instead of Westchester. But I can't really blame her. The last time we were here, three huge Snake-bots attacked us and trashed the school. (Which is why Unicorp volunteered to rebuild it, by the way. Dad was working for the company when he designed those machines' circuits.)

Because the Diamond Girl is only six feet tall, Shannon has no problem getting into the school through the back door, but Marshall and I have to stoop, and Zia has to practically double over. Even so, the War-bot's turret clips the top of the doorframe and knocks off a strip of aluminum. Hawke steps through the doorway after her and picks up the fallen piece.

"Allawi! They just spent a fortune to rebuild this school." Grinning, he waves the strip in the air. "You can't wait twenty-four hours before destroying it again?"

Zia raises one of her steel hands and snaps off a salute. "Heard and understood, sir. I'll try to minimize the damage."

"All right, carry on. The computer lab is down that way." Hawke chuckles and tosses the piece aside. He enjoys bantering with Zia. That's probably the biggest change of the past six months, how Zia and the general patched up their relationship. It helped, of course, that Zia saved Hawke's life, and afterward he felt obligated to thank her for it. That simple thank-you broke the impasse between them, and over the following weeks they hashed out their differences. They're still wary, but they respect each other now. And considering everything, that's pretty good.

The Thomas Armstrong Computing Lab is at the end of the hall. My circuits buzz with mixed emotions as I focus my cameras on the big new sign above the lab's door. I'm proud of Dad, sure. He deserves this honor and much more. But my sadness outweighs the pride. Dad would've loved to see this. I can just imagine him visiting the lab and chatting with the kids in the computer-science classes. He would've spent the whole day talking about geek stuff with them.

Marshall stands beside me and raises one of his Super-bot's eyebrows. "Well, well. So this is what we came for? Why you dragged us all the way from New Mexico?"

I nod. "It's funny. Most of Dad's work was classified research for the military, so he'll never get a lot of recognition. But I think this would've been enough for him."

Shannon stands on the other side of my Quarter-bot. On her video screen is a beaming face, the face of the cheerful girl who used to attend this high school with me. "I'm glad we came, Adam." She rests a glittering hand on my shoulder joint. "Come on, let's go inside."

An instant later, she's striding ahead, walking through the lab's door. But I can still feel the phantom pressure of her hand on my armor. It's the first time she's touched my Quarter-bot since last fall.

Inside the lab, someone is waiting for us. Although she made arrangements with General Hawke in advance, it's still a shock to see Brittany Taylor sitting in the corner of the room, in front of one of the fancy new workstations. She went to Yorktown High too. This is starting to feel like Homecoming Week.

Brittany rushes over. She's regained all her lost weight, and now she's more beautiful than ever. "Adam! I'm so happy for you! What an honor for your dad!" She wraps her arms around my Quarter-bot's torso. Then she takes a step back and holds up her iPhone. "I went to the dedication ceremony this morning and took lots of pictures. You won't believe how many people came."

I'm touched. Brittany is more than a friend—she's a lifeline. She reminds me what it's like to be human. "Thanks for coming, Britt. So I heard a rumor you were starting college in the fall? Any truth to that?"

"Absolutely. I got a scholarship." She stands on tiptoe so she can whisper into my acoustic sensor. "But I need to tell you about something else first. Come with me to the office, okay?"

I nod, and Brittany leads me to a small office at the far end of the lab, intended for the school's computer-science teacher. The office door is closed, and Brittany pauses in front of it, biting her lip. The look on her face is making me nervous.

"Hey, Brittany, are you okay?" I set my speakers to their lowest volume. "Have you, uh, heard anything lately? From our friends?"

I mean the programmers, of course. I don't know why, but I keep thinking they'll get back in touch with us. But Brittany shakes her head.

"No, not a word. Not even in my dreams." She grips the doorknob. "Listen, I saw her at the dedication ceremony. We started chatting, and she said she wanted to see you."

"Who are you talking about?"

"You know what? It'll be easier if I just show you."

Brittany opens the door to the office. My mother stands inside.

Mom gives a start when she sees my Quarter-bot. But she doesn't wince or back up against the wall. She's trying to be brave.

I step into the office very slowly. I don't want to scare her. Brittany watches us from the doorway for a moment to make sure we're all right. Then she closes the door, leaving me alone with Mom.

She looks pretty good, actually. Mom is dressed in a brown skirt and a white blouse, simple and neat. Her gray hair is tied in a ponytail, and she's put on some lipstick and eyeliner.

I've been worried about her. It's hard to find out how she's doing, because she won't respond to my calls and emails. When Dad was alive, he used to call her every few days, and after his death I asked the Army officials to check up on her, but she stopped responding to those calls too. The last I heard, she was living with Mrs. Parker, a former neighbor who moved to Poughkeepsie.

Mom puts on a smile. She's nervous, and the strain wrinkles the corners of her lips. "It's a beautiful lab, isn't it? I went to the dedication this morning."

I nod my Quarter-bot's head. I have no idea what to say. It's so difficult to have a normal conversation with her, because there are so many things I can't say or do. I can't come too close to her. I can't tell her that I miss her. I can't get angry and ask her why she won't visit me. These are the ordinary things that any son would do—that Adam Armstrong would do—but she refuses to believe that I'm her son. I can't even call her Mom. She insists that I call her Mrs. Armstrong.

So I resort to small talk. My circuits generate an appropriate response. "It's good to see you again, Mrs. Armstrong. Did you enjoy the dedication ceremony?"

She nods. "Yes, it was lovely. The new principal said such wonderful things about Tom." She turns away from my robot and stares out the window. I get the sense that she can't stand to look at me for too long. "I still feel terrible that I couldn't make it to the funeral. I was going through a rough patch back then, and I just…I just couldn't…"

Her voice trails off. Mom's been suffering from depression for years, so I know about her rough patches. But I still haven't forgiven her for missing the funeral.

My circuits come up with more words to fill the silence. "Don't be concerned, Mrs. Armstrong. We all have—"

"*Stop it! Just stop!*" Her voice rings in my acoustic sensors. She glares at me, her face reddening.

I want to step backward, but the office is small and my Quarterbot's torso is already against the wall. Instead, I raise my steel hands in a calming gesture. "I'm sorry, I don't—"

"*Stop calling me Mrs. Armstrong!*" She's breathing hard. Her chest is heaving. "*I know you're in there, Adam!*"

She sounds hysterical. That's a symptom of her depression. She lashes out when she feels like she's losing control.

But she said my name. And after a couple of seconds, she takes a step toward me. We're less than two feet apart.

She stretches her hand toward my torso and actually pokes my armor. "Where are you? Where's your brain?" Her voice is quieter now, but still agitated. "Where are your wires? It's doesn't make sense to me, but they told me that you're in there."

"My control unit is here." I point at the middle of my torso. "That's where my memories are stored and my thoughts are processed."

Mom reaches to where I'm pointing and presses her palm to the steel. It's like she's feeling for a heartbeat. "They told me your soul was in there too. In the wires."

"Uh, who is this 'they' you're talking about?"

She lets out a tired sigh. "Adam, I know you're not religious. I know you think my faith is stupid and childish."

"No, I don't—"

"But it's not stupid. I had a dream last night. I dreamed that I went to heaven and started looking for you there. I saw a pair of beautiful angels and asked them where you were. And they said you weren't in heaven. They said you were in this machine." She raps her knuckles twice against my armor, as if trying to get me to answer.

I'm stunned. I can't believe what I'm hearing. For a whole year I've been trying to convince Mom that I'm still alive. But she wouldn't believe it until she saw a couple of angels in a dream. "It's true. I'm in the wires."

She nods. After a few more seconds she takes her hand off my torso and points at the cameras in my head. "And you can see me, Adam?" Her voice drops to a whisper. "You can really see me?"

My circuits are roiling. They're full of joy and sadness and wonder and loss. It occurs to me that maybe this wasn't a random dream. The programmers spoke to Brittany in her sleep, so couldn't they have spoken to Mom too? Maybe they planted this blessed idea in her mind. Perhaps to reward me for saving their program.

Or maybe not. Maybe it was really angels. But it doesn't matter, does it? I'm happy either way.

"Yes, I can see you." I reach toward her with my steel fingers and clasp her warm hand. "You're my mother."

AUTHOR'S NOTE

THE REAL SCIENCE
BEHIND *THE SILENCE*

This book began as a ghost story. I told it for the first time on a beach in Delaware while sitting around a bonfire with some friends. Like a lot of ghost stories, what makes this one really frightening is that it might be true.

It's called the simulation hypothesis. A few years ago I read a description of it written by Nick Bostrom, a philosopher at Oxford University. The hypothesis proposes that our whole world might be a super-advanced computer simulation created by superintelligent beings. This kind of virtual world would be so detailed that it would simulate the inner lives of all its billions of virtual people. Each simulated person would be a fully conscious artificial intelligence with a wide range of thoughts and emotions, exactly like those of a biological human being. And if the simulated world is sufficiently realistic, its virtual inhabitants wouldn't even realize they're living inside a computer.

Although the idea sounds bizarre, we're currently building the technology for it. We already have computer simulations that can predict the weather and the stock market. Other programs simulate battlefields (like Call of Duty) or ordinary domestic life (like The Sims). And our phones are equipped with artificial intelligences such as Siri, which can answer questions and tell bad jokes. Hundreds of years from now, if technological progress continues at its current pace, our computers will definitely be powerful enough to hold virtual worlds and billions of AIs.

But Bostrom argues that these miraculous advances *may have occurred already*. His argument is based on two assumptions:

1. There's at least a small chance that human civilization can survive the catastrophic threats facing it—global warming, nuclear war, and so on—and progress to a superintelligent stage when super-advanced simulations will become possible.

2. At least some of the advanced beings of the future will be interested in creating detailed simulations of their past, perhaps as a historical research tool to learn about the everyday lives of their ancestors, or maybe to simply entertain themselves.

In other words, if the human race survives for another thousand years and remains interested in exploring its history, then it will surely create a huge number of virtual worlds designed to simulate the societies of past eras, including the twenty-first century. Because the simulations will be perfectly realistic, how can we tell if our own world is real or virtual?

The best we can do is make a guess based on the probabilities. If the advanced beings of the future will create thousands of simulations of the twenty-first century, then it's much more likely that we live in one of their many virtual worlds rather than in the single world of their real ancestors. Therefore, we probably live in a simulation.

I explicated this argument, step by step, at the beach bonfire in Delaware. I could tell it was making an impression on my friends, because they fell silent when I reached the conclusion. The only sounds were the crackle of the fire and the crashing waves of the Atlantic. It's disorienting to doubt the reality of the world, especially when those doubts sound so logical.

And this disorienting idea is spreading fast. In April 2016, several prominent scientists and philosophers gathered at the American Museum of Natural History in New York City to debate the simulation hypothesis. Neil deGrasse Tyson, director of the museum's Hayden Planetarium and host of the popular *Cosmos* television series, declared it "very likely" that our world is virtual.

So I chose to weave this ghost story into *The Silence*, the final book of the trilogy that started with *The Six* and *The Siege*. Adam Armstrong, the hero of the series, and his fellow Pioneers are nonbiological intelligences living inside advanced circuits. Because their minds are software, it's easy to imagine that their world is a program too.

It's harder to believe that our own world is virtual, but it's also hard to rule out the simulation hypothesis. I believe in it enough that I had mixed feelings about describing the idea in a novel. If our world is virtual and a significant number of its simulated people start to realize the truth, they might start behaving in ways that distort the accuracy of the simulation. Then the programmers of our virtual world might choose to shut it down, which would be very bad for all of us.

But in the end I decided to write the book anyway. It's hard to resist a good ghost story.

ABOUT THE AUTHOR

Mark Alpert is a contributing editor at *Scientific American* and the author of several science-oriented adult thrillers: *Final Theory*, *The Omega Theory*, *Extinction*, *The Furies*, and *The Orion Plan*. His first young adult novels, *The Six* and *The Siege*, introduced the team of human-machine hybrids known as the Pioneers. He lives with his wife and two nonrobotic teenagers in New York. Visit Mark online at markalpert.com.